PENGUIN BOOKS

A GERMAN REQUIEM

Philip Kerr was born in Edinburgh in 1956 and now lives in London. As a freelance journalist he has written for a number of newspapers and magazines, including the *Sunday Times*. He is the author of the novels *March Violets*, *The Pale Criminal* and *A German Requiem* (also published by Penguin in one volume as *Berlin Noir*). He is also the author of *A Philosophical Investigation*, *Dead Meat* and *Gridiron*, and has edited *The Penguin Book of Lies* and *The Penguin Book of Fights, Feuds and Heartfelt Hatreds*.

PHILIP KERR

A GERMAN REQUIEM

PENGUIN BOOKS

PENGUIN BOOKS

Published by the Penguin Group
Penguin Books Ltd, 27 Wrights Lane, London W8 5TZ, England
Penguin Books USA Inc., 375 Hudson Street, New York, New York 10014, USA
Penguin Books Australia Ltd, Ringwood, Victoria, Australia
Penguin Books Canada Ltd, 10 Alcorn Avenue, Toronto, Ontario, Canada M4V 3B2
Penguin Books (NZ) Ltd, 182–190 Wairau Road, Auckland 10, New Zealand

Penguin Books Ltd, Registered Offices: Harmondsworth, Middlesex, England

First published by Viking 1991
Published in Penguin Books 1992
3 5 7 9 10 8 6 4 2

The lines quoted on p. vii are from 'A German Requiem' by James Fenton,
copyright © James Fenton, published by the Salamander Press

Printed in England by Clays Ltd, St Ives plc

For Jane,
and in memory of my father

It is not what they built. It is what they knocked down.
It is not the houses. It is the spaces between the houses.
It is not the streets that exist. It is the streets that no longer exist.
It is not your memories which haunt you.
It is not what you have written down.
It is what you have forgotten, what you must forget.
What you must go on forgetting all your life.

From 'A German Requiem', by James Fenton

PART ONE

BERLIN, 1947

These days, if you are a German you spend your time in Purgatory before you die, in earthly suffering for all your country's unpunished and unrepented sins, until the day when, with the aid of the prayers of the Powers – or three of them, anyway – Germany is finally purified.

For now we live in fear. Mostly it is fear of the Ivans, matched only by the almost universal dread of venereal disease, which has become something of an epidemic, although both afflictions are generally held to be synonymous.

1

It was a cold, beautiful day, the kind you can best appreciate with a fire to stoke and a dog to scratch. I had neither, but then there wasn't any fuel about and I never much liked dogs. But thanks to the quilt I had wrapped around my legs I was warm, and I had just started to congratulate myself on being able to work from home – the sitting-room doubled as my office – when there was a knock at what passed for the front door.

I cursed and got off my couch.

'This will take a minute,' I shouted through the wood, 'so don't go away.' I worked the key in the lock and started to pull at the big brass handle. 'It helps if you push it from your side,' I shouted again. I heard the scrape of shoes on the landing and then felt a pressure on the other side of the door. Finally it shuddered open.

He was a tall man of about sixty. With his high cheekbones, thin short snout, old-fashioned side-whiskers and angry expression, he reminded me of a mean old king baboon.

'I think I must have pulled something,' he grunted, rubbing his shoulder.

'I'm sorry about that,' I said, and stood aside to let him in. 'There's been quite a bit of subsidence in the building. The door needs rehanging, but of course you can't get the tools.' I showed him into the sitting-room. 'Still, we're not too badly off here. We've had some new glass, and the roof seems to keep out the rain. Sit down.' I pointed to the only armchair and resumed my position on the couch.

The man put down his briefcase, took off his bowler hat and sat down with an exhausted sigh. He didn't loosen his grey overcoat and I didn't blame him for it.

'I saw your little advertisement on a wall on the Kurfürstendamm,' he explained.

'You don't say,' I said, vaguely recalling the words I had used on a small square of card the previous week. Kirsten's idea. With all the notices advertising life-partners and marriage-markets that covered the walls of Berlin's derelict buildings, I had supposed that nobody would bother to read it. But she had been right after all.

'My name is Novak,' he said. 'Dr Novak. I am an engineer. A process metallurgist, at a factory in Wernigerode. My work is concerned with the extraction and production of non-ferrous metals.'

'Wernigerode,' I said. 'That's in the Harz Mountains, isn't it? In the Eastern Zone?'

He nodded. 'I came to Berlin to deliver a series of lectures at the university. This morning I received a telegram at my hotel, the Mitropa – '

I frowned, trying to remember it.

'It's one of those bunker-hotels,' said Novak. For a moment he seemed inclined to tell me about it, and then changed his mind. 'The telegram was from my wife, urging me to cut short my trip and return home.'

'Any particular reason?'

He handed me the telegram. 'It says that my mother is unwell.'

I unfolded the paper, glanced at the typewritten message, and noted that it actually said she was dangerously ill.

'I'm sorry to hear it.'

Dr Novak shook his head.

'You don't believe her?'

'I don't believe my wife ever sent this,' he said. 'My mother may indeed be old, but she is in remarkably good health. Only two days ago she was chopping wood. No, I suspect that this has been cooked up by the Russians, to get me back as quickly as possible.'

'Why?'

'There is a great shortage of scientists in the Soviet Union. I think that they intend to deport me to work in one of their factories.'

I shrugged. 'Then why allow you to travel to Berlin in the first place?'

6

'That would be to grant the Soviet Military Authority a degree of efficiency which it simply does not possess. My guess is that an order for my deportation has only just arrived from Moscow, and that the SMA wishes to get me back at the earliest opportunity.'

'Have you telegraphed your wife? To have this confirmed?'

'Yes. She replied only that I should come at once.'

'So you want to know if the Ivans have got her.'

'I've been to the military police here in Berlin,' he said, 'but – '

His deep sigh told me with what success.

'No, they won't help,' I said. 'You were right to come here.'

'Can you help me, Herr Gunther?'

'It means going into the Zone,' I said, half to myself, as if I needed some persuasion, which I did. 'To Potsdam. There's someone I know I can bribe at the headquarters of the Group of Soviet Forces in Germany. It'll cost you, and I don't mean a couple of candy-bars.'

He nodded solemnly.

'You wouldn't happen to have any dollars, I suppose, Dr Novak?'

He shook his head.

'Then there's also the matter of my own fee.'

'What would you suggest?'

I nodded at his briefcase. 'What have you got?'

'Just papers, I'm afraid.'

'You must have something. Think. Perhaps something at your hotel.'

He lowered his head and uttered another sigh as he tried to recall a possession that might be of some value.

'Look, Herr Doktor, have you asked yourself what you will do if it turns out your wife is being held by the Russians?'

'Yes,' he said gloomily, his eyes glazing over for a moment.

This was sufficiently articulate. Things did not look good for Frau Novak.

'Wait a moment,' he said, dipping his hand inside the breast of his coat, and coming up with a gold fountain-pen. 'There's this.'

He handed me the pen.

'It's a Parker. Eighteen carat.'

I quickly appraised its worth. 'About fourteen hundred dollars on the black market,' I said. 'Yes, that'll take care of Ivan. They love fountain-pens almost as much as they love watches.' I raised my eyebrows suggestively.

'I'm afraid I couldn't part with my watch,' said Novak. 'It was a present – from my wife.' He smiled thinly as he perceived the irony.

I nodded sympathetically and decided to move things along before guilt got the better of him.

'Now, as to my own fee. You mentioned metallurgy. You wouldn't happen to have access to a laboratory, would you?'

'But of course.'

'And a smelter?'

He nodded thoughtfully, and then more vigorously as the light dawned. 'You want some coal, don't you?'

'Can you get some?'

'How much do you want?'

'Fifty kilos would be about right.'

'Very well.'

'Be back here in twenty-four hours,' I told him. 'I should have some information by then.'

Thirty minutes later, after leaving a note for my wife, I was out of the apartment and on my way to the railway station.

In late 1947 Berlin still resembled a colossal Acropolis of fallen masonry and ruined edifice, a vast and unequivocal megalith to the waste of war and the power of 75,000 tonnes of high explosive. Unparalleled was the destruction that had been rained on the capital of Hitler's ambition: devastation on a Wagnerian scale with the Ring come full circle – the final illumination of that twilight of the gods.

In many parts of the city a street map would have been of little more use than a window-cleaner's leather. Main roads meandered like rivers around high banks of debris. Footpaths wound precipitously over shifting mountains of treacherous rubble which sometimes, in warmer weather, yielded a clue unmistakable to the nostrils that something other than house-hold furniture was buried there.

With compasses in short supply you needed a lot of nerve to find your way along facsimile streets on which only the fronts of shops and hotels remained standing unsteadily like some abandoned film-set; and you needed a good memory for the buildings where people still lived in damp cellars, or more precariously on the lower floors of apartment blocks from which a whole wall had been neatly removed, exposing all the rooms and life inside, like some giant doll's house: there were few who risked the upper floors, not least because there were so few undamaged roofs and so many dangerous staircases.

Life amidst the wreckage of Germany was frequently as unsafe as it had been in the last days of the war: a collapsing wall here, an unexploded bomb there. It was still a bit of a lottery.

At the railway station I bought what I hoped might just be a winning ticket.

2

That night, on the last train back to Berlin from Potsdam, I sat in a carriage by myself. I ought to have been more careful, only I was feeling pleased with myself for having successfully concluded the doctor's case: but I was also tired, since this business had taken almost the whole day and a substantial part of the evening.

Not the least part of my time had been taken up in travel. Generally this took two or three times as long as it had done before the war; and what had once been a half-hour's journey to Potsdam now took nearer two. I was closing my eyes for a nap when the train started to slow, and then juddered to a halt.

Several minutes passed before the carriage-door opened and a large and extremely smelly Russian soldier climbed aboard. He mumbled a greeting at me, to which I nodded politely. But almost immediately I braced myself as, swaying gently on his huge feet, he unslung his Mosin Nagant carbine and operated the bolt action. Instead of pointing it at me, he turned and fired his weapon out of the carriage window, and after a brief pause my lungs started to move again as I realized that he had been signalling to the driver.

The Russian burped, sat down heavily as the train started to move again, swept off his lambskin cap with the back of his filthy hand and, leaning back, closed his eyes.

I pulled a copy of the British-run *Telegraf* out of my coat-pocket. Keeping one eye on the Ivan, I pretended to read. Most of the news was about crime: rape and robbery in the Eastern Zone were as common as the cheap vodka which, as often as not, occasioned their commission. Sometimes it seemed as if Germany was still in the bloody grip of the Thirty Years' War.

I knew just a handful of women who could not describe an incident in which they had been raped or molested by a Russian. And even if one makes an allowance for the fantasies of a few neurotics, there was still a staggering number of sex-related crimes. My wife knew several girls who had been attacked only quite recently, on the eve of the thirtieth anniversary of the Russian Revolution. One of these girls, raped by no less than five Red Army soldiers at a police station in Rangsdorff, and infected with syphilis as a result, tried to bring criminal charges, but found herself subjected to a forcible medical examination and charged with prostitution. But there were also some who said that the Ivans merely took by force that which German women were only too willing to sell to the British and the Americans.

Complaints to the Soviet Kommendatura that you had been robbed by Red Army soldiers were equally in vain. You were likely to be informed that 'all the German people have is a gift from the people of the Soviet Union'. This was sufficient sanction for indiscriminate robbery throughout the Zone, and you were sometimes lucky if you survived to report the matter. The depredations of the Red Army and its many deserters made travel in the Zone only slightly less dangerous than a flight on the *Hindenburg*. Travellers on the Berlin–Magdeburg railway had been stripped naked and thrown off the train; and the road from Berlin to Leipzig was so dangerous that vehicles often drove in convoy: the *Telegraf* had reported a robbery in which four boxers, on their way to a fight in Leipzig, had been held up and robbed of everything except their lives. Most notorious of all were the seventy-five robberies committed by the Blue Limousine Gang, which had operated on the Berlin–Michendorf road, and which had included among its leaders the vice-president of the Soviet-controlled Potsdam police.

To people who were thinking of visiting the Eastern Zone, I said 'don't'; and then if they still wanted to go, I said 'Don't wear a wristwatch – the Ivans like to steal them; don't wear anything but your oldest coat and shoes – the Ivans like quality; don't argue or answer back – the Ivans don't mind shooting you: if you must talk to them speak loudly of American fascists; and don't read any newspaper except their own *Taegliche Rund-schau*.'

This was all good advice and I would have done well to have

taken it myself, for suddenly the Ivan in my carriage was on his feet and standing unsteadily over me.

'*Vi vihodeetye* (are you getting off)?' I asked him.

He blinked crapulously and then stared malevolently at me and my newspaper before snatching it from my hands.

He was a hill-tribesman type, a big stupid Chechen with almond-shaped black eyes, a gnarled jaw as broad as the steppes and a chest like an upturned church-bell: the kind of Ivan we made jokes about – how they didn't know what lavatories were and how they put their food in the toilet bowls thinking that they were refrigerators (some of these stories were even true).

'*Lzhy* (lies),' he snarled, brandishing the paper in front of him, his open, drooling mouth showing great yellow kerbstones of teeth. Putting his boot on the seat beside me, he leaned closer. '*Lganyo*,' he repeated in tones lower than the smell of sausage and beer which his breath carried to my helplessly flaring nostrils. He seemed to sense my disgust and rolled the idea of it around in his grizzled head like a boiled sweet. Dropping the *Telegraf* to the floor he held out his horny hand.

'*Ya hachoo padarok*,' he said, and then slowly in German, '. . . I want present.'

I grinned at him, nodding like an idiot, and realized that I was going to have to kill him or be killed myself. '*Padarok*,' I repeated. '*Padarok*.'

I stood up slowly and, still grinning and nodding, gently pulled back the sleeve of my left arm to reveal my bare wrist. The Ivan was grinning too by now, thinking he was on to a good thing. I shrugged.

'*Oo menya nyet chasov*,' I said, explaining that I didn't have a watch to give him.

'*Shto oo vas yest* (what have you got)?'

'*Nichto*,' I said, shaking my head and inviting him to search my coat pockets. 'Nothing.'

'*Shto oo vas yest?*' he said again, more loudly this time.

It was, I reflected, like me talking to poor Dr Novak, whose wife I had been able to confirm was indeed being held by the MVD. Trying to discover what he could trade.

'*Nichto*,' I repeated.

The grin disappeared from the Ivan's face. He spat on the carriage floor.

'*Vroon* (liar),' he growled, and pushed me on the arm.

I shook my head and told him that I wasn't lying.

He reached to push me again, only this time he checked his hand and took hold of the sleeve with his dirty finger and thumb. '*Doraga* (expensive),' he said, appreciatively, feeling the material.

I shook my head, but the coat was black cashmere – the sort of coat I had no business wearing in the Zone – and it was no use arguing: the Ivan was already unbuckling his belt.

'*Ya hachoo vashi koyt*,' he said, removing his own well-patched greatcoat. Then, stepping to the other side of the carriage, he flung open the door and informed me that either I could hand over the coat or he would throw me off the train.

I had no doubt that he would throw me out whether I gave him my coat or not. It was my turn to spit.

'*Nu, nyelzya* (nothing doing),' I said. 'You want this coat? You come and get it, you stupid fucking *svinya*, you ugly, dumb *kryestyan'in*. Come on, take it from me, you drunken bastard.'

The Ivan snarled angrily and picked up his carbine from the seat where he had left it. That was his first mistake. Having seen him signal to the engine-driver by firing his weapon out of the window, I knew that there could not be a live cartridge in the breech. It was a deductive process he made only a moment behind me, but by the time he was working the bolt action a second time I had buried the toe of my boot in his groin.

The carbine clattered to the floor as the Ivan doubled over painfully, and with one hand reached between his legs: with the other he lashed out hard, catching me an agonizing blow on the thigh that left my leg feeling as dead as mutton.

As he straightened up again I swung with my right, and found my fist caught firmly in his big paw. He snatched at my throat and I headbutted him full in the face, which made him release my fist as he instinctively cupped his turnip-sized nose. I swung again and this time he ducked and seized me by the coat lapels. That was his second mistake, but for a brief, puzzled half-second I did not realize it. Unaccountably he cried out and

13

staggered back from me, his hands raised in the air in front of him like a scrubbed-up surgeon, his lacerated fingertips pouring with blood. It was only then that I remembered the razor-blades I had sewn under my lapels many months before, for just this eventuality.

My flying tackle carried him crashing to the floor and half a torso's length beyond the open door of the fast-moving train. Lying on his bucking legs I struggled to prevent the Ivan pulling himself back into the carriage. Hands that were sticky with blood clawed at my face and then fastened desperately round my neck. His grip tightened and I heard the air gurgle from my own throat like the sound of an espresso-machine.

I punched him hard under the chin, not once but several times, and then pressed the heel of my hand against it as I sought to push him back into the racing night air. The skin on my forehead tightened as I gasped for breath.

A terrible roaring filled my ears, as if a grenade had burst directly in front of my face, and, for a second his fingers seemed to loosen. I lunged at his head and connected with the empty space that was now mercifully signalled by an abruptly terminated stump of bloody human vertebra. A tree, or perhaps a telegraph pole, had neatly decapitated him.

My chest a heaving sack of rabbits, I collapsed back into the carriage, too exhausted to yield to the wave of nausea that was beginning to overtake me. But after only a few seconds more I could no longer resist it and summoned forward by the sudden contraction of my stomach, I vomited copiously over the dead soldier's body.

It was several minutes before I felt strong enough to tip the corpse out of the door, with the carbine quickly following. I picked the Ivan's malodorous greatcoat off the seat to throw it out as well, but the weight of it made me hesitate. Searching the pockets I found a Czechoslovakian-made .38 automatic, a handful of wristwatches – probably all stolen – and a half-empty bottle of Moscowskaya. After deciding to keep the gun and the watches, I uncorked the vodka, wiped the neck, and raised the bottle to the freezing night-sky.

'*Alla rasi bo sun* (God save you),' I said, and swallowed a generous mouthful. Then I flung the bottle and the greatcoat off the train and closed the door.

Back at the railway station snow floated in the air like fragments of lint and collected in small ski-slopes in the angle between the station wall and the road. It was colder than it had been all week and the sky was heavy with the threat of something worse. A fog lay on the white streets like cigar smoke drifting across a well starched tablecloth. Close by, a streetlight burned with no great intensity, but it was still bright enough to light up my face for the scrutiny of a British soldier staggering home with several bottles of beer in each hand. The bemused grin of intoxication on his face changed to something more circumspect as he caught sight of me, and he swore with what sounded like fright.

I limped quickly past him and heard the sound of a bottle breaking on the road as it slipped from nervous fingers. It suddenly occurred to me that my hands and face were covered with the Ivan's blood, not to mention my own. I must have looked like Julius Caesar's last toga.

Ducking into a nearby alley I washed myself with some snow. It seemed to remove not only the blood but the skin as well, and probably left my face looking every bit as red as before. My icy toilette completed, I walked on, as smartly as I was able, and reached home without further adventure.

It had gone midnight by the time I shouldered open my front door – at least it was easier getting in than out. Expecting my wife to be in bed, I was not surprised to find the apartment in darkness, but when I went into the bedroom I saw that she was not there.

I emptied my pockets and prepared for bed.

Laid out on the dressing-table, the Ivan's watches – a Rolex, a Mickey Mouse, a gold Patek and a Doxas – were all working and adjusted to within a minute or two of each other. But the sight of so much accurate time-keeping seemed only to underline Kirsten's lateness. I might have been concerned for her but for the suspicion I held as to where she was and what she was doing, and the fact that I was worn through to my tripe.

My hands trembling with fatigue, my cortex aching as if I

had been pounded with a meat-tenderizer, I crawled to bed with no more spirit than if I had been driven from among men to eat grass like an ox.

3

I awoke to the sound of a distant explosion. They were always dynamiting dangerous ruins. A wolf's howl of wind whipped against the window and I pressed myself closer to Kirsten's warm body while my mind slowly decoded the clues that led me back into the dark labyrinth of doubt: the scent on her neck, the cigarette smoke sticking to her hair.

I had not heard her come to bed.

Gradually a duet of pain between my right leg and my head began to make itself felt, and closing my eyes again I groaned and rolled wearily on to my back, remembering the awful events of the previous night. I had killed a man. Worst of all I had killed a Russian soldier. That I had acted in self-defence would, I knew, be a matter of very little consequence to a Soviet appointed court. There was only one penalty for killing soldiers of the Red Army.

Now I asked myself how many people might have seen me walking from Potsdamer Railway Station with the hands and face of a South American headhunter. I resolved that, for several months at least, it might be better if I were to stay out of the Eastern Zone. But staring at the bomb-damaged ceiling of the bedroom I was reminded of the possibility that the Zone might choose to come to me: there was Berlin, an open patch of lathing on an otherwise immaculate expanse of plasterwork, while in the corner of the bedroom was the bag of black-market builder's gypsum with which I was one day intending to cover it over. There were few people, myself included, who did not believe that Stalin was intent on a similar mission to cover over the small bare patch of freedom that was Berlin.

I rose from my side of the bed, washed at the ewer, dressed, and went into the kitchen to find some breakfast.

On the table were several grocery items that had not been there the night before: coffee, butter, a tin of condensed milk and a couple of bars of chocolate – all from the Post Exchange, or PX, the only shops with anything in them, and shops that were restricted to American servicemen. Rationing meant that the German shops were emptied almost as soon as the supplies came in.

Any food was welcome: with cards totalling less than 3,500 calories a day between Kirsten and me, we often went hungry – I had lost more than fifteen kilos since the end of the war. At the same time I had my doubts about Kirsten's method of obtaining these extra supplies. But for the moment I put away my suspicions and fried a few potatoes with ersatz coffee-grounds to give them some taste.

Summoned by the smell of cooking Kirsten appeared in the kitchen doorway.

'Enough there for two?' she asked.

'Of course,' I said, and set a plate in front of her.

Now she noticed the bruise on my face. 'My god, Bernie, what the hell happened to you?'

'I had a run-in with an Ivan last night.' I let her touch my face and demonstrate her concern for a brief moment before sitting down to eat my breakfast. 'Bastard tried to rob me. We slugged it out for a minute and then he took off. I think he must have had a busy evening. He left some watches behind.' I wasn't going to tell her that he was dead. There was no sense in us both feeling anxious.

'I saw them. They look nice. Must be a couple of thousand dollars' worth there.'

'I'll go up to the Reichstag this morning and see if I can't find some Ivans to buy them.'

'Be careful he doesn't come there looking for you.'

'Don't worry. I'll be all right.' I forked some potatoes into my mouth, picked up the tin of American coffee and stared at it impassively. 'A bit late last night, weren't you?'

'You were sleeping like a baby when I got home.' Kirsten checked her hair with the flat of her hand and added, 'We were very busy yesterday. One of the Yanks took the place over for his birthday party.'

'I see.'

18

My wife was a schoolteacher, but worked as a waitress at an American bar in Zehlendorf which was open to American servicemen only. Underneath the overcoat which the cold obliged her to wear about our apartment, she was already dressed in the red chintz frock and tiny frilled apron that was her uniform.

I weighed the coffee in my hand. 'Did you steal this lot?'

She nodded, avoiding my eye.

'I don't know how you get away with it,' I said. 'Don't they bother to search any of you? Don't they notice a shortage in the store-room?'

She laughed. 'You've no idea how much food there is in that place. Those Yanks are on over 4,000 calories a day. A GI eats your monthly meat ration in just one night, and still has room for ice-cream.' She finished her breakfast and produced a packet of Lucky Strike from her coat pocket. 'Want one?'

'Did you steal those as well?' But I took one anyway and bowed my head to the match she was striking.

'Always the detective,' she muttered, adding, rather more irritatedly, 'As a matter of fact these were a present, from one of the Yanks. Some of them are just boys, you know. They can be very kind.'

'I'll bet they can,' I heard myself growl.

'They like to talk, that's all.'

'I'm sure your English must be improving.' I smiled broadly to defuse any sarcasm that was in my voice. This was not the time. Not yet anyway. I wondered if she would say anything about the bottle of Chanel that I had recently found hidden in one of her drawers. But she did not mention it.

Long after Kirsten had gone to the snack bar there was a knock at the door. Still nervous about the death of the Ivan I put his automatic in my jacket pocket before going to answer it.

'Who's there?'

'Dr Novak.'

Our business was swiftly concluded. I explained that my informer from the headquarters of the GSOV had confirmed with one telephone call on the landline to the police in Magdeburg, which was the nearest city in the Zone to Wernigerode, that Frau Novak was indeed being held in 'protective custody' by the MVD. Upon Novak's return home both he and his wife were to be deported immediately for 'work vital to the interests of the peoples of the Union of Soviet Socialist Republics' to the city of Kharkov in the Ukraine.

Novak nodded grimly. 'That would follow,' he sighed. 'Most of their metallurgical research is centred there.'

'What will you do now?' I asked.

He shook his head with such a look of despondency that I felt quite sorry for him. But not as sorry as I felt for Frau Novak. She was stuck.

'Well, you know where to find me if I can be of any further service to you.'

Novak nodded at the bag of coal I had helped him carry up from his taxi and said, 'From the look of your face, I should imagine that you earned that coal.'

'Let's just say that burning it all at once wouldn't make this room half as hot.' I paused. 'It's none of my business Dr Novak, but will you go back?'

'You're right, it's none of your business.'

I wished him luck anyway, and when he was gone carried a shovelful of coal into the sitting-room, and with a care that was only disturbed by my growing anticipation of being once more warm in my home, I built and lit a fire in the stove.

I spent a pleasant morning laid up on the couch, and was almost inclined to stay at home for the rest of the day. But in the afternoon I found a walking-stick in the cupboard and limped up to the Kurfürstendamm where, after queuing for at least half an hour, I caught a tram eastwards.

'Black market,' shouted the conductor when we came within sight of the old ruined Reichstag, and the tram emptied itself.

No German, however respectable, considered himself to be above a little black-marketeering now and again, and with an average weekly income of about 200 marks – enough to buy a packet of cigarettes – even legitimate businesses had plenty of occasions to rely on black-market commodities to pay employees. People used their virtually useless Reichsmarks only to pay the rent and to buy their miserable ration allowances. For the student of classical economics, Berlin presented the perfect model of a business cycle that was determined by greed and need.

In front of the blackened Reichstag on a field the size of a football pitch as many as a thousand people were standing about in little knots of conspiracy, holding what they had come to sell in front of them, like passports at a busy frontier: packets of saccharine, cigarettes, sewing-machine needles, coffee, ration coupons (mostly forged), chocolate and condoms. Others wandered around, glancing with deliberate disdain at the items held up for inspection, and searching for whatever it was they had come to buy. There was nothing that couldn't be bought here: anything from the title-deeds to some bombed-out property to a fake denazification certificate guaranteeing the bearer to be free of Nazi 'infection' and therefore employable in some capacity that was subject to Allied control, be it orchestra conductor or road-sweeper.

But it wasn't just Germans who came to trade. Far from it. The French came to buy jewellery for their girlfriends back home, and the British to buy cameras for their seaside holidays. The Americans bought antiques that had been expertly faked in one of the many workshops off Savignyplatz. And the Ivans came to spend their months of backpay on watches; or so I hoped.

I took up a position next to a man on crutches whose tin leg stuck out of the top of the haversack he was carrying on his back. I held up my watches by their straps. After a while I nodded amicably at my one-legged neighbour who apparently had nothing which he could display, and asked him what he was selling.

He jerked the back of his head at his haversack. 'My leg,' he said without any trace of regret.

'That's too bad.'

His face registered quiet resignation. Then he looked at my watches. 'Nice,' he said. 'There was an Ivan round here about fifteen minutes ago who was looking for a good watch. For 10 per cent I'll see if I can find him for you.'

I tried to think how long I might have to stand there in the cold before making a sale. 'Five,' I heard myself say. 'If he buys.'

The man nodded, and lurched off, a moving tripod, in the direction of the Kroll Opera House. Ten minutes later he was back, breathing heavily and accompanied by not one but two Russian soldiers who, after a great deal of argument, bought the Mickey Mouse and the gold Patek for $1,700.

When they had gone I peeled nine of the greasy bills off the wad I had taken from the Ivans and handed them over.

'Maybe you can hang on to that leg of yours now.'

'Maybe,' he said with a sniff, but later on I saw him sell it for five cartons of Winston.

I had no more luck that afternoon, and having fastened the two remaining watches to my wrists, I decided to go home. But passing close to the ghostly fabric of the Reichstag, with its bricked-up windows and its precarious-looking dome, my mind was changed by one particular piece of graffiti that was daubed there, reproducing itself on the lining of my stomach: 'What our women do makes a German weep, and a GI come in his pants.'

The train to Zehlendorf and the American sector of Berlin dropped me only a short way south of Kronprinzenallee and Johnny's American Bar where Kirsten worked, less than a kilometre from US Military Headquarters.

It was dark by the time I found Johnny's, a bright, noisy place with steamed-up windows, and several jeeps parked in front. A sign above the cheap-looking entrance declared that the bar was only open to First Three Graders, whatever they were. Outside the door was an old man with a stoop like an igloo – one of the city's many thousands of tip-collectors who made a living from picking up cigarette-ends: like prostitutes each tip-collector had his own beat, with the pavements outside American bars and clubs the most coveted of all, where on a good day a man or woman could recover as many as a hundred butts a day: enough for about ten or fifteen whole cigarettes, and worth a total of about five dollars.

'Hey, uncle,' I said to him, 'want to earn yourself four Winston?' I took out the packet I had bought at the Reichstag and tapped four into the palm of my hand. The man's rheumy eyes travelled eagerly from the cigarettes to my face.

'What's the job?'

'Two now, two when you come and tell me when this lady comes out of here.' I gave him the photograph of Kirsten I kept in my wallet.

'Very attractive piece,' he leered.

'Never mind that.' I jerked my thumb at a dirty-looking café further up Kronprinzenallee, in the direction of the US Military HQ. 'See that café?' He nodded. 'I'll be waiting there.'

The tip-collector saluted with his finger and quickly trousering the photograph and the two Winston, he started to turn back to scan his flagstones. But I held him by the grubby handkerchief he wore tied round his stubbly throat. 'Don't forget now, will you?' I said, twisting it tight. 'This looks like a good beat. So I'll know where to go looking if you don't remember to come and tell me. Got that?'

The old man seemed to sense my anxiety. He grinned horribly. 'She might have forgotten you, sir, but you can rest assured that I won't.' His face, a garage floor of shiny spots and oily patches, reddened as for a moment I tightened my grip.

'See that you don't,' I said and let him go, feeling a certain amount of guilt for handling him so roughly. I handed him another cigarette by way of compensation and, discounting his exaggerated endorsements of my own good character, I walked up the street to the dingy café.

For what felt like hours, but wasn't quite two, I sat silently nursing a large and inferior-tasting brandy, smoking several cigarettes and listening to the voices around me. When the tip-collector came to fetch me his scrofulous features wore a triumphant grin. I followed him outside and back into the street.

'The lady, sir,' he said, pointing urgently towards the railway station. 'She went that way.' He paused as I paid him the balance of his fee, and then added, 'With her *schätzi*. A captain, I think. Anyway, a handsome young fellow, whoever he is.'

I didn't stay to hear any more and walked as briskly as I was able in the direction which he had indicated.

I soon caught sight of Kirsten and the American officer who accompanied her, his arm wrapped around her shoulders. I followed them at a distance, the full moon affording me a clear view of their leisurely progress, until they came to a bombed-out apartment block, with six layers of flaky-pastry floors collapsed one on top of the other. They disappeared inside. Should I go in after them, I asked myself. Did I need to see everything?

Bitter bile percolated up from my liver to break down the fatty doubt that lay heavy in my gut.

Like mosquitoes I heard them before I saw them. Their English was more fluent than my understanding, but she seemed to be explaining that she could not be late home two nights in a row. A cloud drifted across the moon, darkening the landscape, and I crept behind an enormous pile of scree, where I thought I might get a better view. When the cloud sailed on, and the moonlight shone undiminished through the bare rafters of the roof, I had a clear sight of them, silent now. For a moment they were a facsimile of innocence as she knelt before him while he laid his hands upon her head as if delivering holy benediction. I puzzled as to why Kirsten's head should be rocking on her shoulders, but when he groaned my understanding of what was happening was as swift as the feeling of emptiness which accompanied it.

I stole silently away and drank myself stupid.

4

I spent the night on the couch, an occurrence which Kirsten, asleep in bed by the time I finally staggered home, would have wrongly attributed to the drink on my breath. I feigned sleep until I heard her leave the apartment, although I could not escape her kissing me on the forehead before she went. She was whistling as she stepped down the stairs and into the street. I got up and watched her from the window as she walked north up Fasanenstrasse towards Zoo Station and her train to Zehlendorf.

When I lost sight of her I set about trying to salvage some remnant of myself with which I could face the day. My head throbbed like an excited Dobermann, but after a wash with an ice-cold flannel, a couple of cups of the captain's coffee and a cigarette, I started to feel a little better. Still, I was much too preoccupied with the memory of Kirsten frenching the American captain and thoughts of the harm I could bring to him to even remember the harm I had already caused a soldier of the Red Army, and I was not as careful in answering a knock at the door as I should have been.

The Russian was short and yet he stood taller than the tallest man in the Red Army, thanks to the three gold stars and light-blue braid border on his greatcoat's silver epaulettes identifying him as a palkovnik, a colonel, of the MVD – the Soviet secret political police.

'Herr Gunther?' he asked politely.

I nodded sullenly, angry with myself for not having been more careful. I wondered where I had left the dead Ivan's gun, and if I dared to make a break for it. Or would he have men waiting at the foot of the stairs for just such an eventuality?

The officer took off his cap, clicked his heels like a Prussian and head-butted the air. 'Palkovnik Poroshin, at your service. May I come in?' He did not wait for an answer. He wasn't the type who was used to waiting for anything other than his own wind.

No more than about thirty years old, the colonel wore his hair long for a soldier. Pushing it clear of his pale blue eyes and back over his narrow head, he rendered the veneer of a smile as he turned to face me in my sitting-room. He was enjoying my discomfort.

'It is Herr Bernhard Gunther, is it not? I have to be sure.'

Knowing my name like that was a bit of a surprise. And so was the handsome gold cigarette-case which he flicked open in front of me. The tan on the ends of his cadaverous fingers suggested that he didn't bother with selling cigarettes as much as smoking them. And the MVD didn't normally bother to share a smoke with a man they were about to arrest. So I took one and owned up to my name.

He fed a cigarette into his lantern jaw and produced a matching Dunhill to light us both.

'And you are a – ' he winced as the smoke billowed into his eye ' – *sh'pek* ... what is the German word – ?'

'Private detective,' I said, translating automatically and regretting my alacrity almost at the very same moment.

Poroshin's eyebrows lifted on his high forehead. 'Well, well,' he remarked with a quiet surprise that turned quickly first to interest and then sadistic pleasure, 'you speak Russian.'

I shrugged. 'A little.'

'But that is not a common word. Not for someone who only speaks a little Russian. *Sh'pek* is also the Russian word for salted pig fat. Did you know that as well?'

'No,' I said. But as a Soviet prisoner of war I had eaten enough of it smeared on coarse black bread to know it only too well. Did he guess that?

'*Nye shooti* (seriously)?' he grinned. 'I bet you do. Just as I'd bet you know that I'm MVD, eh?' Now he laughed out loud. 'Do you see how good at my job I am? I haven't been talking to you for five minutes and already I'm able to say that you are keen to conceal that you speak good Russian. But why?'

'Why don't you tell me what you want, Colonel?'

'Come now,' he said. 'As an Intelligence officer it is only

natural for me to wonder why. You of all people must understand that kind of curiosity, yes?' Smoke trailed from his shark's fin of a nose as he pursed his lips in a rictus of apology.

'It doesn't do for Germans to be too curious,' I said. 'Not these days.'

He shrugged and wandered over to my desk and looked at the two watches that were lying on it. 'Perhaps,' he murmured thoughtfully.

I hoped that he wouldn't presume to open the drawer where I now remembered I had put the dead Ivan's automatic. Trying to steer him back to whatever it was he had wanted to see me about, I said: 'Isn't it true that all private detective and information agencies are forbidden in your zone?'

At last he came away from the desk.

'*Vyerno* (quite right), Herr Gunther. And that is because such institutions serve no purpose in a democracy – '

Poroshin tut-tutted as I started to interrupt.

'No, please don't say it, Herr Gunther. You were going to say that the Soviet Union can hardly be called a democracy. But if you did, the Comrade Chairman might hear you and send terrible men like me to kidnap you and your wife.

'Of course we both know that the only people making a living in this city now are the prostitutes, the black-marketeers and the spies. There will always be prostitutes, and the black-marketeers will last only for as long as the German currency remains unreformed. That leaves spying. That's the new profession to be in, Herr Gunther. You should forget about being a private detective when there are so many new opportunities for people like yourself.'

'That sounds almost as if you are offering me a job, Colonel.'

He smiled wryly. 'Not a bad idea at that. But it isn't why I came.' He looked behind him at the armchair. 'May I sit down?'

'Be my guest. I'm afraid I can't offer you much besides coffee.'

'Thank you, no. I find it a rather excitable drink.'

I arranged myself on the couch and waited for him to start.

'There is a mutual friend of ours, Emil Becker, who has got himself into the devil's kitchen, as you say.'

'Becker?' I thought for a moment and recalled a face from the Russian offensive of 1941; and before that, in the Reichskriminal police – the Kripo. 'I haven't seen him in a long time. I wouldn't call him a friend exactly, but what's he done? What are you holding him for?'

Poroshin shook his head. 'You misunderstand. He isn't in trouble with us, but with the Americans. To be precise, their Vienna military police.'

'So if you haven't got him, and the Americans have, he must have actually committed a crime.'

Poroshin ignored my sarcasm. 'He has been charged with the murder of an American officer, an army captain.'

'Well, we've all felt like doing that at some time.' I shook my head at Poroshin's questioning look. 'No, it doesn't matter.'

'What matters here is that Becker did not kill this American,' he said firmly. 'He is innocent. Nevertheless, the Americans have a good case, and he will certainly hang if someone does not help him.'

'I don't see what I can do.'

'He wishes to engage you in your capacity as a private detective, naturally. To prove him innocent. For this he will pay you generously. Win or lose, the sum of $5,000.'

I heard myself whistle. 'That's a lot of money.'

'Half to be paid now, in gold. The balance payable upon your arrival in Vienna.'

'And what's your interest in all this, Colonel?'

He flexed his neck across the tight collar of his immaculate tunic. 'As I said, Becker is a friend.'

'Do you mind explaining how?'

'He saved my life, Herr Gunther. I must do whatever I can to help him. But it would be politically difficult for me to assist him officially, you understand.'

'How do you come to be so familiar with Becker's wishes in this affair? I can hardly imagine that he telephones you from an American gaol.'

'He has a lawyer, of course. It was Becker's lawyer who asked me to try and find you; and to ask you to help your old comrade.'

'He was never that. It's true we once worked together. But "old comrades", no.'

Poroshin shrugged. 'As you wish.'

'Five thousand dollars. Where does Becker get $5,000?'

'He is resourceful man.'

'That's one word for it. What's he doing now?'

'He runs an import and export business, here and in Vienna.'

'A nice enough euphemism. Black-market, I suppose.'

Poroshin nodded apologetically and offered me another cigarette from his gold case. I smoked it with slow deliberation,
wondering what small percentage of all this might be on the
level.

'Well, what do you say?'

'I can't do it,' I said eventually. 'I'll give you the polite reason
first.'

I stood up and went to the window. In the street below stood
a shiny new BMW with a Russian pennant on the bonnet;
leaning on it was a big, tough-looking Red Army soldier.

'Colonel Poroshin, it wouldn't have escaped your attention
that it's not getting any easier to get in or out of this city. After
all, you have Berlin surrounded with half the Red Army. But
quite apart from the ordinary travel restrictions affecting
Germans, things do seem to have got quite a lot worse during
the last few weeks, even for your so-called allies. And with so
many displaced persons trying to enter Austria illegally, the
Austrians are quite happy that journeys there should be dis-
couraged. All right. That's the polite reason.'

'But none of this is a problem,' Poroshin said smoothly. 'For
an old friend like Emil I will gladly pull a few wires. Rail
warrants, a pink pass, tickets – it can all be easily fixed. You can
trust me to handle all the necessary arrangements.'

'Well, I suppose that's the second reason why I'm not going
to do it. The less polite reason. I don't trust you, Colonel. Why
should I? You talk about pulling a few strings to help Emil. But
you could just as easily pull them the other way. Things are
rather fickle on your side of the fence. I know a man who came
back from the war to find Communist Party officials living in
his house – officials for whom nothing was simpler than to pull

29

a few strings in order to ensure his committal to a lunatic asylum just so they could keep the house.

'And, only a month or two ago, I left a couple of friends drinking in a bar in your sector of Berlin, only to learn later that minutes after I had gone Soviet forces surrounded the place and pressed everyone in the bar into a couple of weeks of forced labour.

'So I repeat, Colonel: I don't trust you and see no reason why I should. For all I know I might be arrested the minute I step into your sector.'

Poroshin laughed out loud. 'But why? Why should you be arrested?'

'I never noticed that you need much of a reason.' I shrugged exasperatedly. 'Maybe because I'm a private detective. For the MVD that's as good as being an American spy. I believe that the old concentration camp at Sachsenhausen which your people took over from the Nazis is now full of Germans who've been accused of spying for the Americans.'

'If you will permit me one small arrogance, Herr Gunther: do you seriously believe that I, an MVD palkovnik, would consider that the matter of your deception and arrest was more important than the affairs of the Allied Control Council?'

'You're a member of the Kommendatura?' I was surprised.

'I have the honour to be Intelligence officer to the Soviet Deputy Military Governor. You may inquire at the council headquarters in Elsholzstrasse if you don't believe me.' He paused, waiting for some reaction from me. 'Come now. What do you say?'

When I still said nothing, he sighed and shook his head. 'I'll never understand you Germans.'

'You speak the language well enough. Don't forget, Marx was a German.'

'Yes, but he was also a Jew. Your countrymen spent twelve years trying to make those two circumstances mutually exclusive. That's one of the things I can't understand. Change your mind?'

I shook my head.

'Very well.'

The Colonel showed no sign of being irritated at my refusal. He looked at his watch and then stood up.

'I must be going,' he said. Taking out a notebook he started to write on a piece of paper. 'If you do change your mind you can reach me at this number in Karlshorst. That's 55-16-44. Ask for General Kaverntsev's Special Security Section. And there's my home telephone number as well: 05-00-19.'

Poroshin smiled and nodded at the note as I took it from him. 'If you should be arrested by the Americans, I wouldn't let them see that if I were you. They'll probably think you're a spy.'

He was still laughing about that as he went down the stairs.

5

For those who had believed in the Fatherland, it was not the defeat which gave the lie to that patriarchal view of society, but the rebuilding. And with the example of Berlin, ruined by the vanity of men, could be learned the lesson that when a war has been fought, when the soldiers are dead and the walls are destroyed, a city consists of its women.

I walked towards a grey granite canyon which might have concealed a heavily worked mine, from where a short train of brick-laden trucks was even now emerging under the supervision of a group of rubble-women. On the side of one of their trucks was chalked 'No time for love'. You didn't need reminding in view of their dusty faces and wrestlers' bodies. But they had hearts as big as their biceps.

Smiling through their catcalls and whistles of derision – where were my hands now that the city needed to be reconstructed? – and waving my walking-stick like a sick-note, I carried on until I came to Pestalozzistrasse where Friedrich Korsch (an old friend from my days with Kripo, and now a Kommissar with Berlin's Communist-dominated police force) had told me that I could find Emil Becker's wife.

Number 21 was a damaged five-storey building of basin-flats with paper windows, and inside the front doorway, smelling heavily of burnt toast, was a sign which warned 'Unsafe Staircase! In use at visitor's own risk'. Fortunately for me, the names and apartment-numbers that were chalked on the wall inside the door told me that Frau Becker lived on the ground floor.

I walked down a dark, dank corridor to her door. Between it and the landing washbasin an old woman was picking large chunks of fungus off the damp wall and collecting them in a cardboard box.

'Are you from the Red Cross?' she asked.

I told her I wasn't, knocked at the door and waited.

She smiled. 'It's all right, you know. We're really quite well-off here.' There was a quiet insanity in her voice.

I knocked again, more loudly this time, and heard a muffled sound, and then bolts being drawn on the other side of the door.

'We don't go hungry,' said the old woman. 'The Lord provides.' She pointed at her shards of fungus in the box. 'Look. There are even fresh mushrooms growing here.' And so saying she pulled a piece of fungus from the wall and ate it.

When the door finally opened, I was momentarily unable to speak from disgust. Frau Becker, catching sight of the old woman, brushed me aside and stepped smartly into the corridor, where with many loud insults she shooed the old woman away.

'Filthy old baggage,' she muttered. 'She's always coming into this building and eating that mould. The woman's mad. A complete spinner.'

'Something she ate no doubt,' I said queasily.

Frau Becker fixed me with the awl of her bespectacled eye. 'Now who are you and what do you want?' she asked brusquely.

'My name is Bernhard Gunther – ' I started.

'Heard of you,' she snapped. 'You're with Kripo.'

'I was.'

'You'd better come in.' She followed me into the icy-cold sitting-room, slammed the door shut and closed the bolts as if in mortal fear of something. Noticing how this took me aback, she added by way of explanation: 'Can't be too careful these days.'

'No indeed.'

I looked around at the loathsome walls, the threadbare carpet and the old furniture. It wasn't much but it was neatly kept. There was little she could have done about the damp.

'Charlottenburg's not too badly off,' I offered by way of mitigation, 'in comparison with some areas.'

'Maybe so,' she said, 'but I can tell you, if you'd come after dark and knocked till kingdom come, I wouldn't have answered. We get all sorts of rats round here at night.' So saying she picked up a large sheet of plywood from off the couch, and for a moment in the gloom of the place I thought she was working on a jigsaw-puzzle. Then I saw the numerous packets of Olleschau cigarette papers, the bags of butts, the piles of salvaged tobacco, and the serried ranks of re-rolls.

I sat down on the couch, took out my Winston and offered her one.

'Thanks,' she said grudgingly, and threaded the cigarette behind her ear. 'I'll smoke it later.' But I didn't doubt that she would sell it with the rest.

'What's the going rate for one of those re-cycled nails?'

'About 5 marks,' she said. 'I pay my collectors five US for 150 tips. That rolls about twenty good ones. Sell them for about ten US. What, are you writing an article about it for the *Tagesspiegel*? Spare me the Victor Gollancz–Save Berlin routine, Herr Gunther. You're here about that lousy husband of mine, aren't you? Well, I haven't seen him in a long while. And I hope I never clap eyes on him again. I expect you know he's in a Viennese gaol, do you?'

'Yes, I do.'

'You may as well know that when the American MPs came to tell me he'd been arrested, I was glad. I could forgive him for deserting me, but not our son.'

There was no telling if Frau Becker had turned witch before or after her husband had jumped his wife's bail. But on first acquaintance she wasn't the type to have persuaded me that her absconding husband had made the wrong choice. She had a bitter mouth, prominent lower jaw and small sharp teeth. No sooner had I explained the purpose of my visit than she started to chew the air around my ears. It cost me the rest of my cigarettes to placate her enough to answer my questions.

'Exactly what happened? Can you tell me?'

'The MPs said that he shot and killed an American army captain in Vienna. They caught him red-handed apparently. That's all I was told.'

'What about this Colonel Poroshin? Do you know anything about him?'

'You want to know if you can trust him or not. That's what you want to know. Well, he's an Ivan,' she sneered. 'That's all you should need to know.' She shook her head and added, impatiently: 'Oh, they knew each other here in Berlin because of one of Emil's rackets. Penicillin, I think it was. Emil said that Poroshin caught syphilis off some girl he was keen on. More like the other way round, I thought. Anyway this was the worst kind of syphilis: the sort that makes you swell up. Salvarsan didn't seem to work. Emil got them some penicillin. Well, you know how rare that is, the good stuff I mean. That could be one reason why Poroshin's trying to help Emil. They're all the same, these Russians. It's not just their brains that are in their balls. It's their hearts too. Poroshin's gratitude comes straight from his scrotum.'

'And another reason?'

Her brow darkened.

'You said that could be one reason.'

'Well of course. It can't simply be a matter of pulling Poroshin's tail out of the fire, can it? I wouldn't be at all surprised if Emil had been spying for him.'

'Got any evidence for that? Did he see much of Poroshin when he was still here in Berlin?'

'I can't say he did, I can't say he didn't.'

'But he's not charged with anything besides murder. He's not been charged with spying.'

'What would be the point? They've got enough to hang him as it is.'

'That's not the way it works. If he had been spying, they would have wanted to know everything. Those American MPs would have asked you a lot of questions about your husband's associates. Did they?'

She shrugged. 'Not that I can remember.'

'If there was any suspicion of spying they would have investigated it, if only to find out what sort of information he might have got hold of. Did they search this place?'

Frau Becker shook her head. 'Either way, I hope he hangs,' she said bitterly. 'You can tell him that if you see him. I certainly won't.'

'When did you last see him?'

'A year ago. He came back from a Soviet POW camp in July and he legged it three months later.'

'And when was he captured?'

'February 1943, at Briansk.' Her mouth tightened. 'To think that I waited three years for that man. All those other men who I turned away. I kept myself for him, and look what happened.' A thought seemed to occur to her. 'There's your evidence for spying, if you need any. How was it that he managed to get himself released, eh? Answer me that. How did he get home when so many others are still there?'

I stood up to leave. Perhaps the situation with my own wife made me more inclined to take Becker's part. But I had heard enough to realize that he would need all the help he could get – possibly more, if this woman had anything to do with it.

I said: 'I was in a Soviet prisoner-of-war camp myself, Frau Becker. For less time than your husband, as it happens. It didn't make me a spy. Lucky maybe, but not a spy.' I went to the door, opened it, and hesitated. 'Shall I tell you what it did make me? With people like the police, with people like you, Frau Becker, with people like my own wife, who's hardly let me touch her since I came home. Shall I tell you what it made me? It made me unwelcome.'

6

It is said that a hungry dog will eat a dirty pudding. But hunger doesn't just affect your standards of hygiene. It also dulls the wits, blunts the memory – not to mention the sex-drive – and generally produces a feeling of listlessness. So it was no surprise to me that there had been a number of occasions during the course of 1947 when, with senses pinched from want of nourishment, I had nearly met with an accident. It was for this very reason I decided to reflect upon my present, rather irrational inclination, which was to take Becker's case after all, with the benefit of a full stomach.

Formerly Berlin's finest, most famous hotel, the Adlon was now little more than a ruin. Somehow it remained open to guests, with fifteen available rooms which, because it was in the Soviet sector, were usually taken by Russian officers. A small restaurant not only survived in the basement, but did brisk business too, a result of it being exclusive to Germans with food coupons who might therefore lunch or dine there without fear of being thrown off a table in favour of some more obviously affluent Americans or British, as happened in most other Berlin restaurants.

The Adlon's improbable entrance was underneath a pile of rubble on Wilhelmstrasse, only a short distance away from the Führerbunker where Hitler had met his death, and which could be toured for the price of a couple of cigarettes in the hand of any one of the policemen who were supposed to keep people out of it. All Berlin's bulls were doubling as touts since the end of the war.

I ate a late lunch of lentil soup, turnip 'hamburger' and tinned fruit; and having sufficiently turned over Becker's problem in my metabolized mind, I handed over my coupons and went up to what passed for the hotel reception desk to use the telephone.

My call to the Soviet Military Authority, the SMA, in

Karlshorst was connected quickly enough, but I seemed to wait forever to be put through to Colonel Poroshin. Nor did speaking in Russian speed the progress of my call; it merely earned me a look of suspicion from the hotel porter. When finally I got through to Poroshin he seemed genuinely pleased that I had changed my mind and told me that I should wait by the picture of Stalin on Unter den Linden, where his staff car would collect me in fifteen minutes.

The afternoon had turned as raw as a boxer's lip and I stood in the door of the Adlon for ten minutes before heading back up the small service stairs and towards the top of the Wilhelmstrasse. Then, with the Brandenburg Gate at my back, I walked up to the house-sized picture of the Comrade Chairman that dominated the centre of the avenue, flanked by two smaller plinths, each bearing the Soviet hammer and sickle.

As I waited for the car, Stalin seemed to watch me, a sensation which, I supposed, was intended: the eyes were as deep, black and unpleasant as the inside of a postman's boot, and under the cockroach moustaches the smile was hard permafrost. It always amazed me that there were people who referred to this mur- dering monster as 'Uncle' Joe: he seemed to me to be about as avuncular as King Herod.

Poroshin's car arrived, its engine drowned by the noise of a squadron of YAK 3 fighters passing overhead. I climbed aboard, and rolled helplessly in the back seat as the broad- shouldered, Tatar-faced driver hit the BMW's accelerator, sending the car speeding east towards Alexanderplatz, and beyond to the Frankfurter Allee and Karlshorst.

'I always thought that German civilians were forbidden to ride in staff cars,' I said to the driver in Russian.

'True,' he said, 'but the colonel said that if we are stopped I'm just to say that you're being arrested.'

The Tatar laughed uproariously at my look of obvious alarm, and I could only console myself with the fact that while we were driving at such a speed, it was unlikely that we could be stopped by anything other than an anti-tank gun.

We reached Karlshorst minutes later.

A villa colony with a steeplechase course, Karlshorst, nicknamed 'the little Kremlin', was now a completely isolated Russian enclave which Germans could only enter by special permit. Or the kind of pennant on the front of Poroshin's car. We were waved through several checkpoints and finally drew up alongside the old St Antonius Hospital on Zeppelin Strasse now housing the SMA for Berlin. The car ground to a halt in the shadow of a five-metre-high plinth on top of which was a big red Soviet star. Poroshin's driver sprang out of his seat, opened my door smartly and, ignoring the sentries, squired me up the steps to the front door. I paused in the doorway for a moment, surveying the shiny new BMW cars and motorcycles in the car park.

'Someone been shopping?' I said.

'From the BMW factory at Eisenbach,' said my driver proudly. 'Now Russian.'

With this depressing thought he left me in a waiting-room that smelled strongly of carbolic. The room's only concession to decoration was another picture of Stalin with a slogan underneath that read: 'Stalin, the wise teacher and protector of the working people'. Even Lenin, portrayed in a smaller frame alongside the wise one, seemed from his expression to have one or two problems with that particular sentiment.

I met these same two popular faces hanging on the wall of Poroshin's office on the top floor of the SMA building. The young colonel's neatly pressed olive-brown tunic was hanging on the back of the glass door, and he was wearing a Circassian-style shirt, belted with a black strap. But for the polish on his soft calf-leather boots he might have passed for a student at Moscow University. He set down his mug and stood up from behind his desk as the Tatar ushered me into his office.

'Sit down, please, Herr Gunther,' said Poroshin, pointing at a bentwood chair. The Tatar waited to be dismissed. Poroshin lifted his mug and held it up for my inspection. 'Would you like some Ovaltine, Herr Gunther?'

'Ovaltine? No, thanks, I hate the stuff.'

'Do you?' He sounded surprised. 'I love it.'

'It's kind of early to be thinking of going to bed, isn't it?'

Poroshin smiled patiently. 'Perhaps you would prefer some

vodka.' He pulled open his desk drawer and took out a bottle
and a glass, which he placed on the desk in front of me.

I poured myself a large one. Out of the corner of my eye I
saw the Tatar rub his thirst with the back of his paw. Poroshin
saw it too. He filled another glass and laid it on the filing cabinet
so that it was immediately next to the man's head.

'You have to train these Cossack bastards like dogs,' he
explained. 'For them drunkenness is an almost religious ordi-
nance. Isn't that so, Yeroshka?'

'Yes, sir,' he said blankly.

'He smashed a bar up, assaulted a waitress, punched a sergeant, and but for me he might have been shot. Still might be
shot, eh, Yeroshka? The minute you touch that glass without
my permission. Understand?'

'Yes, sir.'

Poroshin produced a big, heavy revolver and laid it on the
desk to emphasize his point. Then he sat down again.

'I imagine you know quite a lot about discipline with your
record, Herr Gunther? Where did you say you served during
the war?'

'I didn't say.'

He leaned back in his chair and swung his boots on to the
desk. The vodka trembled over the edge of my glass as they
thudded down on the blotter.

'No, you didn't, did you? But I imagine that with your
qualifications you would have served in some Intelligence capacity.'

'What qualifications?'

'Come now, you're being too modest. Your spoken Russian,
your experience with Kripo. Ah yes, Emil's lawyer told me
about that. I'm told that you and he were once part of the Berlin
Murder Commission. And you a Kommissar, too. That's quite
senior, isn't it?'

I sipped my vodka and tried to keep calm. I told myself that
I ought to have expected something like this.

'I was just an ordinary soldier, obeying orders,' I said. 'I
wasn't even a Party member.'

'So few were, it would now seem. I find that really quite

remarkable.' He smiled and raised a salutary index finger. 'Be as coy as you like Herr Gunther, but I shall find out about you. Mark my words. If only to satisfy my curiosity.'

'Sometimes curiosity is a bit like Yeroshka's thirst,' I said, ' – best left unsatisfied. Unless it's the disinterested, intellectual kind of curiosity that belongs properly to the philosophers. Answers have a habit of disappointing.' I finished the glass and laid it on the blotter next to his boots. 'But I didn't come here with a cipher in my socks to play your afternoon's vexed question, Colonel. So how about you feed me with one of those Lucky Strikes you were smoking this morning and satisfy *my* curiosity at least as far as telling me one or two facts about this case?'

Poroshin leaned forward and knocked open a silver cigarette box on the desk. 'Help yourself,' he said.

I took one and lit it with a fancy silver lighter that was cast in the shape of a field gun; then I looked at it critically, as if judging its value in a pawnshop. He had irritated me and I wanted to kick back at him somehow. 'You've got some nice loot,' I said. 'This is a German field gun. Did you buy it, or was there nobody at home when you called?'

Poroshin closed his eyes, snorted a little laugh, then got up and went over to the window. He drew up the sash and unbuttoned his fly. 'That's the trouble with drinking all that Ovaltine,' he said, apparently unperturbed by my attempt to insult him. 'It goes straight through you.' When he started to pee, he glanced back across his shoulder at the Tatar who remained standing by the filing cabinet and the glass of vodka which stood on it. 'Drink it and get out, pig.'

The Tatar didn't hesitate. He emptied the glass with one jerk of his head and stepped swiftly out of the office, closing the door behind him.

'If you saw how peasants like him leave the toilets here, you would understand why I prefer to piss out of the window,' said Poroshin, buttoning himself. He closed the window and resumed his seat. The boots thudded back on to the blotter. 'My fellow Russians can make life in this sector rather trying at times. Thank God for people like Emil. He is a most amusing man to have around on occasion. And very resourceful too. There is simply nothing that he cannot get hold of. What is the word you have for these black-market types?'

'Swing Heinis.'

'Yes, swings. If one wanted entertainment, Emil would be the swing to arrange it.' He laughed fondly at the thought of him, which was more than I could do. 'I never met a man who knew so many girls. Of course they are all prostitutes and chocoladies, but that is not such a great crime these days, is it?'

'It depends on the chocolady,' I said.

'Also, Emil is most ingenious at getting things across the border – the Green Frontier you call it, don't you?'

I nodded. 'Through the woods.'

'An accomplished smuggler. He's made a great deal of money. Until this happened he was living very well in Vienna. A big house, a fine car and an attractive girlfriend.'

'Have you ever made use of his services? And I don't mean his acquaintance with chocoladies.'

Poroshin confined himself to repeating that Emil could get hold of anything.

'Does that include information?'

He shrugged. 'Now and again. But whatever Emil does, he does for money. I find it hard to believe he would not have also been doing things for the Americans.

'In this case, however, he had a job from an Austrian. A man called König, who was in the advertising and publicity business. The company was called Reklaue & Werbe Zentrale, and they had offices here in Berlin and in Vienna. König wanted Emil to collect layouts from the Vienna office to bring to Berlin, on a regular basis. He said that the work was too important to trust to the post or to a courier, and König couldn't go himself as he was awaiting denazification. Of course Emil suspected that the parcels contained things besides advertisements, but the money was good enough for him to ask no questions, and since he came to and from Berlin on a fairly regular basis anyway, it wasn't going to cause him any extra problems. Or so he thought.

'For a while Emil's deliveries went without a problem. When he was bringing cigarettes or some such contraband into Berlin

42

he would also bring one of König's parcels. He handed them over to a man called Eddy Holl and collected his money. It was as simple as that.

'Well, one night Emil was in Berlin and went to a nightclub in Berlin–Schönberg called the Gay Island. By accident he met this man, Eddy Holl. He was drunk and introduced him to an American army captain called Linden. Eddy described Emil to Captain Linden as "their Vienna courier". The next day Eddy telephoned Emil and apologised for being drunk and suggested that it would be better for all their sakes if Emil forgot all about Captain Linden.

'Several weeks later, when Emil was back in Vienna, he got a call from this Captain Linden, who said that he would like to meet him again. So they met at some bar and the American started to ask questions about the advertising firm, Reklaue & Werbe. There wasn't much that Emil could tell him, but Linden's being there worried him. He thought that if Linden was in Vienna that there might not be any more need for his own services. It would be a shame, he thought, to see the end of such easy money. So he followed Linden around Vienna for a while. After a couple of days Linden met another man, and followed by Emil they went to an old film studio. Minutes later Emil heard a shot and the man came out, alone. Emil waited until this man was gone. Then he went in and found Captain Linden's dead body, and a load of stolen tobacco. Naturally enough he did not inform the police. Emil tries to have as little to do with them as possible.

'The next day, König and a third man came to see him. Don't ask me his name, I don't know. They said that an American friend had gone missing, and that they were worried something might have happened to him. In view of the fact that Emil had once been a detective with Kripo, would he, for a substantial reward, look into it for them. Emil agreed, seeing an easy way to make some money, and perhaps an opportunity to help himself to some of the tobacco.

'After a day or so, and having had the studio watched for a while, Emil and a couple of his boys decided it was safe to go back there with a van. They found the International Patrol

43

waiting for them. Emil's boys were a couple of pleasure-shooters and got themselves killed. Emil was arrested.'

'Does he know who tipped them off?'

'I asked my people in Vienna to find that out. It seems the tip-off was anonymous.' Poroshin smiled appreciatively. 'Now here's the good part. Emil's gun is a Walther P38. He took it with him to the studio. But when he was arrested and surrendered it he noticed that it wasn't his P38 after all. This one had a German eagle on the handgrip. And there was another important difference. The local ballistics expert quickly identified this as the same gun that had shot and killed Captain Linden.'

'Someone switched it for Becker's own gun, eh?' I said. 'Yes, it's not the sort of thing you'd notice right away, is it? Very neat. A man, conveniently carrying the murder weapon, returns to the scene of the crime, ostensibly to collect his stolen tobacco. Quite a strong case there I'd say.'

I took a last puff of my cigarette before extinguishing it in Poroshin's silver desk-ashtray and helping myself to another. 'I'm not sure what I would be able to do,' I said. 'Turning water into wine isn't in my normal line of work.'

'Emil is anxious, so his lawyer, Dr Liebl, tells me, that you should find this man König. He seems to have disappeared.'

'I'll bet he has. Do you think it was König who made the switch, when he came to Becker's house?'

'It certainly looks that way. König or perhaps the third man.'

'Do you know anything about König, or this publicity firm?'

'*Nyet.*'

There was a knock at the door and an officer came into Poroshin's office.

'We have Am Kupfergraben on the line, sir,' he announced in Russian. 'They say it's urgent.'

I pricked up my ears. Am Kupfergraben was the location of Berlin's biggest MVD gaol. With so many displaced and missing persons in my line of work, it paid to keep your ears open.

Poroshin glanced at me, almost as if he knew what I was thinking, and then said to the other officer, 'It will have to wait, Jegoroff. Any other calls?'

44

'Zaisser from K–5.'

'If that Nazi bastard wants to speak to me he can damn well wait outside my door. Tell him that. Now leave us please.' He waited until the door had closed behind his subordinate. 'K–5 mean anything to you, Gunther?'

'Should it?'

'Not yet, no. But in time, who knows?' He did not elaborate, but instead glanced at his wristwatch. 'We really must get on. I have an appointment this evening. Jegoroff will arrange all your necessary papers – pink pass, travel permit, a ration card, an Austrian identity card – do you have a photograph? Never mind. Jegoroff will have one taken. Oh yes, I think it would be a good idea if you were to have one of our new tobacco permits. It allows you to sell cigarettes throughout the Eastern Zone, and obliges all Soviet personnel to be of assistance to you wherever it is possible. It might just get you out of any trouble.'

'I thought the black market was illegal in your zone,' I said, curious as to the reason for this blatant piece of official hypocrisy.

'It is illegal,' Poroshin said, without any trace of embarrassment. 'This is an officially licensed black market. It allows us to raise some foreign currency. Rather a good idea don't you think? Naturally we will supply you with a few cartons of cigarettes to make it look convincing.'

'You seem to have thought of everything. What about my money?'

'It will be delivered to your home at the same time as your papers. The day after tomorrow.'

'And where is the money coming from? This Dr Liebl, or from your cigarette concessions?'

'Liebl will be sending me money. Until then this matter will be handled by the SMA.'

I didn't like this much, but there wasn't much of an alternative. Take money from the Russians, or go to Vienna and trust that the money would be paid in my absence.

'All right,' I said. 'Just one more thing. What do you know about Captain Linden? You said that Becker met him in Berlin. Was he stationed here?'

'Yes. I was forgetting him, wasn't I?' Poroshin stood up and

45

went over to the filing cabinet on which the Tatar had left his empty glass. He opened one of the drawers and fingered his way across the tops of his files until he found the one he was searching for.

'Captain Edward Linden,' he read, coming back to his chair. 'Born Brooklyn, New York, 22 February 1907. Graduated Cornell University, with a degree in German, 1930; serving 970th Counter-Intelligence Corps; formerly 26th Infantry, stationed at Camp King Interrogation Centre, Oberusel as denazification officer; currently attached to US Documents Centre in Berlin as Crowcass liaison officer. Crowcass is the Central Registry of War Crimes and Security Suspects of the United States Army. It's not very much, I'm afraid.'

He dropped the file open in front of me. The strange, Greek-looking letters covered no more than half a sheet of paper.

'I'm not much good with Cyrillic,' I said.

Poroshin did not look convinced.

'What exactly is the United States Documents Centre?'

'It's a building in the American sector, near the edge of the Grünewald. The Berlin Documents Centre is the depository for Nazi ministerial and party documents captured by the Americans and the British towards the end of the war. It's quite comprehensive. They've got the complete NSDAP membership records, which makes it easy to find out when people lie on their denazification questionnaires. I'll bet they've even got your name there somewhere.'

'Like I said, I was never a Party member.'

'No,' he grinned, 'of course not.' Poroshin took the file and returned it to the filing cabinet. 'You were only obeying orders.'

It was plain he didn't believe me any more than he believed that I was unable to decipher St Cyril's Byzantine alphabet: in that at least he would have been justified.

'And now, if you have no more questions, I really must leave you. I am due at the State Opera in the Admiralspalast in half an hour.' He took off his belt and, yelling the names of Yeroshka and Jegoroff, slipped into his tunic.

'Have you ever been to Vienna?' he asked, fixing the cross belt under his epaulette.

'No, never.'

'The people are just like the architecture,' he said, inspecting his appearance in the window's reflection. 'They are all front. Everything that's interesting about them seems to be on the surface. Inside they're very different. Now there's a people I could really work with. All Viennese were born to be spies.'

7

'You were late again last night,' I said.

'I didn't wake you, did I?' She slid naked out of bed and went over to the full-length mirror in the corner of our bedroom. 'Anyway, you were kind of late yourself the other night.' She started to examine her body. 'It's so nice having a warm house again. Where on earth did you find the coal?'

'A client.'

Watching her standing there, stroking her pubic hair and flattening her stomach with the palm of her hand, lifting her breasts, scrutinizing her tight, finely-lined mouth with its waxy sheen, concave cheeks and shrinking gums, and finally twisting around to assess her gently sagging bottom, her bony hand with the rings on the fingers slightly looser than before, pulling at the flesh of one buttock, I didn't need to be told what was going through her mind. She was an attractive, mature woman intent on making full use of what time she had left.

Feeling hurt and irritated, I jack-knifed out of bed to find my leg buckling beneath me.

'You look fine,' I said wearily, and limped into the kitchen.

'That sounds a little short for a love sonnet,' she called out.

There were some more PX goods on the kitchen table: a couple of cans of soup, a bar of real soap, a few saccharine cards and a packet of condoms.

Still naked, Kirsten followed me into the kitchen and watched me examining her haul. Was it just the one American? Or were there more?

'I see you've been busy again,' I said, picking up the packet of Parisians. 'How many calories are these?'

She laughed behind her hand. 'The manager keeps a load under the counter.' She sat down on a chair. 'I thought it would be nice. You know, it's been quite a while since we did anything.'

48

She let her thighs yawn as if to let me see a little more of her. 'There's time now, if you want.'

It was quickly done, expedited with an almost professional nonchalance on her part, as if she had been administering an enema. No sooner had I finished than she was heading towards the bathroom with hardly a blush on her cheek, carrying the used Parisian as if it were a dead mouse she had found under the bed.

Half an hour later, dressed and ready to leave for work, she paused in the sitting-room where I had stoked the ashes in the stove and was now adding some more coal. For a moment she watched me bring the fire to life again.

'You're good at that,' she said. I couldn't tell whether any sarcasm was intended. Then she gave me a peremptory kiss and went out.

The morning was colder than a mohel's knife, and I was glad to start the day in a reading library on Hardenbergstrasse. The library assistant was a man with a mouth so badly scarred that it was impossible to say where his lips were until he started to speak.

'No,' he said, in a voice that belonged properly to a sea-lion, 'there are no books about the BDC. But there have been a couple of newspaper articles published in the last few months. One in the *Telegraf*, I think, and the other in the *Military Government Information Bulletin*.'

He collected his crutches and shouldered his one-legged way to a cabinet housing a large card-index where, as he had remembered, he found references for both these articles: one, published in the *Telegraf* in May, an interview with the Centre's commanding officer, a Lieutenant-Colonel Hans W. Helm; the other an account of the Centre's early history, written by a junior staff member in August.

I thanked the assistant, who told me where to find the library's copies of both publications.

'Lucky for you that you came today,' he said. 'I'm travelling to Giessen tomorrow, to have my artificial leg fitted.'

Reading the articles I realized that I had never thought the Americans were capable of such efficiency. Admittedly, there had been a certain amount of luck involved in the accumulation of some of the Centre's documentary collections. For example, troops of the US Seventh Army had stumbled on the complete Nazi Party membership records at a paper mill near Munich, where they were about to be pulped. But staff at the Centre had set about the creation and organization of the most comprehensive archive, so that it could be determined with complete accuracy exactly who was a Nazi. As well as the NSDAP master files, the Centre included in its collection the NSDAP membership applications, Party correspondence, SS service records, Reich Security Office records, SS racial records, proceedings of the Supreme Party Court and the People's Court – everything from the membership files of the National Socialist Schoolteachers' Organization to a file detailing expulsions from the Hitler Youth.

Another thought occurred to me as I left the library and made my way to the railway station. I would never have believed that the Nazis could have been stupid enough to have recorded their own activities in such comprehensive and incriminating detail.

I left the U–Bahn – a stop too early as it turned out – at a station in the American sector which, for no reason to do with their occupation of the city, was called Uncle Tom's Hut, and walked down Argentinische Allee.

Surrounded by the tall fir trees of the Grünewald, and only a short distance from a small lake, the Berlin Documents Centre stood in well-guarded grounds at the end of Wasserkäfersteig, a cobblestoned cul-de-sac. Inside a wire fence the Centre comprised a number of buildings, but the main part of the BDC appeared to be a two-storey affair at the end of a raised pathway, painted white and with green shutters on the windows. It was a nice-looking place, although I soon remembered it as the headquarters of the old Forschungsamt – the Nazis' telephone-tapping centre.

The soldier at the gatehouse, a big, gap-toothed Negro, eyed me suspiciously as I halted at his checkpoint. He was probably more used to dealing with people in cars, or military vehicles, than with a lone pedestrian.

'What do you want, Fritzy?' he said, clapping his woolly gloves together and stamping his boots to keep warm.

'I was a friend of Captain Linden's,' I said in my halting English. 'I have just heard the terrible news, and I came to say how sorry my wife and I were. He was kind to us both. Gave us PX, you know.' From my pocket I produced the short letter I had composed on the train. 'Perhaps you would be kind enough to deliver this to Colonel Helm.'

The soldier's tone changed immediately.

'Yes sir, I'll give it to him.' He took the letter and regarded it awkwardly. 'Very kind of you to think of him.'

'It is just a few marks, for some flowers,' I said, shaking my head. 'And a card. My wife and I wanted something on Captain Linden's grave. We would go to the funeral if it was in Berlin, but we thought that his family would be taking him home.'

'Well, no, sir,' he said. 'The funeral's in Vienna, this Friday morning. Family wanted it that way. Less trouble than shipping a body all the way home I guess.'

I shrugged. 'For a Berliner that might as well be in America. Travel is not easy these days.' I sighed and glanced at my watch. 'I had better be getting along. I have quite a walk ahead of me.' When I turned to walk away, I groaned, and clutching my knee and affecting a broad grimace, I sat squarely down on the road in front of the barrier, my stick clattering on the cobbles beside me. Quite a performance. The soldier side-stepped his checkpoint.

'Are you all right?' he said, collecting my stick and helping me to my feet.

'A bit of Russian shrapnel. It gives me some trouble now and again. I'll be all right in a minute or two.'

'Hey, come on in to the gatehouse and sit down for a couple of minutes.' He led me round the barrier and through the little door of his hut.

'Thank you. It is very kind of you.'

'Kind, nothing. Any friend of Captain Linden's . . .'

I sat down heavily and rubbed my almost painless knee. 'Did you know him well?'

'Me, I'm just a Pfc. I can't say I knew him, but I used to drive him now and again.'

I smiled and shook my head. 'Could you speak more slowly please? My English is not so good.'

'I drove him now and again,' the soldier said more loudly, and he imitated the action of turning a steering-wheel. 'You say that he gave you PX?'

'Yes, he was very kind.'

'Yeah, that sounds like Linden. Always had plenty of PX to give away.' He paused as a thought occurred to him. 'There was one particular couple – well, he was like a son to them. Always taking them Care packages. Perhaps you know them. The Drexlers?'

I frowned and rubbed my jaw thoughtfully. 'Not the couple who live in – ' I snapped my fingers as if the street name were on the tip of my tongue ' – where is it now?'

'Steglitz,' he said, prompting me. 'Handjery Strasse.'

I shook my head. 'No, I must be thinking of someone else. Sorry.'

'Hey, don't mention it.'

'I suppose the police must have asked you a lot of questions about Captain Linden's murder.'

'Nope. They asked us nothing, on account of the fact that they already got the guy who did it.'

'They've got someone? That is good news. Who is he?'

'Some Austrian.'

'But why did he do it? Did he say?'

'Nope. Crazy, I guess. How d'you meet the captain, anyway?'

'I met him at a nightclub. The Gay Island.'

'Yeah, I know it. Never go there myself. Me, I prefer those places down on the Ku-damm: Ronny's Bar, and the Club Royale. But Linden used to go to the Gay Island a lot. He had a lot of German friends, I guess, and that's where they liked to go.'

'Well, he spoke such good German.'

'That he did, sir. Like a native.'

'My wife and I used to wonder why he never had a regular

girl. We even offered to introduce him to some. Nice girls, from good families.'

The soldier shrugged. 'Too busy, I guess.' He chuckled. 'He sure had plenty of others. Gee, that man liked to frat.'

After a moment I realized he meant fraternize, which was the euphemism in general military usage for what another American officer was doing to my wife. I squeezed my knee experimentally and stood up.

'Sure you're all right now?' said the soldier.

'Yes, thank you. You have been most kind.'

'Kind, nothing. Any friend of Captain Linden's . . .'

8

I inquired after the Drexlers at the Steglitz local post office on Sintenis Platz, a quiet, peaceful square, once covered in grass and now given over to the cultivation of things edible.

The postmistress, a woman with an enormous Ionic curl on either side of her head, informed me crisply that her office knew of the Drexlers and that like most people in the area they collected their mail from the office. Therefore, she explained, their precise address on Handjery Strasse was not known. But she did add that the Drexlers' usually considerable mail was now even larger in view of the fact that it was several days since they had bothered to collect it. She used the word 'bothered' with more than a little distaste, and I wondered if there was some reason she should have disliked the Drexlers. My offer to deliver their mail was swiftly rebuffed. That would not have been proper. But she told me that I could certainly remind them to come and take it away as it was becoming a nuisance.

Next I decided to try at the Schönberg Police Praesidium on nearby Grünewald Strasse. Walking there, under the uneasy shadow of gorgonzola walls that leaned forwards as if permanently on tiptoe, past buildings otherwise unscathed but with just a corner balustrade missing, like an illicitly sampled wedding cake, took me right by the Gay Island nightclub, where Becker had reportedly met Captain Linden. It was a dreary, cheerless-looking place with a cheap neon sign, and I felt almost glad that it was closed.

The bull on the desk at the Police Praesidium had a face as long as a mandarin's thumbnail, but he was an obliging sort of fellow and while he consulted the local registration records he told me that the Drexlers were not unknown to the Schönberg police.

'They're a Jewish couple,' he explained. 'Lawyers. Quite

54

well known around here. You might even say that they were notorious.'

'Oh? Why's that?'

'It's not that they break any laws, you understand.' The sergeant's wurst-sized finger found their name in his ledger and traversed the page to the street and the number. 'Here we are. Handjery Strasse. Number seventeen.'

'Thank you, Sergeant. So what is it about them?'

'Are you a friend of theirs?' He sounded circumspect.

'No, I'm not.'

'Well sir, it's just that people don't like that kind of thing. They want to forget about what happened. I don't think there's any good in raking over the past like that.'

'Forgive me, Sergeant, but what is it that they do exactly?'

'They hunt so-called Nazi war-criminals, sir.'

I nodded. 'Yes, I can see how that might not make them very popular with the neighbours.'

'It was wrong what happened. But we have to rebuild, start again. And we can hardly do that if the war follows us around like a bad smell.'

I needed some more information from him, so I agreed. Then I asked about the Gay Island.

'It's not the sort of place I'd let my missus catch me in, sir. It's run by a sparkler called Kathy Fiege. The place is full of them. But there's never any trouble there, apart from the occasional drunken Yank. Not that you can call that trouble. And if the rumours are true we'll all be Yanks soon – leastways all of us in the American sector, eh?'

I thanked him and walked to the station door. 'One more thing, sergeant,' I said, turning on my heels. 'The Drexlers? Do they ever find any war-criminals?'

The sergeant's long face took on an amused, sly aspect.

'Not if we can help it, sir.'

The Drexlers lived a short way south from the Police Praesidium, in a recently renovated building close to the S–Bahn line and opposite a small school. But there was no reply when I knocked at the door of their top-floor apartment.

I lit a cigarette to rid my nostrils of the strong smell of

disinfectant that hung about the landing, and knocked again. Glancing down I saw two cigarette-ends lying, unaccountably uncollected, on the floor close to the door. It didn't look as if anyone had been through the door in a while. Bending down to pick them up I found the smell even stronger. Dropping into a press-up position I pushed my nose up to the gap between floor and door and retched as the air inside the apartment caught my throat and lungs. I rolled quickly away and coughed half my insides on to the stairs below.

When I had recovered my breath I stood up and shook my head. It seemed hardly possible that anyone could live in such an atmosphere. I glanced down the stairwell. There was nobody about.

I stepped back from the door and kicked hard at the lock with my better leg, but it budged hardly at all. Once more I checked the stairwell to see if the noise had drawn anyone out of their apartment and, finding myself undetected, I kicked again.

The door sprang open and a terrible, pestilent smell flew forth, so strong that I reeled back for a moment and almost fell downstairs. Pulling my coat lapel across my nose and mouth I bounded into the darkened apartment, and, spying the faint outline of a curtain valance, I tore the heavy velvet drapes aside and threw open the window.

Cold air stripped the tears from my eyes as I leaned into the fresh air. Children on their way home from school waved to me and weakly I waved back at them.

When I was sure that the draught between the door and the window had ventilated the room I ducked inside to find whatever I would find. I didn't think it was the kind of smell that was meant to take care of any pest smaller than a rogue elephant.

I went over to the front door and pushed it back and forwards on its hinges to fan some more clean air through while I surveyed the desk, the chairs, the bookcases, the filing cabinets and the piles of books and papers that filled the little room. Beyond was an open door, and the edge of a brass bedstead.

My foot kicked something on the floor as I moved towards the bedroom. A cheap tin tray of the kind you find in a bar or a café.

But for the congestion in the two faces that lay side by side on their pillows, you might have thought they were still sleeping. If your name is on someone's death-card, there are worse ways than asphyxia while asleep to collect it.

I pulled back the quilt and undid Herr Drexler's pyjama top, revealing a well-swollen stomach marbled with veins and blebs like a piece of blue cheese. I pressed it with my forefinger: it felt tight. Sure enough, a harder pressure with my hand produced a fart from the corpse, indicating a gaseous disruption of the internal organs. It appeared as if the pair of them had been dead for at least a week.

I drew the quilt over them again and returned to the front room. For a while I stared hopelessly at the books and papers which lay on the desk, even making a desultory attempt to find some clue or other, but since I had as yet only the vaguest appreciation of the puzzle, I soon abandoned this as a waste of time.

Outside, under a mother-of-pearl-coloured sky, I was just starting up the street towards the S–Bahn when something caught my eye. There was so much discarded military equipment still lying about Berlin that, but for the manner of the Drexlers' death, I should have paid the thing no regard. Lying on a heap of rubble that had collected in the gutter was a gas-mask. An empty tin can rolled to my feet as I tugged at the rubber strap. Rapidly colouring in the outline scenario of the murder, I abandoned the mask and squatted down on to the backs of my legs to read the label on the rusting metallic curve.

'Zyklon–B. Poisonous gas! Danger! Keep cool and dry! Protect from the sun and from naked flame. Open and use with extreme caution. Kaliwerke A. G. Kolin.'

In my mind's eye I pictured a man standing outside the Drexlers' door. It was late at night. Nervously he half-smoked a couple of cigarettes before pulling on the gas-mask, checking the straps to make sure he had a tight fit. Then he opened the can of crystallized prussic acid, tipped the pellets – already liquefying on contact with the air – on to the tray he had brought with him, and quickly slid it under the door, into the Drexlers' apartment. The sleeping couple breathed deeply, lapsing into unconsciousness as the Zyklon–B gas, first used on human beings in the concentration camps, started to block the uptake of oxygen in their blood. Small chance that the Drexlers would have left a window open in this weather. But perhaps the murderer laid something – a coat or a blanket – across the bottom of the door to prevent a draught of fresh air into the apartment, or to prevent anyone else in the building from being killed. One part in two thousand of the gas was lethal. Finally, after fifteen or twenty minutes, when the pellets were fully dissolved, and the murderer was satisfied that the gas had done its silent, deadly work – that two more Jews had, for whatever reason, joined the six million – he would have collected up his coat, his mask and his empty can (perhaps he hadn't meant to leave the tray: not that it mattered, he would surely have worn gloves to handle the Zyklon–B), and walked into the night.

You could almost admire its simplicity.

9

Somewhere, further up the street, a jeep grumbled off into the snow-charged blackness. I wiped the condensation off the window with my sleeve, and saw the reflection of a face that I recognized.

'Herr Gunther,' he said, as I turned in my seat, 'I thought it was you.' A thin layer of snow covered the man's head. With its squared-off skull and prominent, perfectly round ears, it reminded me of an ice-bucket.

'Neumann,' I said, 'I thought you were dead for sure.'

He wiped his head and took off his coat. 'Mind if I join you? My girl hasn't turned up yet.'

'When did you ever have a girl, Neumann? At least, one you hadn't already paid for.'

He twitched nervously. 'Look, if you're going to be – '

'Relax,' I said. 'Sit down.' I waved to the waiter. 'What will you have?'

'Just a beer, thanks.' He sat down and with narrowed eyes regarded me critically. 'You haven't changed much, Herr Gunther. Older-looking, a bit greyer, and rather thinner than you used to be, but still the same.'

'I hate to think what I'd be like if you thought I looked any different,' I said pointedly. 'But what you say sounds like a fairly accurate description of eight years.'

'Is that how long it's been? Since we last met?'

'Give or take a world war. You still listening at keyholes?'

'Herr Gunther, you don't know the half of it,' he snorted. 'I'm a prison warder at Tegel.'

'I don't believe it. You? You're as bent as a stolen rocking-chair.'

'Honest, Herr Gunther, it's true. The Yanks have got me guarding Nazi war-criminals.'

'And you're the hard-labour, right?'

Neumann twitched again.

'Here comes your beer.'

The waiter laid the glass in front of him. I started to speak but the Americans at the next table burst into loud laughter. Then one of them, a sergeant, said something else and this time even Neumann laughed.

'He said that he doesn't believe in fraternization,' Neumann explained. 'He said he doesn't want to treat any fräulein the way he'd treat his brother.'

I smiled and looked over at the Americans. 'Did you learn to speak English working in Tegel?'

'Sure. I learn a lot of things.'

'You were always a good informer.'

'For instance,' he lowered his voice, 'I heard that the Soviets stopped a British military train at the border to take off two cars containing German passengers. The word is that it's in retaliation for the establishment of Bizonia.' He meant the merging of the British and American zones of Germany. Neumann drank some of his beer and shrugged. 'Maybe there will be another war.'

'I don't see how,' I said. 'Nobody's got much stomach for another dose of it.'

'I dunno. Maybe.'

He set his glass down and produced a box of snuff which he offered to me. I shook my head and grimaced as I watched him take a pinch and slide it under his lip.

'Did you see any action during the war?'

'Come on, Neumann, you should know better. Nobody asks a question like that these days. Do you hear me asking how you got a denazification certificate?'

'I'll have you know that I got that quite legitimately.' He fished out his wallet and unfolded a piece of paper. 'I was never involved in anything. Free from Nazi infection this says, and that's what I am, and proud of it. I didn't even join the army.'

'Only because they wouldn't have you.'

'Free from Nazi infection,' he repeated angrily.

'Must be about the only infection you never had.'

'What are you doing here anyway?' he sneered back.

'I love coming to the Gay Island.'

'I've never seen you here before, and I've been coming here a while.'

'Yes, it looks like the kind of place you'd feel comfortable in. But how do you afford it, on a warder's pay?'

Neumann shrugged evasively.

'You must do a lot of errands for people,' I suggested.

'Well, you have to, don't you.' He smiled thinly. 'I'll bet you're here on a case, aren't you?'

'Maybe.'

'I might be able to help. Like I say, I come here a lot.'

'All right then.' I took out my wallet and held up a five-dollar bill. 'You ever hear of a man called Eddy Holl? He comes in here sometimes. He's in the advertising and publicity business. A firm called Reklaue & Werbe Zentrale.'

Neumann swallowed and stared dismally at the bill. 'No,' he said reluctantly, 'I don't know him. But I could ask around. The barman's a friend. He might – '

'I already tried him. Not the talkative type. But from what he did say, I don't think he knew Holl.'

'This advertising mob. What did you say they were called?'

'Reklaue & Werbe Zentrale. They're in Wilmersdorfer Strasse. I was there this afternoon. According to them Herr Eddy Holl is at the offices of their parent company in Pullach.'

'Well, maybe he is. In Pullach.'

'I've never even heard of it. I can't imagine the headquarters of anything being in Pullach.'

'Well, you'd be wrong.'

'All right,' I said. 'I'm ready to be surprised.'

Neumann smiled and nodded at the five dollars I was slipping back into my wallet. 'For five dollars I could tell you everything I know about it.'

'No cold cabbage.'

He nodded and I tossed him the bill. 'This had better be good.'

'Pullach is a small suburb of Munich. It is also the head-quarters of the Postal Censorship Authorities of the United

States Army. The mail for all the GIs at Tegel has to go through there.'

'Is that it?'

'What do you want, the average rainfall?'

'All right, I'm not sure what that tells me, but thanks anyway.'

'Maybe I can keep my eyes open for this Eddy Holl.'

'Why not? I'm off to Vienna tomorrow. When I get there I'll telegraph you with the address where I'll be staying in case you get something. Cash on delivery.'

'Christ, I wish I was going. I love Vienna.'

'You never struck me as the cosmopolitan type, Neumann.'

'I don't suppose you fancy delivering a few letters when you're there, do you? I've got quite a few Austrians on my landing.'

'What, play postman for Nazi war-criminals? No thanks.' I finished my drink and looked at my watch. 'You think she's coming, this girl of yours?' I stood up to leave.

'What time is it?' he said, frowning.

I showed him the face of the Rolex on my wrist. I had more or less decided not to sell it. Neumann winced as he saw the time.

'I expect she got held up,' I said.

He shook his head sadly. 'She won't come now. Women.'

I gave him a cigarette. 'These days the only woman you can trust is another man's wife.'

'It's a rotten world, Herr Gunther.'

'Yeah, well, don't tell anyone, will you.'

10

On the train to Vienna I met a man who talked about what we had done to the Jews.

'Look,' he said, 'they can't blame us for what happened. It was preordained. We were merely fulfilling their own Old Testament prophecy: the one about Joseph and his brothers. There you have Joseph, a repressive father's youngest and most favoured son, and whom we can take to be symbolic of the whole Jewish race. And then you have all the other brothers, symbolic of gentiles everywhere, but let's assume they are Germans who are quite naturally jealous of the little velvet boy. He's better looking than they are. He has a coat of many colours. My God, no wonder they hate him. No wonder they sell him into slavery. But the important point to note is that what the brothers do is as much a reaction against a stern and authoritarian father – a fatherland if you like – as it is against an apparently over-privileged brother.' The man shrugged and started to knead the lobe of one of his question-mark shaped ears thoughtfully. 'Really, when you think about it, they ought to thank us.'

'How do you work that out?' I said, with considerable want of faith.

'Had it not been for what Joseph's brothers did, the children of Israel would never have been enslaved in Egypt, would never have been led to the Promised Land by Moses. Similarly, had it not been for what we Germans did, the Jews would never have gone back to Palestine. Why even now, they are on the verge of establishing a new state.' The man's little eyes narrowed as if he had been one of the few allowed a peek in God's desk-diary. 'Oh yes,' he said, 'it was a prophecy fulfilled, all right.'

'I don't know about any prophecy,' I growled, and jerked my thumb at the scene skimming by the carriage window: an apparently endless Red Army troop convoy, moving south along the autobahn, parallel to the railway line, 'but it certainly looks like we ended up in the Red Sea.'

It was well named, this infinite column of savage, omnivorous red ants, ravaging the land and gathering all that they could carry – more than their individual body weights – to take back to their semi-permanent, worker-run colonies. And like some Brazilian planter who had seen his coffee crop devastated by these social creatures, my hatred of the Russians was tempered by an equal measure of respect. For seven long years I had fought them, killed them, been imprisoned by them, learned their language and finally escaped from one of their labour camps. Seven thin ears of corn blasted with the east wind, devouring the seven good ears.

At the outbreak of the war I had been a Kriminalkommissar in Section 5 of the RSHA, the Reich Main Security Office, and automatically ranked as a full lieutenant in the SS. Apart from the oath of loyalty to Adolf Hitler, my being an SS-Ober-sturmführer had not seemed much of a problem until June 1941, when Arthur Nebe, formerly the director of the Reichs Criminal Police, and newly promoted SS-Gruppenführer, was given command of an Action Group as part of the invasion of Russia.

I was just one of the various police personnel who were drafted to Nebe's group, the aim of which, so I believed, was to follow the Wehrmacht into occupied White Russia and combat lawbreaking and terrorism of whatever description. My own duties at the Group's Minsk headquarters had involved the seizure of the records of the Russian NKVD and the capture of an NKVD death-squad that had massacred hundreds of White Russian political prisoners to prevent them from being liberated by the German Army. But mass murder is endemic in any war of conquest, and it soon became apparent to me that my own side was also arbitrarily massacring Russian prisoners. Then came the discovery that the primary purpose of the Action Groups was not the elimination of terrorists but the systematic murder of Jewish civilians.

In all my four years' service in the first, Great War, I never saw anything which had a more devastating effect on my spirit than what I witnessed in the summer of 1941. Although I was not personally charged with the task of commanding any of these mass-execution squads, I reasoned that it could only be a matter of time before I was so ordered, and, as an inevitable corollary, before I was shot for refusing to obey. So I requested an immediate transfer to the Wehrmacht and the front line.

As the commanding general of the Action Group, Nebe could have had me sent to a punishment battalion. He could even have ordered my execution. Instead he acceded to my request for a transfer, and after several more weeks in White Russia, during which time I assisted General Gehlen's Foreign Armies East Intelligence Section with the organization of the captured NKVD records, I was transferred, not to the front line, but to the War Crimes Bureau of the Military High Command in Berlin. By that time Arthur Nebe had personally supervised the murders of over 30,000 men, women and children.

After my return to Berlin I never saw him again. Years later I met an old friend from Kripo who told me that Nebe, always an ambiguous sort of Nazi, had been executed in early 1945 as one of the members of Count Stauffenberg's plot to kill Hitler.

It always gave me a strange kind of feeling to know that I very possibly owed my life to a mass-murderer.

To my great relief, the man with the curious line in hermeneutics left the train at Dresden, and I slept between there and Prague. But most of the time I thought about Kirsten and the abruptly worded note I had left her, explaining that I would be away for several weeks and accounting for the presence of the gold sovereigns in the apartment, which constituted half of my fee for taking Becker's case, and which Poroshin had taken it upon himself to deliver the previous day.

I cursed myself for not writing more, for failing to say that there was nothing I wouldn't have done for her, no Herculean labour I would not have gladly performed on her behalf. All of this she knew of course, made manifest as it was in the packet of extravagantly worded letters that she kept in her drawer. Next to her unmentioned bottle of Chanel.

11

The journey between Berlin and Vienna is a long time to spend
brooding about the infidelity of your wife, so it was just as well
that Poroshin's aide had got me a ticket on a train that took the
most direct route – nineteen and a half hours, via Dresden,
Prague and Brno – as opposed to the twenty-seven-and-a-half-
hour train which went via Leipzig and Nuremberg. With a
screech of wheels the train drew slowly to a halt in Franz Josefs
Bahnhof, mantling the platform's few occupants in a steamy
limbo.

At the ticket barrier I presented my papers to an American
MP and, having explained my presence in Vienna to his satisfaction, walked into the station, dropped my bag and looked
around for some sign that my arrival was both expected and
welcomed by someone in the small crowd of waiting people.

The approach of a medium-sized, grey-haired man signalled
that I was correct in the first of these calculations, although I
was soon to be apprised of the vanity of the second. He informed
me that his name was Dr Liebl and that he had the honour of
acting as Emil Becker's legal representative.

'I have a taxi waiting,' he said, glancing uncertainly at my
luggage. 'Even so, it isn't very far to my offices and had you
brought a smaller bag we might have walked there.'

'I know it sounds pessimistic,' I said, 'but I rather thought
I'd have to stay overnight.'

I followed him across the station floor.

'I trust that you had a good journey, Herr Gunther.'

'I'm here, aren't I?' I said, forcing an affable sort of chuckle.
'How else does one define a good journey these days?'

'I really couldn't say,' he said crisply. 'Myself, I never leave
Vienna.' He waved his hand dismissively at a group of ragged-
looking DPs who seemed to have camped out in the station.
'Today, with the whole world on some kind of journey, it seems

66

imprudent that I should expect God to look out for the kind of traveller who would only wish to be able to return from whence he started.'

He ushered me to a waiting taxi, and I handed my bag to the driver and climbed into the back seat, only to find the bag come after me again.

'There's an extra charge for luggage carried outside,' Liebl explained, pushing the bag on to my lap. 'As I said, it's not very far and taxis are expensive. While you're here I recommend that you use the tramways – it's a very good service.' The car moved away at speed, the first corner pressing us together like a couple of lovers in a cinema theatre. Liebl chuckled. 'It's also a lot safer, Viennese drivers being what they are.'

I pointed to our left. 'Is that the Danube?'

'Good God, no. That's the canal. The Danube is in the Russian sector, further east.' He pointed to our right, at a grim-looking building. 'That's the police prison, where our client is currently residing. We have an appointment there first thing tomorrow, after which you may wish to attend Captain Linden's funeral at the Central Cemetery.' Liebl nodded back at the prison. 'Herr Becker is not long in there, as it happens. The Americans were initially disposed to treat the case as a matter of military security and as a result they held him in their POW cage at the Stiftskaserne – the headquarters of their military police in Vienna. I had the very devil of a job getting in and out of there, I can tell you. However, the Military Government Public Safety Officer has now decided that the case is one for the Austrian courts, and so he'll be held there until the trial, whenever that may be.'

Liebl leaned forwards, tapped the driver on the shoulder and told him to make a right and head towards the General Hospital.

'Now that we're paying for this, we may as well drop your bag off,' he said. 'It's only a short detour. At least you've seen where your friend is, so you can appreciate the gravity of his situation.

'I don't wish to be rude, Herr Gunther, but I should tell you that I was against you coming to Vienna at all. It isn't as if there aren't any private detectives here. There are. I've used many of them myself, and they know Vienna better than you. I hope you won't mind me saying that. I mean, you don't know this city at all, do you?'

'I appreciate your frankness, Dr Liebl,' I said, not appreciating it much at all. 'And you're right, I don't know this city. As a matter of fact I've never been here in my life. So let me speak frankly. With twenty-five years of police work behind me I'm not particularly disposed to give much of a damn what you think. Why Becker should hire me instead of some local sniffer is his business. The fact that he's prepared to pay me generously is mine. There's nothing in between, for you or anyone else. Not now. When you get to court I'll sit on your lap and comb your hair if you want me to. But until then you read your lawbooks and I'll worry about what you're going to say that'll get the stupid bastard off.'

'Good enough,' Liebl growled, his mouth teetering on the edge of a smile. 'Veracity becomes you rather well. Like most lawyers I have a sneaking admiration for people who seem to believe what they say. Yes, I have a high regard for the probity of others, if only because we lawyers are so brimful of artifice.'

'I thought you spoke plainly enough.'

'A mere feint, I asssure you,' he said loftily.

We left my luggage at a comfortable-looking pension in the 8th Bezirk, in the American sector, and drove on to Liebl's office in the inner city. Like Berlin, Vienna was divided among the Four Powers, with each of them controlling a separate sector. The only difference was that Vienna's inner city, surrounded by the wide open boulevard of grand hotels and palaces that was called the Ring, was under the control of all four Powers at once in the shape of the International Patrol. Another, more immediately noticeable difference was in the Austrian capital's state of repair. It was true the city had been bombed about a bit, but compared with Berlin Vienna looked tidier than an undertaker's shop window.

When at last we were sitting in Liebl's office, he found Becker's files and ran through the facts of the case with me.

'Naturally, the strongest piece of evidence against Herr Becker is his possession of the murder weapon,' Liebl said, handing me a couple of photographs of the gun which had killed Captain Linden.

'Walther P38,' I said. 'SS handgrip. I used one myself in the last year of the war. They rattle a bit, but once the unusual trigger pull is mastered you can generally shoot them fairly accurately. I never much cared for the external hammer though. No, I prefer the PPK myself.' I handed back the pictures. 'Do you have any of the pathologist's snaps of the captain?'

Liebl passed me an envelope with evident distaste.

'Funny how they look when they're all cleaned up again,' I said as I looked at the photographs. 'You shoot a man in the face with a .38 and he looks no worse than if he'd had a mole removed. Good-looking son of a bitch, I'll say that much for him. Did they find the bullet?'

'Next picture.'

I nodded as I found it. Not much to kill a man, I thought.

'The police also found several cartons of cigarettes at Herr Becker's home,' said Liebl. 'Cigarettes of the same kind that were in the old studio where Linden was shot.'

I shrugged. 'He likes to smoke. I don't see what a few boxes of nails can pin on him.'

'No? Then let me explain. These were cigarettes stolen from the tobacco factory on Thaliastrasse, which is quite near the studio. Whoever stole the cigarettes was using the studio to store them. When Becker first found Captain Linden's body he helped himself to a few cartons before he went home.'

'That sounds like Becker, all right,' I sighed. 'He always did have long fingers.'

'Well, it's the length of his neck that matters now. I need not remind you that this is a capital case, Herr Gunther.'

'You can remind me of it as often as you think fit, Herr Doktor. Tell me, who owned the studio?'

'Drittemann Film-und Senderaum GMBH. At least that was the name of the company on the lease. But nobody seems to remember any films being made there. When the police searched the place they didn't find so much as an old spotlight.'

'Could I get a look inside?'

'I'll see if I can arrange it. Now, if you have any more

questions, Herr Gunther, I suggest that you save them until tomorrow morning when we see Herr Becker. Meanwhile, there are one or two arrangements that you and I must conclude, such as the balance of your fee, and your expenses. Please excuse me for a moment while I get your money from the safe.' He stood up and went out of the room.

Liebl's practice, in Judengasse, was on the first floor of a shoemaker's shop. When he came back into his office carrying two bundles of banknotes, he found me standing at the window.

'Two thousand five hundred American dollars, in cash, as agreed,' he said coolly, 'and 1,000 Austrian schillings to cover your expenses. Any more will need to be authorized by Fräulein Braunsteiner – she's Herr Becker's girlfriend. The costs of your accommodation will be taken care of by this office.' He handed me a pen. 'Will you sign this receipt, please?'

I glanced over the writing and signed. 'I'd like to meet her,' I said. 'I'd like to meet all Becker's friends.'

'My instructions are that she will contact you at your pension.'

I pocketed the money and returned to the window.

'I trust that if the police pick you up with all those dollars, I may rely on your discretion? There are currency regulations which –'

'I'll leave your name out of it, don't worry. As a matter of interest, what's to stop me taking the money and returning home?'

'You merely echo my own warning to Herr Becker. In the first place, he said that you were an honourable man, and that if you were paid to do a job, you would do it. Not the type to leave him to hang. He was quite dogmatic about it.'

'I'm touched,' I said. 'And in the second place?'

'Can I be frank?'

'Why stop now?'

'Very well. Herr Becker is one of the worst racketeers in Vienna. Despite his present predicament he is not entirely without influence in certain, shall we say, more nefarious quarters of this city.' His face looked pained. 'I should be reluctant to say any more at the risk of sounding like a common thug.'

'That's quite candid enough, Herr Doktor. Thank you.'

He came over to the window. 'What are you looking at?'

'I think I'm being followed. Do you see that man –?'

'The man reading the newspaper?'

'I'm sure I saw him at the railway station.'

Liebl removed his spectacles from his top pocket and bent them round his furry old ears. 'He doesn't look Austrian,' he pronounced finally. 'What paper is he reading?'

I squinted for a moment. 'The *Wiener Kurier*.'

'Hmm. Not a Communist, anyway. He's probably an American, a field agent from the Special Investigation Section of their military police.'

'Wearing plainclothes?'

'I believe that they are no longer required to wear uniform. At least in Vienna.' He removed his glasses and turned away. 'I dare say it'll be something routine. They'll want to know all about any friend of Herr Becker. You should expect to be pulled in sometime, for questioning.'

'Thanks for the warning.' I started to move away from the window but found my hand lingered on the big shutter, with its solid-looking cross bar. 'They certainly knew how to build these old places, didn't they? This thing looks as if it was meant to keep out an army.'

'Not an army, Herr Gunther. A mob. This was once the heart of the ghetto. In the fifteenth century, when the house was built, they had to be prepared for the occasional pogrom. Nothing changes so very much, does it?'

I sat down opposite him and smoked a Memphis from the packet I had brought from Poroshin's supplies. I waved the packet at Liebl who took one and put it carefully into a cigarette-case. He and I hadn't had the best of starts. It was time to repair a few bridges. 'Keep the pack,' I told him.

'You're very kind,' he said, handing me an ashtray in return.

Watching him light one now, I wondered what genealogy of debauch had jaspered his once handsome face. His grey cheeks were heavily wrinked with almost glacial striations, and his nose was slightly puckered, as if someone had told a sick joke. His lips were very red and very thin and he smiled like a wily old snake, which only served to enhance the look of dissipation that the years, and, most probably, the war had etched on his features. He himself provided an explanation.

'I was in a concentration camp for a while. Before the war I was a member of the Christian Social Party. You know, people prefer to forget, but there was a very great feeling for Hitler in Austria.' He coughed a little as the first smoke filled his lungs. 'It is very convenient for us that the Allies decided that Austria was a victim of Nazi aggression instead of a collaborator with it. But it is also absurd. We are perfect bureaucrats, Herr Gunther. It is remarkable the number of Austrians who came to occupy crucial roles in the organization of Hitler's crimes. And many of these same men – and quite a few Germans – are living right here in Vienna. Even now the Security Directorate for Upper Austria is investigating the theft of a number of identity cards from the Vienna State Printing Office. So you can see that for those who wish to stay here, there is always a means of doing so. The truth is that these men, these Nazis, enjoy living in my country. They have five hundred years of Jew-hatred to make them feel at home.

'I mention these things because as a *pifke –*' he smiled apologetically '– as a Prussian, you may find that you encounter a certain amount of hostility in Vienna. These days Austrians tend to reject everything German. They work very hard at being Austrian. An accent like yours might serve to remind some Viennese that for seven years they were National Socialists. An unpalatable fact that most people now prefer to believe was little more than a bad dream.'

'I'll bear it in mind.'

When I finished my meeting with Liebl I went back to the pension in Skodagasse, where I found a message from Becker's girlfriend to say that that she would drop by around six to make sure that I was comfortable. The Pension Caspian was a first-class little place. I had a bedroom with a small adjoining sitting-room and bathroom. There was even a tiny covered veranda where I might have sat in summer. The place was warm and there seemed to be a never-ending supply of hot water – an unaccustomed luxury. I had not long finished a bath, the duration of which even Marat might have baulked at, when there was a knock at my sitting-room door, and, glancing at my wristwatch, I saw that it was almost six. I slipped into my overcoat and opened the door.

She was small and bright-eyed, with a child's rosy cheeks and dark hair that looked as if it rarely felt a comb. Her well-toothed smile straightened a little as she saw my bare feet.

'Herr Gunther?' she said, hesitantly.

'Fräulein Traudl Braunsteiner.'

She nodded.

'Come in. I'm afraid I spent rather longer in the bath than I should have, but the last time I had really hot water was when I came back from the Soviet labour camp. Have a seat while I throw on some clothes.'

When I came back into the sitting-room I saw that she had brought a bottle of vodka and was pouring two glasses out on a table by the French window. She handed me my drink and we sat down.

'Welcome to Vienna,' she said. 'Emil said I should bring you a bottle.' She kicked the bag by her leg. 'Actually I brought two. They've been hanging out of the window of the hospital all day, so the vodka is nice and cold. I don't like vodka any other way.'

We clinked glasses and drank, the bottom of her glass beating my own to the table-top.

'You're not unwell, I hope? You mentioned a hospital.'

'I'm a nurse, at the General. You can see it if you walk to the top of the street. That's partly why I booked you in here – because it's so near. But also because I know the owner, Frau Blum-Weiss. She was a friend of my mother's. Also I thought you'd prefer to stay close to the Ring, and to the place where the American captain was shot. That's in Dettergasse, on the other side of Vienna's outer ring, the Gürtel.'

'This place suits me very nicely. To be honest it's a lot more comfortable than what I'm used to at home, back in Berlin. Things are quite hard there.' I poured us another drink. 'Exactly how much do you know about what happened?'

'I know everything that Dr Liebl has told you; and everything that Emil will tell you tomorrow morning.'

73

'What about Emil's business?'

Traudl Braunsteiner smiled coyly and uttered a little snigger. 'There's not much I don't know about Emil's business either.' Noticing a button that was hanging by a thread from her crumpled raincoat, she tugged it off and pocketed it. She was like a fine lace handkerchief that was in need of laundering. 'Being a nurse, I guess I'm a little relaxed about that sort of thing: black market. I've stolen a few drugs myself, I don't mind admitting it. Actually, all the girls do it at some time or another. For some it's a simple choice: sell penicillin or sell your body. I guess we are lucky enough to have something else to sell.' She shrugged and swallowed her second vodka. 'Seeing people suffering and dying doesn't breed a very healthy respect for law and order.' She laughed apologetically. 'Money's no good if you're not fit to spend it. God, what are the Krupp family worth? Billions probably. But they've got one of them at an insane asylum here in Vienna.'

'It's all right,' I said. 'I wasn't asking you to justify it to me.' But plainly she was trying to justify it to herself.

Traudl tucked her legs underneath her behind. She sat carelessly in the armchair, not seeming to mind any more than I did that I could see her stocking-tops and garters, and the edge of her smooth, white thighs.

'What can you do?' she said, biting her fingernail. 'Now and again everyone in Vienna has to buy something that's a bit Ressel Park.' She explained that this was the city's main centre for the black market.

'It's the Brandenburg Gate in Berlin,' I said. 'And in front of the Reichstag.'

'How funny,' she chuckled mischievously. 'There would be a scandal in Vienna if that sort of thing went on outside our parliament.'

'That's because you have a parliament. Here the Allies just supervise. But they actually govern in Germany.' My view of her underwear disappeared now as she tugged at the hem of her skirt.

'I didn't know that. Not that it would matter. There would still be a scandal in Vienna, parliament or no parliament. Austrians are such hypocrites. You would think they would feel easier about these things. There's been a black market here since the Habsburgs. It wasn't cigarettes then of course, but favours, patronage. Personal contacts still count for a lot.'

'Speaking of which, how did you meet Becker?'

'He fixed some papers for a friend of mine, a nurse at the hospital. And we stole some penicillin for him. That was when there was still some about. This wasn't long after my mother died.' Her bright eyes widened as if she was struggling to comprehend something. 'She threw herself under a tram.' Forcing a smile and a bemused sort of laugh, she managed to contain her feelings. 'My mother was a very Viennese type of Austrian, Bernie. We're always committing suicide, you know. It's a way of life for us.

'Anyway, Emil was very kind and great fun. He took me away from my grief, really. I've no other family, you see. My father was killed in an air-raid. And my brother died in Yugoslavia, fighting the partisans. Without Emil I really don't know what might have become of me. If something were to happen to him now –' Traudl's mouth stiffened as she pictured the fate that seemed most likely to befall her lover. 'You will do your best for him, won't you? Emil said you were the only person he could trust to find something that might give him half a chance.'

'I'll do everything I can for him, Traudl, you have my word on that.' I lit us both a cigarette and handed one to her. 'It may interest you to know that normally I'd convict my own mother if she were standing over a dead body with a gun in her hand. But for what it's worth I believe Becker's story, if only because it's so plausibly bad. At least until I've heard it from him. That may not surprise you very much, but it sure as hell impresses me.

'Only look at my fingertips. They're a little short on saintly aura. And the hat on the sideboard there? It wasn't meant for stalking deer. So if I'm to guide him out of that condemned cell your boyfriend is going to have to find me a ball of thread. Tomorrow morning, he'd better have something to say for himself or this show won't be worth the price of the greasepaint.'

75

12

The Law's most terrible punishment is always what happens in a man's own imagination: the prospect of one's own, judicially executed killing is food for thought of the most ingeniously masochistic kind. To put a man on trial for his life is to fill his mind with thoughts crueller than any punishment yet devised. And naturally enough the idea of what it must be like to drop metres through a trap-door, to be brought up short of the ground by a length of rope tied round the neck takes its toll on a man. He finds it hard to sleep, loses his appetite, and not uncommonly his heart starts to suffer under the strain of what his own mind has imposed. Even the most dull, unimaginative intellect need only roll his head around on his shoulders, and listen to the crunching gristle sound of his vertebrae in order to appreciate, in the pit of his stomach, the ghastly horror of hanging.

So I was not surprised to find Becker a thinner, etiolated sketch of his former self. We met in a small, barely furnished interview room at the prison on Rossauer Lände. When he came into the room he silently shook me by the hand before turning to address the warder who had stationed himself against the door.

'Hey, Pepi,' Becker said jovially, 'do you mind?' He reached inside his shirt pocket and retrieved a packet of cigarettes which he tossed across the room. The warder called Pepi caught them with the tips of his fingers and inspected the brand. 'Have a smoke outside the door, OK?'

'All right,' said Pepi, and left.

Becker nodded appreciatively as the three of us seated ourselves round the table bolted to the yellow-tiled wall.

'Don't worry,' he said to Dr Liebl. 'All the warders are at it in here. Much better than the Stiftskaserne, I can tell you. None of those fucking Yanks could be greased. There's nothing those bastards want that they can't get for themselves.'

'You're telling me,' I said, and found my own cigarettes. Liebl shook his head when I offered him one. 'These come from your friend Poroshin,' I explained as Becker slipped one out of the pack.

'Quite a fellow, isn't he?'

'Your wife thinks he's your boss.'

Becker lit us both and blew a cloud of smoke across my shoulder. 'You spoke to Ella?' he said, but he didn't sound surprised.

'Apart from the five thousand, she's the only reason I'm here,' I said. 'With her on your case I decided you probably needed all the help you could get. As far as she's concerned you're already swinging.'

'Hates me that bad, eh?'

'Like a cold sore.'

'Well she's got the right, I guess.' He sighed and shook his head. Then he took a long, nervous drag of his cigarette that barely left the paper on the tobacco. For a moment he stared at me, his bloodshot eyes blinking hard through the smoke. After several seconds he coughed and smiled all at once. 'Go ahead and ask me.'

'All right. Did you kill Captain Linden?'

'As God is my witness, no.' He laughed. 'Can I go now, sir?' He took another desperate suck at his smoke. 'You do believe me, don't you, Bernie?'

'I believe you'd have a better story if you were lying. I credit you with that much sense. But as I was saying to your girlfriend –'

'You've met Traudl? Good. She's great, isn't she?'

'Yes, she is. Christ only knows what she sees in you.'

'She enjoys my after-dinner conversation of course. That's why she doesn't like to see me locked up in here. She misses our little fireside chats about Wittgenstein.' The smile disappeared as his hand reached across the table and clutched at my forearm. 'Look, you've got to get me out of here, Bernie. The five thousand was just to get you in the game. You prove that I'm innocent and I'll treble your fee.'

'We both know that it isn't going to be easy.'

Becker misunderstood.

'Money's not a problem: I've got plenty of money. There's a car parked in a garage in Hernals with $30,000 in the boot. It's yours if you get me off.'

Liebl winced as his client continued to demonstrate his apparent lack of business acumen. 'Really, Herr Becker, as your lawyer I must protest. This is not the way to –'

'Shut up,' Becker said savagely. 'When I want your advice I'll ask for it.'

Liebl gave a diplomatic sort of shrug, and leaned back on his chair.

'Look,' I said, 'let's talk about a bonus when you're out. The money's fine. You've already paid me well. I wasn't talking about the money. No, what I'd like now are a few ideas. So how about you start by telling me about Herr König: where you met him, what he looks like and whether you think he likes cream in his coffee. OK?'

Becker nodded and ground his cigarette out on the floor. He clasped and unclasped his hands and started to squeeze his knuckles uncomfortably. Probably he had been over the story too many times to feel happy about repeating it.

'All right. Well then, let's see. I met Helmut König in the Koralle. That's a nightclub in the 9th Bezirk. Porzellangasse. He just came up and introduced himself. Said he'd heard of me, and wanted to buy me a drink. So I let him. We talked about the usual things. The war, me being in Russia, me being in Kripo before the SS, same as you really. Only you left, didn't you, Bernie?'

'Just keep to the point.'

'He said he'd heard of me from friends. He didn't say who. There was some business he'd like to put my way: a regular delivery across the Green Frontier. Cash money, no questions asked. It was easy. All I had to do was collect a small parcel from an office here in Vienna and take it to another office in Berlin. But only when I was going anyway, with a lorry load of cigarettes, that kind of thing. If I'd been picked up they probably wouldn't even have noticed König's parcel. At first I thought it was drugs. But then I opened one of the parcels. It was just a few files: Party files, army files, SS files.

The old stuff. I couldn't see what made it worth money to them.'

'Was it always just files?'

He nodded.

'Captain Linden worked for the US Documents Centre in Berlin,' I explained. 'He was a Nazi-hunter. These files – do you remember any names?'

'Bernie, they were tadpoles, small fry. SS corporals and army pay-clerks. Any Nazi-hunter would just have thrown them back. Those fellows are after the big fish, people like Bormann and Eichmann. Not fucking little pay-clerks.'

'Nevertheless, the files were important to Linden. Whoever it was that killed him also arranged to have a couple of amateur detectives he knew murdered. Two Jews who had survived the camps and were out to settle a few scores. I found them dead a few days ago. They'd been that way a while. Perhaps the files were for them. So it would help if you could try and remember some of the names.'

'Sure, anything you say, Bernie. I'll try to fit it into my busy schedule.'

'You do that. Now tell me about König. What did he look like?'

'Let's see: he was about forty, I'd say. Well-built, dark, thick moustache, weighed about ninety kilos, one-ninety tall; wore a good tweed suit, smoked cigars and always had a dog with him – a little terrier. He was Austrian for sure. Sometimes he had a girl around. Her name was Lotte. I don't know her surname, but she worked at the Casanova Club. Good-looking bitch, blonde. That's all I remember.'

'You said that you talked about the war. Didn't he tell you how many medals he won?'

'Yes, he did.'

'Then don't you think you should tell me?'

'I didn't think it was relevant.'

'I'll decide what's relevant. Come on, unpack it, Becker.'

He stared at the wall and then shrugged. 'As far as I remember, he said he had joined the Austrian Nazi Party when it was still illegal, in 1931. Later he got himself arrested for putting up posters. So he escaped to Germany to avoid arrest and joined the Bavarian police in Munich. He joined the SS in 1933, and stayed in until the end of the war.'

'Any rank?'

'He didn't say.'

'Did he give you any indication of where he served and in what sort of capacity?'

Becker shook his head.

'Not much of a conversation you two had. What were you reminiscing about, the price of bread? All right. What about the second man – the one who came to your home with König and asked you to look for Linden?'

Becker squeezed his temples. 'I've tried to remember his name, but it just won't come,' he said. 'He was a bit more of the senior officer type. You know, very stiff and proper. An aristocrat, maybe. Again he was aged about forty, tall, thin, clean-shaven, balding. Wore a Schiller jacket and a club-tie.' He shook his head. 'I'm not very good on club-ties. It could have been Herrenklub, I don't know.'

'And the man you saw come out of the studio where Linden was killed: what did he look like?'

'He was too far away for me to see much, except that he was quite short and very stocky. He wore a dark hat and coat and he was in a hurry.'

'I'll bet he was,' I said. 'The publicity firm, Reklaue & Werbe Zentrale. It's on Mariahilferstrasse, isn't it?'

'Was,' Becker said gloomily. 'It closed not long after I was arrested.'

'Tell me about it anyway. Was it always König you saw there?'

'No. It was usually a fellow called Abs, Max Abs. He was an academic-looking type, chin-beard, little glasses, you know.' Becker helped himself to another of my cigarettes. 'There was one thing I was meaning to tell you. One time I was there I heard Abs take a telephone call, from a stonemason called Pichler. Maybe he had a funeral. I thought that maybe you could find Pichler and find out about Abs when you go to Linden's funeral this morning.'

'At twelve o'clock,' Liebl said.

'I thought that it might be worth a look, Bernie,' Becker explained.

'You're the client,' I said.

'See if any of Linden's friends show up. And then see Pichler. Most of Vienna's stonemasons are along the wall of the Central Cemetery, so it shouldn't be all that difficult to find him. Maybe you can discover if Max Abs left an address when he ordered his piece of stone.'

I didn't much care for having Becker describe my morning's work for me like this, but it seemed easier to humour him. A man facing a possible death sentence can demand certain indulgences of his private investigator. Especially when there's cash up front. So I said, 'Why not? I love a good funeral.' Then I stood up and walked about his cell a bit, as if I were the one who was nervous about being caged in. Maybe he was just more used to it than me.

'There's one thing still puzzling me here,' I said after a minute's thoughtful pacing.

'What's that?'

'Dr Liebl told me that you're not without friends and influence in this city.'

'Up to a point.'

'Well, how is it that none of your so-called friends tried to find König? Or for that matter his girlfriend Lotte?'

'Who's saying they didn't?'

'Are you going to keep it to yourself, or do I have to give you a couple of bars of chocolate?'

Becker's tone turned placatory. 'Now, it's not certain what happened here, Bernie, so I don't want you getting the wrong idea about this job. There's no reason to suppose that –'

'Cut the cold cabbage and just tell me what happened.'

'All right. A couple of my associates, fellows who knew what they were doing, asked around about König and the girl. They checked a few of the nightclubs. And . . .' he winced uncomfortably '. . . they haven't been seen since. Maybe they double-crossed me. Maybe they just left town.'

'Or maybe they got the same as Linden,' I suggested.

81

'Who knows? But that's why you're here, Bernie. I can trust you. I know the kind of fellow you are. I respect what you did back in Minsk, really I did. You're not the kind to let an innocent man hang.' He smiled meaningfully. 'I can't believe I'm the only one who's had a use for a man of your qualifications.'

'I do all right,' I said quickly, not caring much for flattery, least of all from clients like Emil Becker. 'You know, you probably deserve to hang,' I added. 'Even if you didn't kill Linden, there must have been plenty of others.'

'But I just didn't see it coming. Not until it was too late. Not like you. You were clever, and got out while you still had a choice. I never had that chance. It was obey orders, or face a court martial and a firing squad. I didn't have the courage to do anything other than what I did.'

I shook my head. I really didn't care any more. 'Perhaps you're right.'

'You know I am. We were at war, Bernie.' He finished his cigarette and stood up to face me in the corner where I was leaning. He lowered his voice, as if he meant Liebl not to hear.

'Look,' he said, 'I know this is a dangerous job. But only you can do it. It needs to be done quietly, and privately, the way you do it best. Do you need a lighter?'

I had left the gun I'd taken off the dead Russian in Berlin, having had no wish to risk arrest for crossing a border with a pistol. I doubted that Poroshin's cigarette pass could have sorted that out. So I shrugged and said, 'You tell me. This is your city.'

'I'd say you'll need one.'

'All right,' I said, 'but for Christ's sake make it a clean one.'

When we were outside the prison again Liebl smiled sarcastically and said: 'Is a lighter what I think it is?'

'Yes. But it's just a precaution.'

'The best precaution you can take while you're in Vienna is to stay out of the Russian sector. Especially late at night.'

I followed Liebl's gaze across the road and beyond, to the other side of the canal, where a red flag fluttered in the early morning breeze.

'There are a number of kidnapping gangs working for the

Ivans in Vienna,' he explained. 'They snatch anyone they think might be spying for the Americans, and in return they're given black-market concessions to operate out of the Russian sector, which effectively puts them beyond the reach of the law. They took one woman out of her own house rolled up in a carpet, just like Cleopatra.'

'Well, I'll be careful not to fall asleep on the floor,' I said. 'Now, how do I get to the Central Cemetery?'

'It's in the British sector. You need to take a 71 from Schwarzenbergplatz, only your map calls it Stalinplatz. You can't miss it: there's an enormous statue to the Soviet soldier as liberator that we Viennese call the Unknown Plunderer.'

I smiled. 'Like I always say, Herr Doktor, we can survive defeat, but heaven help us from another liberation.'

13

'The city of the other Viennese' was how Traudl Braunsteiner had described it. This was no exaggeration. The Central Cemetery was bigger than several towns of my acquaintance and quite a bit more affluent too. There was no more chance of the average Austrian doing without a headstone than there was of him staying out of his favourite coffee house. It seemed there was nobody who was too poor for a decent piece of marble, and for the first time I began to appreciate the attractions of the undertaking business. A piano keyboard, an inspired muse, the introductory bars of a famous waltz – there was nothing too ornate for Vienna's craftsmen, no flatulent fable or overstated allegory that was beyond the dead hand of their art. The huge necropolis even mirrored the religious and political divisions of its living counterpart, with its Jewish, Protestant and Catholic sections, not to mention those of the Four Powers.

There was quite a turnover of services at the first-wonder-of-the-world-sized chapel where Linden's obsequies were heard, and I found that I had missed the captain's mourners there by only a few minutes.

The little cortège wasn't difficult to spot as it drove slowly across the snowbound park to the French sector where Linden, a Catholic, was to be buried. But for one on foot, as I was, it was rather more difficult to catch up: by the time I did the expensive casket was already being lowered slowly into the dark-brown trench like a dinghy let down into a dirty harbour. The Linden family, arms interlinked in the manner of a squad of riot-police, faced its grief as indomitably as if there had been medals to be won.

The colour party raised their rifles and took aim at the floating snow. It gave me an uncomfortable feeling as they fired, and for just a moment I was back in Minsk when, on a walk to staff headquarters, I had been summoned by the sound of gunshots:

climbing up an embankment I had seen six men and women kneeling at the edge of a mass grave already filled with innumerable bodies, some of whom were still alive, and behind them an SS firing squad commanded by a young police officer. His name was Emil Becker.

'Are you a friend of his?' said a man, an American, appearing behind me.

'No,' I said. 'I came over because you don't expect to hear gunfire in a place like this.' I couldn't tell if the American had been at the funeral already or if he had followed me from the chapel. He didn't look like the man who had been standing outside Liebl's office. I pointed at the grave. 'Tell me, who's the –'

'A fellow called Linden.'

It is difficult for someone who does not speak German as a first language, so I might have been mistaken, but there seemed to be no trace of emotion in the American's voice.

When I had seen enough, and having ascertained that there was nobody even vaguely resembling König among the mourners – not that I really expected to see him there – I walked quietly away. To my surprise I found the American walking alongside me.

'Cremation is so much kinder to the thoughts of the living,' he said. 'It consumes all sorts of hideous imaginings. For me the putrefaction of a loved one is quite unthinkable. It remains in the thoughts with the persistence of a tapeworm. Death is quite bad enough without letting the maggots make a meal of it. I should know. I've buried both parents and a sister. But these people are Catholics. They don't want anything to jeopardize their chances of bodily resurrection. As if God is going to bother with –' he waved his arm at the whole cemetery '– all this. Are you a Catholic, Herr –?'

'Sometimes,' I said. 'When I'm hurrying to catch a train, or trying to sober up.'

'Linden used to pray to St Anthony,' said the American. 'I believe he's the patron saint of lost things.'

Was he trying to be cryptic, I wondered. 'Never use him myself,' I said.

He followed me on to the road that led back to the chapel. It was a long avenue of severely pruned trees on which the gobbets of snow sitting on the sconce-like ends of the branches resembled the stumps of melted candles from some outsized requiem.

Pointing at one of the parked cars, a Mercedes, he said: 'Like a lift to town? I've got a car here.'

It was true that I wasn't much of a Catholic. Killing men, even Russians, wasn't the kind of sin that was easy to explain to one's maker. All the same I didn't have to consult St Michael, the patron saint of policemen, to smell an MP.

'You can drop me at the main gate, if you like,' I heard myself reply.

'Sure, hop in.'

He paid the funeral and the mourners no more attention. After all he had me, a new face, to interest him now. Perhaps I was someone who might shed some light on a dark corner of the whole affair. I wondered what he would have said if he could have known that my intentions were the same as his own; and that it was in the vague hope of just such an encounter that I had allowed myself to be persuaded to come to Linden's funeral in the first place.

The American drove slowly, as if he were part of the cortège, no doubt hoping to spin out his chance to discover who I was and why I was there.

'My name is Shields,' he volunteered. 'Roy Shields.'

'Bernhard Gunther,' I answered, seeing no reason to tease him with it.

'Are you from Vienna?'

'Not originally.'

'Where, originally?'

'Germany.'

'No, I didn't think you were Austrian.'

'Your friend – Herr Linden,' I said, changing the subject. 'Did you know him well?'

The American laughed and found some cigarettes in the top pocket of his sports jacket. 'Linden? I didn't know him at all.' He pulled one clear with his lips and then handed me the packet.

'He got himself murdered a few weeks back, and my chief thought it would be a good idea if I were to represent our department at the funeral.'

'And what department is that?' I asked, although I was almost certain I already knew the answer.

'The International Patrol.' Lighting his cigarette he mimicked the style of the American radio broadcasters. 'For your protection, call A29500.' Then he handed me a book of matches from somewhere called the Zebra Club. 'Waste of valuable time if you ask me, coming all the way down here like this.'

'It's not that far,' I told him; and then: 'Perhaps your chief was hoping that the murderer would put in an appearance.'

'Hell, I should hope not,' he laughed. 'We've got that guy in gaol. No, the chief, Captain Clark, is the kind of fellow who likes to observe the proper protocols.' Shields turned the car south towards the chapel. 'Christ,' he muttered, 'this place is like a goddamned gridiron.'

'You know, Gunther, that road we just turned off is almost a kilometre, as straight as an arrow. I caught sight of you when you were still a couple of hundred metres short of Linden's funeral, and it looked to me like you were in a hurry to join us.' He grinned, to himself it seemed. 'Am I right?'

'My father is buried only a short way from Linden's grave. When I got there and saw the colour party I decided to come back a little later, when it's quieter.'

'You walked all that way and you didn't bring a wreath?'

'Did you bring one?'

'Sure did. Cost me fifty schillings.'

'Cost you, or cost your department?'

'I guess we did pass a hat round at that.'

'And you need to ask me why I didn't bring a wreath.'

'Come on, Gunther,' Shields laughed. 'There isn't one of you people who isn't involved in some kind of a racket. You're all exchanging schillings for dollar scrip, or selling cigarettes on the black market. You know, I sometimes think that the Austrians are making more from breaking the rules than we are.'

'That's because you're a policeman.'

We passed through the main gate on Simmeringer Haupt-strasse and drew up in front of the tram stop, where several men were already clinging to the outside of the packed tram car like a litter of hungry piglets on a sow's belly.

'Are you sure you don't want that lift into town?' said Shields.

'No thanks. I have some business with some of the stone-masons.'

'Well, it's your funeral,' he said with a grin, and sped away.

I walked along the high wall of the cemetery, where it seemed that most of Vienna's market gardeners and stonemasons had their premises, and found a pathetic old woman standing in my way. She held up a penny candle and asked me if I had a light.

'Here,' I said, and gave her Shields' book of matches.

When she made as if to take only one I told her to keep the whole book. 'I can't afford to pay you for it,' she said, with real apology.

Just as surely as you know that a man waiting for a train will look at his watch, I knew that I would be seeing Shields again. But I wished him back right then and there so that I could have shown him one Austrian who didn't have the price of a match, let alone a fifty-schilling wreath.

Herr Josef Pichler was a fairly typical Austrian: shorter and thinner than the average German, with pale, soft-looking skin, and a sparse, immature sort of moustache. The hangdog expression on his drawn-out muzzle of a face gave him the appearance of one who had consumed too much of the absurdly young wine that Austrians apparently consider drinkable. I met him standing in his yard, comparing the sketch-plan of a stone's inscription with its final execution.

'God's greeting to you,' he said sullenly. I replied in kind.

'Are you Herr Pichler, the celebrated sculptor?' I asked. Traudl had advised me that the Viennese have a passion for overblown titles and flattery.

'I am,' he said, with a slight swell of pride. 'Does the gallant gentleman wish to consider ordering a piece?' He spoke as if he had been the curator of an art-gallery on Dorotheergasse. 'A fine headstone perhaps.' He indicated a large slice of polished black marble on which names and a date had been inscribed and

88

painted in gold. 'Something marmoreal? A carved figure? A statue perhaps?'

'To be honest, I am not entirely sure, Herr Pichler. I believe you recently created a fine piece for a friend of mine, Dr Max Abs. He was so delighted with it that I wondered if I might have something similar.'

'Yes, I think I remember the Herr Doktor.' Pichler took off his little chocolate cake of a hat and scratched the top of his grey head. 'But the particular design escapes me for the moment. Do you remember what kind of piece it was he had?'

'Only that he was delighted with it, I'm afraid.'

'No matter. Perhaps the honourable gentleman would care to return tomorrow, by which time I should have been able to find the Herr Doktor's specifications. Permit me to explain.' He showed me the sketch in his hand, one for a deceased whose inscription described him as an 'Engineer of Urban Conduits and Conservancy'.

'Take this customer,' he said, warming to the theme of his own business. 'I have a design with his name and order number here. When this piece is completed the drawing will be filed away according to the nature of the piece. From then on I must consult my sales book to find the name of the customer. But right now I'm in something of a hurry to complete this piece and really –' he patted his stomach '– I'm dead today.' He shrugged apologetically. 'Last night, you understand. I'm short of staff, too.'

I thanked him and left him to his Engineer of Urban Conduits and Conservancy. That was presumably what you called yourself if you were one of the city's plumbers. What sort of title, I wondered, did the private investigators give themselves? Balanced on the outside of the tram car back to town, I kept my mind off my precarious position by constructing a number of elegant titles for my rather vulgar profession: Practitioner of Solitary Masculine Lifestyle; Non-metaphysical Inquiry Agent; Interrogative Intermediary to the Perplexed and Anxious; Confidential Solicitor for the Displaced and the Misplaced; Bespoke Grail-Finder; Seeker after Truth. I liked the last one best of all. But, at least as far as my client in the particular case before me was concerned, there was nothing which seemed properly to reflect the sense of working for a lost cause that might have deterred even the most dogmatic Flat Earther.

14

According to all the guidebooks, the Viennese love dancing almost as passionately as they love music. But then the books were all written before the war, and I didn't think that their authors could ever have spent a whole evening at the Casanova Club in Dorotheergasse. There the band was led in a way that put you in mind of the most ignominious retreat, and the shit-kicking that passed for something approximately terpsichorean looked as if it might have been performed more in imitation of a polar bear kept in a very small cage. For passion you had to look to the sight of the ice yielding noisily to the spirit in your glass.

After an hour in the Casanova I was feeling as sour as a eunuch in a bathful of virgins. Counselling myself to be patient, I leaned back into my red velvet-and-satin booth and stared unhappily at the tent-like drapes on the ceiling: the last thing to do, unless I wanted to end up like Becker's two friends (whatever he said, I hadn't much doubt that they were dead), was to bounce around the place asking the regulars if they knew Helmut König, or maybe his girlfriend Lotte.

On its ridiculously plush surface, the Casanova didn't look like the kind of place which a fearful angel might have preferred to avoid. There were no extra-large tuxedoes at the door, nor anyone about who looked as if he could be carrying anything more lethal than a silver toothpick, and the waiters were all commendably obsequious. If König no longer frequented the Casanova it wasn't because he was afraid of having his pocket fingered.

'Has it started turning yet?'

She was a tall, striking girl with the sort of exaggeratedly made body that might have adorned a sixteenth-century Italian fresco: all breasts, belly and backside.

'The ceiling,' she explained, jerking her cigarette-holder vertically.

'Not yet, anyway.'

'Then you can buy me a drink,' she said, and sat down beside me.

'I was starting to worry you wouldn't show up.'

'I know, I'm the kind of girl you've been dreaming about. Well, here I am now.'

I waved to the waiter and let her order herself a whisky and soda.

'I'm not one for dreaming much,' I told her.

'Well, that's a pity, isn't it?'

She shrugged.

'What do you dream about?'

'Listen,' she said, shaking her head of long, shiny brown hair, 'this is Vienna. It doesn't do to describe your dreams to anyone here. You never know, you might just be told what they really mean, and then where would you be?'

'That sounds almost as if you have something to hide.'

'I don't see you wearing sandwich boards. Most people have something to hide. Especially these days. What's in their heads most of all.'

'Well, a name ought to be easy enough. Mine's Bernie.'

'Short for Bernhard? Like the dog that rescues mountaineers?'

'More or less. Whether or not I do any rescuing depends on how much brandy I'm carrying. I'm not as loyal when I'm loaded.'

'I never met a man who was.' She jerked her head down at my cigarette. 'Can you spare me one of those?'

I handed her a pack and watched as she screwed one into her holder. 'You didn't tell me your name,' I said, thumb-nailing a match alight for her.

'Veronika, Veronika Zártl. Pleased to meet you, I'm sure. I don't think I've ever seen your face in here. Where are you from? You sound like a *pifke*.'

'Berlin.'

'I thought so.'

'Anything wrong with that?'

92

'Not if you like *pifkes*. Most Austrians don't, as it happens.' She spoke in the slow, almost yokelish drawl that seemed typical of the modern Viennese. 'But I don't mind them. I get mistaken for a *pifke* myself sometimes. That's because I won't speak like the rest of them.' She chuckled. 'It's so funny when you hear some lawyer or dentist speaking like he was a tram-driver or a miner just so as he doesn't get mistaken for a German. Mostly they only do it in shops, to make sure that they get the good service that all Austrians think that they are entitled to. You want to try it yourself, Bernie, and see the difference it makes to the way you're treated. Viennese is quite easy, you know. Just speak like you're chewing something and add 'ish' onto the end of everything you say. Cleverish, eh?'

The waiter returned with her drink which she regarded with some disapproval. 'No ice,' she muttered as I tossed a banknote on to the silver tray and left the change under Veronika's questioning eyebrow.

'With a tip like that you must be planning on coming back here.'

'You don't miss much, do you?'

'Are you? Planning on coming back here, I mean.'

'It could be that I am. But is it always like this? The trade here's about as busy as an empty fireplace.'

'Just wait until it gets crowded, and then you'll wish it was like this again.' She sipped her drink and leaned back on the red-velvet-and-gilt chair, stroking the buttonback satin upholstery that covered the wall of our booth with the palm of her outstretched hand.

'You should be grateful for the quiet,' she told me. 'It gives us a chance to get to know each other. Just like those two.' She waved her holder meaningfully at a couple of girls who were dancing with each other. With their gaudy outfits, tight buns and flashing paste necklaces they looked like a pair of circus horses. Catching Veronika's eye they smiled and then whinnied a little confidence to each other at a coiffure's distance.

I watched them turn in elegant little circles. 'Friends of yours?'

'Not exactly.'

'Are they – together?'

She shrugged. 'Only if you made it worth their while.' She laughed some smoke out of her pert little nose. 'They're just giving their high-heels some exercise, that's all.'

'Who's the taller one?'

'Ibolya. That's Hungarian for a violet.'

'And the blonde?'

'That's Mitzi.' Veronika was bristling a little as she named the other girl. 'Maybe you'd prefer to talk to them.' She took out her powder-compact and scrutinized her lipstick in the tiny mirror. 'I'm expected soon anyway. My mother will be getting worried.'

'There's no need to play the Little Red Riding Hood with me,' I told her. 'We both know that your mother doesn't mind if you leave the path and walk through the woods. And as for those two sparklers over there, a man can look in the window, can't he?'

'Sure, but there's no need to press your nose up against it. Not when you're with me, anyway.'

'It seems to me, Veronika,' I said, 'that you wouldn't have to try very hard to sound like someone's wife. Frankly, it's the sort of sound that drives a man to a place like this in the first place.' I smiled just to let her know I was still friendly. 'And then along you come with the rolling-pin in your voice. Well, it could put a man right back to where he was when he walked through the door.'

She smiled back at me. 'I guess you're right at that,' she said. 'You know, it strikes me that you're new at this chocolady thing.'

'Christ,' she said, her smile turning bitter, 'isn't everyone?'

But for the fact that I was tired I might have stayed longer at the Casanova, might even have gone home with Veronika. Instead I gave her a packet of cigarettes for her company and told her that I would be back the following evening.

On the town, late at night, was not the best time to compare Vienna to any metropolis, with the possible exception of the lost city of Atlantis. I had seen a moth-eaten umbrella stay open for longer than Vienna. Veronika had explained, over several more drinks, that Austrians preferred to spend their evenings at home, but that when they did choose to make a night of it, they traditionally made an early start – as early as six or seven o'clock. Which left me trailing back to the Pension Caspian along an empty street at only 10.30, with just my shadow and the sound of my half-intoxicated footsteps for company.

After the combusted atmosphere of Berlin, Vienna's air tasted as pure as birdsong. But the night was a cold one, and shivering inside my overcoat I quickened my step, disliking the quiet, and remembering Dr Liebl's warning about the Soviet predilection for nocturnal kidnappings.

At the same time, however, crossing Heldenplatz in the direction of the Volksgarten, and beyond the Ring, Josefstadt and home, it was easy to find one's thoughts turning to the Ivans. As far away from the Soviet sector as I was, there was still ample evidence of their omnipresence. The Imperial Palace of the Habsburgs was one of the many public buildings in the internationally run city centre that was occupied by the Red Army. Over the main door was a colossal red star in the centre of which was a picture of Stalin in profile, set against a significantly dimmer one of Lenin.

It was as I passed the ruined Kunsthistorische that I felt there was someone behind me, someone hanging back between the shadows and the piles of rubble. I stopped in my tracks, looked around and saw nothing. Then, about thirty metres away, next to a statue of which only the torso remained, like something I had once seen in a mortuary drawer, I heard a noise, and a moment later saw some small stones roll down a high bank of rubble.

'Are you feeling a bit lonely?' I called out, having drunk just enough not to feel stupid asking such a ridiculous question. My voice echoed up the side of the ruined museum. 'If it's the museum you're interested in, we're closed. Bombs, you know: dreadful things.' There was no reply, and I found myself laughing. 'If you're a spy, you're in luck. That's the new profession to be in. Especially if you're a Viennese. You don't have to take my word for it. One of the Ivans told me.'

Still laughing to myself, I turned and walked away. I didn't bother to see if I was followed, but crossing onto Mariahilfer-strasse I heard footsteps again as I paused to light a cigarette.

As anyone who knows Vienna could have told you, this wasn't exactly the most direct route back to Skodagasse. I even told myself. But there was a part of me, probably the part most affected by alcohol, that wanted to find out exactly who was following me and why.

The American sentry who stood out in front of the Stifts-kaserne was having a cold time of it. He watched me carefully as I passed by on the other side of the empty street and I reflected that he might even recognize the man on my tail as a fellow American and member of the Special Investigations Section of his own military police. Probably they were in the same baseball team or whatever game it was that American soldiers played when they weren't eating or chasing women.

Further up the slope of the wide street I glanced to my left and through a doorway saw a narrow covered passage that seemed to lead down several flights of steps to an adjoining street. Instinctively I ducked inside. Vienna might not have been blessed with a fabulous nightlife but it was perfect for anyone on foot. A man who knew his way around the streets and the ruins, who could remember these convenient passages, would, I thought, provide even the most determined police cordon with a better chase than Jean Valjean.

Ahead of me, beyond my sight, someone else was making his way down the steps, and thinking that my tail might take these for my own footsteps, I pressed myself against a wall and waited for him in the dark.

After less than a minute I heard the approaching sound of a man running lightly. Then the footsteps halted at the top of the passageway as he stood trying to judge whether or not it was safe to come after me. Hearing the other man's footsteps, he started forward.

I stepped out of the shadows and punched him hard in the stomach – so hard I thought I would have to bend down and retrieve my knuckles – and while he lay gasping on the steps where he had fallen, I tugged his coat off his shoulders and pulled it down to hold his arms. He wasn't carrying a gun, so I helped myself to the wallet in his breast pocket and picked out an ID card.

'"Captain John Belinsky",' I read. '"430th United States CIC". What's that? Are you one of Mr Shields's friends?'

The man sat up slowly. 'Fuck you, kraut,' he said biliously.

'Have you orders to follow me?' I tossed the card on to his lap and searched the other compartments of his wallet. 'Because you'd better ask for another assignment, Johnny. You're not very good at this sort of thing – I've seen less conspicuous striptease dancers than you.' There wasn't much of interest in his wallet: some dollar scrip, a few Austrian schillings, a ticket for the Yank Movie Theatre, some stamps, a room card from Sacher's Hotel and a photograph of a pretty girl.

'Have you finished with that?' he said in German.

I tossed him the wallet.

'That's a nice-looking girl you have there, Johnny,' I said. 'Did you follow her as well? Maybe I should give you my snapshot. Write my address on the back. Make it easier for you.'

'Fuck you, kraut.'

'Johnny,' I said, starting back up the steps to Mariahilfer-strasse, 'I'll bet you say that to all the girls.'

15

Pichler lay under a massive piece of stone like some primitive car mechanic repairing a neolithic stone-axle, with the tools of his trade – a hammer and a chisel – held tight in his dusty, blood-stained hands. It was almost as if while carving the black rock's inscription he had paused for a moment to draw breath and decipher the words that seemed to emerge vertically from his chest. But no mason ever worked in such a position, at right angles to his legend. And draw breath he never would again, for although the human chest is sufficiently strong a cage for those soft, mobile pets that are the heart and lungs, it is easily crushed by something as heavy as half a tonne of polished marble.

It looked like an accident, but there was one way to be sure. Leaving Pichler in the yard where I had found him, I went into the office.

I retained very little memory of the dead man's description of his business-accounting system. To me, the niceties of double-entry bookkeeping are about as useful as a pair of brogue galoshes. But as someone who ran a business himself, albeit a small one, I had a rudimentary knowledge of the petty, fastidious way in which the details of one ledger are supposed to correspond with those in another. And it didn't take William Randolph Hearst to see that Pilcher's books had been altered, not by any subtle accounting, but by the simple expedient of tearing out a couple of pages. There was only one financial analysis that was worth a spit, and that was that Pichler's death had been anything but accidental.

Wondering whether his murderer had thought to steal the sketch-design for Dr Max Abs' headstone, as well as the relevant pages from the ledgers, I went back into the yard to see if I might be able to find it. I had a good look round, and after a few minutes discovered a number of dusty art-files propped up against a wall in the workshop at the back of the yard. I untied the first file and started to sort through the draughtsman's drawings, working quickly since I had no wish to be found searching the premises of a man who lay crushed to death less than ten metres away. And when at last I found the drawing I was looking for I gave it no more than a cursory glance before folding it up and slipping it into my coat pocket.

I caught a 71 back to town and went to the Café Schwarzenberg, close to the tram terminus on the Kärtner Ring. I ordered a mélange and then spread the drawing out on the table in front of me. It was about the size of a double-page spread in a newspaper, with the customer's name – Max Abs – clearly marked on an order copy stapled to the top right-hand corner of the paper.

The mark-up for the inscription read: 'SACRED TO THE MEMORY OF MARTIN ALBERS, BORN 1899, MARTYRED 9 APRIL 1945. BELOVED OF WIFE LENI, AND SONS MANFRED AND ROLF. BEHOLD, I SHEW YOU A MYSTERY; WE SHALL NOT ALL SLEEP, BUT WE SHALL ALL BE CHANGED, IN A MOMENT, IN THE TWINKLING OF AN EYE, AT THE LAST TRUMP: FOR THE TRUMPET SHALL SOUND, AND THE DEAD SHALL BE RAISED INCORRUPTIBLE, AND WE SHALL BE CHANGED. I CORINTHIANS 15: 51–52.'

On Max Abs' order was written his address, but beyond the fact that the doctor had paid for a headstone in the name of a man who was dead – a brother-in-law perhaps? – and which had now occasioned the murder of the man who had carved it, I could not see that I had learned very much.

The waiter, wearing his grey frizzy hair on the back of his balding head like a halo, returning with the small tin tray that carried my mélange and the glass of water customarily served with coffee in Viennese cafés. He glanced down at the drawing before I folded it away to make room for the tray, and said, with a sympathetic sort of smile: 'Blessed are they that mourn, for they shall be comforted.'

I thanked him for his kind thought and, tipping him generously, asked him first from where I might send a telegram, and then where Berggasse was.

'The Central Telegraph Office is on Börseplatz,' he answered, 'on the Schottenring. You'll find Berggasse just a couple of blocks north of there.'

An hour or so later, after sending my telegrams to Kirsten and to Neumann, I walked up to Berggasse, which ran between the police prison where Becker was locked up and the hospital where his girlfriend worked. This coincidence was more remarkable than the street itself, which seemed largely to be occupied by doctors and dentists. Nor did I think it particularly remarkable to discover from the old woman who owned the building in which Abs had occupied the mezzanine floor that only a few hours earlier he had told her he was leaving Vienna for good.

'He said his job urgently required him to go to Munich,' she explained in the kind of tone that left me feeling she was still a bit puzzled by this sudden departure. 'Or at least somewhere near Munich. He mentioned the name but I'm afraid that I've forgotten it.'

'It wasn't Pullach, was it?'

She tried to look thoughtful but only succeeded in looking bad-tempered. 'I don't know if it was or if it wasn't,' she said finally. The cloud lifted from her face as she returned to her normal bovine expression. 'Anyway, he said he would let me know where he was when he got himself settled.'

'Did he take all his things with him?'

'There wasn't much to take,' she said. 'Just a couple of suitcases. The apartment is furnished, you see.' She frowned again. 'Are you a policeman or something?'

'No, I was wondering about his rooms.'

'Well why didn't you say? Come in, Herr – ?'

'It's Professor, actually,' I said with what I thought sounded like a typically Viennese punctiliousness. 'Professor Kurtz.' There was also the possibility that by giving myself the academic handle I might appeal to the snob in the woman. 'Dr Abs and myself are mutually acquainted with a Herr König, who told me that he thought the Herr Doktor might be about to vacate some excellent rooms at this address.'

I followed the old woman through the door and into the big hallway which led to a tall glass door. Beyond the open door lay a courtyard with a solitary plane tree growing there. We turned up the wrought-iron staircase.

'I trust you will forgive my discretion,' I said. 'Only I wasn't sure how much credence to place on my friend's information. He was most insistent that they were excellent rooms, and I'm sure I don't have to tell you, madam, how difficult it can be for a gentleman to find an apartment of any quality in Vienna these days. Perhaps you know Herr König?'

'No,' she said firmly. 'I don't think I ever met any of Dr Abs' friends. He was a very quiet man. But your friend is well informed. You won't find a better set of rooms for 400 schillings a month. This is a very good neighbourhood.' At the door to the apartment she lowered her voice. 'And entirely Jew-free.' She produced a key from the pocket of her jacket and slipped it into the keyhole of the great mahogany door. 'Of course, we had a few of them here before the Anschluss. Even in this house. But by the time the war came most of them had gone away.' She opened the door and showed me into the apartment.

'Here we are,' she said proudly. 'There are six rooms in total. It's not as big as some of the apartments in the street, but then not as expensive either. Fully furnished as I think I said.'

'Lovely,' I said looking about me.

'I'm afraid that I haven't yet had time to clean the place,' she apologized. 'Doctor Abs left a lot of rubbish to throw out. Not that I mind really. He gave me four weeks' money in lieu of notice.' She pointed at one door which was closed. 'There's still quite a bit of bomb damage showing in there. We had an incendiary in the courtyard when the Ivans came, but it's due to be repaired very soon.'

'I'm sure it's fine,' I said generously.

'Right then. I'll leave you to have a little look around on your own, Professor Kurtz. Let you get a feel for the place. Just lock up after you and knock on my door when you've seen everything.'

When the old woman had gone I wandered among the rooms, finding only that for a single man Abs seemed to have received an extraordinarily large number of Care parcels, those food parcels that came from the United States. I counted the empty cardboard boxes that bore the distinctive initials and the Broad Street, New York address and found that there were over fifty of them.

It didn't look like Care so much as good business.

When I had finished looking around I told the old woman that I was looking for something bigger and thanked her for allowing me to see the place. Then I strolled back to my pension in Skodagasse.

I wasn't back very long before there was a knock at my door.

'Herr Gunther?' said the one wearing the sergeant's stripes.

I nodded.

'I'm afraid you'll have to come with us, please.'

'Am I being arrested?'

'Excuse me, sir?'

I repeated the question in my uncertain English. The American MP shifted his chewing-gum around impatiently.

'It will be explained to you down at headquarters, sir.'

I picked up my jacket and slipped it on.

'You will remember to bring your papers, won't you, sir?' he smiled politely. 'Save us coming back for them.'

'Of course,' I said, collecting my hat and coat. 'Have you got transport? Or are we walking?'

'The truck's right outside the front door.'

The landlady caught my eye as we came through her lobby. To my surprise she looked not at all perturbed. Maybe she was used to her guests getting pulled in by the International Patrol. Or perhaps she just told herself that someone else was paying for my room whether I slept there or in a cell at the police prison.

We climbed into the truck and drove a few metres north before a short turn to the right took us south down Lederergasse, away from the city centre and the headquarters of the IMP.

'Aren't we going to Kärtnerstrasse?' I said.

'It isn't an International Patrol matter, sir,' the sergeant explained. 'This is American jurisdiction. We're going to the Stiftskaserne, on Mariahilferstrasse.'

'To see who? Shields or Belinsky?'

'It will be explained –'

'– when we get there, right.'

The mock-baroque entrance to the Stiftskaserne, the head-quarters of the 796th Military Police, with its half-relief Doric columns, griffins and Greek warriors, was situated, somewhat incongruously, between the twin entrances of Tiller's department store, and was part of a four-storey building that fronted onto Mariahilferstrasse. We passed through the massive arch of this entrance and beyond the rear of the main building and a parade ground to another building, which housed a military barracks.

The truck drove through some gates and pulled up outside the barracks. I was escorted inside and up a couple of flights of stairs to a big bright office which commanded an impressive view of the anti-aircraft tower that stood on the other side of the parade ground.

Shields stood up from behind a desk and grinned like he was trying to impress the dentist.

'Come on in and sit down,' he said as if we were old friends. He looked at the sergeant. 'Did he come peaceably, Gene? Or did you have to beat the shit out of his ass?'

The sergeant grinned a little and mumbled something which I didn't catch. It was no wonder that one could never understand their English, I thought: Americans were forever chewing something.

'You better stick around a while, Gene,' Shields added. 'Just in case we have to get tough with this guy.' He uttered a short laugh and, hitching up his trousers, sat squarely in front of me, his heavy legs splayed apart like some samurai lord, except that he was probably twice as large as any Japanese.

'First of all, Gunther, I have to tell you that there's a Lieutenant Canfield, a real asshole Brit, down at International Headquarters who would love somebody to help him with a little problem he's got. It seems like some stonemason in the British sector got himself killed when a rock fell on his tits. Mostly everyone, including the lieutenant's boss, believes that it was probably an accident. Only the lieutenant's the keen type. He's read Sherlock Holmes and he wants to go to detective school when he leaves the army. He's got this theory that someone tampered with the dead man's books. Now I don't know if that's sufficient motive to kill a man or not, but I do remember seeing you go into Pichler's office yesterday morning after Captain Linden's funeral.' He chuckled. 'Hell, I admit it, Gunther. I was spying on you. Now what do you say to that?'

'Pichler's dead?'

'How about it you try it with a little more surprise? "Don't tell me Pichler is dead!" or "My God, I don't believe what you are telling me!" You wouldn't know what happened to him, would you, Gunther?'

I shrugged. 'Maybe the business was getting on top of him.'

Shields laughed at that one. He laughed like he had once taken a few classes in laughing, showing all his teeth, which were mostly bad, in a blue boxing-glove of a jaw that was wider than the top of his dark and balding head. He seemed loud, like most Americans, and then some. He was a big, brawny man with shoulders like a rhinoceros, and wore a suit of light-brown flannel with lapels that were as broad and sharp as two Swiss halberds. His tie deserved to hang over a café terrace, and his shoes were heavy brown Oxfords. Americans seemed to have an attraction for stout shoes in the same way that Ivans loved wristwatches: the only difference was that they generally bought them in shops.

'Frankly, I don't give a damn for that lieutenant's problems,' he said. 'It's shit in the British backyard, not mine. So let them sweep it up. No, I'm merely explaining your need to cooperate with me. You may have nothing at all to do with Pichler's death, but I'm sure that you don't want to waste a day explaining that to Lieutenant Canfield. So you help me and I'll help you: I'll forget I ever saw you go into Pichler's shop. Do you understand what I'm saying to you?'

'There's nothing wrong with your German,' I said. All the same it struck me with what venom he attacked the accent, tackling the consonants with a theatrical degree of precision, almost as if he regarded the language as one which needed to be spoken cruelly. 'I don't suppose it would matter if I said that I know absolutely nothing about what happened to Herr Pichler?'

Shields shrugged apologetically. 'As I said, it's a British problem, not mine. Maybe you are innocent. But like I say, it sure would be a pain in the ass explaining it to those British. I swear they think every one of you krauts is a goddam Nazi.'

I threw up my hands in defeat. 'So how can I help you?'

'Well, naturally, when I heard that before coming to Captain Linden's party you visited his murderer in prison, my inquiring nature could not be constrained.' His tone grew sharper. 'Come on, Gunther. I want to know what the hell is going on between you and Becker.'

'I take it you know Becker's side of the story.'

'Like it was engraved on my cigarette-case.'

'Well, Becker believes it. He's paying me to investigate it. And, he hopes, to prove it.'

'You're investigating it, you say. So what does that make you?'

'A private investigator.'

'A shamus? Well, well.' He leaned forwards on his chair, and taking hold of the edge of my jacket, felt the material with his finger and thumb. It was fortunate that there were no razor blades sewn on that particular number. 'No, I can't buy that. You're not half greasy enough.'

'Greasy or not, it's true.' I took out my wallet and showed him my ID. And then my old warrant disc. 'Before the war I was with the Berlin Criminal Police. I'm sure I don't have to tell you that Becker was too. That's how I know him.' I took out my cigarettes. 'Mind if I smoke?'

'Smoke, but don't let it stop your lips moving.'

'Well, after the war I didn't want to go back to the police. The force was full of Communists.' I was throwing him a line with that one. There wasn't one American I had met who seemed to like Communism. 'So I set up in business on my own. Actually, I had a period out of the force during the mid-thirties, and did a bit of private work then. So I'm not exactly new at this game. With so many displaced persons since the war, most people can use an honest bull. Believe me, thanks to the Ivans they're few and far between in Berlin.'

'Yeah, well it's the same here. Because the Soviets got here first they put all their own people in the top police jobs. Things are so bad that the Austrian government had to look to the chief of the Vienna Fire Service when they were trying to find a straight man to become the new vice-president of police.' He shook his head. 'You're one of Becker's old colleagues. How about that? What kind of cop was he, for Christ's sake?'

'The crooked kind.'

'No wonder this country's in such a mess. I suppose you were SS as well then?'

'Briefly. When I found out what was going on I asked for a transfer to the front. People did, you know.'

'Not enough of them. Your friend didn't, for one.'

'He's not exactly a friend.'

'So why did you take the case?'

'I needed the money. And I needed to get away from my wife for a while.'

'Do you mind telling me why?'

I paused, realizing that it was the first time I had talked about it. 'She's been seeing someone else. One of your brother officers. I thought that if I wasn't around for a while she might decide what was more important: her marriage or this *schätzi* of hers.'

Shields nodded and then made a sympathetic-sounding grunt.

'Naturally all your papers are in order?'

'Naturally.' I handed them over and watched him examine my identity card and my pink pass.

'I see you came through the Russian Zone. For a man who doesn't like Ivans you must have some pretty good contacts in Berlin.'

'Just a few dishonest ones.'

'Dishonest Russkies?'

'What other kind is there? Sure I had to grease some people, but the papers are genuine.'

Shields handed them back. 'Do you have your *Fragebogen* with you?'

I fished my denazification certificate out of my wallet and handed it over. He only glanced at it, having no desire to read through the 133 questions and answers it recorded. 'An exonerated person, eh? How come you weren't classed as an offender? All SS were automatically arrested.'

'I saw out the end of the war in the army. On the Russian front. And, like I said, I got a transfer out of the SS.'

Shields grunted and handed back the *Fragebogen*. 'I don't like SS,' he growled.

'That makes two of us.'

Shields examined the big fraternity ring which gracelessly adorned one of his well-tufted fingers. He said: 'We checked Becker's story, you know. There was nothing in it.'

'I don't agree.'

'And what makes you think that?'

'Do you think he'd be willing to pay me $5,000 to dig around if his story were just hot air?'

'Five thousand?' Shields let out a whistle.

'Worth it if your head's in a noose.'

'Sure. Well, maybe you can prove that the guy was somewhere else when we actually caught him. Maybe you can find something that'll persuade the judge that his friends didn't shoot at us. Or that he wasn't carrying the gun that shot Linden. You got any bright ideas yet, shamus? Like maybe the one that took you to see Pichler?'

'It was a name that Becker remembered as having been mentioned by someone at Reklaue & Werbe Zentrale.'

'By who?'

'Dr Max Abs?'

Shields nodded, recognizing the name.

'I'd say it was him who killed Pichler. Probably he went to see him not long after I did and found out that someone claiming to be a friend of his had been asking questions. Maybe Pichler told him that he'd said I should come back the following day. So before I did Abs killed him and took away the paperwork with his name and address on. Or so he thought. He forgot something which led me to his address. Only by the time I got there he'd cleared out. According to his landlady he's halfway to Munich by now. You know, Shields, it might not be a bad idea if you were to have someone meet him off that train.'

Shields stroked his poorly-shaven jaw. 'It might not be at that.'

He stood up and went behind his desk where he picked up the telephone and proceeded to make a number of calls, but using a vocabulary and an accent that I was unable to comprehend. When finally he replaced the receiver in its cradle, he looked at his wristwatch and said: 'The train to Munich takes eleven and a half hours, so there's plenty of time to make sure he gets a warm hello when he gets off.'

The telephone rang. Shields answered it, staring at me open-mouthed and unblinking, as if there wasn't much of my story he had believed. But when he put down the telephone a second time he was grinning.

'One of my calls was to the Berlin Documents Centre,' he said. 'I'm sure you know what that is. And that Linden worked there?'

I nodded.

'I asked them if they had anything on this Max Abs guy. That was them calling back just now. It seems that he was SS too. Not actually wanted for any war crimes, but something of a coincidence, wouldn't you say? You, Becker, Abs, all former pupils of Himmler's little Ivy League.'

'A coincidence is all it is,' I said wearily.

Shields settled back in his chair. 'You know, I'm perfectly prepared to believe that Becker was just the trigger-man for Linden. That your organization wanted him dead because he had found out something about you.'

'Oh?' I said without much enthusiasm for Shields's theory. 'And which organization is that?'

'The Werewolf Underground.'

I found myself laughing out loud. 'That old Nazi fifth-column story? The stay-behind fanatics who were going to continue a guerrilla war against our conquerors? You have to be joking, Shields.'

'Something wrong with that, you think?'

'Well, they're a bit late for a start. The war's been over for nearly three years. Surely you Americans have screwed enough of our women by now to realize that we never planned to cut your throats in bed. The Werewolves ...' I shook my head pityingly. 'I thought they were something that your own intelligence people had dreamed up. But I must say I certainly never thought there was anyone who actually believed that shit. Look, maybe Linden did find out something about a couple of war-criminals, and maybe they wanted him out of the way. But not the Werewolf Underground. Let's try and find something a little more original, can we?' I started another cigarette and watched Shields nod and think his way through what I had said.

'What does the Berlin Documents Centre have to stay about Linden's work?' I said.

'Officially, he was no more than the Crowcass liaison officer – the Central Registry of War Crimes and Security Suspects of the United States Army. They insist that Linden was simply an administrator and not a field agent. But then, if he were working in intelligence, those boys wouldn't tell us anyway. They've got more secrets than the surface of Mars.'

He got up from behind the desk and went to the window.

'You know, the other day I had eyes of a report that said as many as two out of every thousand Austrians were spying for the Soviets. Now there are over 1.8 million people in this city, Gunther. Which means that if Uncle Sam has as many spies as Uncle Joe there are over 7,000 spies right on my doorstep. To say nothing of what the British and the French are doing. Or what the Vienna state police get up to – that's the Commie-run political police, not the ordinary Vienna police, although they're a bunch of Communists as well of course. And then only a few months ago we had a whole bunch of Hungarian state police infiltrated into Vienna in order to kidnap or murder a few of their own dissident nationals.'

He turned away from the window and came back to the seat in front of me. Grasping the back of it as if he were planning to pick it up and crash it over my head, he sighed and said: 'What I'm trying to say, Gunther, is that this is a rotten town. I believe Hitler called it a pearl. Well, he must have meant one that was as yellow and worn as the last tooth in a dead dog. Frankly, I look out of that window and I see about as much that's precious about this place as I can see blue when I'm pissing in the Danube.'

Shields straightened up. Then he leaned across and took hold of my jacket lapels, pulling me up to my feet.

'Vienna disappoints me, Gunther, and that makes me feel bad. Don't you do the same, old fellow. If you turn up something I think I should know about and you don't come and tell me, I'll get real sore. I can think of a hundred good reasons to haul your ass out of this town even when I'm in a good mood, like I am now. Am I making myself clear?'

'Like you were made of crystal.' I brushed his hands off my jacket and straightened it on my shoulders. Halfway to the door I stopped and said: 'Does this new cooperation with the American Military Police extend as far as removing the tail you put on me?'

'Someone's following you?'

'He was until I took a poke at him last night.'

'This is a weird city, Gunther. Maybe he's queer for you.'

'That must be why I presumed he was working for you. The man's an American named John Belinsky.'

Shields shook his head, his eyes innocently wide. 'I never heard of him. Honest to God, I never ordered anyone to tail you. If someone's following you it has nothing to do with this office. You know what you should do?'

'Surprise me.'

'Go home to Berlin. There's nothing here for you.'

'Maybe I would, except that I'm not sure that there's anything there either. That's one of the reasons I came, remember?'

16

It was late by the time I got to the Casanova Club. The place was full of Frenchmen and they were full of whatever it is that Frenchmen drink when they want to get good and stiff. Veronika had been right after all: I did prefer the Casanova when it was quiet. Failing to spot her in the crowd I asked the waiter I had tipped so generously the previous night if she had been in the place.

'She was here only ten, fifteen minutes ago,' he said. 'I think she went to the Koralle, sir.' He lowered his voice, and dipped his head towards me. 'She doesn't much care for Frenchmen. And to tell the truth, neither do I. The British, the Americans, even the Russians, one can at least respect armies that took a hand in our defeat. But the French? They are bastards. Believe me, sir, I know. I live in the 15th Bezirk, in the French sector.' He straightened the tablecloth. 'And what will the gentleman have to drink?'

'I think I might take a look at the Koralle myself. Where is it, do you know?'

'It's in the 9th Bezirk sir. Porzellangasse, just off Berggasse, and close to the police prison. Do you know where that is?'

I laughed. 'I'm beginning to.'

'Veronika is a nice girl,' the waiter added. 'For a chocolady.'

Rain blew into the Inner City from the east and the Russian sector. It turned to hail in the cold night air and stung the four faces of the International Patrol as they pulled up outside the Casanova. Nodding curtly to the doorman, and without a word, they passed me by and went inside to look for soldierly vice, that compromising manifestation of lust exacerbated by a combination of a foreign country, hungry women and a never-ending supply of cigarettes and chocolate.

At the now-familiar Schottenring I crossed on to Währinger

Strasse and headed north across Rooseveltplatz in the moonlit shadow of the twin towers of the Votivkirche which, despite its enormous, sky-piercing height, had somehow survived all the bombs. I was turning into Berggasse for the second time that day when, from a large ruined building on the opposite side of the road, I heard a cry for help. Telling myself that it was none of my business I stopped for only a brief moment, intending to keep to my route. But then I heard it again: an almost recognizably contralto voice.

I felt fear crawl across my skin as I walked quickly in the direction of the sound. A high bank of rubble was piled against the building's curved wall and, having climbed to the top of it, I stared through an empty arched window into a semi-circular room that was of the proportions of a small-sized theatre.

There were three of them struggling in a little spot of moonlight against a straight wall that faced the windows. Two were Russian soldiers, filthy and ragged and laughing uproariously as they attempted forcibly to strip the clothes from the third figure, which was a woman. I knew it was Veronika even before she lifted her face to the light. She screamed and was slapped hard by the Russian who held her arms and the two flap sides of her dress that his comrade, kneeling on her toes, had torn open.

'*Pakazhitye, dushka* (show me, darling),' he guffawed, wrenching Veronika's underwear down over her knocking knees. He sat back on his haunches to admire her nakedness. '*Pryekrasnaya* (beautiful),' he said, as if he had been looking at a painting, and then pushed his face into her pubic hair. '*Vkoosnaya, tozhe* (tasty, too),' he growled.

The Russian looked round from between her legs as he heard my footfall on the debris that littered the floor, and seeing the length of lead pipe in my hand he stood up beside his friend, who now pushed Veronika aside.

'Get out of here, Veronika,' I shouted.

Needing little encouragement, she grabbed her coat and ran towards one of the windows. But the Russian who had licked her seemed to have other ideas, and snatched at her mane of hair. In the same moment I swung the pipe, which hit the side of his lousy-looking head with an audible clang, numbing my hand with the vibration from the blow. The thought was just crossing my mind that I had hit him much too hard when I felt a sharp kick in the ribs, and then a knee thudded into my groin. The pipe fell on to the brick-strewn floor and there was a taste of blood in my mouth as I slowly followed it. I drew my legs up to my chest and tensed myself as I waited for the man's great boot to smash into my body again and finish me. Instead I heard a short, mechanical punch of a sound, like the sound of a rivet-gun, and when the boot swung again it was well over my head. With one leg still in the air, the man staggered for a second like a drunken ballet-dancer and then fell dead beside me, his forehead neatly trepanned with a well-aimed bullet. I groaned and for a moment shut my eyes. When I opened them again and raised myself on to my forearm, there was a third man squatting in front of me, and for a chilling moment he pointed the silenced barrel of his Luger at the centre of my face.

'Fuck you, kraut,' he said, and then, grinning broadly, helped me to my feet. 'I was going to belt you myself, but it looks like those two Ivans have saved me the trouble.'

'Belinsky,' I wheezed, holding my ribs. 'What are you, my guardian angel?'

'Yeah. It's a wonderful life. You all right, kraut?'

'Maybe my chest would feel better if I quit smoking. Yes, I'm all right. Where the hell did you come from?'

'You didn't see me? Great. After what you said about tailing someone I read a book about it. I disguised myself as a Nazi so as you wouldn't notice me.'

I looked around. 'Did you see where Veronika went?'

'You mean you know that lady?' He meandered over to the soldier I had felled with the pipe, and who lay senseless on the floor. 'I thought you were just the Don Quixote type.'

'I only met her last night.'

'Before you met me, I guess. Belinsky stared down at the soldier for a moment, then levelled the Luger at the back of the man's head and pulled the trigger. 'She's outside,' he said with no more emotion than if he had shot at a beer-bottle.

'Shit,' I breathed, appalled at this display of callousness. 'They could certainly have used you in an Action Group.'

'What?'

'I said I hope I didn't make you miss your tram last night. Did you have to kill him?'

He shrugged and started to unscrew the Luger's silencer. 'Two dead is better than one left alive to testify in court. Believe me, I know what I'm talking about.' He kicked the man's head with the toe of his shoe. 'Anyway, these Ivans won't be missed. They're deserters.'

'How do you know?'

Belinsky pointed out two bundles of clothes and equipment that lay near the doorway, and next to them the remains of a fire and a meal.

'It looks like they've been hiding here for a couple of days. I guess they got bored and fancied some –' he searched for the right word in German and then, shaking his head, completed the sentence in English '– cunt.' He holstered the Luger and dropped the silencer into his coat pocket. 'If they're found before the rats eat them up, the local boys will just figure that the MVD did it. But my bet is on the rats. Vienna's got the biggest rats you ever saw. They come straight up out of the sewers. Come to think of it, from the smell of these two, I'd say they'd been down there themselves. The main sewer comes out in the Stadt Park, just by the Soviet Kommendatura and the Russian sector.' He started towards the window. 'Come on, kraut, let's find this girl of yours.'

Veronika was standing a short way back down Währinger Strasse and looked ready to make a run for it if it had been the two Russians who came out of the building. 'When I saw your friend go in,' she explained, 'I waited to see what would happen.'

She had buttoned her coat to the neck, and, but for a slight bruise on her cheek and the tears in her eyes, I wouldn't have said she looked like a girl who had narrowly missed being raped. She glanced nervously back at the building with a question in her eyes.

'It's all right,' said Belinsky. 'They won't bother us no more.'

When Veronika had finished thanking me for saving her, and

Belinsky for saving me, he and I walked her home to the half-ruin in Rotenturmstrasse where she had her room. There she thanked us some more and invited us both to come up, an offer which we declined, and only after I had promised to visit her in the morning could she be persuaded to close the door and go to bed.

'From the look of you I'd say that you could use a drink,' Belinsky said. 'Let me buy you one. The Renaissance Bar is just around the corner. It's quiet there, and we can talk.'

Close by St Stephen's Cathedral, which was now being restored, the Renaissance in Singerstrasse was an imitation Hungarian tavern with gypsy music. The kind of place you see depicted on a jigsaw-puzzle, it was no doubt popular with the tourists, but just a concertina-squeeze too premeditated for my simple, gloomy taste. There was one significant compensation, as Belinsky explained. They served Csereszne, a clear Hungarian spirit made from cherries. And for one who had recently been subjected to a kicking, it tasted even better than Belinsky had promised.

'That's a nice girl,' he said, 'but she ought to be a bit more careful in Vienna. So should you for that matter. If you're going to go around playing Errol-fucking-Flynn you should have more than just a bit of hair under your arm.'

'I guess you're right.' I sipped at my second glass. 'But it seems strange you telling me that, you being a bull and all. Carrying a gun's not strictly legal for anyone but Allied personnel.'

'Who said I was a bull?' He shook his head. 'I'm CIC. The Counter-Intelligence Corps. The MPs don't know shit about what we get up to.'

'You're a spy?'

'No, we're more like Uncle Sam's hotel detectives. We don't run spies, we catch them. Spies and war-criminals.' He poured some more of the Csereszne.

'So why are you following me?'

'It's hard to say, really.'

'I'm sure I could find you a German dictionary.'

Belinsky withdrew a ready-filled pipe from his pocket and

while he explained what he meant he suck-started the thing into yielding a steady smoke.

'I'm investigating the murder of Captain Linden,' he said.

'What a coincidence. So am I.'

'We want to try and find out what it was that brought him to Vienna in the first place. He liked to keep things pretty close to his chest. Worked on his own a lot.'

'Was he in the CIC too?'

'Yes, the 970th, stationed in Germany. I'm 430th. We're stationed in Austria. Really he should have let us know he was coming on to our patch.'

'And he didn't send so much as a postcard, eh?'

'Not a word. Probably because there was no earthly reason why he should have come. If he was working on anything that affected this country he should have told us.' Belinsky let out a balloon of smoke and waved it away from his face. 'He was what you might call a desk-investigator. An intellectual. The sort of fellow you could let loose on a wall full of files with instructions to find Himmler's optical prescription. The only problem is that because he was such a bright guy, he kept no case notes.' Belinsky tapped his forehead with the stem of his pipe. 'He kept everything up here. Which makes it a nuisance to find out what he was investigating that got him a lead lunch.'

'Your MPs think that the Werewolf Underground might have had something to do with it.'

'So I heard.' He inspected the smouldering contents of his cherrywood pipe bowl, and added: 'Frankly, we're all scraping around in the dark a bit on this one. Anyway, that's where you walk into my life. We thought maybe you'd turn up something that we couldn't manage ourselves, you being a native, comparatively speaking. And if you did, I'd be there for the cause of free democracy.'

'Criminal investigation by proxy, eh? It wouldn't be the first time that it's happened. I hate to disappoint you, only I'm kind of in the dark myself.'

'Maybe not. After all, you already got the stonemason killed. In my book that rates as a result. It means you got someone upset, Kraut.'

I smiled. 'You can call me Bernie.'

'The way I figure it, Becker wouldn't bring you into the game without dealing you a few cards. Pichler's name was probably one of them.'

'You might be right,' I conceded. 'But all the same it's not a hand I'd care to put my shirt on.'

'Want to let me take a peek?'

'Why should I?'

'I saved your life, kraut,' he growled.

'Too sentimental. Be a little more practical.'

'All right then, maybe I can help.'

'Better. Much better.'

'What do you need?'

'Pichler was more than likely murdered by a man named Abs, Max Abs. According to the MPs he used to be SS, but small-time. Anyway, he boarded a train to Munich this afternoon and they were going to have someone meet him: I expect that they'll tell me what happens. But I need to find out more about Abs. For instance, who this fellow was.' I took out Pichler's drawing of Martin Albers' gravestone and spread it on the table in front of Belinsky. 'If I can find out who Martin Albers was and why Max Abs was willing to pay for his headstone I might be on my way to establishing why Abs thought it necessary to kill Pichler before he spoke to me.'

'Who is this Abs guy? What's his connection?'

'He used to work for an advertising firm here in Vienna. The same place that König managed. König's the man that briefed Becker to run files across the Green Frontier. Files that went to Linden.'

Belinsky nodded.

'All right then,' I said. 'Here's my next card. König had a girlfriend called Lotte who hung around the Casanova. It could be that she sparkled there a bit, nibbled a little chocolate, I don't know yet. Some of Becker's friends crashed around there and a few other places and didn't come home for tea. My idea is to put the girl on to it. I thought I'd have to get to know her a bit first of all. But of course now that she's seen me on my white horse and wearing my Sunday suit of armour I can hurry that along.'

'Suppose Veronika doesn't know this Lotte. What then?'

'Suppose you think of a better idea.'

Belinsky shrugged. 'On the other hand, your scheme has its points.'

'Here's another thing. Both Abs and Eddy Holl, who was Becker's contact in Berlin, are working for a company that's based in Pullach, near Munich. The South German Industries Utilization Company. You might like to try and find out something about it. Not to mention why Abs and Holl decided to move there.'

'They wouldn't be the first two krauts to go and live in the American Zone,' said Belinsky. 'Haven't you noticed? Relations are starting to get a shade difficult with our Communist allies. The news from Berlin is that they've started to tear up a lot of the roads connecting the east and west sectors of the city.' His face made plain his lack of enthusiasm, and then added: 'But I'll see what I can turn up. Anything else?'

'Before I left Berlin I came across a couple of amateur Nazi-hunters named Drexler. Linden used to take them Care parcels now and again. I wouldn't be surprised if they were working for him: everyone knows that's how the CIC pays its way. It would help if we knew who they had been looking for.'

'Can't we ask them?'

'It wouldn't do much good. They're dead. Someone slipped a tray-load of Zyklon–B pellets underneath their door.'

'Give me their address anyway.' He took out a notepad and pencil.

When I had given it to him he pursed his lips and rubbed his jaw. His was an impossibly broad face, with thick horns of eyebrows that curved halfway round his eye-sockets, some small animal's skull for a nose and intaglio laugh-lines which, added to his square chin and sharply angled nostrils, completed a perfectly septagonal figure: the overall impression was of a ram's head resting on a V-shaped plinth.

'You were right,' he admitted. 'It's not much of a hand, is it? But it's still better than the one I folded on.'

With the pipe clenched tight between his teeth, he crossed his arms and stared down at his glass. Perhaps it was his choice of drink, or perhaps it was his hair, styled longer than the crew-cut favoured by the majority of his countrymen, but he seemed curiously un-American.

'Where are you from?' I said eventually.

'Williamsburg, New York.'

'Belinsky,' I said, measuring each syllable. 'What kind of a name is that for an American?'

The man shrugged, unperturbed. 'I'm first-generation American. My dad's from Siberia originally. His family emigrated to escape one of the Tsar's Jewish pogroms. You see, the Ivans have got a tradition of anti-Semitism that's almost as good as yours. Belinsky was Irving Berlin's name before he changed it. And as names for Americans go, I don't think a yid-name like that sounds any worse than a kraut-name like Eisenhower, do you?'

'I guess not.'

'Talking of names, if you do speak to the MPs again it might be better if you didn't mention me, or the CIC, to them. On account of the fact that they recently screwed up an operation we had going. The MVD managed to steal some US Military Police uniforms from the battalion HQ at the Stiftskaserne. They put them on and persuaded the MPs at the 19th Bezirk station to help them arrest one of our best informers in Vienna. A couple of days later another informant told us that the man was being interrogated at MVD headquarters in Mozartgasse. Not long after that we learned he had been shot. But not before he talked and gave away several other names.

'Well, there was an almighty row, and the American High Commissioner had to kick some ass for the poor security of the 796th. They court-martialled a lieutenant and broke a sergeant back to the ranks. As a result of which me being CIC is tantamount to having leprosy in the eyes of the Stiftskaserne. I suppose you might find that hard to understand, you being German.'

'On the contrary,' I said. 'I'd say being treated like lepers is something we krauts understand only too well.'

17

The water arriving in the tap from the Styrian Alps tasted cleaner than the squeak of a dentist's fingers. I carried a glassful of it from the bathroom to answer the telephone ringing in my sitting-room, and sipped some more while I waited for Frau Blum-Weiss to switch the call through.

'Well, good-morning,' Shields said with affected enthusiasm. 'I hope I got you out of bed.'

'I was just cleaning my teeth.'

'And how are you today?' he said, still refusing to come to the point.

'A slight headache, that's all.' I had drunk too much of Belinsky's favourite liquor.

'Well, blame it on the föhn,' suggested Shields, referring to the unseasonably warm and dry wind that occasionally descended on Vienna from the mountains. 'Everyone else in this city blames all kinds of strange behaviour on it. But all I notice is that it makes the smell of horseshit even worse than usual.'

'It's nice to talk to you again, Shields. What do you want?'

'Your friend Abs didn't get to Munich. We're pretty sure he got on the train, only there was no sign of him at the other end.'

'Maybe he got off somewhere else.'

'The only stop that train makes is in Salzburg, and we had that covered too.'

'Perhaps someone threw him off. While the train was still moving.' I knew only too well how that happened.

'Not in the American Zone.'

'Well, that doesn't start until you get to Linz. There's over a hundred kilometres of Russian Lower Austria between here and your zone. You said yourself that you're sure he got on the train. So what else does that leave?' Then I recalled what Belinsky had said about the poor security of the US Military Police. 'Of course, it's possible he simply gave your men the slip. That he was too clever for them.'

Shields sighed. 'Sometime, Gunther, when you're not too busy with your old Nazi comrades, I'll drive you out to the DP camp at Auhof and you can see all the illegal Jewish emigrants who thought they were too smart for us.' He laughed. 'That is, if you're not scared that you might be recognized by someone from a concentration camp. It might even be fun to leave you there. Those Zionists don't have my sense of humour about the SS.'

'I'd certainly miss that, yes.'

There was a soft, almost furtive knock at the door.

'Look, I've got to go.'

'Just watch your step. If I so much as think that I can smell shit on your shoes I'll throw you in the cage.'

'Yes, well, if you do smell something it'll probably just be the föhn.'

Shields laughed his ghost-train laugh and then hung up.

I went to the door and let in a short, shifty-looking type who brought to mind the print of a portrait by Klimt that was hanging in the breakfast-room. He wore a brown, belted rain-coat, trousers that seemed a little short of his white socks and, barely covering his head of long fair hair, a small, black Tyrolean that was loaded with badges and feathers. Somewhat incongruously, his hands were enclosed in a large woollen muff.

'What are you selling, swing?' I asked him.

The shifty look turned suspicious. 'Aren't you Gunther?' he drawled in an improbable voice that was as low as a stolen bassoon.

'Relax,' I said, 'I'm Gunther. You must be Becker's personal gunsmith.'

'S'right. Name's Rudi.' He glanced around and grew easier. 'You alone in this watertight?'

'Like a hair on a widow's tit. Have you brought me a pre-sent?'

Rudi nodded and with a sly grin pulled one of his hands out of the muff. It held a revolver and it was pointed at my morning croissant. After a short, uncomfortable moment his grin widened and he released the handgrip to let the gun hang by the trigger-guard on his forefinger.

'If I stay in this city I'm going to have to shop for a new sense of humour,' I said, taking the revolver from him. It was a .38 Smith with a six-inch barrel and the words 'Military and Police' clearly engraved in the black finish. 'I suppose the bull who owned this let you have it for a few packets of cigarettes.' Rudi started to answer, but I got there first. 'Look, I told Becker a clean gun, not Exhibit A in a murder trial.'

'That's a new gun,' Rudi said indignantly. 'Squeeze your eye down the barrel. It's still greased: hasn't been fired yet. I swear them at the top don't even know it's missing.'

'Where did you get it?'

'The Arsenal Warehouse. Honest, Herr Gunther, that gun's as clean as they come these days.'

I nodded reluctantly. 'Did you bring any ammunition?'

'There's six in it,' he said, and taking his other hand out of the muff laid a miserly handful of cartridges on to the sideboard, next to my two bottles from Traudl. 'And these.'

'What, did you buy them off the ration?'

Rudi shrugged. 'All I could get for the moment, I'm afraid.' Eyeing the vodka he licked his lips.

'I've had my breakfast,' I told him, 'but you help yourself.'

'Just to keep the cold out, eh?' he said and poured a nervous glassful, which he quickly swallowed.

'Go ahead and have another. I never stand between a man and a good thirst.' I lit a cigarette and went over to the window. Outside, a Pan's pipes of icicles hung from the edge of the terrace roof. 'Especially on a day as chilly as this one.'

'Thanks,' said Rudi, 'thanks a lot.' He smiled thinly, and poured a second, steadier glass, which he sipped at slowly. 'So how's it coming along? The investigation, I mean.'

'If you've got any ideas I'd love to hear them. Right now the fish aren't exactly jumping on to the riverbank.'

Rudi flexed his shoulders. 'Well, the way I see it is that this Ami captain, the one that took the 71 – '

He paused while I made the connection: the number 71 was

122

the tram that went to the Central Cemetery. I nodded for him to continue.

'Well, he must have been involved in some kind of racket. Think about it,' he instructed, warming to his subject. 'He goes to a warehouse with some coat, and the place is stacked high with nails. I mean, why did they go there in the first place? It couldn't have been because the killer planned to shoot him there. He wouldn't have done it near his stash, would he? They must have gone to look at the merchandise, and had an argument.'

I had to admit there was something in what he said. I thought for a minute. 'Who sells cigarettes in Austria, Rudi?'

'Apart from everyone?'

'The main black-siders.'

'Excepting Emil, there's the Ivans; a mad American staff sergeant who lives in a castle near Salzburg; a Romanian Jew here in Vienna; and an Austrian named Kurtz. But Emil was the biggest. Most people have heard the name of Emil Becker in that particular connection.'

'Do you think it's possible that one of them could have framed Emil, to take him out of competition?'

'Sure. But not at the expense of losing all those nails. Forty cases of cigarettes, Herr Gunther. That's a big loss for someone to take.'

'When exactly was this tobacco factory on Thaliastrasse robbed?'

'Months ago.'

'Didn't the MPs have any idea who could have done it? Didn't they have any suspects?'

'Not a chance. Thaliastrasse is in the 16th Bezirk, part of the French sector. The French MPs couldn't catch drip in this city.'

'What about the local bulls – the Vienna police?'

Rudi shook his head firmly. 'Too busy fighting with the state police. The Ministry of the Interior has been trying to have the state mob absorbed into the regular force, but the Russians don't like it and are trying to fuck the thing up. Even if it means wrecking the whole force.' He grinned. 'I can't say I'd be sorry.

No, the locals are almost as bad as the Frenchies. To be honest, the only bulls that are worth a damn in this city are the Amis. Even the Tommies are pretty stupid if you ask me.'

Rudi glanced at one of the several watches he had strapped to his arm. 'Look, I've got to go, otherwise I'll miss my pitch at Ressel. That's where you'll find me every morning if you need to, Herr Gunther. There, or at the Hauswirth Café on Favoritenstrasse during the afternoon.' He drained his glass. 'Thanks for the drink.'

'Favoritenstrasse,' I repeated, frowning. 'That's in the Russian sector, isn't it?'

'True,' said Rudi. 'But it doesn't make me a Communist.' He raised his little hat and smiled. 'Just prudent.'

The sad aspect to her face, with its downcast eyes and the tilt of her thickening jaw, not to mention her cheap and secondhand-looking clothes, made me think that Veronika could not have made much out of being a prostitute. And certainly there was nothing about the cold, cavern-sized room she rented in the heart of the city's red-light district that indicated anything other than an eked-out, hand-to-mouth kind of existence.

She thanked me again for helping her and, having inquired solicitously after my bruises, proceeded to make a pot of tea while she explained that one day she was planning to become an artist. I looked through her drawings and watercolours without much enjoyment.

Profoundly depressed by my gloomy surroundings, I asked her how it was that she had ended up on the sledge. This was foolish, because it never does to challenge a whore about anything, least of all her own immorality, and my only excuse was that I felt genuinely sorry for her. Had she once had a husband who had seen her frenching an Ami in a ruined building for a couple of bars of chocolate?

'Who said I was on the sledge?' she responded tartly.

I shrugged. 'It's not coffee that keeps you up half the night.'

'Maybe so. All the same, you won't find me working in one of those places on the Gürtel where the numbers just walk up the stairs. And you won't find me selling it on the street outside the American Information Office, or the Atlantis Hotel. Choco-lady I may be, but I'm no sparkler. I have to like the gentle-man.'

'That won't stop you getting hurt. Like last night, for instance. Not to mention venereal disease.'

'Listen to yourself,' she said with amused contempt. 'You sound just like one of those bastards in the vice squad. They pick you up, have a doctor examine you for a dose and then give you a lecture on the perils of drip. You're beginning to sound like a bull.'

'Maybe the police are right. Ever think of that?'

'Well, they never found anything wrong with me. Nor will they.' She smiled a shrewd little smile. 'Like I said, I'm careful. I have to like the gentleman. Which means I won't do Ivans or niggers.'

'Nobody ever heard of an Ami or a Tommy with syphilis, I suppose.'

'Look, you play the percentages.' She scowled. 'What the hell do you know about it anyway? Saving my ass doesn't give you the right to read me the Ten Commandments, Bernie.'

'You don't have to be a swimmer to throw someone a life-preserver. I've met enough snappers in my time to know that most of them started out as selective as you. Then someone comes along and beats the shit out of them, and the next time, with the landlord chasing for his rent, they can't afford to be quite as choosy. You talk about percentages. Well, there's not much percentage in french for ten schillings when you're forty. You're a nice girl, Veronika. If there were a priest around he'd maybe think you were worth a short homily, but since there isn't you'll have to make do with me.'

She smiled sadly and stroked my hair. 'You're not so bad. Not that I have any idea why you think it necessary. I'm really quite all right. I've got money saved. Soon I'll have enough to get myself into an art-school somewhere.'

I thought it just as likely that she would win a contract to repaint the Sistine Chapel, but I felt my mouth force its way up to a politely optimistic sort of smile. 'Sure you will,' I said. 'Look, maybe I can help. Maybe we can help each other.' It was a hopelessly flat-footed way of manoeuvring the conversation back to the main purpose of my visit.

'Maybe,' she said, serving the tea. 'One more thing and then you can give me a blessing. The vice squad has got files on over 5,000 girls in Vienna. But that's not even half of it. These days everyone has to do things that were once unthinkable. You too, probably. There's not much percentage in going hungry. And even less in going back to Czechoslovakia.'

'You're Czech?'

She sipped some of her tea, then took a cigarette from the packet I had given her the night before and collected a light.

'According to my papers I was born in Austria. But the fact is that I'm Czech: a Sudeten German-Jew. I spent most of the war hiding out in lavatories and attics. Then I was with the partisans for a while, and after that a DP camp for six months before I escaped across the Green Frontier.

'Have you heard of a place called Wiener Neustadt? No? Well, it's a town about fifty kilometres outside Vienna, in the Russian Zone, with a collection centre for Soviet repatriations. There are 60,000 of them waiting there at any one time. The Ivans screen them into three groups: enemies of the Soviet Union are sent to labour camps; those they can't actually prove are enemies are sent to work outside the camps – so either way you end up as some kind of slave labour; unless, that is, you're the third group and you're sick or old or very young, in which case you're shot right away.'

She swallowed hard and took a long drag of her cigarette. 'Do you want to know something? I think I would sleep with the whole of the British Army if it meant that the Russians couldn't claim me. And that includes the ones with syphilis.' She tried a smile. 'But as it happens I have a medical friend who got me a few bottles of penicillin. I dose myself with it now and again just to be on the safe side.'

'That sounds expensive.'

'Like I said, he's a friend. It costs me nothing that could be spent on the reconstruction.' She picked up the teapot. 'Would you like some more tea?'

I shook my head. I was anxious to be out of that room. 'Let's go somewhere,' I suggested.

'All right. It beats staying here. How's your head for heights? Because there's only one place to go on a Sunday in Vienna.'

The amusement park of the Prater, with its great wheel, merry-go-rounds and switchback-railway, was somehow incongruous in that part of Vienna which, as the last to fall to the Red Army, still showed the greatest effects of the war and the clearest evidence of our being in an otherwise less amusing sector. Broken tanks and guns still littered the nearby meadows, while on every one of the dilapidated walls of houses all along the Ausstellungsstrasse was the faded chalk outline of the Cyrillic word '*Atak'ivat*' (searched), which really meant 'looted'.

From the top of the big wheel Veronika pointed out the piers of the Red Army Bridge, the star on the Soviet obelisk close by it and, beyond these, the Danube. Then, as the cabin carrying the two of us started its slow descent to the ground, she reached inside my coat and took hold of my balls, but snatched her hand away again when I sighed uncomfortably.

'It could be that you would have preferred the Prater before the Nazis,' she said peevishly, 'when all the dolly-boys came here to pick up some trade.'

'That's not it at all,' I laughed.

'Maybe that's what you meant when you said that I could help you.'

'No, I'm just the nervous type. Try it again sometime when we're not sixty metres up in the air.'

'Highly strung, eh? I thought you said you had a head for heights.'

'I lied. But you're right, I do need your help.'

'If vertigo's your problem, then getting horizontal is the only treatment I'm qualified to prescribe.'

'I'm looking for someone, Veronika: a girl who used to hang around the Casanova Club.'

'Why else do men go to the Casanova except to look for a girl?'

'This is one particular girl.'

'Maybe you hadn't noticed. None of the girls at the Casanova are that particular.' She threw me a narrow-eyed look, as if she suddenly distrusted me. 'I thought you sounded like them at the top. All that shit about drip and all. Are you working with that American?'

'No, I'm a private investigator.'

'Like the Thin Man?'

She laughed when I nodded.

'I thought that stuff was just for the films. And you want me to help you with something you're investigating, is that it?'

I nodded again.

'I never saw myself quite like Myrna Loy,' she said, 'but I'll help you if I can. Who is this girl you're looking for?'

'Her name is Lotte. I don't know her last name. You might have seen her with a man called König. He wears a moustache and has a small terrier.'

Veronika nodded slowly. 'Yes, I remember them. Actually I used to know Lotte reasonably well. Her name is Lotte Hartmann, but she hasn't been around in a few weeks.'

'No? Do you know where she is?'

'Not exactly. They went skiing together – Lotte and Helmut König, her *schätzi*. Somewhere in the Austrian Tyrol, I believe.'

'When was this?'

'I don't know. Two, three weeks ago. König seems to have plenty of money.'

'Do you know when they're coming back?'

'I have no idea. I do know she said she'd be away for at least a month if things worked out between them. Knowing Lotte, that means it would depend on how much of a good time he showed her.'

'Are you sure she's coming back?'

'It would take an avalanche to stop her coming back here. Lotte's Viennese right up to her earlobes; she doesn't know how to live anywhere else. I guess you want me to keep my eye close to the keyhole for them.'

'That's about the size of it,' I said. 'Naturally I'll pay you.'

She shrugged. 'There's no need,' she said, and pressed her nose against the windowpane. 'People who save my life get themselves all sorts of generous discounts.'

'I ought to warn you. It could be dangerous.'

'You don't have to tell me,' she said coolly. 'I've met König. He's all smooth and charming at the club but he doesn't fool me. Helmut's the kind of man who takes his brass knuckles to confession.'

When we were on the ground again I used some of my coupons to buy us a bag of lingos, a Hungarian snack of fried dough sprinkled with garlic, from one of the stalls near the great wheel. After this modest lunch we took the Lilliput Railway down to the Olympic Stadium and walked back in the snow through the woods on Hauptallee.

Much later on, when we were in her room again, she said, 'Are you still feeling nervous?'

I reached for her gourd-like breasts and found her blouse damp with perspiration. She helped me to unbutton her and while I enjoyed the weight of her bosom in my hand she unfastened her skirt. I stood back to give her room to step out of it. And when she had laid it over the back of a chair I took her by the hand and drew her towards me.

For a brief moment I held her tight, enjoying her short, husky breath on my neck, before searching down for the curve of her girdled behind, her membrane-tight stocking-tops, and then the soft, cool flesh between her gartered thighs. And after she had engineered the subtraction of what little remained to cover her, I kissed her and allowed an intrepid finger to enjoy a short exploration of her hidden places.

In bed she held a smile on her face as slowly I strove to fathom her. Catching sight of her open eyes, which were no more than dreamy, as if she was unable to forget my satisfaction in search of her own, I found that I was too excited to care much beyond what seemed polite. When at last she felt the wound I was making in her become more urgent, she raised her thighs on to her chest and, reaching down, spread herself open with the flats of her hands, as if holding taut a piece of cloth for the needle of a sewing-machine, so that I might see myself periodically drawn tight into her. A moment later I flexed against her as life worked its independent and juddering propulsion.

It snowed hard that night, and then the temperature fell into the sewers, freezing the whole of Vienna, to preserve it for a better day. I dreamed, not of a lasting city, but of the city which was to come.

PART TWO

19

'A date for Herr Becker's trial has now been set,' Liebl told me, 'which makes it absolutely imperative that we make all haste with the preparation of our defence. I trust you will forgive me, Herr Gunther, if I impress upon you the urgent need for evidence to substantiate our client's account. While I have faith in your ability as a detective, I should very much like to know exactly what progress you have made so far, in order that I may best advise Herr Becker how we are to conduct his case in court.'

This conversation took place several weeks after my arrival in Vienna – but it was not the first time that Liebl had pressed me for some indication of my progress.

We were sitting in the Café Schwarzenberg, which had become the nearest thing I'd had to an office since before the war. The Viennese coffee house resembles a gentleman's club, except in so far as that a day's membership costs little more than the price of a cup of coffee. For that you can stay for as long as you like, read the papers and magazines that are provided, leave messages with waiters, receive mail, reserve a table for appointments and generally run a business in total confidence before all the world. The Viennese respect privacy in the same way that Americans worship antiquity, and a fellow patron of the Schwarzenberg would no more have stuck his nose over your shoulder than he would have stirred a cup of mocha with his forefinger.

On previous occasions I had told Liebl that an exact idea of progress was not something that existed in the world of the private investigator: that it was not the kind of business in which one might report that a specific course of action would definitely occur within a certain period. That's the trouble with lawyers. They expect the rest of the world to work like the Code Napoléon. On this particular occasion however, I had rather more to tell Liebl.

'König's girlfriend, Lotte, is back in Vienna,' I said.

'She's returned from her skiing holiday at long last?'

'It looks like that.'

'But you haven't yet found her.'

'Someone I know from the Casanova Club has a friend who spoke to her just a couple of days ago. She may even have been back for a week or so.'

'A week?' Liebl repeated. 'Why has it taken so long to find that out?'

'These things take time,' I shrugged provocatively. I was fed up with Liebl's constant quizzing and had started to take a childish delight in teasing him with these displays of apparent insouciance.

'Yes,' he grumbled, 'so you've said before.' He did not sound convinced.

'It's not like we have addresses for these people,' I said. 'And Lotte Hartmann hasn't been near the Casanova since she's been back. The girl who spoke to her said that Lotte had been trying to get a small part in a film at Sievering Studios.'

'Sievering? Yes, that's in the 19th Bezirk. The studio is owned by a Viennese called Karl Hartl. He used to be a client of mine. Hartl's directed all the great stars: Pola Negri, Lya de Putti, Maria Corda, Vilma Banky, Lilian Harvey. Did you see *The Gypsy Baron*? Well that was Hartl.'

'You don't suppose he could know anything about the film studio where Becker found Linden's body?'

'Drittemann Film?' Liebl stirred his coffee absently. 'If it were a legitimate film company, Hartl would know about it. There's not much that happens in Viennese film-production that Hartl doesn't know about. But this wasn't anything more than a name on a lease. There weren't actually any films made there. You checked it out yourself, didn't you?'

'Yes,' I said, recalling the fruitless afternoon I had spent there two weeks before. It turned out that even the lease had expired, and that the property had now reverted to the state. 'You're right. Linden was the first and last thing to be shot there.' I shrugged. 'It was just a thought.'

'So what will you do now?'

134

'Try and trace Lotte Hartmann at Sievering. That shouldn't be too difficult. You don't go after a part in a film without leaving an address where you can be contacted.'

Liebl sipped his coffee noisily, and then dabbed daintily at his mouth with a spinnaker-sized handkerchief.

'Please waste no time in tracing this person,' he said. 'I'm sorry to have to press you like this, but until we discover Herr König's whereabouts, we have nothing. Once you find him we might at least try and oblige him to be called as a material witness.'

I nodded meekly. There was more I could have told him but his tone irritated me, and any further explanation would have generated questions I was simply not equipped to answer yet. I could, for instance, have given him an account of what I had learned from Belinsky, at that same table in the Schwarzenberg, about a week after he had saved my skin – information that I was still turning over in my mind, and trying to make sense of. Nothing was as straightforward as Liebl somehow imagined.

'First of all,' Belinsky had explained, 'the Drexlers were what they seemed. She survived Matthausen Concentration Camp, while he came out of the Lodz Ghetto and Auschwitz. They met in a Red Cross hospital after the war, and lived in Frankfurt for a while before they went to Berlin. Apparently they worked pretty closely with the Crowcass people and the public prosecutor's office. They maintained a large number of files on wanted Nazis and pursued many cases simultaneously. Consequently our people in Berlin weren't able to determine if there had been any one investigation which related to their deaths, or to Captain Linden's. The local police are baffled, as they say. Which is probably the way they prefer it. Frankly, they don't give much of a damn who killed the Drexlers, and the American MP investigation doesn't look as if it's going to get anywhere.

'But it doesn't seem likely that the Drexlers would have been very interested in Martin Albers. He was SS and SD clandestine operations chief in Budapest until 1944, when he was arrested for his part in Stauffenberg's plot to kill Hitler, and hanged at Flossenburg Concentration Camp in April 1945. But I dare say he had it coming to him. From all accounts, Albers was a bit of a bastard, even if he did try and get rid of the Führer. A lot of you guys were a hell of a long time about that, you know. Our Intelligence people even think that Himmler knew about the plot all along and let it go ahead in the hope that he could take Hitler's place himself.

'Anyway, it turns out that this Max Abs guy was Albers' servant, driver and general dogsbody, so it kind of looks as if he was honouring his old boss. The Albers family was killed in an air-raid, so I guess there was no one else to erect a stone in his memory.'

'Rather an expensive gesture, wouldn't you say?'

'You think so? Well, I'd sure hate to get killed minding your ass, kraut.'

Then Belinsky told me about the Pullach company.

'It's an American-sponsored organization, run by the Germans, set up with the aim of rebuilding German commerce throughout Bizonia. The whole idea is that Germany should become economically self-supporting as quickly as possible so that Uncle Sam won't have to keep baling you all out. The company itself is located at an American mission called Camp Nicholas, which until a few months ago was occupied by the postal censorship authorities of the US Army. Camp Nicholas is a big compound that was originally built for Rudolf Hess and his family. But after he went AWOL Bormann had it for a while. And then Kesselring and his staff. Now it's ours. There's just enough security about the place to convince the locals that the camp is home to some kind of technical research establishment, but that's no surprise given the history of the place. Anyway, the good people of Pullach give it a wide berth, preferring not to know too much about what's happening there, even if it is something as harmless as an economic and commercial think-tank. I guess they're good at that, what with Dachau just a few miles away.'

That seemed to take care of Pullach, I thought. But what of Abs? It didn't seem to be in character for a man who wished to commemorate the memory of a hero of the German Resistance (such as it had existed), to kill an innocent man merely in order to remain anonymous. And how could Abs be connected with Linden, the Nazi-hunter, except as some kind of informer? Was it possible that Abs had also been killed, just like Linden and the Drexlers?

I finished my coffee, lit a cigarette and for the present moment I was content that these and other questions could not be asked in any forum other than my own mind.

The number 39 ran west along Sieveringer Strasse into Döbling and stopped just short of the Vienna Woods, a spur of the Alps which reaches as far as the Danube.

A film studio is not a place where you are likely to see any great evidence of industry. Equipment lies forever idle in the vans hired to transport it. Sets are never more than half-built even when they are finished. But mostly there are lots of people, all drawing a wage, who seem to do little more than stand around, smoking cigarettes and nursing cups of coffee; and these only stand because they are not considered important enough to be provided with a seat. For anyone foolish enough to have financed such an apparently profligate undertaking, film must seem like the most expensive length of material since Chinese silk, and would, I reflected, surely have driven Dr Liebl half-mad with impatience.

I inquired after the studio manager from a man with a clip-board, and he directed me to a small office on the first floor. There I found a tall, paunchy man with dyed hair, wearing a lilac-coloured cardigan and having the manner of an eccentric maiden aunt. He listened to my mission with one hand clasped on top of the other as if I had been requesting the hand of his warded niece.

'What are you, some kind of policeman?' he said combing an unruly eyebrow with his fingernail. From somewhere in the building came the sound of a very loud trumpet, which caused him to wince noticeably.

'A detective,' I said, disingenuously.

'Well, we always like to cooperate with them at the top, I'm sure. What did you say this girl was casting for?'

'I didn't. I'm afraid I don't know. But it was in the last two or three weeks.'

He picked up the telephone and pressed a switch.

'Willy? It's me, Otto. Could you be a love and step into my office for a moment?' He replaced the receiver, and checked his hair. 'Willy Reichmann's a production manager here. He may be able to help you.'

'Thanks,' I said and offered him a cigarette.

He threaded it behind his ear. 'How kind. I'll smoke it later.'

'What are you filming at the moment?' I inquired while we waited. Whoever was playing the trumpet hit a couple of high notes that didn't seem to match.

Otto emitted a groan and stared archly at the ceiling. 'Well, it's called *The Angel with the Trumpet*,' he said with a conspicuous lack of enthusiasm. 'It's more or less finished now, but this director is such a perfectionist.'

'Would that be Karl Hartl?'

'Yes. Do you know him?'

'Only *The Gypsy Baron*.'

'Oh,' he said sourly. 'That.'

There was a knock at the door and a short man with bright red hair came into the office. He reminded me of a troll.

'Willy, this is Herr Gunther. He's a detective. If you're willing to forgive the fact that he liked *The Gypsy Baron* you might like to give him some assistance. He's looking for a girl, an actress who was at a casting session here not so long ago.'

Willy smiled uncertainly, revealing small uneven teeth that looked like a mouthful of rock salt, nodded and said in a high-pitched voice: 'You'd best come into my office, Herr Gunther.'

'Don't keep Willy too long, Herr Gunther,' Otto instructed as I followed Willy's diminutive figure into the corridor. 'He has an appointment in fifteen minutes.'

Willy turned on his heel and looked blankly at the studio manager. Otto sighed exasperatedly. 'Don't you ever write anything in your diary, Willy? We've got that Englishman coming from London Films. Mr Lyndon-Haynes? Remember?'

Willy grunted something and then closed the door behind us. He led the way along the corridor to another office, and ushered me inside.

'Now, what is this girl's name?' he said, pointing me to a chair.

'Lotte Hartmann.'

'I don't suppose you know the name of the production company?'

'No, but I know that she came here within the last couple of weeks.'

He sat down and opened one of the desk drawers. 'Well, there were only three films casting here this past month, so it shouldn't be too difficult.' His short fingers picked out three files which he laid on the blotter and started to sort through their contents. 'Is she in trouble?'

'No. It's just that she may know someone who can help the police with an inquiry we are making.' This was true at least.

'Well if she's been up for a part this last month or so, she'll be in one of these files. We may be short of attractive ruins in Vienna, but one thing we've got plenty of is actresses. Half of them are chocoladies, mind you. Even at the best of times an actress is just a chocolady by another name.' He came to the end of one pile of papers and started on another.

'I can't say I miss your lack of ruins,' I remarked. 'I'm from Berlin myself. We've got ruins on an epic scale.'

'Don't I know it. But this Englishman I have to see wants lots of ruins here in Vienna. Just like Berlin. Just like Rosellini.' He sighed disconsolately. 'I ask you: what is there apart from the Ring and the Opera district?'

I shook my head sympathetically.

'What does he expect? The war's been over for three years. Does he imagine that we delayed rebuilding just in case an English film crew turned up? Perhaps these things take longer in England than in Austria. It wouldn't surprise me, considering the amount of red-tape the British generate. Never known such a bureaucratic lot. Christ knows what I'm going to tell this fellow. By the time they start filming they'll be lucky to find a broken window.'

He skimmed a sheet of paper across the desk. Pinned to its top left-hand corner was a passport-sized photograph. 'Lotte Hartmann,' he announced.

I glanced at the name and the photograph. 'It looks like it.'

'Actually I remember her,' he said. 'She wasn't quite what we were looking for on that occasion, but I said I could probably find her something in this English production. Good-looking, I'll say that much for her. But to be frank with you, Herr Gunther, she isn't much of an actress. A couple of walk-on parts at the Burgtheater during the war and that's about it. Still, the English are making a film about the black market and so they want lots of chocoladies. In view of Lotte Hartmann's particular experience I thought she could be one of them.'

'Oh? What experience is that?'

'She used to be a greeter at the Casanova Club. And now she's a croupier at the Casino Oriental. At least that's what she told me. For all I know she could be one of the exotic dancers they have there. Anyway, if you're looking for her, that's the address she gave.'

'Mind if I borrow this sheet?'

'Be my guest.'

'One more thing: if for any reason Fräulein Hartmann gets in contact with you I'd be grateful if you would keep this under your hat.'

'Like it was a new toupee.'

I stood up to leave. 'Thanks,' I said, 'you've been very helpful. Oh, and good luck with your ruins.'

He grinned wryly. 'Yes, well, if you see any weak walls, give them a shove, there's a good fellow.'

I was at the Oriental that evening, just in time for the first show at 8.15. The girl dancing naked on the pagoda-like dance floor, to the accompaniment of a six-piece orchestra, had eyes that were as cold and hard as the blackest piece of Pichler's porphyry. Contempt was written into her face as indelibly as the birds tattooed on her small, girlish breasts. A couple of times she had to stifle a yawn, and once she grimaced at the gorilla who was detailed to watch over her in case anyone wanted to show the girl his appreciation. When after forty-five minutes she came to the end of her act, her curtsy was a mockery of those of us who had watched it.

I waved to a waiter and transferred my attention to the club itself. 'The wonderful Egyptian Night Cabaret' was how the Oriental described itself on the book of matches I had collected from the brass ashtray, and it was certainly greasy enough to have passed for something Middle Eastern, at least in the clichéd eye of some set-designer from Sievering Studios. A long, curving stairway led down into the Moorish-style interior with its gilt pillars, cupola'd ceiling and many Persian tapestries on the mock-mosaic walls. The dank, basement smell, cheap Turkish tobacco-smoke and number of prostitutes only added to the authentic Oriental atmosphere. I half expected to see the thief of Baghdad sit down at the wooden marquetry table I had taken. Instead I got a Viennese garter-handler.

'You looking for a nice girl?' he asked.

'If I were I wouldn't have come here.'

The pimp read this the wrong way up, and pointed out a big redhead who was seated at the anachronistic American bar. 'I can get you nice and cosy with that one there.'

'No thanks. I can smell her pants from here.'

'Listen, *pifke,* that little chocolady is so clean you could eat your supper off her crotch.'

'I'm not that hungry.'

'Perhaps something else, then. If it's drip you're worried about, I know where I can find some nice fresh snow, with no footprints. Know what I mean?' He leaned forwards across the table. 'A girl who hasn't even finished school yet. How does a splash like that sound to you?'

'Disappear, swing, before I shut your flap.'

He leaned back suddenly. 'Slow your blood down, *pifke,*' he sneered. 'I was only trying to – ' He yelped with pain as he found himself drawn to his feet by one sideburn held between Belinsky's forefinger and thumb.

'You heard my friend,' he said with quiet menace, and pushing the man away he sat down opposite me. 'God, I hate pimps,' he muttered, shaking his head.

'I'd never have guessed,' I said, and waved again at the waiter, who seeing the pimp's manner of departure approached the table with more obsequiousness than an Egyptian houseboy. 'What'll you have?' I asked the American.

'A beer,' he said.

'Two Gossers,' I told the waiter.

'Immediately, gentlemen,' he said, and scuttled away.

'Well that's certainly made him more attentive,' I observed.

'Yeah, well, you don't come to the Casino Oriental for ritzy service. You come to lose money on the tables or in a bed.'

'What about the floor-show? You forgot the show.'

'The hell I did.' He laughed obscenely and proceeded to explain that he usually tried to catch the show at the Oriental at least once a week.

When I told him about the girl with the tattoos on her breasts he shook his head with worldly indifference, and for a while I was obliged to listen to him tell me about the strippers and exotic dancers he'd seen in the Far East, where a girl with a tattoo was considered nothing to write home about. This kind of conversation was of little interest to me, and when after several minutes Belinsky ran out of unholy anecdote, I was glad to be able to change the subject.

'I found König's girlfriend, Fräulein Hartmann,' I announced.

'Yes? Where?'

'In the next room. Dealing cards.'

'The croupier? The blonde piece with the tan and the icicle up her ass?'

I nodded.

'I tried to buy her a drink,' he said, 'only I might as well have been selling brushes. If you're going to ingratiate yourself with that one you've got your work cut out, kraut. She's so cold her perfume makes your nostrils ache. Perhaps if you were to kidnap her you might stand some chance.'

'I was thinking along similar lines. Seriously, how low is your credit with the MPs here in Vienna?'

Belinsky shrugged. 'It's a real snake's ass. But say what you've got in mind and I'll tell you for sure.'

'How's this then? The International Patrol comes in here one night and arrests me and the girl on some pretext. Then they take us down to Kärtnerstrasse where I start talking tough about how a mistake has been made. Maybe some money even changes hands to make it look really convincing. After all, people like to believe that all police are corrupt, don't they? So she and König might appreciate that little bit of fine detail. Anyway, when the police let us go I make out to Lotte Hartmann that the reason I helped her was because I find her attractive. Well naturally she's grateful and would like me to know it, only she's got this gentleman friend. Maybe he can repay me somehow or other. Put some business my way, that kind of thing.' I paused and lit a cigarette. 'Well, what do you think?'

'In the first place,' Belinsky said thoughtfully, 'the IP isn't allowed in this joint. There's a big sign at the front door to that effect. Your ten-schilling entrance buys a night's membership to what is, after all, a private club, which means the IP just can't come marching in here dirtying the carpet and scaring the flower-lady.'

'All right then,' I said, 'they wait outside and work a spot-check on people as they leave the club. Surely there's nothing to stop them doing that? They pull Lotte and me in on suspicion: her of being a chocolady, and me of working some racket.'

The waiter arrived with our beers. Meanwhile the second show was starting. Belinsky swallowed a mouthful of his drink and sat back in his seat to watch.

'I like this one,' he growled, lighting his pipe. 'She's got an ass like the west coast of Africa. Just you wait until you see it.' Puffing contentedly, his pipe fixed between his grinning teeth, Belinsky kept his eyes on the girl peeling off her brassière.

'It might just work at that,' he said eventually. 'Only forget trying to bribe one of the Americans. No, if it's grease you're trying to simulate then it really has to be an Ivan or a Frenchy. As it happens the CIC has turned a Russian captain in the IP. Apparently he's trying to work his passage to the United States, so he's good for service manuals, identity-papers, tip-offs, the usual kind of thing. A fake arrest ought to be within his abilities. And by a happy coincidence the Russians are in the chair this month, so it should be easy enough to arrange a night when he's on duty.'

Belinsky's grin widened as the dancing girl eased her pants over her substantial backside to reveal a tiny G-string.

'Oh, will you look at that?' he chuckled, with schoolboyish glee. 'Put a nice frame around her ass and I could hang it on my wall.' He tossed back his beer and winked lasciviously at me. 'I'll say one thing for you krauts. You build your women every bit as well as you build your automobiles.'

20

My clothes actually seemed to fit me better. My trousers had stopped hanging loose around my waist like a clown's pantaloons. Slipping into my jacket was no longer reminiscent of a schoolboy optimistically trying on his dead father's suits. And my shirt-collar was as snug about my neck as the bandage on a coward's arm. There was no doubt that a couple of months in Vienna had put some weight on me, so that I now looked more like the man who had gone to a Soviet POW camp and less like the man who had returned from one. But while this pleased me, I saw it as no excuse to get out of condition, and I had resolved to spend less time sitting in the Café Schwarzenberg, and to take more exercise.

It was the time of year when winter's denuded trees were starting to bud, and when the decision to wear an overcoat was no longer automatic. With only a chalk-mark of cloud on an otherwise uniformly blue board of sky, I decided to take a walk around the Ring and expose my pigments to the warm spring sunshine.

Like a chandelier that is too big for the room in which it hangs, so the official buildings on the Ringstrasse, built at a time of overbearing Imperial optimism, were somehow too grand, too opulent for the geographical realities of the new Austria. A country of six million people, Austria was little more than the butt-end of a very large cigar. It wasn't a Ring I went walking on so much as a wreath.

The American sentry outside the US-requisitioned Bristol Hotel had his pink face lifted up to catch the rays of the morning sun. His Russian counterpart guarding the similarly requisitioned Grand Hotel next door looked as if he had spent his whole life outdoors, so dark were his features.

Crossing on to the south side of the Ring in order to be close to the park as I came up the Schubertring, I found myself near the Russian Kommendatura, formerly the Imperial Hotel, as a large Red Army staff car drew up outside the enormous red star and four caryatids that marked the entrance. The car door opened and out stepped Colonel Poroshin.

He did not seem in any way surprised to see me. Indeed, it was almost as if he had expected to find me walking there, and for a moment he simply looked at me as if it had been only a few hours since I had sat in his office in the little Kremlin in Berlin. I suppose my jaw must have dropped, because after a second he smiled, murmured '*Dobraye ootra* (Good-morning)', and then carried on into the Kommendatura followed closely by a couple of junior officers who stared suspiciously back at me, while I stood there, simply lost for words.

More than a little puzzled as to why Poroshin should have turned up in Vienna now, I wandered back across the road to the Café Schwarzenberg, narrowly escaping being hit by an old lady on a bicycle who rang her bell furiously at me.

I sat down at my usual table to give some thought to Poroshin's arrival on the scene, and ordered a light snack, my new fitness resolution already ruined.

The colonel's presence in Vienna seemed easier to explain with some coffee and cake inside of me. There was, after all, no reason why he should not have come. As an MVD colonel he could probably go wherever he liked. That he had not said more to me or inquired as to how my efforts were going on behalf of his friend I thought was probably due to the fact that he had no wish to discuss the matter in front of the two other officers. And he had only to pick up the telephone and ring the headquarters of the International Patrol in order to discover if Becker was still in prison or not.

All the same I had a feeling on the sole of my shoe that Poroshin's arrival from Berlin was connected with my own investigation, not necessarily for the better. Like a man who has breakfasted on prunes, I told myself I was certain to notice something before very long.

21

Each one of the Four Powers took administrative responsibility for the policing of the Inner City for a month at a time. 'In the chair' was how Belinsky had described it. The chair in question was located in a meeting-room at the combined forces head-quarters in the Palais Auersperg, although it also affected who sat next to the driver in the International Patrol vehicle. But though the IP was an instrument of the Four Powers and subject in theory to orders from the combined forces, for all practical purposes it was American operated and supplied. All vehicles, petrol and oil, radios, radio spares, maintenance of the vehicles and the radios, operation of the radio network system and organization of the patrols were the responsibility of the US 796th. This meant that the American member of the patrol always drove the vehicle, operated the radio and performed the first-echelon maintenance. Thus, at least as far as the patrol itself was concerned, the idea of 'the chair' was a bit of a movable feast.

Although the Viennese referred to 'the four men in the jeep', or sometimes 'the four elephants in the jeep', in reality 'the jeep' had long been abandoned as too small to accommodate a patrol of four men, their short-wave transmitter, not to mention any prisoners; and a three-quarter-ton Command and Reconnais-sance vehicle was now the favoured mode of transport.

All this I learned from the Russian corporal commanding the IP truck parked a short distance from the Casino Oriental on Petersplatz, in which I sat under arrest, waiting for the kapral's colleagues to pick up Lotte Hartmann. Speaking neither French nor English, and with only a smattering of German, the kapral was delighted to find someone with whom he could have a conversation, even if it was a Russian-speaking prisoner.

'I'm afraid I can't tell you very much about why you're being arrested, apart from the fact that it's for black-marketeering,' he apologised. 'You'll find out more when we get to the Kärt-nerstrasse. We'll both find out, eh? All I can tell you about is the procedure. My captain will fill out an arrest-form, in duplicate – everything's in duplicate – and leave both copies with the Austrian police. They'll forward one copy to the Military Government Public-Safety Officer. If you're held for trial in a military court, a charge sheet will be prepared by my captain; and if you're held for trial in an Austrian court, the local police will be instructed accordingly.' The kapral frowned. 'To be honest with you, we don't bother much with black-market offences these days. Or vice for that matter. It's smugglers we're generally after, or illegal emigrants. Those other three bastards think I've gone mad, I can tell. But I've got my orders.'

I smiled sympathetically and said how I appreciated him explaining. I was thinking of offering him a cigarette when the door of the truck opened and the French patrolman helped a very pale-looking Lotte Hartmann to climb up beside me. Then he and the Englishman came after her, locking the door from the inside. The smell of her fear was only marginally weaker than the cloying scent of her perfume.

'Where are they taking us?' she whispered to me.

I told her we were going to the Kärtnerstrasse.

'No talking is allowed,' said the English MP in appalling German. 'Prisoners will keep quiet until we reach headquarters.'

I smiled quietly to myself. The language of bureaucracy was the only second language that an Englishman would ever be capable of speaking well.

The IP was headquartered in an old palace within a cigarette-end's flick of the State Opera. The truck drew up outside and we were marched through huge glass doors and into a baroque-style hall, where an assortment of atlantes and caryatids showed the omnipresent hand of the Viennese stonemason. We went up a staircase that was as wide as a railway track, past urns and busts of forgotten noblemen, through a pair of doors that were longer than the legs of a circus tall-man and into an arrangement of glass-fronted offices. The Russian kapral opened the door of one of them, ushered his two prisoners inside and told us to wait there.

148

'What did he say?' Fräulein Hartmann asked as he closed the door behind him.

'He said to wait.' I sat down, lit a cigarette and looked about the room. There was a desk, four chairs and on the wall a large wooden noticeboard of the kind you see outside churches, except that this one was in Cyrillic, with columns of chalked numbers and names, headed 'Wanted Persons', 'Absentees', 'Stolen Vehicles', 'Express Messages', 'Part I Orders' and 'Part II Orders'. In the column headed 'Wanted Persons' appeared my own name and that of Lotte Hartmann. Belinsky's pet Russian was making things look very convincing.

'Have you any idea what this is all about?' she asked tremulously.

'No,' I lied. 'Have you?'

'No, of course not. There must be some kind of mistake.'

'Evidently.'

'You don't seem all that concerned. Or maybe you just don't understand that it's the Russians who ordered us to be brought here.'

'Do you speak Russian?'

'No, of course not,' she said impatiently. 'The American MP who arrested me said that this was a Russian call and nothing to do with him.'

'Well, the Ivans are in the chair this month,' I said reflectively. 'What did the Frenchman say?'

'Nothing. He just kept looking down the front of my dress.'

'He would.' I smiled at her. 'It's worth a look.'

She gave me a sarcastic sort of smile. 'Yes, well, I don't think they brought me here just to see the wood stacked in front of the cabin, do you?' She spoke with crisp distaste, but accepted the cigarette I offered her all the same.

'I can't think of a better reason.'

She swore under her breath.

'I've seen you, haven't I?' I said. 'At the Oriental?'

'What were you during the war – an air spotter?'

'Be nice. Maybe I can help you.'

'Better help yourself first.'

'You can depend on that.'

149

When the office door finally opened it was a tall, burly-looking Red Army officer who came into the room. He introduced himself as Captain Rustaveli and took a seat behind the desk.

'Look here,' demanded Lotte Hartmann, 'would you mind telling me why I've been brought here in the middle of the night? What the hell is going on?'

'All in good time, Fräulein,' he replied in flawless German. 'Please sit down.'

She slumped on to a chair beside me and regarded him sullenly. The captain looked at me.

'Herr Gunther?'

I nodded and told him in Russian that the girl spoke only German. 'She'll think I'm a more impressive son-of-a-bitch if you and I confine ourselves to a language she can't understand.'

Captain Rustaveli stared coldly back at me and for a brief moment I wondered if something had gone wrong and Belinsky had not managed to make it clear to this Russian officer that our arrests were a put-up job.

'Very well,' he said after a long moment. 'Nevertheless, we shall at least have to go through the motions of an interrogation. May I see your papers please, Herr Gunther?' From his accent I took him for a Georgian. The same as Comrade Stalin.

I reached inside my jacket and handed over my identity card into which, at Belinsky's suggestion, I had inserted two $100 bills while sitting in the truck. Rustaveli quickly slipped the money into his breeches pocket without blinking, and out of the corner of my eye I saw Lotte Hartmann's jaw drop on to her lap.

'Very generous,' he murmured, turning over my identity card in his hairy fingers. Then he opened a file with my name on it. 'Although quite unnecessary, I can assure you.'

'There's her feelings to think of, Captain. You wouldn't want me to disappoint her prejudice, would you?'

'No indeed. Good-looking, wouldn't you say?'

'Very.'

'A whore, do you think?'

'That, or something pretty close to it. I'm only guessing of course, but I'd say she was the type that likes to strip a man of a lot more than ten schillings and his underwear.'

'Not the sort of girl to fall in love with, eh?'

'It would be like putting your tail on an anvil.'

It was warm in Rustaveli's office and Lotte started to fan herself with her jacket, allowing the Russian several glimpses of her ample cleavage.

'It's rare that an interrogation is quite so amusing,' he said, and looking down at his papers added: 'She has nice tits. That's the kind of truth I can really respect.'

'I guess it's a lot easier for you Russians to look at.'

'Well, whatever this little show has been laid on to achieve, I hope you get to have her. I can't think of a better reason to go to all this trouble. Me, I've got a sexual disease: my tail swells up every time I see a woman.'

'I guess that makes you a fairly typical Russian.'

Rustaveli smiled wryly. 'Incidentally, you speak excellent Russian, Herr Gunther. For a German.'

'So do you, Captain. For a Georgian. Where are you from?'

'Tbilisi.'

'Stalin's birthplace?'

'No, thank God. That's Gori's misfortune.' Rustaveli closed my file. 'That should be enough to impress her, don't you think?'

'Yes.'

'What shall I tell her?'

'You have information that she's a whore,' I explained, 'so you're reluctant to let her go. But you let me talk you into it.'

'Well, that seems to be in order, Herr Gunther,' Rustaveli said, reverting to German again. 'My apologies for having detained you. Now you may leave.'

He handed back my identity card, and I stood up and made for the door.

'But what about me?' Lotte moaned.

Rustaveli shook his head. 'I'm afraid you must stay, Fräulein. The vice squad doctor will be here shortly. He will question you regarding your work at the Oriental.'

'But I'm a croupier,' she wailed, 'not a chocolady.'

'That is not our information.'

'What information?'

'Your name has been mentioned by several other girls.'

'What other girls?'

'Prostitutes, Fräulein. Possibly you may have to submit your-self for a medical examination.'

'A medical? What for?'

'For venereal disease, of course.'

'Venereal disease – ?'

'Captain Rustaveli,' I said above Lotte's rising cry of outrage, 'I can vouch for this woman. I wouldn't say I knew her very well, but I've known her long enough to be able to state, quite categorically, that she is not a prostitute.'

'Well – ' he cavilled.

'I ask you: does she look like a prostitute?'

'Frankly, I've yet to meet an Austrian girl who isn't selling it.' He closed his eyes for a second, and then shook his head. 'I can't go against the protocol. These are serious charges. Many Russian soldiers have been infected.'

'As I recall, the Oriental where Fräulein Hartmann was arrested is off limits to the Red Army. I was under the impression that your men tended to go to the Moulin Rouge in Walfischgasse.'

Rustaveli pursed his lips and shrugged. 'That is true. But nevertheless – '

'Perhaps if I were to meet you again, Captain, we might discuss the possibility of me compensating the Red Army for any embarrassment regarding a breach of the protocol. In the meantime, would you be able to accept my personal surety for the Fräulein's good character?'

Rustaveli scratched his stubble thoughtfully. 'Very well,' he said, 'your personal surety. But remember, I have your addresses. You can always be re-arrested.' He turned to Lotte Hartmann and told her that she was also free to leave.

'Thank God,' she breathed, and sprang to her feet.

Rustaveli nodded at the kapral standing guard on the other side of the grimy glass door, and then ordered him to escort us out of the building. Then the captain clicked his heels and apologised for 'the mistake', as much for the benefit of his kapral as for any effect it might have had on Lotte Hartmann.

She and I followed the kapral back down the big staircase, our steps echoing up to the ornate cornice-work on the high ceiling, and through the arched glass doors into the street where he leaned over the pavement and spat copiously into the gutter.

'A mistake, eh?' He uttered a bitter laugh. 'Mark my words, I'll be the one that gets the blame for it.'

'I hope not,' I said, but the man just shrugged, adjusted his lambskin hat and trudged wearily back into his headquarters.

'I suppose I ought to thank you,' Lotte said, tying up the collar of her jacket.

'Forget it,' I said, and started walking towards the Ring. She hesitated for a moment and then tripped after me.

'Wait a minute,' she said.

I stopped and faced her again. Frontally her face was even more attractive than its profile, as the length of her nose seemed less noticeable. And she was not cold at all. Belinsky had been wrong about that, mistaking cynicism for general indifference. Indeed, I thought she seemed more apt to entice men, although an evening of watching her in the Casino had established that she was probably one of those unsatisfactory women who dangle intimacy, only to withdraw it at a later stage.

'Yes? What is it?'

'Look, you've already been very kind,' she said, 'but would you mind walking me home? It is very late for a decent girl to be on the streets, and I doubt if I'll be able to find a taxi at this time of night.'

I shrugged and looked at my watch. 'Where do you live?'

'It's not very far. The 3rd Bezirk, in the British sector.'

'All right.' I sighed with a conspicuous lack of enthusiasm. 'Lead the way.'

We walked eastwards, along streets that were as quiet as a house of Franciscan tertiaries.

'You haven't explained why you helped me,' she said, breaking the silence after a while.

'I wonder if that's what Andromeda said when Perseus had saved her from the sea-monster.'

'You seem a little less obviously heroic, Herr Gunther.'

'Don't be fooled by my manners,' I told her. 'I've got a whole chestful of medals down at my local pawnshop.'

'So you're not the sentimental type either.'

'No, I like sentiment. It looks fine on needlework and Christmas cards. Only it doesn't make much of an engraving on the Ivans. Or perhaps you weren't looking.'

'Oh, I was looking all right. It was very impressive the way you handled him. I never knew the Ivans could be greased like that.'

'You just have to know the right spot on the axle. That kapral would probably have been too scared to take some drop, and a major too proud. Not to mention the fact that I'd met our Captain Rustaveli before, when he was plain Lieutenant Rustaveli and both he and his girlfriend had a dose of drip. I got them some good penicillin, for which he was very grateful.'

'You don't look like any swing Heini.'

'I don't look like a swing, I don't look like a hero. What are you, the head of casting at Warner Brothers?'

'I only wish I were,' she murmured. And then: 'Anyway, you started it. You said to that Ivan that I didn't look like a chocolady. Coming from you I'd say it almost sounded like a compliment.'

'Like I said, I've seen you at the Oriental, selling nothing worse than bad luck. Incidentally, I hope you're a good cardplayer, because I'm supposed to go back and give him something for your liberty. Assuming you actually want to stay out of the cement.'

'How much will that be?'

'A couple of hundred dollars ought to do it.'

'A couple of hundred?' Her words echoed around Schwarzenbergplatz as we came past a great fountain, and crossed onto Rennweg. 'Where am I going to get that kind of mouse?'

'Same place you got the suntan and nice jacket, I imagine. Failing that you could ask him to the club and deal him a few aces off the bottom of the deck.'

'I could if I were that good. But I'm not.'

'That's too bad.'

She was quiet for a moment as she gave the matter some thought. 'Maybe you could persuade him to take less. After all, you seem to speak pretty good Russkie.'

'Maybe,' I allowed.

'I don't suppose it would do much good to go to court and protect my innocence, would it?'

'With the Ivans?' I laughed harshly. 'You might just as well appeal to the goddess Kali.'

'No, I didn't think so.'

We came up a side street or two and stopped outside an apartment building that was close by a small park.

'Would you like to come in for a drink?' She fumbled in her handbag for her key. 'I know I could use one.'

'I could suck one out of the rug,' I said, and followed her through the door, upstairs and into a cosy, solidly furnished apartment.

There was no ignoring the fact that Lotte Hartmann was attractive. Some women, you look at them and calculate what modest length of time you would be willing to settle for. Generally, the better-looking the girl the less time with which you tell yourself you would be satisfied. After all, a really attractive woman might have to accommodate a lot of similar wishes. Lotte was the kind of girl with whom you could have been persuaded to settle for five steamy, unfettered minutes. Just five minutes for her to let you and your imagination do what you wanted. Not too much to ask, you would have thought. The way things happened, though, it looked like she might actually have granted me rather longer than that. Perhaps even the full hour. But I was dog-tired, and perhaps I drank a little too much of her excellent whisky to pay much attention to the way she bit her bottom-lip and stared at me through those black-widow eyelashes. I was probably supposed to lie quietly on her bed with my muzzle resting on her impressively convex lap and let her fold my big, floppy ears, only I ended up falling asleep on the sofa.

22

When I awoke later that same morning, I scribbled my address and telephone number on a piece of paper and, leaving Lotte asleep in bed, I caught a taxi back to my pension. There I washed, changed my clothes and ate a large breakfast, which did much to restore me. I was reading the morning's *Wiener Zeitung* when the telephone rang.

A man's voice, with only the smallest trace of a Viennese accent, asked me if it was speaking to Herr Bernhard Gunther. When I identified myself the voice said:

'I'm a friend of Fräulein Hartmann. She tells me that you very kindly helped her out of an awkward spot last night.'

'She's not exactly out of it yet,' I said.

'Quite so. I was hoping that we could meet and discuss the matter. Fräulein Hartmann mentioned the sum of $200 for this Russian captain. Also that you had offered to act as her intermediary.'

'Did I? I suppose I might have.'

'I was hoping I might give you the money to give to this wretched fellow. And I should like to thank you, personally.'

I felt sure that this was König, but I stayed silent for a moment, not wishing to seem too eager to meet him.

'Are you still there?'

'Where do you suggest?' I asked reluctantly.

'Do you know the Amalienbad, on Reumannplatz?'

'I'll find it.'

'Shall we say in one hour? In the Turkish baths?'

'All right. But how will I recognize you? You haven't even told me your name yet.'

'No I haven't,' he said mysteriously, 'but I'll be whistling this tune.' And with that he proceeded to whistle it down the line.

'Bella, bella, bella Marie,' I said, recognizing a melody that had been irritatingly ubiquitous some months before.

'Precisely that,' said the man, and hung up.

It seemed a curiously conspiratorial mode of recognition, but I told myself that if it was König, he had good reason to be cautious.

The Amalienbad was in the 10th Bezirk, in the Russian sector, which meant catching a number 67 south down Favoritenstrasse. The district was a working-class quarter with lots of dirty old factories, but the municipal baths on Reumannplatz was a seven-storeyed building of comparatively recent construction which, without any apparent exaggeration, advertised itself as the largest and most modern baths in Europe.

I paid for a bath and a towel, and after I had changed I went to find the men's steam-room. This was at the far end of a swimming pool that was as big as a football field, and possessed only a few Viennese who, wrapped in their bath-sheets, were trying to sweat off some of the weight that was rather easy to gain in the Austrian capital. Through the steam, at the far end of the luridly-tiled room, I heard someone whistling intermittently. I walked towards the source of the tune, and took it up as I approached.

I came upon the seated figure of a man with a uniformly white body and a uniformly brown face: it looked almost as if he had blacked-up, like Jolson, but of course this disparity in colour was a souvenir of his recent skiing holiday.

'I hate that tune,' he said, 'but Fräulein Hartmann is always humming it and I couldn't think of anything else. Herr Gunther?'

I nodded, circumspectly, as if I had come there only reluctantly.

'Permit me to introduce myself. My name is König.' We shook hands and I sat down beside him.

He was a well-built man, with thick dark eyebrows and a large, flourishing moustache: it looked like some rare species of marten that had escaped on to his lip from some colder, more northerly clime. Drooping over König's mouth, this small sable completed a generally lugubrious expression which started with his melancholy brown eyes. He was much as Becker had described him but for the absence of the small dog.

'I hope you like a Turkish bath, Herr Gunther?'

'Yes, when they're clean.'

'Then it's lucky I chose this one,' he said, 'instead of the Dianabad. Of course the Diana's war-damaged, but the place does seem to attract rather more than its fair share of incurables and other assorted lower humans. They go for the thermal pools they have there. You take a dip at your peril. You could go in with eczema and come out with syphilis.'

'It doesn't sound very healthy.'

'I dare say that I'm exaggerating a little,' König smiled. 'You're not from Vienna, are you?'

'No, I'm from Berlin,' I said. 'I come and go from Vienna.'

'How is Berlin these days? From what one hears the situation there is getting worse. The Soviet delegation walked out of the Control Commission, did it not?'

'Yes,' I said, 'soon the only way in or out will be by military air transport.'

König made a tutting noise and rubbed his big hairy chest wearily. 'Communists,' he sighed, 'that's what happens when you make deals with them. It was terrible what happened at Potsdam and Yalta. The Amis just let the Ivans take what they wanted. A great mistake, which makes another war a virtual certainty.'

'I doubt if anyone's got the stomach for another one,' I said, repeating the same line I had used on Neumann in Berlin. This was a fairly automatic reaction with me, but I genuinely believed it to be true.

'Not yet, maybe. But people forget, and in time – ' he shrugged ' – who knows what may happen? Until then, we carry on with our lives and our businesses, doing the best that we can.' For a moment he rubbed his scalp furiously. Then he said: 'What business are you in? The only reason I ask is that I hoped that there might be some way in which I could repay you for helping Fräulein Hartmann. Such as putting a little business your way, perhaps.'

I shook my head. 'It's not necessary. If you really want to know, I'm in imports and exports. But to be frank with you, Herr König, I helped her because I liked the smell of her scent.'

He nodded appreciatively. 'That's natural enough. She is very lovely.' But slowly, rapture gave way to perplexity. 'Strange though, don't you think? The way you were both picked up like that.'

'I can't answer for your friend, Herr König, but in my line of work there are always business rivals who would be glad to see me out of the way. An occupational hazard, you might say.'

'By Fräulein Hartmann's account, it's a hazard to which you seem more than equal. I heard that you handled that Russian captain quite expertly. And she was most impressed that you could speak Russian.'

'I was a plenny,' I said, 'a POW in Russia.'

'That would certainly explain it. But tell me, do you believe that this Russian can be serious? That there were charges made against Fräulein Hartmann?'

'I'm afraid he was very serious.'

'Have you any idea where he could have got his information?'

'No more than I have about how he came to have my name. Perhaps the lady has someone with a tooth against her.'

'Maybe you could find out who. I'd be prepared to pay you.'

'Not my line,' I said, shaking my head. 'The chances are that it was an anonymous tip-off. Probably done out of spite. You'd be wasting your money. If you'll take my advice you'll just give the Ivan what he wants and pay up. Two hundred is not a lot of coal to get a name off a file. And when the Ivans decide to keep a dog away from a bitch it's best to settle the account without any trouble.'

König smiled and then nodded. 'Perhaps you are right,' he said. 'But you know, it has occurred to me that you and this Ivan are in it together. It would after all be a nice way of raising money, wouldn't it? The Russian puts the squeeze on innocent people, and you offer to act as intermediary.' He kept on nodding as he surveyed the subtlety of his own scheme. 'Yes, it could be very profitable for someone with the right kind of background.'

'Keep going,' I laughed. 'Maybe you can make an ox out of an egg.'

'Surely you admit that it's possible.'

'Anything is possible in Vienna. But if you think I'm trying to give you some chocolate for a lousy two hundred, that's your affair. It may have escaped your attention, König, but it was your ladyfriend who asked me to walk her home, and you who asked me to come here. Frankly, I've got better things to polish.' I stood up and made as if to leave.

'Please, Herr Gunther,' he said, 'accept my apologies. Perhaps I was allowing my imagination to run away with me. But I must confess that this whole affair has me intrigued. And even at the best of times, I find myself suspicious with regard to so many things that happen today.'

'Well, that sounds like a recipe for a long life,' I said, sitting down again.

'In my own particular line of work, it pays to be a little sceptical.'

'What line of work is that?'

'I used to be in advertising. But that is an odious, unrewarding business, full of very small minds with no real vision. I dissolved the company I owned and moved into business research. The flow of accurate information is essential in all walks of commerce. But it is something that one must treat with a degree of caution. Those who wish to be well-informed must first equip themselves with doubt. Doubt breeds questions, and questions beg answers. These things are essential to the growth of any new enterprise. And new enterprise is essential to the growth of a new Germany.'

'You sound like a politician.'

'Politics.' He smiled wearily, as if the subject was too childish for him to contemplate. 'A mere sideshow to the main event.'

'Which is?'

'Communism against the free world. Capitalism is our only hope of withstanding the Soviet tyranny, wouldn't you agree?'

'I'm no friend of the Ivans,' I said, 'but capitalism comes with its own particular faults.'

But König was hardly listening. 'We fought the wrong war,' he said, 'the wrong enemy. We should have fought the Soviets, and only the Soviets. The Amis know that now. They know the mistake they made in letting Russia have a free hand in Eastern

Europe. And they're not about to let Germany or Austria go the same way.'

I stretched my muscles in the heat and yawned wearily. König was beginning to bore me.

'You know,' he said, 'my company could use a man with your special talents. A man with your background. Which part of the SS was it that you were in?' Noting the surprise that must have appeared on my face, he added: 'The scar under your arm. Doubtless you too were keen to remove your SS tattoo before being captured by the Russians.' He lifted his own arm to reveal an almost identical scar in his armpit.

'I was with Military Intelligence – the Abwehr – when the war ended,' I explained, 'not the SS. That was much earlier.'

But he had been right about the scar, the result of an obliterating and excrutiatingly painful burn sustained from the muzzle flash of an automatic pistol I had fired underneath my upper arm. It had been that or risk discovery and death at the hands of the NKVD.

König himself offered no explanation for the removal of his own tattoo. Instead he proceeded to expand on his offer of employment.

This was all much more than I had hoped for. But I still had to be careful: it was only a few minutes since he had all but accused me of working in consort with Captain Rustaveli.

'It's not that working for someone else gives me the livers or anything,' I said, 'but right now I've got another bottle to finish.' I shrugged. 'Maybe when that's empty ... who knows? But thanks anyway.'

He did not seem offended that I had declined his offer, and merely shrugged philosophically.

'Where can I find you if I ever change my mind?'

'Fräulein Hartmann at the Casino Oriental will know where to contact me.' He collected a folded newspaper from beside his thigh and handed it to me. 'Open it carefully when you get outside. There are two $100 bills to pay off the Ivan, and one for your trouble.'

At that moment he groaned and took hold of his face, baring incisors and canines that were as even as a row of tiny milk-bottles. Observing my eyebrows and mistaking their inquiry for concern he explained that he was quite all right but that he had recently been fitted with two dental plates.

'I can't seem to get used to having them in my mouth,' he said, and briefly allowed the blind, slow worm that was his tongue to squirm along the upper and lower galleries of his jaw. 'And when I see myself in a mirror, it's like having some perfect stranger grinning back at me. Most disconcerting.' He sighed and shook his head sadly. 'A pity really. I always had such perfect teeth.'

He stood up, adjusting the sheet around his chest, and then shook my hand.

'It was a pleasure meeting you, Herr Gunther,' he said with easy Viennese charm.

'No, the pleasure was all mine,' I replied.

König chuckled. 'We'll make an Austrian out of you yet, my friend.' Then he walked off into the steam, whistling that same maddening tune.

23

There's nothing the Viennese love more than getting 'cosy'. They look to achieve this conviviality in bars and restaurants, to the accompaniment of a musical quartet comprising a bass, a violin, an accordion and a zither – a strange instrument which resembles an empty box of chocolates with thirty or forty strings that are plucked like a guitar. For me, this omnipresent combination embodies everything that was phoney about Vienna, like the syrupy sentiment and the affected politeness. It did make me feel cosy. Only it was the kind of cosiness you might have experienced after you had been embalmed, sealed in a lead-lined coffin, and tidily deposited in one of those marble mausoleums up at the Central Cemetery.

I was waiting for Traudl Braunsteiner, in the Herrendorf, a restaurant on Herrengasse. The place was her choice, but she was late. When at last she arrived her face was red because she had been running, and also because of the cold.

'You have a less than Catholic air about you, the way you sit there in the shadows,' she said, sitting down at the dinner table.

'I work at that,' I said. 'Nobody wants a detective who looks as honest as the village postmaster. Being dimly lit is good for business.'

I waved to a waiter and we quickly ordered.

'Emil's upset that you haven't been to see him lately,' Traudl said, giving up her menu.

'If he wants to know what I've been doing, tell him I'll be sending him a bill for a shoe-repair. I've walked all over this damned city.'

'You know he goes to trial next week, don't you?'

'I'm not likely to be able to forget it, what with Liebl telephoning nearly every day.'

'Emil's not about to forget it either.' She spoke quietly, obviously upset.

'I'm sorry,' I said, 'that was a stupid thing to say. Look, I do have some good news. I've finally spoken to König.'

Her face lit up with excitement. 'You have?' she said. 'When? Where?'

'This morning,' I said. 'At the Amalienbad.'

'What did he say?'

'He wanted me to work for him. I think it might not be a bad idea, as a way of getting close enough to him to find some sort of evidence.'

'Couldn't you just tell the police where he is so that they can arrest him?'

'On what charge?' I shrugged. 'As far as the police are concerned they've already got their man cold. Anyway, even if I could persuade them to do it, König wouldn't be so easy to clip. The Americans can't go into the Russian sector and arrest him, even if they wanted to. No, Emil's best chance is that I gain König's confidence as quickly as possible. And that's why I turned down his offer.'

Traudl bit her lip with exasperation. 'But why? I don't understand.'

'I have to make sure that König believes I don't want to work for him. He was slightly suspicious of the way in which I got to meet his girlfriend. So here's what I want to do. Lotte's a croupier at the Oriental. I want you to give me some money to lose there tomorrow night. Enough to make it look like I've been cleaned out. Which would give me a reason to reconsider König's offer.'

'This counts as legitimate expenses, does it?'

'I'm afraid it does.'

'How much?'

'Three or four thousand schillings ought to do it.'

She thought for a minute and then the waiter arrived with a bottle of Riesling. When he had filled our glasses Traudl sipped some of her wine and said: 'All right then. But only on one condition: that I'm there to watch you lose it.'

From the set of her jaw I judged her to be quite determined. 'I don't suppose it would do much good to remind you that it could be dangerous. It's not as if you could accompany me. I can't afford to be seen with you in case somebody recognizes you as Emil's girl. If this weren't such a quiet place I would have insisted that we met at your house.'

'Don't worry about me,' she said firmly. 'I'll treat you like you were a sheet of glass.'

I started to speak again, but she held her hands over her small ears.

'No, I'm not listening to any more. I'm coming, and that's final. You're a spinner if you think that I'm just going to hand over 4,000 schillings without keeping an eye on what happens to it.'

'You have a point.' I stared at the limpid disc of wine in my glass for a moment, and then said, 'You love him a lot, don't you?'

Traudl swallowed hard, and nodded vigorously. After a short pause, she added, 'I'm carrying his child.'

I sighed and tried to think of something encouraging to say to her.

'Look,' I mumbled, 'don't worry. We'll get him out of this mess. There's no need to be the cockroach. Come on, come out of the dumps. Everything will work out, for you and the baby, I'm sure of it.' A pretty inadequate speech I thought and lacking any real conviction.

Traudl shook her head, and smiled. 'I'm all right, really I am. I was just thinking how the last time I was here was with Emil, when I told him that I was pregnant. We used to come here a lot. I never meant to fall in love with him, you know.'

'Nobody ever means to do it.' I noticed that my hand was on hers. 'It just happens that way. Like a car accident.' But looking at her elfin face I wasn't sure if I agreed with what I was saying. Her beauty wasn't the kind that's left smeared on your pillowcase in the morning, but the kind that would make a man proud that his child should have such a mother. I realized how much I envied Becker this woman, how much I myself would have wanted to fall in love with her if she had come my way. I let go her hand and quickly lit a cigarette to hide behind some smoke.

24

The next evening found me hurrying from its sharp edge and hint of snow, although the calendar suggested something less inclement, and into the warm, lubricious fug of the Casino Oriental, my pockets packed tight with wads of Emil Becker's easy money.

I bought quite a lot of the highest denomination chips and then wandered over to the bar to await Lotte's arrival at one of the card-tables. Having ordered a drink, all I had to do was shoo away the sparklers and the chocoladies that buzzed around, intent on keeping me and my wallet company, which left me with a keener appreciation of what it must be like to be a horse's ass in high summer. It was ten o'clock before Lotte showed up at one of the tables, by which time the flick of my tail was becoming more apathetic. I delayed another few minutes for appearance's sake before carrying my drink over to Lotte's stretch of green baize and sitting down directly opposite her.

She surveyed the pile of chips that I neatly arranged in front of me and made an equally neat purse of her lips. 'I didn't figure you for a quirk,' she said, meaning a gambler. 'I thought you had more sense.'

'Maybe your fingers will be lucky for me,' I said brightly.

'I wouldn't bet on it.'

'Yes, well, I'll certainly bear that in mind.'

I'm not much of a card-player. I couldn't even have named the game I was playing. So it was with some considerable surprise that, at the end of twenty minutes' play, I realized that I had almost doubled my original stock of chips. It seemed a perverse logic that trying to lose money at cards should be every bit as difficult as trying to win it.

Lotte dealt from the shoe and once again I won. Glancing up from the table I noticed Traudl seated opposite me, nursing a small pile of chips. I hadn't seen her come into the club, but by now the place was so busy that I would have missed Rita Hayworth.

'I guess it's my lucky night,' I remarked to no one in particular as Lotte raked my winnings towards me. Traudl merely smiled politely as if I had been a stranger to her, and prepared to make her next modest bet.

I ordered another drink and, concentrating hard, tried to make a go of being a real loser, taking a card when I should have stayed, betting when I should have folded and generally trying to sidestep luck at every available opportunity. Now and again I tried to play sensibly in order to make what I was doing appear less obvious. But after another forty minutes I had succeeded in losing all of what I had won, as well as half my original capital. When Traudl left the table, having seen me lose enough of her boyfriend's money to be satisfied that it had been used for the purpose I had stated, I finished my drink and sighed exasperatedly.

'It looks as if it's not my lucky night after all,' I said grimly.

'Luck's got nothing to do with the way you play,' Lotte murmured. 'I just hope you were more skilful in dealing with that Russian captain.'

'Oh, don't worry about him, he's taken care of. You won't have any more problems there.'

'I'm glad to hear it.'

I gambled my last chip, lost it and then stood up from the table saying that maybe I was going to be grateful for König's offer of a job after all. Smiling ruefully, I walked back to the bar where I ordered a drink and for a while watched a topless girl dancing in a parody of a Latin American step on the floor to the tinny, jerking sound of the Oriental's jazz band.

I didn't see Lotte leave the table to make a telephone call but after a while König came down the stairs into the club. He was accompanied by a small terrier, which stayed close to his heels, and a taller, more distinguished-looking man who was wearing a Schiller jacket and a club-tie. This second man disappeared through a bead curtain at the back of the club while König made a pantomime of catching my eye.

He walked over to the bar, nodding to Lotte and producing

a fresh cigar from the top pocket of his green tweed suit as he came.

'Herr Gunther,' he said, smiling, 'how nice to meet you again.'

'Hello, König,' I said. 'How are your teeth?'

'My teeth?' His smile vanished as if I had asked him how his chancre was.

'Don't you remember?' I explained. 'You were telling me about your plates.'

His face relaxed. 'So I was. They're much better, thank you.' Tipping in a smile again, he added, 'I hear you've had some bad luck at the tables.'

'Not according to Fräulein Hartmann. She told me that luck has nothing at all to do with the way I play cards.'

König finished lighting his four-schilling corona and chuckled. 'Then you must allow me to buy you a drink.' He waved the barman over, ordered a scotch for himself and whatever I was drinking. 'Did you lose much?'

'More than I could afford,' I said unhappily. 'About 4,000 schillings.' I drained my glass and pushed it across the bartop for a refill. 'Stupid, really. I shouldn't play at all. I have no real aptitude for cards. So I'm cleaned out now.' I toasted König silently and swallowed some more vodka. 'Thank God I had the good sense to pay my hotel bill well in advance. Apart from that, there's very little to feel happy about.'

'Then you must allow me to show you something,' he said, and puffed at his cigar vigorously. He blew a large smoke ring into the air above his terrier's head and said, 'Time for a smoke, Lingo,' whereupon, and much to its owner's amusement, the brute leaped up and down, sniffing excitedly at the tobacco-enriched air like the most craven nicotine addict.

'That's a neat trick,' I smiled.

'Oh, it's no trick,' said König. 'Lingo loves a good cigar almost as much as I do.' He bent down and patted the dog's head. 'Don't you, boy?' The dog barked by way of reply.

'Well, whatever you call it, it's money, not laughs I need right now. At least until I can get back to Berlin. You know it's fortunate you happened to come along. I was sitting here wondering how I might manage to broach the subject of that job with you again.'

'My dear fellow, all in good time. There's someone I want you to meet first. He is the Baron von Bolschwing and he runs a branch of the Austrian League for the United Nations here in Vienna. It's a publishing house called Österreichischer Verlag. He's an old comrade too, and I know he would be interested to meet a man like yourself.'

I knew König was referring to the SS.

'He wouldn't be associated with this research company of yours, would he?'

'Associated? Yes, associated,' he allowed. 'Accurate information is essential to a man like the Baron.'

I smiled and shook my head wryly. 'What a town this is for saying "going-away party" when what you really mean is "a requiem mass". Your "research" sounds rather like my "imports and exports", Herr König: a fancy ribbon round a rather plain cake.'

'I can't believe that a man who served with the Abwehr could be much of a stranger to these necessary euphemisms, Herr Gunther. However, if you wish me to do so, I will, as the saying goes, uncover my batteries for you. But let us first move away from the bar.' He led me to a quiet table and we sat down.

'The organization of which I am a member is fundamentally an association of German officers, the primary aim and purpose of which is the collection of research – excuse me, intelligence – as to the threat that the Red Army poses to a free Europe. Although military ranks are seldom used, nevertheless we exist under military discipline and we remain officers and gentlemen. The fight against Communism is a desperate one, and there are times when we must do things we may find unpleasant. But for many old comrades struggling to adjust to civilian life, the satisfaction of continuing to serve in the creation of a new free Germany outweighs such considerations. And there are of course generous rewards.'

It sounded as if König had said these words or their equivalent on a number of other occasions. I was beginning to think that there were more old comrades whose struggle to adjust to civilian life was remedied by the simple expedient of continuing under a form of military discipline than I could guess at. He spoke a lot more, most of which went in one ear and out of the other, and after a while he drained the remainder of his drink and said that if I were interested in his proposition then I should meet the Baron. When I told him that I was very much interested, he nodded satisfiedly and steered me towards the bead curtain. We came along a corridor and then went up two flights of stairs.

'These are the premises of the hat shop next door,' explained König. 'The owner is a member of our Org, and allows us to use them for recruiting.'

He stopped outside a door and knocked gently. Hearing a shout, he ushered me into a room which was lit only by a lamppost outside. But it was enough to make out the face of the man seated at a desk by the window. Tall, thin, clean-shaven, dark-haired and balding, I judged him to be about forty.

'Sit down, Herr Gunther,' he said and pointed at a chair on the other side of the desk.

I removed the stack of hat-boxes that lay on it while König went over to the window behind the Baron and sat on the deep sill.

'Herr König believes you might make a suitable representative for our company,' said the Baron.

'You mean an agent, don't you?' I said and lit a cigarette.

'If you like,' I saw him smile. 'But before that can happen it's up to me to learn something of your personality and circumstances. To question you in order that we might determine how best to use you.'

'Like a *Fragebogen*? Yes, I understand.'

'Let's start with your joining the SS,' said the Baron.

I told him all about my service with Kripo and the RSHA, and how I had automatically become an officer in the SS. I explained that I had gone to Minsk as a member of Arthur Nebe's Action Group, but, having no stomach for the murder of women and children, I had asked for a transfer to the front and how instead I had been sent to the Wehrmacht War Crimes Bureau. The Baron questioned me closely but politely, and he seemed the perfect Austrian gentleman. Except that there was also about him an air of false modesty, a surreptitious aspect to his gestures and a way of speaking that seemed to indicate something of which any true gentleman might have felt less than proud.

'Tell me about your service with the War Crimes Bureau.'

'This was between January 1942 and February 1944,' I explained. 'I had the rank of Oberleutnant conducting investigations into both Russian and German atrocities.'

'And where was this, exactly?'

'I was based in Berlin, in Blumeshof, across from the War Ministry. From time to time I was required to work in the field. Specifically in the Crimea and the Ukraine. Later on, in August 1943, the OKW moved its offices to Torgau because of the bombing.'

The Baron smiled a supercilious smile and shook his head. 'Forgive me,' he said, 'it's just that I had no idea that such an institution had existed within the Wehrmacht.'

'It was no different to what happened within the Prussian Army during the Great War,' I told him. 'There have to be some accepted humanitarian values, even in wartime.'

'I suppose there do,' sighed the Baron, but he did not sound convinced of this. 'All right. Then what happened?'

'With the escalation of the war it became necessary to send all the able-bodied men to the Russian front. I joined General Schorner's northern army in White Russia in February 1944, promoted Hauptmann. I was an Intelligence officer.'

'In the Abwehr?'

'Yes. I spoke a fair bit of Russian by then. Some Polish too. The work was mostly interpreting.'

'And you were finally captured where?'

'Königsberg, in East Prussia. April 1945. I was sent to the copper mines in the Urals.'

'Where exactly in the Urals, if you don't mind?'

'Outside Sverdlovsk. That's where I perfected my Russian.'

'Were you questioned by the NKVD?'

'Of course. Many times. They were very interested in anyone who had been an Intelligence officer.'

'And what did you tell them?'

'Frankly, I told them everything I knew. The war was over by that stage and so it didn't seem to matter much. Naturally I left out my previous service with the SS, and my work with the OKW. The SS were taken to a separate camp where they were either shot or persuaded to work for the Soviets in the Free Germany Committee. That seems to be how most of the German People's Police were recruited. And I dare say the Staatspolizei here in Vienna.'

'Quite so.' His tone was testy. 'Do carry on, Herr Gunther.'

'One day a group of us were told that we were to be transferred to Frankfurt an der Oder. This would be in December 1946. They said they were sending us to a rest camp there. As you can imagine we thought that was pretty funny. Well, on the transport train I overheard a couple of the guards say that we were bound for a uranium mine in Saxony. I don't suppose either of them realized I could speak Russian.'

'Can you remember the name of this place?'

'Johannesgeorgenstadt, in the Erzebirge, on the Czech border.'

'Thank you,' the Baron said crisply, 'I know where it is.'

'I jumped the train as soon as I saw a chance, not long after we crossed the German–Polish border, and then I made my way back to Berlin.'

'Were you at one of the camps for returning POWs?'

'Yes. Staaken. I wasn't there for very long, thank God. The nurses there didn't think much of us plennys. All they were interested in was American soldiers. Fortunately the Social Welfare Office of the Municipal Council found my wife at my old address almost immediately.'

'You've been very lucky, Herr Gunther,' said the Baron. 'In several respects. Wouldn't you say so, Helmut?'

'As I told you Baron, Herr Gunther is a most resourceful man,' said König, stroking his dog absently.

'Indeed he is. But tell me, Herr Gunther, did no one debrief you about your experiences in the Soviet Union?'

'Like who, for instance?'

It was König who answered. 'Members of our Organization

have interrogated a great many returning plennys,' he said. 'Our people present themselves as social workers, historical researchers, that kind of thing.'

I shook my head. 'Perhaps if I had been officially released, instead of escaping ...'

'Yes,' said the Baron. 'That must be the reason. In which case you must count yourself as doubly fortunate, Herr Gunther. Because if you had been officially released we should now almost certainly have been obliged to take the precaution of having you shot, in order to protect the security of our group. You see, what you said about the Germans who were persuaded to work for the Free Germany Committee was absolutely right. It is these traitors who were usually released first of all. Sent to a uranium mine in Erzebirge as you were, eight weeks is as long as you could have been expected to have lived. Being shot by the Russians would have been easier. So you see we can now be confident of you, knowing that the Russians were happy for you to die.'

The Baron stood up now, the interrogation evidently over. I saw that he was taller than I had supposed. König slid off his window sill and stood beside him.

I pushed myself off my chair and silently shook the Baron's outstretched hand, and then König's. Then König smiled and handed me one of his cigars. 'My friend,' he said, 'welcome to the Org.'

25

During the next couple of days König met me at the hat shop next to the Oriental on several occasions in order to school me in the many elaborate and secret working methods of the Org. But first I had to sign a solemn declaration agreeing, on my honour as a German officer, not to disclose anything of the Org's covert activities. The declaration also stipulated that any breach of secrecy would be severely punished, and König said that I would be well-advised to conceal my new employment not only from any friends and relatives but 'even' – and these were his precise words – 'even from our American colleagues'. This, and one or two other remarks he made, led me to believe that the Org was in fact fully funded by American Intelligence. So when my training – considerably shortened in view of my experience with the Abwehr – was complete I irately demanded of Belinsky that we should talk as quickly as possible.

'What's eating you, kraut?' he said when we met at a table I had reserved for us in a quiet corner at the Café Schwarzenberg.

'If I'm not in my plate, it's only because you've been showing me the wrong map.'

'Oh? And how's that?' He set to work with one of his clove-scented toothpicks.

'You know damned well. König's part of a German intelligence organization set up by your own people, Belinsky. I know because they've just finished recruiting me. So either you put me in the picture or I go to the Stiftskaserne and explain how I now believe that Linden was murdered by an American-sponsored organization of German spies.'

Belinsky looked around for a moment and then leaned purposefully across the table, his big arms framing it as if he was planning to pick it up and drop it on my head.

'I don't think that would be a very good idea,' he said quietly.

'No? Perhaps you think you can stop me. Like the way you

stopped that Russian soldier. I might just mention that as well.'

'Perhaps I will kill you, kraut,' he said. 'It shouldn't be too difficult. I have a gun with a silencer. I could probably shoot you in here and nobody would notice. That's one of the nice things about the Viennese. With someone's brains spattered in their coffee cups, they'd still try and mind their own fucking business.' He chuckled at the idea and then shook his head, talking over me when I tried to reply.

'But what are we talking about?' he said. 'There's no need for us to fall out. No need at all. You're right. Maybe I should have explained before now, but if you have been recruited by the Org then you've undoubtedly been obliged to sign a secrecy declaration. Am I right?'

I nodded.

'Maybe you don't take it very seriously, but at least you can understand when I tell you that my government required me to sign a similar declaration, and that I take it very seriously indeed. It's only now that I can take you into my complete confidence, which is ironic: I'm investigating the very same organization which your membership of now enables me to treat you as someone who no longer poses a security risk. How's that for a bit of cock-eyed logic?'

'All right,' I said. 'You've given me your excuse. Now how about telling me the whole story.'

'I mentioned Crowcass before now, right?'

'The War Crimes Commission? Yes.'

'Well, how shall I put it? The pursuit of Nazis and the employment of German intelligence personnel are not exactly separate considerations. For a long time the United States has been recruiting former members of the Abwehr to spy on the Soviets. An independent organization was set up at Pullach, headed by a senior German officer, to gather intelligence on behalf of CIC.'

'The South German Industrial Utilization Company?'

'The same. When the Org was set up they had explicit instructions about exactly who they might recruit. This is supposed to be a clean operation, you understand. But for some time now we've had the suspicion that the Org is also recruiting SS, SD and Gestapo personnel in violation of its original mandate. We wanted intelligence people, for God's sake, not war-criminals. My job is to find out the level of penetration that these outlawed classes of personnel have achieved within the Org. You with me?'

I nodded. 'But where did Captain Linden fit into this?'

'As I explained before, Linden worked in records. It's possible that his position at the US Documents Centre enabled him to act as a consultant to members of the Org with regard to recruitment. Checking out people to see if their stories matched what could be discovered from their service records, that kind of thing. I am sure I don't have to tell you that the Org is keen to avoid any possible penetration by Germans who may have already been recruited by the Soviets in their prison camps.'

'Yes,' I said, 'I've already had that explained to me in no uncertain terms.'

'Maybe Linden even advised them on who might have been worth recruiting. But that's the bit we're not sure about. That and what this stuff your friend Becker was playing courier with.'

'Maybe he lent them some files when they were interrogating potential recruits who might have been under some suspicion,' I suggested.

'No, that simply couldn't have happened. Security at the Centre is tighter than a clam's ass. You see, after the war the army was scared your people might try to take the contents of the centre back. That or destroy them. You just don't walk out of that place with an armful of files. All documentary examinations are on-site and must be accounted for.'

'Then perhaps Linden altered some of the files.'

Belinsky shook his head. 'No, we've already thought of that and checked back from the original log to every single one of the files which Linden had sight of. There's no sign of anything having been removed or destroyed. It seems our best chance of finding out what the hell he was up to depends on your membership of the Org, kraut. Not to mention your best chance of finding something that will put your friend Becker in the clear.'

'I'm almost out of time with that. He goes to trial at the beginning of next week.'

Belinsky looked thoughtful. 'Maybe I could help you to cut a few corners with your new colleagues. If I were to provide you with some high-grade Soviet intelligence it could put you well in with the Org. Of course it would have to be stuff that my people had seen already, but the boys in the Org wouldn't know that. If I dressed it up with the right kind of provenance, that would make you look like a pretty good spy. How does that sound?'

'Good. While you're in such an inspired mood you can help me out of another fix. After König had got through instructing me in the use of the dead-letter box, he gave me my first assignment.'

'He did? Good. What was it?'

'They want me to kill Becker's girlfriend, Traudl.'

'That pretty little nurse?' He sounded quite outraged. 'The one at the General Hospital? Did they say why?'

'She came into the Casino Oriental to oversee me losing her boyfriend's money. I warned her about it, but she wouldn't listen. I guess it must have made them nervous or something.'

But this wasn't the reason that König had given me.

'A bit of wet-work is often used as an early test of loyalty,' Belinsky explained. 'Did they say how to do it?'

'I'm to make it look like an accident,' I said. 'So naturally I'll need to get her out of Vienna as quickly as possible. And that's where you come in. Can you organize a travel warrant and a rail ticket for her?'

'Sure,' he said, 'but try and persuade her to leave as much behind as possible. We'll drive her across the zone and get her on a train at Salzburg. That way we can make it look as if she's disappeared, maybe dead. Which would help you, right?'

'Let's just make sure that she gets safely out of Vienna,' I told him. 'If anyone has to take risks I'd rather it was me than her.'

'Leave it to me, kraut. It'll take a few hours to arrange, but the little lady is as good as out of here. I suggest that you go back to your hotel and wait for me to bring her papers. Then we'll go and pick her up. In which case, perhaps it would be better if you didn't speak to her before then. She might not want to leave your friend Becker to face the music on his own. It would be better if we could just pick her up and drive out of here. That way if she decides to protest about it there won't be much that she can do.'

After Belinsky had left to make the necessary arrangements, I wondered if he would have been so willing to help get Traudl safely out of Vienna if he had seen the photograph which König had given to me. He had told me that Traudl Braunsteiner was an MVD agent. Knowing the girl as I did it seemed utterly absurd. But for anyone else – most of all a member of CIC – looking at the photograph that had been taken in a Vienna restaurant, in which Traudl was evidently enjoying the company of a Russian colonel of MVD, whose name was Poroshin, things might have seemed rather less than clear-cut.

26

There was a letter from my wife waiting for me when I returned to the Pension Caspian. Recognizing the tight, almost child-like writing on the cheap manilla envelope, crushed and grimy from a couple of weeks at the mercy of a haphazard postal service, I balanced it on the mantelpiece in my sitting-room and stared at it for a while, recollecting the letter to her that I had positioned similarly on our own mantelpiece at home in Berlin, and regretting its peremptory tone.

Since then I had sent her only two telegrams: one to say that I had arrived safely in Vienna and giving my address; and the other telling her that the case might take a little longer than I had first anticipated.

I dare say a graphologist could easily have analysed Kirsten's hand and made a pretty good job of convincing me that it indicated the letter inside had been written by an adulterous woman who was in the frame of mind to tell her inattentive husband that despite his having left her $2,000 in gold she nevertheless intended divorcing him and using the money to emigrate to the United States with her handsome American *schätzi*.

I was still looking at the unopened envelope with some trepidation when the telephone rang. It was Shields.

'And how are we doing today?' he asked in his over-precise German.

'I am doing very well, thank you,' I said, mocking his way of speaking, but he didn't seem to notice. 'Exactly how may I be of service to you, Herr Shields?'

'Well, with your friend Becker about to go to trial, frankly I wondered what kind of detective you were. I was asking myself whether you had come up with anything pertinent to the case: if your client was going to get his $5,000 worth?'

He paused, waiting for me to reply, and when I said nothing he continued, rather more impatiently.

'So? What's the answer? Have you found the vital piece of evidence that will save Becker from the hangman's noose? Or does he take the drop?'

'I've found Becker's witness, if that's what you mean, Shields. Only I haven't got anything that connects him with Linden. Not yet anyway.'

'Well, you had better work fast, Gunther. When trials commence in this city they're apt to be a mite quick. I'd hate to see you get round to proving a dead man innocent. That looks bad all round, I'm sure you would agree. Bad for you, bad for us, but worst of all for the man on the rope.'

'Suppose I could set this other fellow up for you to arrest him as a material witness.' It was an almost desperate suggestion, but I thought it worth a try.

'There's no other way he'd show up in court?'

'No. At least it would give Becker someone to point the finger at.'

'You're asking me to make a dirty mark on a shiny floor.' Shields sighed. 'I hate not to give the other side a chance, you know. So I tell you what I'm going to do. I'll have a word with my Executive Officer, Major Wimberley, and see what he recommends. But I can't promise anything. Chances are, the major will tell me to go balls out and get a conviction, and to hell with your man's witness. There's a lot of pressure on us to get a quick result here, you know. The Brig doesn't like it when American officers are murdered in his city. That's Brigadier-General Alexander O. Gorder, commanding the 796th. One tough son-of-a-bitch. I'll be in touch.'

'Thanks, Shields. I appreciate it.'

'Don't thank me yet, mister,' he said.

I replaced the receiver and picked up my letter. After I'd fanned myself with it, and used it to clean my fingernails, I tore it open.

Kirsten was never much of a letter-writer. She was more one for a postcard, only a postcard from Berlin was no longer likely to inspire much in the way of wishful thinking. A view of the ruined Kaiser-Wilhelm church? Or one of the bombed-out Opera House? The execution shed at Plotzensee? I thought that it would be a good long while before there were any postcards sent from Berlin. I unfolded the paper and started to read:

Dear Bernie,

I hope this letter reaches you, but things are so difficult here that it may not, in which case I may also try to send you a telegram, if only to tell you that everything is all right. Sokolovsky has demanded that the Soviet military police should control all traffic from Berlin to the West, and this may mean that the mail does not get through.

The real fear here is that this will all turn into a full-scale siege of the city in an effort to push the Americans, the British and the French out of Berlin – although I don't suppose anyone would mind if we saw the back of the French. Nobody objects to the Amis and the Tommies bossing us around – at least they fought and beat us. But Franz? They are such hypocrites. The fiction of a victorious French army is almost too much for a German to bear.

People say that the Amis and the Tommies won't stand by and see Berlin fall to the Ivans. I'm not so sure about the British. They've got their hands full in Palestine right now (all books on Zionist Nationalism have been removed from Berlin bookshops and libraries, which seems only too familiar). But just when you think that the British have more important things to do, one hears that they've been destroying more German shipping. The sea is full of fish for us to eat, and they're blowing up boats! Do they want to save us from the Russians in order that they can starve us?

One still hears rumours of cannibalism. There's a story going around Berlin that the police were called to a house in Kreuzberg where downstairs neighbours had heard the sounds of a terrible commotion, and found blood seeping through their ceiling. They burst in and found an old couple dining off the raw flesh of a pony that they had dragged off the street and killed with rocks. It may or may not be true, but I have the terrible feeling that it is. What is certain is that morale has sunk to new depths. The skies are full of transport planes and troops of all four Powers are increasingly jumpy.

You remember Frau Fersen's son, Karl? He came back from a

Russian POW camp last week, but in very poor health. Apparently the doctor says that his lungs are finished, poor boy. She was telling me what he'd said about his time in Russia. It sounds awful! Why ever didn't you talk to me about it, Bernie? Perhaps I would have been more understanding. Perhaps I could have helped. I am conscious that I haven't been much of a wife to you since the war. And now that you are no longer here, this seems harder to bear. So when you come back I thought that maybe we could use some of the money you left – so much money! did you rob a bank? – to go on holiday somewhere. To leave Berlin for a while, and spend time together.

Meanwhile, I have used some of the money to repair the ceiling. Yes, I know you had planned on doing it yourself, but I know how you kept putting it off. Anyway, it's done now, and it looks very nice.

Come home and see it soon. I miss you.

> Your loving wife,
> Kirsten.

So much for my imaginary graphologist, I reflected happily, and poured myself the last of Traudl's vodka. This had the immediate effect of melting my nervousness of telephoning Liebl to report on my almost imperceptible progress. To hell with Belinsky, I said to myself, and resolved to solicit Liebl's opinion as to whether Becker would or would not be best served by trying to obtain König's immediate arrest in order that he be forced to give evidence.

When Liebl finally came on the line he sounded like a man who had just come to the telephone after falling down a flight of stairs. His normally forthright and irascible manner was cowed and his voice was balanced precariously at the very edge of breakdown.

'Herr Gunther,' he said, and swallowed his way to a more decorous silence. Then I heard him take a deep breath as he took control of himself again. 'There's been the most terrible accident. Fräulein Braunsteiner has been killed.'

'Killed?' I repeated dumbly. 'How?'

'She was run over by a car,' Liebl said quietly.

'Where?'

'It happened virtually on the doorstep of the hospital where she worked. Apparently it was instantaneous. There was nothing they could do for her.'

'When was this?'

'Just a couple of hours ago, when she was coming off duty. Unfortunately the driver did not stop.'

That part I could have guessed for myself.

'He was scared probably. Possibly he had been drinking. Who knows? Austrians are such bad drivers.'

'Did anyone see the – the accident?' The words sounded almost angry in my mouth.

'There are no witnesses so far. But someone seems to recollect having seen a black Mercedes driving rather too fast much farther along Alser Strasse.'

'Christ,' I said weakly, 'that's just around the corner. To think I might even have heard the squeal of those car-tyres.'

'Yes, indeed, quite so,' Liebl murmured. 'But there was no pain. It was so quick that she could not have suffered. The car struck her in the middle of her back. The doctor I spoke to said that her spine was completely shattered. Probably she was dead before she hit the ground.'

'Where is she now?'

'In the morgue at the General Hospital,' Liebl sighed. I heard him light a cigarette and take a long drag of smoke. 'Herr Gunther,' he said, 'we shall of course have to inform Herr Becker. Since you know him so much better than I – '

'Oh no,' I said quickly, 'I get enough rotten jobs without contracting to do that one as well. Take her insurance policy and her will along if it makes it any easier for you.'

'I can assure you that I'm every bit as upset about this as you are, Herr Gunther. There's no need to be – '

'Yes, you're right. I'm sorry. Look, I hate to sound callous, but let's see if we can't use this to get an adjournment.'

'I don't know if this quite qualifies as compassionate,' Liebl hummed. 'It's not as if they were married or anything.'

'She was going to have his baby, for Christ's sake.'

There was a brief, shocked silence. Then Liebl spluttered, 'I had no idea. Yes, you're right, of course. I'll see what I can do.'

'Do that.'

'But however am I going to tell Herr Becker?'

'Tell him she was murdered,' I said. He started to say something, but I was not in a mood to be contradicted. 'It was no accident, believe me. Tell Becker it was his old comrades who did it. Tell him that precisely. He'll understand. See if it doesn't jog his memory a little. Perhaps now he'll remember something he should have told me earlier. Tell him that if this doesn't make him give us everything he knows then he deserves a crushed windpipe.' There was a knock at the door. Belinsky with Traudl's travel papers. 'Tell him that,' I snapped and banged the receiver back onto its cradle. Then I crossed the floor of the room and hauled the door open.

Belinsky held Traudl's redundant travel papers in front of him and gave them a jaunty wave as he came into the room, too pleased with himself to notice my mood.

'It took a bit of doing, getting a pink as quickly as this,' he said, 'but old Belinsky managed it. Just don't ask me how.'

'She's dead,' I said flatly, and watched his big face fall.

'Shit,' he said, 'that's too bad. What the hell happened?'

'A hit-and-run driver.' I lit a cigarette and slumped into the armchair. 'Killed her outright. I've just had Becker's lawyer on the phone telling me. It happened not far from here, a couple of hours ago.'

Belinsky nodded and sat down on the sofa opposite me. Although I avoided his eye I still felt it trying to look into my soul. He shook his head for a while and then produced his pipe which he set about filling with tobacco. When he had finished he started to light the thing and in between fire-sustaining sucks of air, he said, 'Forgive me – for asking – but you didn't – change your mind – did you?'

'About what?' I growled belligerently.

He removed the pipe from his mouth and glanced into the bowl before replacing it between his big irregular teeth. 'I mean, about killing her yourself.'

Finding the answer on my rapidly colouring face he shook his head quickly. 'No, of course not. What a stupid question. I'm sorry.' He shrugged. 'All the same, I had to ask. You must agree, it's a bit of a coincidence, isn't it? The Org asks you to arrange an accident for her, and then almost immediately she gets herself knocked down and killed.'

'Maybe you did it,' I heard myself say.

'Maybe.' Belinsky sat forward on the sofa. 'Let's see now: I waste all afternoon getting this unfortunate little fräulein a pink and a ticket out of Austria. Then I knock her down and kill her in cold blood on my way here to see you. Is that it?'

'What kind of car do you drive?'

'A Mercedes.'

'What colour?'

'Black.'

'Someone saw a black Mercedes speeding further up the street from the scene of the accident.'

'I dare say. I've yet to see the car which drives slowly in Vienna. And in case you hadn't noticed, just about every other non-military vehicle in this city is a black Mercedes.'

'All the same,' I persisted, 'maybe we should take a look at the front fenders, and check for dents.'

He spread his hands innocently, as if he had been about to give the sermon on the mount. 'Be my guest. Only you'll find dents all over the car. There seems to be a law against careful driving here.' He sucked some more of his pipe smoke. 'Look, Bernie, if you don't mind me saying so I think we're in danger of throwing the handle after the axe-head here. It's a real shame that Traudl's dead, but there's no sense in you and me falling out over it. Who knows? Maybe it was an accident. You know it's true what I said about Viennese drivers. They're worse than the Soviets, and they take some beating. Jesus, it's like a chariot-race on these roads. Now I agree that it's a hell of a coincidence, but it's not an impossible one, by any stretch of the imagination. You must admit that, surely.'

I nodded slowly. 'All right. I admit it's not impossible.'

'On the other hand maybe the Org briefed more than one agent to kill her so that if you missed, somebody else was bound to get her. It's not unusual for assassinations to be handled that way. Certainly not in my own experience, anyway.' He paused, and then pointed his pipe at me. 'You know what I think? I

185

think that the next time you see König, you should simply keep quiet about it. If he mentions it then you can assume that it probably was an accident and feel confident of taking the credit for it.' He searched in his jacket pocket and drew out a buff-coloured envelope which he threw into my lap. 'It makes this a little less necessary, but that can't be helped.'

'What's this?'

'From an MVD station near Sopron, close to the Hungarian border. It's the details of MVD personnel and methods throughout Hungary and Lower Austria.'

'And how am I supposed to account for this little lot?'

'I rather thought that you could handle the man who gave it to us. Frankly it's just the sort of material that they're keen on. The man's name is Yuri. That's all you need to know. There are map references and the location of the dead-letter box he's been using. There's a railway bridge near a little town called Mattersburg. On the bridge is a footpath and about two-thirds of the way along the handrail is broken. The top part is hollow cast metal. All you have to do is collect your information from there once a month, and leave some money and instructions.'

'How do I account for my relationship with him?'

'Until quite recently Yuri was stationed in Vienna. You used to buy identity papers for him. But now he's getting more ambitious, and you haven't the money to buy what he's got to offer. So you can offer him to the Org. CIC has already assessed his worth. We've had all we're going to get out of him, at least in the short term. There's no harm done if he gives all the same stuff to the Org.' Belinsky re-lit his pipe and puffed vigorously while he awaited my reaction.

'Really,' he said, 'there's nothing to it. An operation of this sort is hardly deserving of the word "intelligence". Believe me, very few of them are. But all in all a source like this and an apparently successful bit of murder leaves you pretty well accredited, old man.'

'You'll forgive my lack of enthusiasm,' I said drily, 'only I'm beginning to lose sight of what I'm doing here.'

Belinsky nodded vaguely. 'I thought you wanted to clear your old pitman.'

'Maybe you haven't been listening. Becker was never my friend. But I really think he is innocent of Linden's murder. And so did Traudl. So long as she was alive this case really felt as if it was worthwhile, there seemed to be some point in trying to prove Becker innocent. Now I'm not so sure.'

'Come on, Gunther,' Belinsky said. 'Becker's life without his girl is still better than no life at all. Do you honestly think that Traudl would have wanted you to give up?'

'Maybe, if she knew the kind of crap he was into. The kind of people he was dealing with.'

'You know that's not true. Becker was no altar-boy, that's for sure. But from what you've told me about her I'd bet she knew that. There's not much innocence left anymore. Not in Vienna.'

I sighed and rubbed my neck wearily. 'Maybe you're right,' I conceded. 'Maybe it's just me. I'm used to having things being a little more well-defined than this. A client came along, paid my fee and I'd point my suit in whatever direction seemed appropriate. Sometimes I even got to solve a case. That's a pretty good feeling, you know. But right now it's like there are too many people near me, telling me how to work. As if I've lost my independence. I've stopped feeling like a private investigator.'

Belinsky rocked his head on his shoulders like a man who has sold out of something. Explanations probably. He made a stab at one all the same. 'Come on, surely you must have worked undercover before now.'

'Sure,' I said. 'Only it was with a sharper sense of purpose. At least I got to see a criminal's picture. I knew what was right. But this isn't clear-cut anymore, and it's beginning to peel my reed.'

'Nothing stays the same, kraut. The war changed everything for everyone, private investigators included. But if you want to see criminals' photographs I can show you a hundred. Thousands probably. War-criminals, all of them.'

'Photographs of krauts? Listen, Belinsky, you're an American and you're a Jew. It's a lot easier for you to see the right here. Me? I'm a German. For one brief, dirty moment I was even in the SS. If I met one of your war-criminals he'd probably shake me by the hand and call me an old comrade.'

He had no answer for that.

I found another cigarette and smoked it in silence. When it was finished I shook my head ruefully. 'Maybe it's just Vienna. Maybe it's being away from home for so long. My wife wrote to me. We weren't getting along too well when I left Berlin. Frankly I couldn't wait to leave, and so I took this case against my better judgement. Anyway she says that she hopes we can start again. And do you know, I can't wait to get back to her and give it a try. Maybe – ' I shook my head. 'Maybe I need a drink.'

Belinsky grinned enthusiastically. 'Now you're talking, kraut,' he said. 'One thing I've learned in this job: if in doubt, pickle it in alcohol.'

27

It was late when we drove back from the Melodies Bar, a nightclub in the 1st Bezirk. Belinsky drew up outside my pension and as I got out of the car a woman stepped quickly out of the shadow of a nearby doorway. It was Veronika Zartl. I smiled thinly at her, having drunk rather too much to care for any company.

'Thank God you've come,' she said. 'I've waited hours.' Then she flinched as through the open car door we both heard Belinsky utter an obscene remark.

'What's the matter?' I asked her.

'I need your help. There's a man in my room.'

'So what's new?' said Belinsky.

Veronika bit her lip. 'He's dead, Bernie. You've got to help me.'

'I'm not sure what I can do,' I said uncertainly, wishing that we'd stayed longer in the Melodies. I said to myself: 'A girl ought not to trust anyone these days.' To her I said: 'You know, it's really a job for the police.'

'I can't tell the police,' she groaned impatiently. 'That would mean the vice squad, the Austrian criminal police, public health officials and an inquest. I'd probably lose my room, everything. Don't you see?'

'All right, all right. What happened?'

'I think he had a heart attack.' Her head dropped. 'I'm sorry to bother you, only there is no one else I can turn to.'

I cursed myself again and then stuck my head back into Belinsky's car. 'The lady needs our help,' I grunted, without much enthusiasm.

'That's not all she needs.' But he started the engine and added: 'Come on, hop in, the pair of you.'

He drove to Rotenturmstrasse and parked outside the bomb-damaged building where Veronika had her room. When we got out of the car I pointed across the darkened cobbles of Stephansplatz to the partly restored cathedral.

'See if you can't find a tarpaulin over on the building site,' I told Belinsky. 'I'll go up and take a look. If there's something suitable, bring it up to the second floor.'

He was too drunk to argue. Instead he nodded dully and walked back towards the Cathedral scaffolding, while I turned and followed Veronika up the stairs to her room.

A large, lobster-coloured man of about fifty lay dead in her big oak bed. Vomiting is quite common in cases of congestive heart failure. It covered his nose and mouth like a bad facial burn. I pressed my fingers against the man's clammy neck.

'How long has he been here?'

'Three or four hours.'

'It's lucky you kept him covered up,' I told her. 'Close that window.' I stripped the bedclothes from the dead man's body and started to raise the upper part of his torso. 'Give me a hand here,' I ordered.

'What are you doing?' She helped me to bend the torso over the legs as if I had been trying to shut an overstuffed suitcase.

'I'm keeping this bastard in shape,' I said. 'A bit of chiro-practic ought to slow up the stiffening and make it easier for us to get him in and out of the car.' I pressed down hard on the back of his neck, and then, blowing hard from my exertions, pushed the man back against the puke-strewn pillows. 'Uncle here's been getting extra food-stamps,' I breathed. 'He must weigh more than a hundred kilos. It's lucky we've got Belinsky along to help.'

'Is Belinsky a policeman?' she asked.

'Sort of,' I said, 'but don't worry, he's not the kind of bull who cares much for the crime figures. Belinsky's got other fish to fry. He hunts Nazi war-criminals.' I started to bend the dead man's arms and legs.

'What are you going to do with him?' she said nauseously.

'Drop him on the railway line. With him being naked it will look like the Ivans gave him a little party and then threw him off a train. With any luck the express will go over him and fit him with a good disguise.'

190

'Please don't,' she said weakly. '... He was very kind to me.'

When I'd finished with the body I stood up and straightened my tie. 'This is hard work on a vodka supper. Now where the hell is Belinsky?' Spotting the man's clothes which were laid neatly over the back of a dining-chair by the grimy net curtains, I said: 'Have you been through his pockets yet?'

'No, of course not.'

'You *are* new at this game, aren't you?'

'You don't understand at all. He was a good friend of mine.'

'Evidently,' Belinsky said coming through the door. He held up a length of white material. 'I'm afraid that this was all I could find.'

'What is it?'

'An altar-cloth, I think. I found it in a cupboard inside the cathedral. It didn't look like it was being used.'

I told Veronika to help Belinsky wrap her friend in the cloth while I searched his pockets.

'He's good at that,' Belinsky told her. 'He went through my pockets once while I was still breathing. Tell me, honey, were you and fat boy actually doing it when he was scythed out?'

'Leave her alone, Belinsky.'

'Blessed are the dead which die in the Lord from henceforth,' he chuckled. 'But me? I just hope I die in a good woman.'

I opened the man's wallet and thumbed a fold of dollar bills and schillings on to the dressing-table.

'What are you looking for?' asked Veronika.

'If I'm going to dispose of a man's body I like to know at least a little more about him than just the colour of his underwear.'

'His name was Karl Heim,' she said quietly.

I found a business card. 'Dr Karl Heim,' I said. 'A dentist, eh? Is he the one who got you the penicillin?'

'Yes.'

'A man who liked to take precautions, eh?' Belinsky murmured. 'From the look of this room, I can understand why.' He nodded at the money on the dressing-table. 'You had better keep that money, sweetheart. Get yourself a new decorator.'

There was another business card in Heim's wallet. 'Belinsky,'

191

I said. 'Have you ever heard of a Major Jesse P. Breen? From something called the DP Screening Project?'

'Sure I have,' he said, coming over and taking the card out of my fingers. 'The DPSP is a special section of the 430th. Breen is the CIC's local liaison officer for the Org. If any of the Org's men get into trouble with the US military police, Breen is supposed to try and help them sort it out. That is unless it's anything really serious, like a murder. And I wouldn't put it past him to fix that as well, providing the victim was anyone but an American or an Englishman. It looks as if our fat friend might have been one of your old comrades, Bernie.'

While Belinsky talked I quickly searched Heim's trouser pockets and found a set of keys.

'In that case it might be an idea if you and I were to take a look around the good doctor's surgery,' I said. 'I've got a feeling in my socks that we might just find something interesting there.'

We dumped Heim's naked body on a quiet stretch of railway track near the Ostbahnhof in the Russian sector of the city. I was keen to leave the scene as quickly as possible, but Belinsky insisted on sitting in the car and waiting to see the train finish the job. After about fifteen minutes a goods train bound for Budapest and the Orient came rumbling by, and Heim's corpse was lost under its many hundreds of pairs of wheels.

'For all flesh is grass,' Belinsky intoned, 'and all the goodliness thereof is as the flower of the field: The grass withereth, and the flower fadeth.'

'Cut that out, will you?' I said. 'It makes me nervous.'

'But the souls of the righteous are in the hand of God and there shall no torment touch them. Anything you say, kraut.'

'Come on,' I said. 'Let's get away from here.'

We drove north to Währing in the 18th Bezirk, and an elegant three-storey house on Türkenschanzplatz, close to a decent-sized park which was bisected by a small railway line.

'We could have dropped our passenger out here,' said Belinsky, 'on his own doorstep. And saved ourselves a trip into the Russian sector.'

'This is the American sector,' I reminded him. 'The only way to get thrown off a train round here is to travel without a ticket. They even wait until the train stops moving.'

'That's Uncle Sam for you, hey? No, you're right, Bernie. He's better off with the Ivans. It wouldn't be the first time they threw one of our people off a train. But I'd sure hate to be one of their trackmen. Damned dangerous, I'd say.'

We left the car and walked towards the house.

There was no sign that anyone was at home. Above the broad, toothy grin of a short wooden fence the darkened windows on the white stuccoed house stared back like the empty sockets in a great skull. A tarnished brass plate on the gatepost which, with typical Viennese exaggeration, bore the name of Dr Karl Heim, Consultant Orthodontic Surgeon, not to mention most of the letters of the alphabet, indicated two separate entrances: one to Heim's residence, and the other to his surgery.

'You look in the house,' I said, opening the front door with the keys. 'I'll go round the side and check the surgery.'

'Anything you say.' Belinsky produced a flashlight from his overcoat pocket. Seeing my eyes fasten on the torch, he added: 'What's the matter? You scared of the dark or something?' He laughed. 'Here, you take it. I can see in the dark. In my line of work you have to.'

I shrugged and relieved him of the light. Then he reached inside his jacket and took out his gun.

'Besides,' he said, screwing on the silencer. 'I like to keep one hand free for turning door handles.'

'Just watch who you shoot,' I said and walked away.

Round the side of the house I let myself in through the surgery door and, after closing it quietly behind me again. switched on the torch. I kept the light on the linoleum floor and away from the windows in case a nosy neighbour happened to be keeping an eye on the place.

I found myself in a small reception and waiting area which was home to a number of potted plants and a tankful of terrapins: it made a change from goldfish, I told myself, and mindful of the fact that their owner was now dead, I sprinkled some of the foul-smelling food that they ate on to the surface of their water.

That was my second good deed of the day. Charity was beginning to be a bit of a habit with me.

Behind the reception desk I opened the appointment-book and pointed the torch beam on to its pages. It didn't look like Heim had much of a practice to leave to his competition, always assuming he had any. There wasn't a lot of spare money around for curing toothache these days, and I didn't doubt that Heim would have made a better living selling drugs on the black market. Turning back the pages I could see that he averaged no more than two or three appointments a week. Several months back in the book I came across two names I knew: Max Abs and Helmut König. Both of them were marked down for full extractions within a few days of each other. There were lots of other names listed for full extractions, but none that I recognized.

I went over to the filing cabinets and found them mostly empty, with the exception of one that contained details only of patients prior to 1940. The cabinet didn't look as if it had been opened since then, which struck me as odd as dentists tend to be quite meticulous about such things; and indeed, the Heim of pre-1940 had been conscientious with his patients' records, detailing residual teeth, fillings and denture-fitting marks for each one of them. Had he just got sloppy, I wondered, or had an inadequate volume of business ceased to make such careful records worthwhile? And why so many full extractions of late? It was true, the war had left a great many men, myself included, with poor teeth. In my case this was one legacy of a year's starvation as a Soviet prisoner. But nevertheless I had still managed to keep a full set. And there were plenty of others like me. What need for König then, who I remembered telling me that he had had such good teeth, to have had all of his teeth extracted? Or did he simply mean that his teeth had been good before they went bad? While none of this was enough for Conan Doyle to have turned into a short story, it certainly left me puzzled.

The surgery itself was much like any other I had ever been in. A little dirtier perhaps, but then nothing was as clean as it had been before the war. Beside the black-leather chair stood a large cylinder of anaesthetic gas. I turned the tap at the neck of the bottle and, hearing a hissing sound, switched it off again. Everything looked like it was in proper working order.

Beyond a locked door was a small store-room, and it was there that Belinsky found me.

'Find anything?' he said.

I told him about the lack of records.

'You're right,' Belinsky said with what sounded like a smile, 'that doesn't sound at all German.'

I flashed the torch over the shelves in the store-room.

'Hello,' he said, 'what have we got here?' He reached out to touch a steel drum on the side of which was painted in yellow the chemical formula $H_2 SO_4$.

'I wouldn't, if I were you,' I said. 'That stuff's not from a schoolboy's chemistry set. Unless I'm very much mistaken, it's sulphuric acid.' I moved the torch beam up the side of the drum to where the words EXTREME CAUTION were also painted. 'Enough to turn you into a couple of litres of animal fat.'

'Kosher, I hope,' Belinsky said. 'What does a dentist want with a drum-load of sulphuric acid?'

'For all I know he soaks his false teeth in it overnight.'

On a shelf beside the drum, piled one on top of the other, were several kidney-shaped steel trays. I picked one of them up and brought it under the beam of the torch. The two of us stared at what looked like a handful of odd-shaped peppermints, all stuck together as if they had been half-sucked and then saved by some disgusting small boy. But there was also dried blood on some of them.

Belinsky's nose wrinkled with disgust. 'What the hell are these?'

'Teeth.' I handed him the torch and picked one of the spiky white objects out of the tray to hold it up to the light. 'Extracted teeth. And several mouthfuls of them too.'

'I hate dentists,' Belinsky hissed. He fumbled in his waistcoat and found one of his picks to chew.

'I'd say these normally end up in the drum of acid.'

'So?' But Belinsky had noticed my interest.

'What kind of dentist does nothing but full extractions?' I

asked. 'The appointment-book is booked for nothing but full extractions.' I turned the tooth in my fingers. 'Would you say that there was much wrong with this molar? It hasn't even been filled.'

'It looks like a perfectly healthy tooth,' agreed Belinsky.

I stirred the sticky mass in the tray with my forefinger. 'Same as the rest of them,' I observed. 'I'm no dentist, but I don't see the point of pulling teeth that haven't even been filled yet.'

'Maybe Heim was on some kind of piece work. Maybe the guy just liked to pull teeth.'

'Better than he liked keeping records. There are no records for any of his recent patients.'

Belinsky picked up another kidney-tray and inspected its contents. 'Another full set,' he reported. But something rolled in the next tray. It looked like several tiny ball bearings. 'Well, what have we here?' He picked one up and regarded it with fascination. 'Unless I'm very much mistaken, I should say each one of these little confections contains a dose of potassium cyanide.'

'Lethal pills?'

'That's right. They were very popular with some of your old comrades, kraut. Especially the SS and senior state and party officials who might have had the guts to prefer suicide to being captured by the Ivans. I believe that these were originally developed for German secret agents, but Arthur Nebe and the SS decided that the top brass had a greater need of them. A man would have his dentist make him a false tooth, or use an existing cavity, and then put this little baby inside. Nice and snug – you'd be surprised. When he was captured he might even have a decoy cyanide brass cartridge in his pocket, which meant our people wouldn't bother with a dental examination. And then, when the man had decided the right time had come, he would work off the false tooth, tongue out this capsule and chew the thing until it broke. Death is almost instantaneous. That's how Himmler killed himself.'

'Goering too, I heard.'

'No,' said Belinsky, 'he used one of the decoys. An American officer smuggled it back to him while he was in gaol. How about that, eh? One of our own people going soft on the fat bastard like that.' He dropped the capsule back into the tray and handed it to me.

I poured a few into my hand to get a closer look. It seemed almost astonishing that things which were so small could also be so deadly. Four tiny seed pearls for the deaths of four men. I did not think I could have carried one in my mouth, false tooth or not, and still enjoyed my dinner.

'You know what I think, kraut? I think we've got ourselves a lot of toothless Nazis running round Vienna.' I followed him back into the surgery. 'I take it that you're familiar with dental techniques for the identification of the dead.'

'As familiar as the next bull,' I said.

'It was damned useful after the war,' he said. 'The best way we had of establishing the identity of a corpse. Naturally enough there were many Nazis who were keen for us to believe that they were dead. And they went to a great deal of trouble to try and persuade us of it. Half-charred bodies carrying false papers, you know the sort of thing. Well of course the first thing we did was have a dentist take a look at a corpse's teeth. Even if you don't have a man's dental records you can at least determine his age from his teeth: periodontosis, root resorption, etc. – you can say for sure that a corpse isn't who it is supposed to be.'

Belinsky paused and looked about the surgery. 'You finished looking around in here?'

I told him I was and asked if he had found anything in the house. He shook his head and said he hadn't. Then I said that we had better get the hell out of there.

He resumed his explanation as we climbed into the car.

'Take the case of Heinrich Müller, chief of the Gestapo. He was last seen alive in Hitler's bunker in April 1945. Müller was supposed to have been killed in the battle for Berlin in May 1945. But when after the war his body was exhumed, a dental expert specializing in jawbone surgery at a Berlin hospital in the British sector couldn't identify the teeth in the corpse as those belonging to a forty-four-year-old male. He thought that the corpse was more probably that of a man of no more than twenty-five.' Belinsky turned the ignition, gunned the engine for a second or two, and then slipped the car into gear.

Crouched over the steering-wheel, he drove badly for an American, double-declutching, missing his gears and generally over-steering. It was clear to me that driving required all of his attention, but he continued with his calm explanation, even after we had almost killed a passing motorcyclist.

'When we catch up with some of these bastards, they've got false papers, new hairstyles, moustaches, beards, glasses, you name it. But teeth are as good as a tattoo, or sometimes a fingerprint. So if any of them have had all their teeth pulled it removes yet another possible means of identification. After all, a man who can explode a cartridge under his arm to remove an SS number probably wouldn't baulk at wearing false teeth, would he?'

I thought of the burn scar under my own arm and reflected that he was probably right. To disguise myself from the Russians I would certainly have resorted to having my teeth out, assuming that I would have the same opportunity for painless extraction as Max Abs and Helmut König.

'No, I guess not.'

'You can bet your life on it. Which is why I stole Heim's appointment-book.' He patted the breast of his coat where I assumed he was now keeping it. 'It might be interesting to find out who these men with bad teeth really are. Your friend König, for instance. And Max Abs too. I mean, why would a little SS chauffeur feel the need to disguise what he had in his mouth? Unless he wasn't an SS corporal at all.' Belinsky chuckled enthusiastically at the thought of it. 'That's why I have to be able to see in the dark. Some of your old comrades really know how to mix the maps. You know, I wouldn't be at all surprised if we're still chasing some of these Nazi bastards when their kids are having to sugar their strawberries for them.'

'All the same,' I said, 'the longer it is before you catch them, the harder it will be to get a positive identification.'

'Don't you worry,' he snarled vindictively. 'There won't be a shortage of witnesses willing to come forward and testify against these shits. Or perhaps you think people like Müller and Globocnik should be allowed to get away with it?'

'Who's Globocnik, when he's having a party?'

'Odilo Globocnik. He headed up Operation Reinhard, establishing most of the big death camps in Poland. Another one who is supposed to have committed suicide in '45. So come on, what do you think? There's a trial going on in Nuremberg right now. Otto Ohlendorf, commander of one of those SS special action groups. Do you think he should hang for his war crimes?'

'War crimes?' I repeated wearily. 'Listen, Belinsky, I worked in the Wehrmacht's War Crimes Bureau for three years. So don't think you can lecture me about fucking war crimes.'

'I'm just interested to know where you stand, kraut. Exactly what kind of war crimes did you Jerries investigate anyway?'

'Atrocities, by both sides. You've heard of Katyn Forest?'

'Of course. You investigated that?'

'I was part of the team.'

'How about that?' He seemed genuinely surprised. Most people were.

'Frankly, I think that the idea of charging fighting men with war crimes is absurd. The murderers of women and children should be punished, yes. But it wasn't just Jews and Poles who were killed by people like Müller and Globocnik. They murdered Germans, too. Perhaps if you'd given us half a chance we could have brought them to justice ourselves.'

Belinsky turned off Währinger Strasse and drove south, past the long edifice of the General Hospital and on to Alser Strasse where, encountering the same recollection as myself, he slowed the car to a more respectful pace. I could tell he had been about to answer my point, but now he grew quiet, almost as if he felt obliged to avoid giving me any cause for offence. Drawing up outside my pension, he said: 'Did Traudl have any family?'

'Not that I know of. There's just Becker.' I wondered at that, though. The photograph of her and Colonel Poroshin still preyed on my mind.

'Well, that's all right. I'm not going to lose any sleep worrying about his grief.'

'He's my client, in case you'd forgotten. In helping you I'm supposed to be working to prove him innocent.'

'And you're convinced of that?'

'Yes, I am.'

'But surely you must know he's on the Crowcass list.'

'You're pretty cute,' I said dumbly, 'letting me make all the running like this, only to tell me that. Supposing that I do get lucky and win the race, am I going to be allowed to collect the prize?'

'Your friend is a murdering Nazi, Bernie. He commanded an execution squad in the Ukraine, massacring men, women and children. I'd say that he deserved to hang whether he killed Linden or not.'

'You're pretty cute, Belinsky,' I repeated bitterly, and started to get out of the car.

'But as far as I'm concerned, he's small fry. I'm after bigger fish than Emil Becker. You can help me. You can try and repair some of the damage that your country has done. A symbolic gesture, if you like. Who knows – if enough Germans do the same then maybe the account could be settled.'

'What are you talking about?' I said, from the road. 'What account?' I leaned on the car door and bent forward to see Belinsky take out his pipe.

'God's account,' he said quietly.

I laughed and shook my head in disbelief.

'What's the matter? Don't you believe in God?'

'I don't believe in trying to make a deal with him. You speak about God as if he sells secondhand cars. I've misjudged you. You're much more of an American than I thought you were.'

'Now that's where you're wrong. God likes making deals. Look at that covenant he made with Abraham, and with Noah. God's a huckster, Bernie. Only a German could mistake a deal for a direct order.'

'Get to the point, will you? There is a point, isn't there?' His manner seemed to indicate as much.

'I'm going to level with you – '

'Oh? I seem to remember you doing that a little earlier on.'

'Everything I told you was true.'

'There's just more to come, right?'

Belinsky nodded and lit his pipe. I felt like smacking it out of his mouth. Instead I got back into the car and closed the door.

'With your penchant for selective truth, you should get a job in an advertising agency. Let's hear it.'

'Just don't make a hot throat at me until I'm through, right?'

I nodded curtly.

'All right. For a start, we – Crowcass – believe Becker is innocent of Linden's murder. You see, the gun which killed him was used to kill somebody else in Berlin almost three years ago. The ballistics people matched that bullet with the one that killed Linden, and they were both fired from the same gun. For the time of the first killing Becker has a pretty good alibi: he was a Russian prisoner of war. Of course he could have acquired the gun since then, but I haven't come to the interesting part yet, the part that actually makes me want Becker to be innocent.

'The gun was a Standard SS-issue Walther P38. We traced the serial-number records held at the US Documents Centre and discovered that this same pistol was one of a batch that was issued to senior officers within the Gestapo. This particular weapon was given to Heinrich Müller. It was a long shot but we compared the bullet that killed Linden with the one that killed the man we dug up who was supposed to be Müller, and what do you know? Jackpot. Whoever killed Linden might also have been responsible for putting a false Heinrich Müller in the ground. Do you see, Bernie? It's the best clue that we've ever had that Gestapo Müller is still alive. It means that only a few months ago he might have been right here in Vienna, working for the Org, of which you are now a member. He may even still be here.

'Do you know how important that is? Think about it, please. Müller was the architect of the Nazi terror. For ten years he controlled the most brutal secret police the world has ever known. This was a man almost as powerful as Himmler himself. Can you imagine how many people he must have tortured? How many deaths he must have ordered? How many Jews, Poles –

even how many Germans he must have killed? Bernie, this is your opportunity to help avenge all those dead Germans. To see that justice is done.'

I laughed scornfully. 'Is that what you call it when you let a man hang for something he didn't do? Correct me if I'm wrong, Belinsky, but isn't that part of your plan: to let Becker take the drop?'

'Naturally I hope that it doesn't come to that. But if it's necessary, then so be it. So long as the military police have Becker, Müller won't be spooked. And if that includes hanging him, yes. Knowing what I know about Emil Becker, I won't lose much sleep.' Belinsky watched my face carefully for some sign of approval. 'Come on, you're a cop. You appreciate how these things work. Don't tell me you've never had to nail a man for one thing because you couldn't prove another. It all evens up, you know that.'

'Sure, I've done it. But not when a man's life was involved. I've never played games with a man's life.'

'Provided you help us to find Müller we're prepared to forget about Becker.' The pipe emitted a short smoke signal, which seemed to bespeak a growing impatience on its owner's part. 'Look, all I'm suggesting is that you put Müller in the dock instead of Becker.'

'And if I do find Müller, what then? He's not about to let me walk up and put the cuffs on him. How am I supposed to bring him in without getting my head blown off?'

'You can leave that to me. All you have to do is establish exactly where he is. Telephone me and my Crowcass team will do the rest.'

'How will I recognize him?'

Belinsky reached behind his seat and brought back a cheap leather briefcase. He unzipped it and took out an envelope from which he removed a passport-sized photograph.

'That's Müller,' he said. 'Apparently he speaks with a very pronounced Munich accent, so even if he should have radically changed his appearance, you'll certainly have no trouble recognizing his voice.' He watched me turn the photograph towards the streetlight and stare at it for a while.

'He'd be forty-seven now. Not very tall, big peasant hands. He may still even be wearing his wedding ring.'

The photograph didn't say much about the man. It wasn't a very revealing face; and yet it was a remarkable one. Müller had a squarish skull, a high forehead, and tense, narrow lips. But it was the eyes that really got to you, even on that small photograph. Müller's eyes were like the eyes of a snowman: two black, frozen coals.

'Here's another one,' Belinsky said. 'These are the only two photographs of him known to exist.'

The second picture was a group shot. There were five men seated round an oak table as if they had been having dinner in a comfortable restaurant. Three of them I recognized. At the head of the table was Heinrich Himmler, playing with his pencil and smiling at Arthur Nebe on his right. Arthur Nebe: my old comrade, as Belinsky would have said. On Himmler's left, and apparently hanging on every one of the Reichsführer-SS's words, was Reinhard Heydrich, chief of the RSHA, assassinated by Czech terrorists in 1942.

'When was this picture taken?' I asked.

'November 1939.' Belinsky leaned across and tapped one of the two other men in the picture with the stem of his pipe. 'That's Müller there,' he said, 'sitting beside Heydrich.'

Müller's hand had moved in the same half-second that the camera-shutter had opened and closed: it was blurred as if covering the order paper on the table, but even so, the wedding ring was clearly visible. He was looking down, almost not listening to Himmler at all. By comparison with Heydrich, Müller's head was small. His hair was closely cropped, shaven even until it reached the very top of the cranium, where it had been permitted to grow a little in a small, carefully tended allotment.

'Who's the man sitting opposite Müller?'

'The one taking notes? That's Franz Josef Huber. He was chief of the Gestapo here in Vienna. You can hang on to those pictures if you want. They're only prints.'

'I haven't agreed to help you yet.'

'But you will. You have to.'

'Right now I ought to tell you to go and fuck yourself,

Belinsky. You see, I'm like an old piano – I don't much like being played. But I'm tired. And I've had a few. Maybe I'll be able to think a little more clearly tomorrow.' I opened the car door and got out again.

Belinsky was right: the body work of the big black Mercedes was covered in dents.

'I'll call you in the morning,' he said.

'You do that,' I said, and slammed the door shut.

He drove away like he was the devil's own coachman.

28

I did not sleep well. Troubled by what Belinsky had said, my thoughts made my limbs restless, and after only a few hours I woke before dawn in a cold sweat and did not sleep again. If only he hadn't mentioned God, I said to myself.

I was not a Catholic until I became a prisoner in Russia. The regime in the camp was so hard that it seemed to me that there was an even chance it would kill me, and, wishing to make my peace with the back of my mind, I had sought out the only churchman among my fellow prisoners, a Polish priest. I had been brought up as a Lutheran, but religious denomination seemed like a matter of small account in that dreadful place.

Becoming a Catholic in the full expectation of death only made me more tenacious of life, and after I'd escaped and returned to Berlin I continued to attend mass and to celebrate the faith that had apparently delivered me.

My newfound Church did not have a good record in its relation to the Nazis, and had now also distanced itself from any imputation of guilt. It followed that if the Catholic Church was not guilty, nor were its members. There was, it seemed, some theological basis for a rejection of German collective guilt. Guilt, said the priests, was really something personal between a man and his God, and its attribution to one nation by another was blasphemy, for this could only be a matter of divine prerogative. After that, all that there remained to do was pray for the dead, for those who had done wrong, and for the whole dreadful and embarrassing epoch to be forgotten as quickly as possible.

There were many who remained uneasy at the way the moral dirt was swept under the carpet. But it is certain that a nation cannot feel collective guilt, that each man must encounter it personally. Only now did I realize the nature of my own guilt – and perhaps it was really not much different from that of many others: it was that I had not said anything, that I had not lifted my hand against the Nazis. I also realized that I had a personal sense of grievance against Heinrich Müller, for as chief of the Gestapo he had done more than any other man to achieve the corruption of the police force of which I had once been a proud member. From that had flowed wholesale terror.

Now it seemed it was not too late to do something after all. It was just possible that, by seeking out Müller, the symbol not just of my own corruption but Becker's too, and bringing him to justice, I might help to clear my own guilt for what had happened.

Belinsky rang early, almost as if he had already guessed my decision, and I told him that I would help him to find Gestapo Müller not for Crowcass, nor for the United States Army, but for Germany. But mostly, I told him, I would help him to get Müller for myself.

29

First thing that morning, after telephoning König and arranging
a meeting to hand over Belinsky's ostensibly secret material, I
went to Liebl's office in Judengasse in order that he might
arrange for me to see Becker at the police prison.

'I want to show him a photograph,' I explained.

'A photograph?' Liebl sounded hopeful. 'Is this a photograph
that might become an item of evidence?'

I shrugged. 'That depends on Becker.'

Liebl made a couple of swift telephone calls, trading on the
death of Becker's fiancée, the possibility of new evidence and
the proximity of the trial, which gained us almost immediate
access to the prison. It was a fine day and we made our way
there by foot, with Liebl walking his umbrella like a colour
sergeant in an imperial regiment of guards.

'Did you tell him about Traudl?' I asked.

'Last night.'

'How did he take it?'

The grey brow on the old lawyer's head shifted uncertainly.
'Surprisingly well, Herr Gunther. Like you, I had supposed
our client would be devastated by the news.' The brow shifted
again, more in consternation this time. 'But he was not. No, it
was his own unfortunate situation that seemed to preoccupy
him. As well as your progress, or lack of it. Herr Becker does
seem to have an extraordinary amount of faith in your powers
of detection. Powers for which, if I may be frank with you, sir,
I have seen little or no evidence.'

'You're entitled to your opinion, Dr Liebl. I guess you're like
most lawyers I've met: if your own sister sent you an invitation
to her wedding you'd be happy only if it was signed under seal
and in the presence of two witnesses. Perhaps if our client had
been a little more forthcoming...'

'You suspect he's been holding something back? Yes, I

remember you said as much on the telephone yesterday. Without knowing quite what you were talking about I did not feel able to take advantage of Herr Becker's – ' he hesitated for a second while he debated whether or not he could reasonably use the word, and then decided that he could ' – grief, to make such an allegation.'

'Very sensitive of you, I'm sure. But perhaps this photograph will jog his memory.'

'I do hope so. And perhaps his bereavement will have sunk in, and he will make a better show of his grief.'

It seemed like a very Viennese sort of sentiment.

But when we saw Becker he appeared hardly affected. After a packet of cigarettes had persuaded the guard to leave the three of us alone in the interview room I tried to find out why.

'I'm sorry about Traudl,' I said. 'She was a really lovely girl.'

He nodded expressionlessly, as if he had been listening to some boring point of legal procedure as explained by Liebl.

'I must say you don't seem very upset by it,' I remarked.

'I'm dealing with it in the best way I know how,' he said quietly. 'There's not a lot I can do here. Chances are they won't even let me attend the funeral. How do you think I feel?'

I turned to Liebl and asked him if he wouldn't mind leaving the room for a minute. 'There's something I wish to say to Herr Becker in private.'

Liebl glanced at Becker, who nodded curtly back at him. Neither of us spoke until the heavy door had closed behind the lawyer.

'Spit it out, Bernie,' Becker said, half-yawning at the same time. 'What's on your mind?'

'It was your friends in the Org who killed your girl,' I said, watching his long thin face closely for some sign of emotion. I wasn't sure if this was true or not, but I was keen to see what it might make him reveal. But there was nothing. 'They actually asked me to kill her.'

'So,' he said, with his eyes narrowing, 'you're in the Org.' His tone was cautious. 'When did this happen?'

'Your friend König recruited me.'

His face seemed to relax a little. 'Well, I guessed it was only a matter of time. To be honest, I wasn't at all sure whether or not you were in the Org when you first came to Vienna. With your background you're the kind of man they're quick to recruit. If you're in now, you have been busy. I'm impressed. Did König say why he wanted you to kill Traudl?'

'He told me she was an MVD spy. He showed me a photograph of her talking to Colonel Poroshin.'

Becker smiled sadly. 'She was no spy,' he said, shaking his head, 'and she was not my girlfriend. She was Poroshin's girl. Originally she posed as my fiancée so that I could stay in contact with Poroshin while I was in prison. Liebl knew nothing about it. Poroshin said that you hadn't been all that keen to come to Vienna. Said you didn't seem to have a very good opinion of me. He wondered if you would stay very long when you did come. So he thought it would be a good idea if Traudl worked on you a little and persuaded you that there was someone who loved me on the outside, someone who needed me. He's a shrewd judge of character, Bernie. Go on, admit it, she's half the reason why you've stuck to my case. Because you thought that mother and baby deserved the benefit of the doubt, even if I didn't.'

It was Becker who was watching me now, looking for some reaction. Oddly enough, I found I wasn't angry at all. I was used to discovering that at any one time I only ever had half the truth.

'So I don't suppose she was a nurse at all.'

'Oh, she was a nurse all right. She used to steal penicillin for me to sell on the black market. It was me who introduced her to Poroshin.' He shrugged. 'I didn't know about the two of them for a while. But I wasn't surprised. Traudl liked a good time, like most of the women in this city. She and I were even lovers for a brief while, but nothing like that lasts for very long in Vienna.'

'Your wife said that you got Poroshin some penicillin for a dose of drip? Was that true?'

'I got him some penicillin, sure, but it wasn't for him. It was for his son. He had cerebro-spinal fever. There's quite an epidemic of it, I believe. And a shortage of antibiotics, especially in Russia. There's a shortage of everything but manpower in the Soviet Union.

'After that, Poroshin did me one or two favours. Fixed papers, gave me a cigarette concession, that sort of thing. We became quite friendly. And when the Org's people got round to recruiting me, I told him all about it. Why not? I thought König and his friends were a bunch of spinners. But I was happy to make money from them, and frankly I wasn't much involved with the Org beyond that odd bit of courier-work to Berlin. Poroshin was keen that I get closer to them however, and when he offered me a lot of money, I agreed to try. But they're absurdly suspicious, Bernie, and when I expressed some interest in doing more work for them they insisted that I subject myself to an interrogation about my service with the SS and my imprisonment in a Soviet POW camp. It bothered them a lot that I was released. They didn't say anything about it at the time, but in view of what has happened since, I guess they must have decided that they couldn't trust me, and put me out of the way.' Becker lit one of his cigarettes and leaned back on the hard chair.

'Why didn't you tell this to the police?'

He laughed. 'You think I didn't? When I told them about the Org those stupid bastards thought I was telling them about the Werewolf Underground. You know, that shit about a Nazi terrorist group.'

'So that's where Shields got the idea.'

'Shields?' Becker snorted. 'He's a fucking idiot.'

'All right, why didn't you tell me about the Org?'

'Like I said, Bernie, I wasn't sure if they hadn't already recruited you in Berlin. Ex-Kripo, ex-Abwehr, you'd have been exactly what they were looking for. But if you hadn't been in the Org and I'd told you, you might well have gone round Vienna asking questions about it, in which case you would have ended up dead, like my two business partners. And if you were in the Org I thought that maybe that would just be in Berlin. Here in Vienna you'd be just another detective, albeit one I knew and trusted. Do you see?'

I grunted an affirmative and found my own cigarettes.

'You still should have told me.'

'Perhaps.' He drew fiercely on his cigarette. 'Listen, Bernie. My original offer still stands. Thirty thousand dollars if you can dig me out of this hole. So if you've got anything up your sleeve . . .'

'There's this,' I said, cutting across him. I produced Müller's photograph, the one that was passport-sized. 'Do you recognize him?'

'I don't think so. But I've seen this picture before, Bernie. At least I think I have. Traudl showed it to me before you came to Vienna.'

'Oh? Did she say how she came by it?'

'Poroshin, I guess.' He studied the picture more carefully. 'Oak-leaf collar patches, silver braid on the shoulders. An SS-Brigadeführer by the look of him. Who is it, anyway?'

'Heinrich Müller.'

'Gestapo Müller?'

'Officially he's dead, so I'd like you to keep quiet about all this for the moment. I've teamed up with this American agent from the War Crimes Commission who is interested in the Linden case. He worked for the same department. Apparently the gun that was used to kill Linden belonged to Müller, and was used to kill the man who was supposed to be Müller. Which might leave Müller still alive. Naturally the War Crimes people are anxious to get hold of Müller at any price. Which leaves you firmly on the spot I'm afraid, at least for the moment.'

'I wouldn't mind if it was firmly. But the particular spot they have in mind has hinges on it. Do you mind explaining what this means exactly?'

'It means they're not prepared to do anything that might scare Müller out of Vienna.'

'Assuming he's here.'

'That's right. Because this is an intelligence operation, they're not prepared to let the military police in on it. If the charges against you were to be dropped now, it might persuade the Org that the case was about to be reopened.'

'So where does that leave me, for Christ's sake?'

'This American agent I'm working with has promised to let you go if we can put Müller in your place. We're going to try and draw him out into the open.'

'Until then they're just going to let the trial go ahead, maybe even the sentence too?'

'That's about the size of it.'

'And you're asking me to keep my mouth shut in the meantime.'

'What can you say? That Linden was possibly murdered by a man who's been dead for three years?'

'It's just so – ' Becker flung his cigarette into the corner of the room ' – so damned callous.'

'Do you want to take that biretta off your head? Look, they know about what you did in Minsk. Playing a game with your life isn't something they feel squeamish about. To be honest, they don't much care whether you swing or not. This is your only chance, and you know it.'

Becker nodded sullenly. 'All right,' he said.

I stood up to leave, but a sudden thought stopped me from walking to the door.

'As a matter of interest,' I said, 'why did they release you from the Soviet POW camp?'

'You were a prisoner. You know what it was like. Always scared they were going to find out you were in the SS.'

'That's why I'm asking.'

He hesitated for a moment. Then he said: 'There was a man who was due to be released. He was very sick, and would have died soon enough. What was the point in repatriating him?' He shrugged, and looked me square in the eye. 'So I strangled him. Ate some camphor to make myself sick – damn near killed myself – and took his place.' He stared me out. 'I was desperate, Bernie. You remember what it was like.'

'Yes, I remember.' I tried to conceal my distaste, and failed. 'All the same, if you'd told me that before today I'd have let them hang you.' I reached for the door handle.

'There's still time. Why don't you?'

If I'd told him the truth Becker wouldn't have understood what I was talking about. He probably thought that metaphysics was something you used to manufacture cheap penicillin for the black market. So instead I shook my head, and said, 'Let's just say that I made a deal with someone.'

30

I met König at the Café Sperl in Gumpendorfer Strasse, which was in the French sector but close to the Ring. It was a big, gloomy place which the many art-nouveau-style mirrors on the walls did nothing to brighten, and was home to several half-size billiard tables. Each one of these was illuminated by a light which was fixed to the yellowing ceiling above with a brass fitting that looked like something out of an old U–boat.

König's terrier sat a short way off from its master like the dog on the record label, watching him play a solitary but thoughtful game. I ordered a coffee and approached the table.

He judged his shot at a careful cue's length, and then applied a screw of chalk to the tip, silently acknowledging my presence with a short nod of his head.

'Our own Mozart was particularly fond of this game,' he said, lowering his eyes to the felt. 'Doubtless he found it a very congenial facsimile of the very precise dynamism of his intellect.' He fixed his eye on the cue-ball like a sniper taking aim, and after a long, painstaking moment, rifled the white on to one red and then the other. This second red coasted down the length of the table, teetered on the lip of the pocket and, enticing a small murmur of satisfaction from its trans-lator – for there exists no more graceful manifestation of the laws of gravity and motion – slipped noiselessly out of sight.

'I, on the other hand, enjoy the game for rather more sensuous reasons. I love the sound of the balls hitting each other, and the way they run so smoothly.' He retrieved the red from the pocket and replaced it to his own satisfaction. 'But most of all I love the colour green. Did you know that among Celtic peoples the colour green is considered unlucky? No? They believe green is followed by black. Probably because the English used to hang

Irishmen for wearing green. Or was it the Scots?' For a moment König stared almost insanely at the surface of the billiard table, as if he could have licked it with his tongue.

'Just look at it,' he breathed. 'Green is the colour of ambition, and of youth. It's the colour of life, and of eternal rest. *Requiem aeternam dona eis*.' Reluctantly he laid his cue down on the cloth, and conjuring a large cigar from one of his pockets, turned away from the table. The terrier stood up expectantly. 'You said on the telephone that you had something for me. Something important.'

I handed him Belinsky's envelope. 'Sorry it's not in green ink,' I said, watching him take out the papers. 'Do you read Cyrillic?'

König shook his head. 'I'm afraid it might as well be in Gaelic.' But he went ahead and spread the papers out on the billiard table and then lit his cigar. When the dog barked he ordered it to be quiet. 'Perhaps you would be good enough to explain exactly what I am looking at?'

'These are details of MVD dispositions and methods in Hungary and Lower Austria.' I smiled coolly and sat down at an adjacent table where the waiter had just laid my coffee.

König nodded slowly, stared uncomprehendingly at the papers for another few seconds, then scooped them up, replaced them in their envelope and slipped the papers inside his jacket pocket.

'Very interesting,' he said, sitting down at my table. 'Assuming for a moment that they're genuine – '

'Oh, they're genuine all right,' I said quickly.

He smiled patiently, as if I could have had no idea of the lengthy process whereby such information was properly verified. 'Assuming they're genuine,' he repeated firmly, 'how exactly did you come by them?'

A couple of men came over to the billiard table and started a game. König drew his chair away and jerked his head at me to follow him. 'It's all right,' said one of the players. 'There's plenty of room to get by.' But we moved our chairs anyway. And when we were at a more discreet distance from the table I started to give him the story I had rehearsed with Belinsky.

Only now König shook his head firmly and picked up his dog, which licked his ear playfully.

'This isn't the right time or place,' he said. 'But I'm impressed at how busy you have been.' He raised his eyebrows and watched the two men at the billiard table with an air of distraction. 'I learned this morning that you had been successful in procuring some petrol coupons for that medical friend of mine. The one at the General Hospital.' I realized that he was talking about Traudl's murder. 'And so soon after we had discussed the matter too. It really was most efficient of you, I'm sure.' He puffed smoke at the dog on his lap which sniffed and then sneezed. 'It's so difficult to obtain reliable supplies of anything in Vienna these days.'

I shrugged. 'You just have to know the right people, that's all.'

'As you clearly do, my friend.' He patted the breast pocket of his green tweed suit, where he had put Belinsky's documents. 'In these special circumstances I feel I ought to introduce you to someone in the company who will be better able than I to judge the quality of your source. Someone who, as it happens, is keen to meet you, and decide how best a man of your skills and resourcefulness may be used. We had thought to wait a few weeks before making the introduction, but this new information changes everything. However, first I must make a telephone call. I shall be a few minutes.' He looked down the café and pointed to one of the other free billiard tables. 'Why don't you try a few shots while I'm away?'

'I've not much use for games of skill,' I said. 'I distrust a game that relies on anything but luck. That way I needn't blame myself if I lose. I have a tremendous capacity for self-recrimination.'

A twinkle came into König's eye. 'My dear fellow,' he said standing up from the table, 'that seems hardly German.'

I watched him as he walked into the back of the café to use the phone, the terrier trotting faithfully after him. I wondered who it was that he was calling: the one who was better able to judge the quality of my source might even be Müller. It seemed too much to hope for so soon.

When König returned a few minutes later, he seemed excited. 'As I thought,' he said, nodding enthusiastically, 'there is someone who is keen to have immediate sight of this material, and to meet you. I have a car outside. Shall we go?'

König's car was a black Mercedes, like Belinsky's. And like Belinsky he drove too fast for safety on a road that had seen a heavy morning rain. I said that it would be better to arrive late than not to arrive at all, but he paid no attention. My feeling of discomfort was made worse by König's dog, which sat on his master's lap and barked excitedly at the road ahead for the whole of the journey, as if the brute had been giving directions on where we were going. I recognized the road as the one which led to Sievering Studios, but at that same moment the road forked and we turned north again on to Grinzinger Allee.

'Do you know Grinzing?' König shouted over the dog's incessant barking. I said that I did not. 'Then you really don't know the Viennese,' he opined. 'Grinzing is famous for its wine production. In the summer everyone comes up here in the evening to go to one of the taverns selling the new vintage. They drink too much, listen to a Schrammel quartet and sing old songs.'

'It sounds very cosy,' I said, without much enthusiasm.

'Yes, it is. I own a couple of vineyards up here myself. Just two small fields you understand. But it's a start. A man must have some land, don't you think? We'll come back here in the summer and then you can taste the new wine yourself. The lifeblood of Vienna.'

Grinzing seemed hardly a suburb of Vienna at all, more a charming little village. But because of its proximity to the capital, its cosy country charm somehow appeared as false as one of the film sets they built over at Sievering. We drove up a hill on a narrow winding lane which led between old Heurige Inns and cottage gardens, with König declaring how pretty he thought it all was now that spring was here. But the sight of so much storybook provinciality merely served to stimulate my city-bred parts to contempt, and I restricted myself to a sullen grunt and a muttered sentence about tourists. To one more used to the perennial sight of rubble, Grinzing with its many trees and vineyards looked very green. However I made no mention of this impression for fear that it might set König off on one of his queer little monologues about that sickly colour.

He stopped the car in front of a high yellow-brick wall which enclosed a large, yellow-painted house and a garden that looked as if it had spent all day in the beauty parlour. The house itself was a tall, three-storey building with a high-dormered roof. Apart from its bright colour, there was a certain austerity of detail about the façade which lent the house an institutional appearance. It looked like a rather opulent sort of town hall.

I followed König through the gates and up an immaculately bordered path to a heavy studded oak door of the kind that expected you to be holding a battle-axe when you knocked. We walked straight into the house and on to a creaking wooden floor that would have given a librarian a heart attack.

König led me into a small sitting-room, told me to wait there and then left, closing the door behind him. I took a good look round, but there wasn't much to see beyond the fact of the owner's bucolic taste in furniture. A rough-hewn table blocked the French window, and a couple of cartwheel farmhouse chairs were ranged in front of an empty fireplace that was as big as a mineshaft. I sat down on a slightly more comfortable-looking ottoman and re-tied my shoelaces. Then I polished my toes with the edge of the threadbare rug. I must have waited there for an indifferent half-hour before König came back to fetch me. He led me through a maze of rooms and corridors and up a flight of stairs to the back of the house, with the manner of a man whose jacket is lined with oak panelling. Hardly caring if I insulted him or not now that I was about to meet someone more important, I said, 'If you changed that suit you'd make someone a wonderful butler.'

König did not turn around, but I heard him bare his dentures and utter a short, dry laugh. 'I'm glad you think so. You know, although I like a sense of humour I would not advise you to exercise it with the general. Frankly, his character is most severe.' He opened a door and we came into a bright, airy room with a fire in the grate and hectares of empty bookshelves. Against the broad window, behind a long library table, stood a grey-suited figure with a closely-cropped head I half recognized. The man turned and smiled, his hooked nose unmistakably belonging to a face from my past.

'Hello, Gunther,' said the man.

König looked quizzically at me as I blinked speechlessly at the grinning figure.

'Do you believe in ghosts, Herr König?' I said.

'No. Do you?'

'I do now. If I'm not mistaken, the gentleman by the window was hanged in 1945 for his part in the plot to kill the Führer.'

'You can leave us, Helmut,' said the man at the window. König nodded curtly, turned on his heel and left.

Arthur Nebe pointed at a chair in front of the table on which Belinsky's documents lay spread out beside a pair of spectacles and a fountain pen. 'Sit down,' he said. 'Drink?' He laughed. 'You look as though you need one.'

'It's not every day I get to see a man raised from the dead,' I said quietly. 'Better make it a large one.'

Nebe opened a large carved-wood drinks cabinet, revealing a marble interior filled with several bottles. He took out a bottle of vodka and two small glasses, which he filled to the top.

'To old comrades,' he said, raising his glass. I smiled uncertainly. 'Drink up. It won't make me disappear again.'

I tossed the vodka back and breathed deeply as it hit my stomach. 'Death agrees with you, Arthur. You look well.'

'Thanks. I've never felt better.'

I lit a cigarette and left it on my lip for a while.

'Minsk, wasn't it?' he said. 'In 1941. The last time we saw each other?'

'That's right. You got me transferred to the War Crimes Bureau.'

'I ought to have had you put on a charge for what you asked. Even had you shot.'

'From what I hear, you were keen on shooting that summer.' Nebe let that one pass. 'So why didn't you?'

'You were a damned good policeman. That's why.'

219

'So were you.' I sucked hard at my cigarette. 'At least, you were before the war. What made you change, Arthur?'

Nebe savoured his drink for a moment and then finished it with one swallow. 'This is good vodka,' he remarked quietly, almost to himself. 'Bernie, don't expect me to give you an explanation. I had my orders to carry out, and so it was them or me. Kill or be killed. That's how it always was with the SS. Ten, twenty, thirty thousand – after you've calculated that to save your own life you must kill others then the number makes little or no difference. That was my final solution, Bernie: the final solution to the pressing problem of my own continued survival. You were fortunate that you were never required to make that same calculation.'

'Thanks to you.'

Nebe shrugged modestly, before pointing at the papers spread before him. 'I'm rather glad that I didn't have you shot, now that I've seen this lot. Naturally this material will have to be assessed by an expert, but on the face of it you appear to have won the lottery. All the same, I'd like to hear more about your source.'

I repeated my story, after which Nebe said:

'Can he be trusted, do you think? Your Russian?'

'He never let me down before,' I said. 'Of course, he was just fixing papers for me then.'

Nebe refilled our glasses and frowned.

'Is there a problem?' I asked.

'It's just that in the ten years I've known you Bernie, I can't find anything that can persuade me that you're now a common black-marketeer.'

'That shouldn't be any more difficult than the problem I have persuading myself that you're a war-criminal, Arthur. Or for that matter, accepting that you're not dead.'

Nebe smiled. 'You have a point. But with so many opportunities presented by the vast number of displaced persons, I'm surprised you didn't return to your old trade and become a private investigator again.'

'Private investigation and the black market are not mutually exclusive,' I said. 'Good information is just like penicillin or cigarettes. It has its price. And the better, the more illicit the information, the higher that price. It's always been like that. Incidentally, my Russian will want to be paid.'

'They always do. Sometimes I think that the Ivans have more confidence in the dollar than the Americans themselves.' Nebe clasped his hands and laid both forefingers along the length of his shrewd-looking nose. Then he pointed them at me as if he had been holding a pistol. 'You've done very well, Bernie. Very well indeed. But I must confess I am still puzzled.'

'About me as a black Peter?'

'I can accept the idea of that rather more easily than I can accept the idea of you killing Traudl Braunsteiner. Murder was never in your line.'

'I didn't kill her,' I said. 'König told me to do it, and I thought I could, because she was a Communist. I learned to hate them while I was in a Soviet prison-camp. Even enough to kill one. But when I thought about it, I realized I couldn't do it. Not in cold blood. Maybe I could have done it if it had been a man, but not a girl. I was going to tell him that this morning, but when he congratulated me on having done it, I decided to keep my mouth shut and take the credit. I figured there might be some money in it.'

'So somebody else killed her. How very intriguing. You've no idea who, I suppose?'

I shook my head.

'A mystery, then.'

'Just like your resurrection, Arthur. How exactly did you manage it?'

'I'm afraid that I can't take any of the credit,' he said. 'It was something the intelligence people dreamed up. In the last few months of the war they simply doctored the service records of senior SS and party personnel, to the effect that we were dead. Most of us were executed for our part in Count Stauffenberg's plot to kill the Führer. Well, what were another hundred or so executions on a list that was already thousands of names long? And then some of us were listed as killed in a bombing raid, or in the battle for Berlin. Then all that remained was to make sure that these records fell into the hands of the Americans.

'So the SS transported the records to a paper mill near Munich, and the owner – a good Nazi – was briefed to wait until the Amis were on his doorstep before he started to destroy anything.' Nebe laughed. 'I remember reading in the newspaper how pleased with themselves the Amis were. What a coup they thought they had scored. Of course, most of what they captured was genuine enough. But for those of us who were most at risk from their ridiculous war-crimes investigations, it provided a real breathing space, and enough time to establish a new identity. There's nothing quite like being dead for giving one a little room.' He laughed again. 'Anyway, that US Documents Centre of theirs in Berlin is still working for us.'

'How do you mean?' I asked, wondering if I was about to learn something that would throw light on why Linden had been killed. Or perhaps he had simply found out that the records had been doctored before they fell into Allied hands? Wouldn't that have been enough to justify killing him?

'No, I've said enough for the moment.' Nebe drank some more vodka and licked his lips appreciatively. 'These are interesting times we live in, Bernie. A man can be whoever he wants to be. Take me: my new name is Nolde, Arthur Nolde, and I make wine on this estate. Resurrected, you said. Well you're not so very far away from it there. Only our Nazi dead are raised incorruptible. We're changed, my friend. It's the Russians who are wearing the black hats and trying to take over the town. Now that we're working for the Americans, we're the good boys. Dr Schneider – he's the man who set the Org up with the help of their CIC – he has regular meetings with them at our headquarters in Pullach. He's even been to the United States to meet their Secretary of State. Can you imagine it? A senior German officer working with the President's number two? You don't get more incorruptible than that, not these days.'

'If you don't mind,' I said, 'I find it hard to think of the Amis as saints. When I got back from Russia my wife was getting an extra ration from an American captain. Sometimes I think they're no better than the Ivans.'

Nebe shrugged. 'You're not the only one in the Org who thinks that,' he said. 'But for my part, I never heard of the Ivans asking a lady's permission or giving her a few bars of chocolate first. They're animals.' He smiled as a thought came into his head. 'All the same, I will admit that some of those women ought to be grateful to the Russians. But for them, they might never have known what it was like.'

It was a poor joke, and in bad taste, but I laughed along with him anyway. I was still sufficiently nervous of Nebe to want to be good company for him.

'So what did you do, about your wife and this American captain?' he asked when his laughter has subsided.

Something made me check myself before I replied. Arthur Nebe was a clever man. Before the war, as chief of the criminal police, he had been Germany's most outstanding policeman. It would have been too risky to give an answer which suggested that I had wanted to kill an American Army captain. Nebe saw common factors worthy of investigation where other men only saw the hand of a capricious god. I knew him too well to believe that he would have forgotten how once he had assigned Becker to a murder inquiry I was leading. Any hint of an association, no matter how accidental, between the death of one American officer affecting Becker and the death of another affecting me and I didn't doubt that Nebe would have given orders to have had me killed. One American officer was bad enough. Two would have been too much of a coincidence. So I shrugged, lit a cigarette and said: 'What can you do but make sure it's her and not him who gets the slap in the mouth? American officers don't take kindly to being socked, least of all by krauts. It's one of the small privileges of conquest that you don't have to take any shit from your defeated enemy. I can't imagine you've forgotten that, Herr Gruppenführer. You of all people.'

I watched his grin with an extra curiosity. It was a cunning smile, in an old fox's face, but his teeth looked real enough.

'That was very wise of you,' he said. 'It doesn't do to go around killing Americans.' Confirming my nervousness of him, he added, after a long pause: 'Do you remember Emil Becker?'

It would have been stupid to have tried to affect a show of protracted remembering. He knew me better than that.

'Of course,' I said.

'It was his girlfriend that König told you to kill. One of his girlfriends anyway.'

'But König said she was MVD,' I frowned.

'And so she was. So was Becker. He killed an American officer. But not before he'd tried to infiltrate the Org.'

I shook my head slowly. 'A crook, maybe,' I said, 'but I can't see Becker as one of Ivan's spies.' Nebe nodded insistently. 'Here in Vienna?' He nodded again. 'Did he know about you being alive?'

'Of course not. We used him to do a little courier work now and again. It was a mistake. Becker was a black-marketeer, like you, Bernie. Rather a successful one, as it happens. But he had delusions regarding his own worth to us. He thought he was at the centre of a very big pond. But he was nowhere near it. Quite frankly if a meteorite had landed in the middle of it, Becker wouldn't even have noticed the fucking ripple.'

'How did you find out about him?'

'His wife told us,' Nebe said. 'When he came back from a Soviet POW camp, our people in Berlin sent someone round to his house to see if we could recruit him to the Org. Well, they missed him, and by the time they got to speak to Becker's wife he had left home and was living here in Vienna. The wife told them about Becker's association with a Russian colonel of MVD. But for one reason and another – actually it was sheer bloody inefficiency – it was quite a while before that information reached us here in Vienna section. And by that time he had been recruited by one of our collectors.'

'So where is he now?'

'Here in Vienna. In gaol. The Americans are putting him on trial for murder, and he will most certainly hang.'

'That must be rather convenient for you,' I said, sticking my neck out a little way. 'Rather too convenient, if you ask me.'

'Professional instinct, Bernie?'

'Better just call it a hunch. That way, if I'm wrong it won't make me look like an amateur.'

'Still trusting your guts, eh?'

'Most of all now that I've got something inside them again, Arthur. Vienna's a fat city after Berlin.'

'So you think we killed the American?'

'That would depend on who he was, and if you had a good reason. Then all you would have to do is make sure they got someone's coat for it. Someone you might want out of the way. That way you could get to hit two flies with one swat. Am I right?'

Nebe inclined his head to one side a little. 'Perhaps. But don't ever try to remind me of just how good a detective you were by doing something as stupid as proving it. It's still a very sore point with some people in this section, so it might be best if you were to nail your beak about it altogether.

'You know, if you really felt like playing detective, you might like to give us the benefit of your advice as to how we should go about finding one of our own missing persons. His name is Dr Karl Heim and he's a dentist. A couple of our people were supposed to take him to Pullach early this morning, but when they went to his house there was no sign of him. Of course he may just have gone on the local cure,' Nebe meant a tour of the bars, 'but in this city there is always the possibility that the Ivans have snatched him. There are a couple of freelance gangs that the Russians have working here. In return they get concessions to sell black-market cigarettes. As far as we've been able to find out, both these gangs report to Becker's Russian colonel. That's probably how he got most of his supplies in the first place.'

'Sure,' I said, unnerved by this latest revelation of Becker's involvement with Colonel Poroshin. 'What do you want me to do?'

'Speak to König,' Nebe instructed, 'give him some advice on how he might try and find Heim. If you get time, you could even give him some help.'

'That's simple enough,' I said. 'Anything else?'

'Yes, I'd like you to come back here tomorrow morning. There's one of our people who has specialized in all matters relating to the MVD. I have a feeling that he will be especially keen to talk to you about this source of yours. Shall we say ten o'clock?'

'Ten o'clock,' I repeated.

Nebe stood up and came round the table to shake my hand. 'It's good to see an old face, Bernie, even if it does look like my conscience.'

I smiled weakly and clasped his hand. 'What's past is past,' I said.

'Exactly so,' he said, dropping a hand on to my shoulder. 'Until tomorrow then. König will drive you back to town.' Nebe opened the door and led the way down the stairs back to the front of the house. 'I'm sorry to hear about that problem with your wife. I could arrange to have her sent some PX if you wanted.'

'Don't bother,' I said quickly. The last thing I wanted was anyone from the Org turning up at my apartment in Berlin and asking Kirsten awkward questions she wouldn't know how to answer. 'She works in an American café and gets all the PX she needs.'

In the hallway we found König playing with his dog.

'Women,' Nebe laughed. 'It was a woman who bought König his dog, isn't that so, Helmut?'

'Yes, Herr General.'

Nebe bent down to tickle the dog's stomach. It rolled over and presented itself submissively to Nebe's fingers.

'And do you know why she bought him a dog?' I caught König's embarrassed little crease of a smile, and I sensed that Nebe was about to crack a joke. 'To teach the man obedience.'

I laughed right along with the two of them. But after only a few days' closer acquaintance with König I thought that Lotte Hartmann would as soon have taught her boyfriend to recite the Torah.

31

The sky was grey by the time I got back to my rooms. I heard a handful of rain against the french windows, and seconds later there was a short flash and a huge clap of thunder that sent the pigeons on my terrace flying for cover. I stood and watched the storm as it rocked the trees and flooded the drains, discharging the atmosphere of all its surplus electrical energy until the air was clear and comfortable again.

Ten minutes later the birds were singing in the trees, as if in celebration of the purgative squall. There seemed much to envy them in this swift climatic cure, and I wished the pressure I felt on my own nerves could have been as easily resolved. Trying to keep one step ahead of all the lies, my own included, I was rapidly coming to the end of my own ingenuity, and I was in danger of losing the tempo of the whole affair. Not to mention my life.

It was about eight o'clock when I called Belinsky at Sacher's, a hotel on Philharmonikerstrasse requisitioned by the military. I thought it might be too late to catch him, but he was there. He sounded relaxed, like he'd known all along that the Org would take his bait.

'I said I'd call,' I reminded him. 'It's a bit late, but I've been busy.'

'No problem. Did they buy it? The information?'

'Damn near took my hand off. König drove me to a house in Grinzing. Possibly it's their headquarters here in Vienna, I'm not sure. It's certainly grand enough.'

'Good. Did you see anything of Müller?'

'No. But I saw someone else.'

'Oh? And who was that?' Belinsky's voice got cool.

'Arthur Nebe.'

'Nebe? Are you sure of that?' He was excited now.

'Of course I'm sure. I knew Nebe before the war. I thought

he was dead. But this afternoon we spoke for almost an hour. He wants me to help König find our dentist friend, and to go back to Grinzing for a meeting tomorrow morning to discuss your Russian's love letters. I've a hunch that Müller's going to be there.'

'How do you make that out?'

'Nebe said that there would be someone there who specialized in all matters relating to the MVD.'

'Yes, coming from Arthur Nebe that description might well fit Müller. What time is this meeting?'

'Ten o'clock.'

'That only gives me tonight to get things organized. Let me think for a minute.' He was silent for so long that I wondered if he was still on the line. But then I heard him take a deep breath. 'How far is the house from the road?'

'Twenty or thirty metres at the front and the north side. Behind the house to the south is a vineyard. I couldn't tell you how far the road is on that side. There's a row of trees between the house and the vineyard. Some outbuildings as well.' I gave him directions to the house as best I remembered them.

'All right,' he said briskly. 'Here's what we'll do. After ten, I'll start to have my men surround the place at a discreet distance. If Müller is there, you signal to us and we'll close in and pick him up. That's going to be the difficult part because they'll be watching you closely. While you were there, did you happen to use the lavatory?'

'No, but I walked past one on the first floor. If the meeting is in the library where I met Nebe, as I imagine it will be, that will be the one in use. It faces north, towards Josefstadt and the road. And there's a window, with a beige roller blind. Perhaps I could use the blind to signal.'

There was another short silence. Then he said: 'Twenty minutes past the hour, or as near as you can manage, you go to the music-room. When you're in there you pull the blind down and count for five seconds, and then push it up for five seconds. Do it three times. I'll be watching the place through binoculars, and when I see your signal I'll sound the car horn three times.

That will be the signal for my men to move in. Then you rejoin the meeting, sit tight and wait for the cavalry.'

'It sounds simple enough. A bit too simple really.'

'Look, kraut, I would suggest that you hang your ass out of the window and whistle "Dixie" but that might attract attention.' He gave an irritated sort of sigh. 'A swoop like this needs a lot of paperwork, Gunther. I have to work out code names and get all kinds of special authorizations for a major field operation. And then there's an investigation if the whole thing turns out to be a false alarm. I hope you're right about Müller. You know, I'm going to be up all night arranging this little party.'

'That really knocks over the heap,' I said. 'I'm the one on the beach and you're bitching about some sand in the oil. Well, I'm really blue about your damned paperwork.'

Belinsky laughed. 'Come on, kraut. Don't get a hot throat about it. I just meant that it would be nice if we could be sure that Müller will be there. Be reasonable. We still don't know for sure that he's part of the Org's set-up in Vienna.'

'Sure we do,' I lied. 'This morning I went to the police prison and showed Emil Becker one of Müller's snapshots. He identified him immediately as the man who was with König when he asked Becker to try and find Captain Linden. Unless Müller is just sweet on König, that means he must be part of the Org's Vienna section.'

'Shit,' said Belinsky, 'why didn't I think of doing that? It's so simple. He's certain it was Müller?'

'No doubt whatsoever.' I strung him along like that for a while until I was sure of him. 'All right, slow your blood down. As a matter of fact, Becker didn't identify him at all. But he had seen the photograph before. Traudl Braunsteiner showed it to him. I just wanted to make sure it wasn't you who gave it to her.'

'You still don't trust me yet, do you, kraut?'

'If I'm going to walk into the lion's den for you, I'm entitled to give you an eye-test beforehand.'

'Yes, well that still leaves us with the problem of where Traudl Braunsteiner got hold of a picture of Gestapo Müller.'

'From a Colonel Poroshin of MVD, I expect. He gave Becker a cigarette concession here in Vienna in return for information and the occasional bit of kidnapping. When Becker was approached by the Org he told Poroshin all about it and agreed to try and find out everything he could. After Becker was arrested, Traudl was their go-between. She just posed as his girlfriend.'

'You know what this means, kraut?'

'It means the Ivans are after Müller as well, right?'

'But have you thought what would happen if they got him? Frankly there's not much chance of him going on trial in the Soviet Union. Like I said before, Müller's made a special study of Soviet police methods. No, the Russians want Müller because he can be very useful to them. He could, for instance, tell them who all the Gestapo's agents in the NKVD were. Men who are probably still in place in the MVD.'

'Let's hope he's there tomorrow then.'

'You'd better tell me how to find this place.'

I gave him clear directions, and told him not to be late. 'These bastards scare me,' I explained.

'Hey, you want to know something? All you krauts scare me. But not as much as the Russians.' He chuckled in a way that I had almost started to like. 'Goodbye, kraut,' he said, 'and good luck.'

Then he hung up, leaving me staring at the purring receiver with the curious sensation that the disembodied voice to which I had been speaking belonged nowhere outside my own imagination.

32

Smoke drifted up to the vaulted ceiling of the nightclub like the thickest underworld fog. It wreathed the solitary figure of Belinsky like Bela Lugosi emerged from a churchyard as he strode up to the table where I sat. The band I had been listening to could hold a beat about as well as a one-legged tap-dancer, but somehow he managed to walk to the rhythm it was generating. I knew he was still angry with me for doubting him, and that he was well aware of how, even now, I was trying to fathom why it was that he hadn't thought to show Müller's photograph to Becker. So I wasn't very surprised when he took hold of my hair and banged my head twice on the table, telling me that I was just a suspicious kraut. I got up and staggered away from him towards the door, but found my exit blocked by Arthur Nebe. His presence there was so unexpected that I was momentarily unable to resist Nebe grasping me by both ears and banging my skull once against the door, and then once again for good luck, saying that if I hadn't killed Traudl Braunsteiner then perhaps I ought to find out who had. I twisted my head free of his hands and said that I might as soon have guessed that Rumpelstiltskin's name was Rumpelstiltskin.

I shook my head again, unwillingly, and blinked hard at the dark. There was another knock at the door, and I heard a half-whispered voice.

'Who is it?' I said, reaching for the bedside light, and then my watch. The name made no impression on me as I swung my legs out of bed and went into the sitting-room.

I was still swearing as I opened the door a little wider than was safe. Lotte Hartmann stood in the corridor, in the glistening black evening dress and astrakhan jacket I remembered her wearing from our last evening together. She had a questioning, impertinent sort of look in her eye.

'Yes?' I said. 'What is it? What do you want?'

She sniffed with cool contempt and pushed the door lightly with her gloved hand, so I stepped back into the room. She came in, closed the door behind her and, leaning on it, looked around while my nostrils got a little exercise thanks to the smell of smoke, alcohol and perfume she carried on her venal body. 'I'm sorry if I woke you up,' she said. She didn't look at me so much as the room.

'No you're not,' I said.

Now she took a little trip around the floor, peering into the bedroom and then the bathroom. She moved with an easy grace and as confidently as any woman who is used to the constant sensation of having a man's eyes fixed on her behind.

'You're right,' she grinned, 'I'm not sorry at all. You know, this place isn't as bad as I thought it would be.'

'Do you know what time it is?'

'Very late.' She giggled. 'Your landlady wasn't impressed with me at all. So I had to tell her I was your sister and that I had come all the way from Berlin to give you some bad news.' She giggled again.

'And you're it?'

She pouted for a moment. But it was just an act. She was still too amused with herself to take much umbrage. 'When she asked me if I had any luggage I said that the Russians had stolen it on the train. She was extremely sympathetic, and really rather sweet. I hope you're not going to be different.'

'Oh? I thought that's why you were here. Or are the vice squad giving you problems again?'

She ignored the insult, always supposing she had even bothered to notice it. 'Well, I was just on my way home from the Flottenbar – that's on Mariahilferstrasse, do you know it?'

I didn't say anything. I lit a cigarette and fixed it in a corner of my mouth to stop me snarling something at her.

'Anyway, it's not far from here. And I thought that I'd just drop by. You know – ' her tone grew softer and more seductive ' – I haven't had a chance to thank you properly,' she let that one hang in the air for a second, and I suddenly wished that I was wearing a dressing-gown, 'for getting me out of that little spot of bother with the Ivans.' She untied the ribbon of her jacket and let it slip to the floor. 'Aren't you even going to offer me a drink?'

'I'd say you've had enough.' But I went ahead and found a couple of glasses anyway.

'Don't you think you'd like to find that out for yourself?' She laughed easily and sat down without any hint of unsteadiness. She looked like the type who could take the stuff through the vein and still walk a chalk line without so much as a hiccup.

'Do you want anything in it?' I held a glass of vodka up as I asked the question.

'Perhaps,' she said ruminatively, 'after I've had my drink.'

I handed her the drink and put one quickly down into the pit of my stomach to hold the fort. I took another drag on my cigarette and hoped that it might fill me up enough to kick her out.

'What's the matter?' she said, almost triumphantly. 'Do I make you nervous or something?'

I guessed it was probably the something. 'Not me,' I said, 'just my pyjamas. They're not used to mixed company.'

'From the look of them I'd say they were more used to mixing concrete.' She helped herself to one of my cigarettes and blew a cord of smoke straight at my groin.

'I could get rid of them if they bothered you,' I said, stupidly. My lips were dry when they sucked at my cigarette again. Did I want her to leave or not? I wasn't making a very good job of throwing her out on her perfect little ear.

'Let's talk a little first. Why don't you sit down?'

I sat down, relieved that I could still fold in the middle.

'All right,' I said, 'how about you tell me where your boy-friend is tonight?'

She grimaced. 'Not a good subject, Perseus. Pick another.'

'You two have a rattle?'

She groaned. 'Do we have to?'

I shrugged. 'It doesn't make me itch a lot.'

'The man's a bastard,' she said, 'but I still don't want to talk about it. Especially today.'

'What's so special about today?'

'I got a part in a movie.'

'Congratulations. What's the role?'

'It's an English film. Not a very big part, you understand. But there are going to be some big stars in it. I play the role of a girl at a nightclub.'

'Well, that sounds simple enough.'

'Isn't it exciting?' she squealed. 'Me acting with Orson Welles.'

'*The War of the Worlds* fellow?'

She shrugged blankly. 'I never saw that film.'

'Forget it.'

'Of course they're not actually sure about Welles. But they think there's a good chance they can persuade him to come to Vienna.'

'That all sounds very familiar to me.'

'What's that?'

'I didn't even know you were an actress.'

'You mean I didn't tell you? Listen, that job at the Oriental is just temporary.'

'You seem pretty good at it.'

'Oh, I've always been good with numbers and money. I used to work in the local tax department.' She leaned forward and her expression became just a little too quizzical, as if she meant to question me about my year-end business expenses. 'I've been meaning to ask you,' she said, 'that night when you dropped all that mouse. What were you trying to prove?'

'Prove? I'm not sure I follow you.'

'No?' She turned her smile up a couple of stops to shoot me a knowing, conspiratorial sort of look. 'I see a lot of quirks, mister. I get to recognize the types. One day I'm even going to write a book about it. Like Franz Josef Gall. Ever hear of him?'

'I can't say that I have.'

'He was an Austrian doctor who founded the science of phrenology. Now you've heard of that, haven't you?'

'Sure,' I said. 'And what can you tell from the bumps I'm wearing on my head?'

'I can tell you're not the kind to drop that sort of money without a good reason.' She stretched an eyebrow of draughtsman's quality up her smooth forehead. 'I've got an idea about that too.'

'Let's hear it,' I urged, and poured myself another drink. 'Maybe you'll make a better go of reading my mind than you did of reading my cranium.'

'Don't act so hard to get,' she told me. 'We both know you're the kind of man that likes to make an impression.'

'And did I? Make an impression?'

'I'm here, aren't I? What do you want – Tristan and Isolde?'

So that was it. She thought that I had lost the money for her benefit. To look like a big-shot.

She drained her glass, stood up and handed it back to me. 'Pour me some more of that love potion of yours while I powder my nose.'

While she was in the bathroom I refilled the glasses with hands that were none too steady. I didn't particularly like the woman, but I had nothing against her body: it was just fine. I had an idea that my head was going to object to this little skylark when my libido had released the controls, but at that particular moment I could do nothing more than sit back and enjoy the flight. Even so, I was unprepared for what happened next.

I heard her open the bathroom door and say something ordinary about the perfume she was wearing, but when I turned round with the drinks I saw that the perfume was all that she was wearing. Actually she had kept her shoes on, but it took my eyes a little while to work their way down past her breasts and her pubic equilateral. Except for those high-heels, Lotte Hartmann was as naked as an assassin's blade, and probably just as treacherous.

She stood in the doorway of my bedroom, her hands hanging by her bare thighs, glowing with delight as my tongue licked my lips rather too obviously for me to have contemplated using it on anything but her. Maybe I could have given her a pompous little lecture at that. I'd seen enough naked women in my time, some of them in fair shape too. I ought to have tossed her back like a fish, but the sweat starting out on my palms, the flare of my nostrils, the lump in my throat and the dull, insistent ache in my groin told me that the machina had other ideas as to the next course of action than the deus which called it home.

Delighted with the effect she was having on me, Lotte smiled happily and took the glass from my hand.

'I hope you don't mind me undressing,' she said, 'only the gown is an expensive one and I had the strangest feeling that you were about to tear it off my back.'

'Why should I mind? It's not as if I haven't finished reading the evening paper. Anyway, I like having a naked woman about the place.' I watched the slight wobble of her behind as she walked lazily to the other side of the sitting-room where she swallowed her drink and dropped the empty glass on to the sofa.

Suddenly I wanted to see her bottom shaking like a jelly against the rut of my abdomen. She seemed to sense this and, bending forwards, took hold of the radiator like a wrestler pulling against the ring ropes in his corner. Then she stood with her feet a short way apart and stood quietly with her backside towards me, as if waiting for a thoroughly unnecessary body-search. She glanced back over her shoulder, flexed her buttocks and then faced the wall again.

I'd had more eloquent invitations, but with the blood buzzing in my ears and battering those few brain cells not yet affected by alcohol or adrenalin, I really couldn't remember when. Probably I didn't even care. I tore off my pyjamas and stalked after her.

I'm no longer young enough, nor quite thin enough, to share a single bed with anything other than a hangover or a cigarette. So it was perhaps a sense of surprise that woke me from an unexpectedly comfortable sleep at around six o'clock. Lotte, who might otherwise have caused me a restless night, was no longer lying in the crook of my arm and for a brief, happy moment I supposed that she must have gone home. It was then that I heard a small, stifled sob coming from the sitting-room. Reluctantly I slipped out from under the covers and into my overcoat, and went to see what was wrong.

Still naked, Lotte had made a little ball of herself on the floor by the radiator where it was warm. I squatted down beside her and asked why she was crying. A fat tear rolled down a stained cheek and hung on her top lip like a translucent wart. She licked it away and sniffed as I handed her my handkerchief.

'What do you care?' she said bitterly. 'Now that you've had your fun.'

She had a point, but I went ahead and protested, enough to be polite. Lotte heard me out and when her vanity was satisfied she tried a crippled sort of smile that reminded me of the way an unhappy child will cheer up when you hand over 50 pfennigs or a penny-chew.

'You're very sweet,' she allowed finally, and wiped her red eyes. 'I'll be all right now, thank you.'

'Do you want to tell me about it?'

Lotte glanced at me out of the corner of one eye. 'In this town? Better tell me your rates first, doctor.' She blew her nose and then uttered a short, hollow laugh. 'You might make a good screw doctor.'

'You seem quite sane to me,' I said, helping her to an arm-chair.

'I wouldn't bet on it.'

'Is that your professional advice?' I lit a couple of cigarettes and handed her one. She smoked it desperately, and without much apparent pleasure.

'That's my advice as a woman who's mad enough to have been having an affair with a man who just slapped her round like a circus clown.'

'König? I never saw him as the violent type.'

'If he seems urbane that's only the morphine he uses.'

'He's an addict?'

'I don't know if he's an addict exactly. But whatever it was he did while he was in the SS, he needed morphine to get through the war.'

'So why did he paste you?'

She bit her lip fiercely. 'Well, it wasn't because he thought I could use a little colour.'

I laughed. I had to hand it to her, she was a tough one. I said, 'Not with that tan anyway.' I picked up the astrakhan jacket from the floor where she had dropped it and draped it around

237

her shoulders. Lotte drew it close to her throat and smiled bitterly.

'Nobody puts his hand on my jaw,' she said, 'not if he ever wants to put his hand any place else. Tonight was the first and last time that he'll give me a pair of slaps, so help me.' She blew smoke from her nostrils as fiercely as a dragon. 'That's what you get when you try to help someone, I guess.'

'Help who?'

'König came into the Oriental at around ten last night,' she explained. 'He was in a foul mood and when I asked him why, he wanted to know if I remembered a dentist who used to come into the club and gamble a bit.' She shrugged. 'Well, I did remember him. A bad player but certainly not half as bad as you like to pretend you are.' Her eyes flicked at me uncertainly.

I nodded, urgently. 'Go on.'

'Helmut wanted to know if Dr Heim, the dentist, had been in the place during the last couple of days. I told him I didn't think he had. Then he wanted me to ask some of the girls if they remembered him being there. Well, there was one particular girl I said he should be sure to speak to. A bit of a hard-luck case, but pretty with it. The doctors always went for her. I guess it was because she always looked that little bit more vulnerable, and there are some men who quite like that sort of thing. It so happened she was sitting at the bar, so I pointed her out to him.'

I felt my stomach turning to quicksand. 'What was this girl's name?' I asked.

'Veronika something,' she said, and noticing my concern, added, 'Why? Do you know her?'

'A little,' I said. 'What happened then?'

'Helmut and one of his friends took Veronika next door.'

'To the hat shop?'

'Yes.' Her voice was soft now and just a little ashamed. 'Helmut's temper –' she flinched at the memory of it ' – I was worried. Veronika's a nice girl. A doofy, but nice, you know. She's had a bit of a hard life but she's got plenty of guts. Perhaps too many for her own good. I thought with Helmut the way he was, the mood he was in, it would be better for her to tell him if she knew anything or not, and to tell him quickly. He's not a very patient man. Just in case he turned nasty.' She grimaced. 'Not much of a corner to turn, when you know Helmut.'

'So I went after them. Veronika was crying when I found them. They'd already slapped her around quite hard. She'd had enough, and I told them to stop it. That was when he slapped me. Twice.' She held her cheeks as if the pain lingered with the memory. 'Then he shoved me out into the corridor and told me to mind my own business and stay out of his.'

'What happened after that?'

'I went to the Ladies, a couple of bars and came here, in that order.'

'Did you see what happened to Veronika?'

'They left with her, Helmut and the other man.'

'You mean they took her away somewhere?'

Lotte shrugged glumly. 'I guess so.'

'Where would they have taken her?' I stood up and walked into the bedroom.

'I don't know.'

'Try and think.'

'You're going after her?'

'Like you said, she's been through a lot already.' I started to dress. 'And what's more, I got her into this.'

'You. How come?'

While I finished dressing I described how, coming back from Grinzing with König, I had explained how I would have gone about trying to find a missing person, in this case Dr Heim.

'I told him how we could check Heim's usual haunts if he could tell me where they were,' I told her. But I left out how I had thought it would never have got that far: how I assumed that with Müller – possibly Nebe and König too – arrested by Belinsky and the people from Crowcass, the need actually to look for Heim would never have arisen: how I thought that I had stalled König into waiting until the meeting at Grinzing was over before we started to look for his dead dentist.

'Why should they have thought that you could find her?'

'Before the war I was a detective with the Berlin police.'

'I should have known,' she snorted.

'Not really,' I said, straightening my tie, and jabbing a

239

cigarette into my sour-tasting mouth, 'but I should certainly have known that your boyfriend was arrogant enough to go and look for Heim on his own. It was stupid of me to think that he would wait.' I climbed back into my overcoat and picked up my hat. 'Do you think they would have taken her to Grinzing?' I asked her.

'Now I come to think of it, I had the idea they were going to Veronika's room, wherever that is. But if she's not there, Grinzing would be as good a place to look as any.'

'Well, let's hope she's home.' But even as I said it, I knew in my guts that this was unlikely.

Lotte stood up. The jacket covered her chest and her upper torso, but left bare the burning bush which earlier had spoken so persuasively and left me feeling as sore as a skinned rabbit.

'What about me?' she said quietly. 'What shall I do?'

'You?' I nodded down at her nakedness. 'Put the magic away and go home.'

33

The morning was bright, clear and chilly. Crossing the park in front of the new town hall on my way to the Inner City, a couple of squirrels bounded up to say hello and check me out for breakfast. But before they got close they caught the cloud on my face and the smell of fear on my socks. Probably they even made a mental note of the heavy shape in my coat pocket and thought better of it. Smart little creatures. After all, it wasn't so very long since small mammals were being shot and eaten in Vienna. So they hurried on their way, like living scribbles of fur.

At the dump where Veronika lived they were used to people, mostly men, coming and going at all hours of the day and night, and even if the landlady had been the most misanthropic of lesbians, I doubt she would have paid me much attention if she had met me on the stairs. But as it happened there was nobody about, and I made my way up to Veronika's room unchallenged.

I didn't need to break the door in. It was wide open, just like all the drawers and cupboards. I wondered why they had bothered when all the evidence they needed was still hanging on the back of the chair where Doctor Heim had left it.

'The stupid bitch,' I muttered angrily. 'What's the point of getting rid of a man's body if you leave his suit in your room?' I slammed a drawer shut. The force dislodged one of Veronika's pathetic sketches from off the chest of drawers, and it floated to the floor like a huge dead leaf. König had probably turned the place over out of pure spite. And then taken her to Grinzing. With an important meeting there that morning I couldn't see that they would have gone anywhere else. Assuming that they didn't kill her outright. On the other hand, if Veronika told them the truth about what had happened – that a couple of friends had helped her to dispose of Heim's body after his suffering a heart attack, then (if she had omitted mentioning

Belinsky's name and my own) perhaps they would let her go. But there was a real possibility that they might still kick her around to make sure she had told them everything she knew: that by the time I arrived to try and help her I would already be exposed as the man who had dumped Heim's body.

I remembered how Veronika had told me about her life as a Sudeten Jew during wartime. How she had hid in lavatories, dirty basements, cupboards and attics. And then a DP camp for six months. 'A bit of hard life,' was how Lotte Hartmann had described it. The more I thought about it, the more it seemed to me that she'd had very little of what could properly be called life at all.

I glanced at my wristwatch and saw that it was seven o'clock. There were still three hours to go before the meeting started: longer before Belinsky could be expected with 'the cavalry', as he put it. And because the men who had taken Veronika were who they were, I began to think that there was a real possibility that she wouldn't live that long. It looked as if I had no choice but to go and get her myself.

I took out my revolver, thumbed open the six-shot cylinder and checked that it was fully loaded before heading back downstairs. Outside, I hailed a taxi at the rank on Kärtnerstrasse and told the driver to go to Grinzing.

'Whereabouts in Grinzing?' he asked, accelerating away from the kerb.

'I'll tell you when we get there.'

'You're the boss,' he said, speeding on to the Ring. 'Only reason I asked was that everything there will be shut at this time of the morning. And you don't look like you're going hill-walking. Not in that coat.' The car shuddered as we hit a couple of enormous potholes. 'And you're no Austrian. I can tell that from your accent. You sound like a *pifke*, sir. Am I right?'

'Skip the university-of-life class, will you? I'm not in the mood.'

'That's all right, sir. Only reason I asked was in case you were looking for a little bit of fun. You see, sir, only a few minutes further on from Grinzing, on the road to Cobenzl, there's this hotel – the Schloss-Hotel Cobenzl.' He wrestled with the wheel as the car hit another pothole. 'Right now it's being used as a DP camp. There's girls there you can have for just a few cigarettes. Even at this hour of the morning if you fancy it. A man wearing a good coat like yours could have two or three together maybe. Get them to put a nice show on for you between themselves if you know what I mean.' He laughed coarsely. 'Some of these girls, sir. They've grown up in DP camps. Got the morals of rabbits, so they have. They'll do anything. Believe me, sir, I know what I'm talking about. I keep rabbits myself.' He chuckled warmly at the thought of it all. 'I could arrange something for you, sir. In the back of the car. For a small commission of course.'

I leaned forwards on the seat. I don't know why I bothered with him. Maybe I just don't like garter-handlers. Maybe I just didn't much care for his Trotsky-lookalike face.

'That would be just great,' I said, very tough. 'If it weren't for a Russian table-trap I found in the Ukraine. Partisans put a tension-release grenade behind a drawer that they left half-open with a bottle of vodka in there, just to get your attention. I came along, pulled the drawer, the pressure was released and the grenade detonated. It took the meat and two vegetables clean off at my belly. I nearly died of shock, then I nearly died from loss of blood. And when finally I came out of the coma I nearly died of grief. I tell you if I so much as see a bit of plum I'm liable to go mad with the frustration of it. I'd probably kill the nearest man to me out of plain envy.'

The driver glanced back over his shoulder. 'Sorry,' he said nervously, 'I didn't mean to – '

'Forget it,' I said, almost smiling now.

When we came past the yellow house I told the driver to keep going to the top of the hill. I had decided to approach Nebe's house from the back, through the vineyards.

Because the meters on Vienna's taxis were old and out of date, it was customary to multiply the tariff shown by five to give the total sum payable. There were six schillings on the clock when I told him to stop, and this was all the driver asked me for, his hand trembling as he took the money. The car was already roaring away by the time I realized he had forgotten his arithmetic.

I stood there, on a muddy track by the side of the road, wondering why I hadn't kept my mouth shut, having intended to tell the man to wait a while. Now if I did find Veronika, I would have the problem of how to get away. Me and my smart mouth, I thought. The poor bastard was only offering a service, I told myself. But he was wrong about one thing. There was something open, a café further up Cobenzlgasse: the Rudelshof. I decided that if I was going to get shot I'd prefer to collect it with something in my stomach.

The café was a cosy little place if you didn't mind taxidermy. I sat down under the beady eye of an anthraxic-looking weasel and waited for the badly stuffed proprietor to shamble up to my table.

'God's greeting to you, sir,' he said. 'It's a lovely morning.'

I reeled away from his distilled breath. 'I can tell you're already enjoying it,' I said, using my smart mouth yet again. He shrugged, uncomprehending, and took my order.

The five-schilling Viennese breakfast I gobbled tasted like the taxidermist had cooked it during his time off between jobs: the coffee had grounds in it, the roll was about as fresh as a piece of scrimshaw and the egg was so hard it might have come from a quarry. But I ate it. I had so much on my mind I'd probably have eaten the weasel if only they'd sat it on a slice of toast.

Outside the café I walked down the road awhile and then climbed over a wall into what I thought must be Arthur Nebe's vineyard.

There wasn't much to see. The vines themselves, planted in neat rows, were still only young shoots, hardly higher than my knee. Here and there on high trolleys were what looked like abandoned jet engines but were in fact the rapid burners they used at night to heat the atmosphere around the shoots and protect them from late frost. They were still warm to the touch. The field itself was perhaps a hundred metres square and offered little in the way of cover. I wondered exactly how Belinsky would manage to deploy his men. Apart from crawling the length of the field on your belly, you could only stay close to the wall while you worked your way down to the trees immediately behind the yellow house and its outbuildings.

When I got as far as the trees I looked for some sign of life, and seeing none I edged my way forwards until I heard voices. Next to the largest of the outbuildings, a long half-timbered affair that resembled a barn, two men, neither of whom I recognized, were standing talking. Each man wore a metal drum on his back, and this was connected by a rubber hose to a long thin tube of metal he held in his hand which I presumed to be some kind of crop-spraying contraption.

At last they finished their conversation and walked towards the opposite side of the vineyard, as if to start their attack on the bacteria, fungi and insects which plagued their lives. I waited until they were well across the field before leaving the cover of the trees and entering the building.

A musty fruit smell hit my nostrils. Large oak vats and storage tanks were ranged under the open rafters of the ceiling like enormous cheeses. I walked the length of the stone floor and emerged at the other end of this first building to be faced with the door to another, built at right angles to the house.

This second outhouse contained hundreds of oak barrels, which lay on their sides as if awaiting the giant St Bernard dogs to come and collect them. Stairs led down into the darkness. It seemed like a good place to imprison someone, so I switched on the light and went downstairs to take a look. But there were only thousands of bottles of wine, each rack marked by a small blackboard on which were chalked a few numbers that must have meant something to somebody. I came back upstairs, switched off the light and stood by the barrel-room window. It was beginning to look as if Veronika might be in the house after all.

From where I was standing I had a clear view across a short cobbled yard, to the west side of the house. In front of an open door a big black cat sat staring at me. Beside the door was the window of what looked like the kitchen. There was a large, shiny shape on the kitchen ledge which I thought was probably a pot or a kettle. After a while the cat walked slowly up to the outbuilding where I was hiding and mewed loudly at something beside the window where I was standing. For a second or two it fixed me with its green eyes, and then for no apparent reason ran off. I looked back towards the house and continued to watch the kitchen door and window. After a few more minutes I judged it safe to leave the barrel room, and started across the yard.

I had not gone three paces when I heard the ratchet sound of an automatic-slide and almost simultaneously felt the cold steel of a gun muzzle pressed hard against my neck.

'Clasp your hands behind your head,' said a voice, none too distinctly.

I did as I was told. The gun pressed under my ear felt heavy enough to be a .45. Enough to dispose of a large part of my skull. I winced as he screwed the gun between my jaw and my jugular vein.

'Twitch and you're tomorrow morning's pig swill,' he said, smacking my pockets, and relieving me of my revolver.

'You'll find that Herr Nebe is expecting me,' I said.

'Don't know a Herr Nebe,' he said thickly, almost as if his mouth didn't work properly. Naturally I was reluctant to turn round and take a good look to make sure.

'Yes, that's right, he changed his name, didn't he?' I tried hard to remember Nebe's new surname. Meanwhile I heard the man behind me step back a couple of steps.

'Now walk to your right,' he told me. 'Towards the trees. And don't trip on your shoelaces or anything.'

He sounded big and not too bright. And it was a strangely accented German he spoke: like Prussian, but different; more like the Old Prussian I had heard my grandfather speak; almost like the German I had heard spoken in Poland.

'Look, you're making a mistake,' I said. 'Why don't you check with your boss? My name is Bernhard Gunther. There's a meeting at ten o'clock this morning. I'm supposed to be at it.'

'It's not even eight yet,' grunted my captor. 'If you're here for a meeting, how come you're so early? And how come you don't come to the front door like normal visitors? How come you walk across the fields? How come you snoop around in the outhouses?'

246

'I'm early because I own a couple of wineshops in Berlin,' I said. 'I thought it might be nice to take a look around the estate.'

'You were taking a look all right. You're a snooper.' He chuckled cretinously. 'I got orders to shoot snoopers.'

'Now wait a minute –' I turned into a clubbing blow from his gun, and as I fell I caught a glimpse of a big man with a shaven head and a lopsided sort of jaw. He grabbed me by the scruff of my neck and hauled me back on to my feet, and I wondered why I had never thought to sew a razor blade under that part of my coat collar. He pushed me through the line of trees and down a slope to a small clearing where several large dustbins were standing. A trail of smoke and a sweet sickly smell arose through the roof of a small brick hut: it was where they incinerated the rubbish. Next to several bags of what looked like cement, a sheet of rusting corrugated iron lay on some bricks. The man ordered me to draw it aside.

Now I had it. He was a Latvian. A big, stupid Latvian. And I decided that if he was working for Arthur Nebe he was probably from a Latvian SS division, that had served in one of the Polish death camps. They had used a lot of Latvians at places like Auschwitz. Latvians were enthusiastic anti-Semites when Moses Mendelssohn was one of Germany's favourite sons.

I hauled the iron sheet away from what was revealed as some kind of old drain, or cesspit. Certainly it smelt every bit as bad. It was then that I saw the cat again. It emerged from between two paper sacks labelled calcium oxide close by the pit. It mewed contemptuously, as if to say, 'I warned you there was someone standing in that yard, but you wouldn't listen to me.' An acrid, chalky smell came up from the pit and made my skin crawl. 'You're right,' mewed the cat, like something from Edgar Allan Poe, 'calcium oxide is a cheap alkali for treating acid soil. Just the sort of thing you would expect to see in a vineyard. But it's also called quicklime, and that's an extremely efficient compound for speeding human decomposition.'

With horror I realized that the Latvian really did mean to kill me. And there I was trying to place his accent like some sort of philologist, and to recall the chemical formulas I had learned at school.

Then I got my first good look at him. He was big and as burly as a circus horse, but you hardly noticed that for looking at his face: its whole right side was crooked like he had a big chew of tobacco in his cheek; his right eye stared wide as if it had been made of glass. He could probably have kissed his own earlobe. Starved of affection, as any man with such a face would have been, he probably had to.

'Kneel down by the side of the pit,' he snarled, sounding like a Neanderthal short of a couple of vital chromosomes.

'You're not going to kill an old comrade, are you?' I said desperately trying to remember Nebe's new name, or even one of the Latvian regiments. I considered shouting for help except that I knew he would have shot me without hesitation.

'You're an old comrade?' he sneered, without much apparent difficulty.

'Obersturmführer with the First Latvian,' I said with a poor show of nonchalance.

The Latvian spat into the bushes and regarded me blankly with his pop eye. The gun, a big blue steel Colt automatic, remained pointed squarely at my chest.

'First Latvian, eh? You don't sound like a Lat.'

'I'm Prussian,' I said. 'Our family lived in Riga. My father was a shipworker from Danzig. He married a Russian.' I offered a few words of Russian by way of confirmation, although I could not remember if Riga was predominantly Russian or German-speaking.

His eyes narrowed, one rather more than the other. 'So what year was the First Latvian founded?'

I swallowed hard and racked my memory. The cat mewed encouragingly. Reasoning that the raising of a Latvian SS regiment would have to have followed Operation Barbarossa in 1941, I said, '1942.'

He grinned horribly, and shook his head with slow sadism. '1943,' he said, advancing a couple of paces. 'It was 1943. Now get down on your knees or I'll give it to you in the guts.'

Slowly I sank down on my knees on the edge of the pit, feeling the ground wet through the material of my trousers. I had seen more than enough of SS murder to know what he intended: a

248

shot in the back of the neck, my body collapsing neatly into a ready-made grave, and a few spadefuls of quicklime on top. He came around behind me in a wide circle. The cat settled down to watch, its tail wrapping neatly around its behind as it sat. I closed my eyes and waited.

'Rainis,' said a voice, and several seconds passed. I hardly dared to look around and see if I had been saved.

'It's all right, Bernie. You can get up now.'

My breath came out in one huge burp of fright. Weakly, my knees knocking, I picked myself up from the edge of the pit and turned to see Arthur Nebe standing a few metres behind the Latvian ugly. To my annoyance he was grinning.

'I'm glad you find it so amusing, Dr Frankenstein,' I said. 'Your fucking monster nearly killed me.'

'What on earth were you thinking of, Bernie?' Nebe said. 'You should know better. Rainis here was only doing his job.'

The Latvian nodded sullenly and holstered his Colt. 'He was snooping,' he said dully. 'I caught him.'

I shrugged. 'It's a nice morning. I thought I'd take a look at Grinzing. I was just admiring your estate when Lon Chaney here stuck a gun in my ear.'

The Latvian took my revolver out of his jacket pocket and handed it to Nebe. 'He was carrying a lighter, Herr Nolde.'

'Planning to shoot small game, is that it, Bernie?'

'You can't be too careful these days.'

'I'm glad you think so,' said Nebe. 'It saves me the trouble of apologizing.' He weighed my gun in his hand and then pocketed it. 'All the same, I'll hang on to this for now if you don't mind. Guns make some of our friends nervous. Remind me to return it to you before you leave.' He turned to the Latvian.

'All right, Rainis, that's all. You were only doing your job. I suggest that you go and get yourself some breakfast.'

The monster nodded and walked back towards the house, with the cat following him.

'I'll bet he can eat his weight in peanuts.'

Nebe smiled thinly. 'Some people keep savage dogs to protect them. I have Rainis.'

'Yes, well I hope he's house-trained.' I took off my hat and wiped my brow with my handkerchief. 'Me, I wouldn't let him past the front door. I'd keep him on a chain in the yard. Where does he think he is? Treblinka? The bastard couldn't wait to shoot me, Arthur.'

'Oh, I don't doubt it. He enjoys killing people.'

Nebe shook his head to my offer of a cigarette, but he had to help me light mine as my hand was shaking like it was talking to a deaf Apache.

'He's a Latvian,' Nebe explained. 'He was a corporal at the Riga concentration camp. When the Russians captured him they stamped on his head and broke his jaw with their boots.'

'Believe me, I know how they must have felt.'

'They paralysed half his face, and left him slightly soft in the head. He was always a brutal killer. But now he's more like an animal. And just as loyal as any dog.'

'Well, naturally I was thinking he'd have his good points too. Riga eh?' I jerked my head at the open pit and the incinerator. 'I bet that little waste-disposal set-up makes him feel quite at home.' I sucked gratefully at my cigarette and added, 'If it comes to that, I bet it makes you both feel at home.'

Nebe frowned. 'I think you need a drink,' he said quietly.

'I wouldn't be at all surprised. Just make sure it doesn't have any lime in it. I think I lost my taste for lime, for ever.'

34

I followed Nebe into the house and up to the library where we had talked the day before. He fetched me a brandy from the drinks-cabinet and set it down on the table in front of me.

'Forgive me for not joining you,' he said, watching me down it quickly. 'Normally I quite enjoy a cognac with my breakfast but this morning I must keep a clear head.' He smiled indulgently as I replaced the empty glass on the table. 'Better now?'

I nodded. 'Tell me, have you found your missing dentist yet? Dr Heim?' Now that I no longer had to worry about my own immediate prospects for survival, Veronika was once again at the front of my mind.

'He's dead, I'm afraid. That's bad enough, but it's not half as bad as not knowing what had happened to him was. At least we now know that the Russians haven't got him.'

'What did happen to him?'

'He had a heart attack.' Nebe uttered the familiar, dry little laugh I remembered from my days at the Alex, the headquarters of Berlin's criminal police. 'It seems that he was with a girl at the time. A chocolady.'

'You mean it was while they were – ?'

'I mean precisely that. Still, I can think of worse ways to go, can't you?'

'After what I've just been through, that's not particularly difficult for me, Arthur.'

'Quite.' He smiled almost sheepishly.

I spent a moment searching for a frame of words that might enable me to innocently inquire as to Veronika's fate. 'So what did she do? The chocolady, I mean. Phone the police?' I frowned. 'No, I expect not.'

'Why do you say that?'

I shrugged at the apparent simplicity of my explanation. 'I can't imagine she'd have risked a run-in with the vice squad.

No, I'll bet she tried to have him dumped somewhere. Got her garter-handler to do it.' I raised my eyebrows questioningly. 'Well? Am I right?'

'Yes, you're right.' He sounded almost as if he admired my thinking. 'As usual.' Then he uttered a wistful sort of sigh. 'What a pity that we're no longer with Kripo. I can't tell you how much I miss it all.'

'Me too.'

'But you, you could rejoin. Surely you're not wanted for anything, Bernie?'

'And work for the Communists? No thanks.' I pursed my lips and tried to look rueful. 'Anyway, I'd rather stay out of Berlin for a while. A Russian soldier tried to rob me on a train. It was self-defence, but I'm afraid I killed him. I was seen leaving the scene of the crime covered in blood.'

'"The scene of the crime",' quoted Nebe, rolling the phrase round his mouth like a fine wine. 'It's good to talk to a detective again.'

'Just to satisfy my professional curiosity, Arthur: how did you find the chocolady?'

'Oh, it wasn't me, it was König. He tells me that it was you who told him how best to go about looking for poor Heim.'

'It was just routine stuff, Arthur. You could have told him.'

'Maybe so. Anyway, it seems that König's girlfriend recognized Heim from a photograph. Apparently he used to frequent the nightclub where she works. She remembered that Heim used to be especially keen on one of the snappers who worked there. All Helmut had to do was persuade her to come clean about it. It was as simple as that.'

'Getting information out of a snapper is never "as simple as that",' I said. 'It can be like getting a curse out of a nun. Money is the only way to get a party-girl to talk that doesn't leave a bruise.' I waited for Nebe to contradict me, but he said nothing. 'Of course, a bruise is cheaper, and leaves no margin for error.' I grinned at him as if to say that I had no particular scruples when it came to slapping a chocolady in the interests of efficient investigation. 'I'd say König wasn't the type to waste money: am I right?'

To my disappointment, Nebe merely shrugged and then glanced at his watch. 'You'd better ask him yourself when you see him.'

'Is he coming to this meeting too?'

'He'll be here.' Nebe consulted his watch again. 'I'm afraid I have to leave you now. I've still one or two things to do before ten. Perhaps it would be better if you stayed in here. Security is tight today, and we wouldn't want another incident, would we? I'll have someone bring you some coffee. Build a fire if you like. It's rather cold in here.'

I tapped my glass. 'I can't say that I'm noticing it much now.'

Nebe regarded me patiently. 'Yes, well, do help yourself to some more brandy, if you think you need it.'

'Thanks,' I said, reaching for the decanter, 'I don't mind if I do.'

'But stay sharp. You'll be asked a lot of questions about your Russian friend. I wouldn't like your opinion of his worth to be doubted merely because you had too much to drink.' He walked across the creaking floor to the door.

'Don't worry about me,' I said, surveying the empty shelves, 'I'll read a book.'

Nebe's considerable nose wrinkled with disapproval. 'Yes, it's such a pity that the library is gone. Apparently the previous owners left a superb collection, but when the Russians came they used them all as fuel for the boiler.' He shook his head sadly. 'What can you do with subhumans like that?'

When Nebe had left the library I did as he had suggested and built a fire in the grate. It helped me to focus my mind on my next course of action. As the flames took hold of the small edifice of logs and sticks I had constructed, I reflected that Nebe's apparent amusement at the circumstances of Heim's death seemed to indicate that the Org was satisfied Veronika had told the truth.

It was true, I was no wiser as to where she might be, but I had gained the impression that König was not yet at Grinzing, and without my gun I did not see that I could now leave and look for her elsewhere. With only two hours to go before the Org's meeting, it appeared that my best course of action was to wait for König to arrive, and hope that he could put my mind at rest. And if he had killed or injured Veronika, I would settle his account personally when Belinsky arrived with his men.

I collected the poker off the hearth and stoked the fire negligently. Nebe's man arrived with the coffee, but I paid him no attention, and after he had gone again I stretched out on the sofa and closed my eyes.

The fire stirred, clapped its hands a couple of times, and warmed my side. Behind my closed lids, bright red turned to deep purple, and then something more restful . . .

'Herr Gunther?'

I jerked my head up from the sofa. Sleeping in an awkward position, even for only a few minutes, had made my neck as stiff as new leather. But when I looked at my watch I saw that I had been sleeping for more than an hour. I flexed my neck.

Sitting beside the sofa was a man wearing a grey flannel suit. He leaned forward and held out his hand for me to shake. It was a broad, strong hand and surprisingly firm for such a short man. Gradually I recognized his face, although I had never met him before.

'I am Dr Moltke,' he said. 'I've heard a great deal about you, Herr Gunther.' You could have blown froth from the top of his accent it was so Bavarian.

I nodded uncertainly. There was something about his gaze I found deeply disconcerting. His were the eyes of a music-hall hypnotist.

'I'm pleased to meet you, Herr Doktor.' Here was another one who had changed his name. Another one who was supposed to be dead, like Arthur Nebe. And yet this was no ordinary Nazi fugitive from justice, if indeed justice existed anywhere in Europe during 1948. It gave me a strange feeling to consider that I had just shaken hands with a man who, but for the mysterious circumstances surrounding his 'death', might well have been the world's most wanted man. This was 'Gestapo' Heinrich Müller, in person.

'Arthur Nebe has been telling me about you,' he said. 'You know, you and I are quite alike it seems. I was a police detective,

254

like yourself. I began on the beat and I learnt my profession in the hard school of ordinary police work. Like you I also specialized: while you worked for the murder commission, I was led to the surveillance of Communist Party functionaries. I even made a special study of Soviet Russian police methods. I found much there to admire. As a policeman yourself, you would surely appreciate their professionalism. The MVD, which used to be the NKVD, is probably the finest secret police force anywhere in the world. Better even than the Gestapo. For the simple reason, I think, that National Socialism was never able to offer a faith capable of commanding such a consistent attitude towards life. And do you know why?'

I shook my head. His broad Bavarian speech seemed to suggest a natural geniality which I knew the man himself could not possibly have possessed.

'Because, Herr Gunther, unlike Communism, we never really appealed to the intellectuals as well as to the working classes. You know, I myself did not join the Party until 1939. Stalin does these things better. Today I see him in quite a different light than I did of old.'

I frowned, wondering whether this was Müller's idea of a test, or a joke. But he seemed to be perfectly serious. Pompously so.

'You admire Stalin?' I asked, almost incredulously.

'He stands head and shoulders above any of our Western leaders. Even Hitler was a small man by comparison. Just think what Stalin and his Party have stood up to. You were in one of their camps. You know what they're like. Why, you even speak Russian. You always know where you are with the Ivans. They put you up against a wall and shoot you, or they give you the Order of Lenin. Not like the Americans or the British.' Müller's face suddenly took on an expression of intense dislike. 'They talk about morality and justice and yet they allow Germany to starve. They write about ethics and yet they hang old comrades one day, and recruit them for their own security services the next. You can't trust people like that, Herr Gunther.'

'Forgive me, Herr Doktor, but I was under the impression that we were working for the Americans.'

'That is wrong. We work *with* the Americans. But in the end we are working *for* Germany. For a new Fatherland.'

Looking more thoughtful now, he got up and went over to the window. His manner of expressing deliberation was a silent rhapsody more characteristic of a peasant priest wrestling with his conscience. He folded his thick hands thoughtfully, unclasped them again and finally pressed his temples between both fists.

'There is nothing to admire in America. Not like Russia. But the Amis do have power. And what gives them this power is the dollar. That is the only reason why we must oppose Russia. We need the American dollars. All that the Soviet Union can give us is an example: an example of just what loyalty and dedication can achieve, even without money. So then, think what Germans might do with similar devotion and American cash.'

I tried and failed to stifle a yawn. 'Why are you telling me this Herr – Herr Doktor?' For one ghastly second I had almost called him Herr Müller. Did anyone but Arthur Nebe, and perhaps von Bolschwing, who had interrogated me, know who Moltke really was?

'We are working for a new tomorrow, Herr Gunther. Germany may be divided between them now. But there will come a time when we are a great power again. A great economic power. So long as our Organization works alongside the Amis to oppose Communism, they will be persuaded to allow Germany to rebuild herself. And with our industry and our technology we shall achieve what Hitler could never have achieved. And what Stalin – yes, even Stalin with his massive five-year plans – what he can still only dream of. The German may never rule militarily, but he can do it economically. It is the mark, not the swastika, that will conquer Europe. You doubt what I say?'

If I looked surprised it was only because the idea of German industry being on top of anything but a scrapheap seemed perfectly ludicrous.

'It's just that I wonder if everyone in the Org thinks the same way as you?'

He shrugged. 'Not precisely, no. There are a variety of opinions as to the worth of our allies, and the evil of our enemies. But all are agreed on one thing, and that is the new Germany. Whether it takes five years, or fifty-five years.'

Absently, Müller started to pick his nose. It occupied him for several seconds, after which he inspected his thumb and forefinger and then wiped them on Nebe's curtains. It was, I considered, a poor indicator of the new Germany he had been speaking of.

'Anyway, I just wanted this opportunity to thank you personally for your initiative. I've had a good look at the documents that your friend has provided, and there's no doubt in my mind – it's first-class material. The Americans will be beside themselves with excitement when they see it.'

'I'm pleased to hear it.'

Müller strolled back to his chair by my sofa and sat down again. 'How confident are you that he can carry on providing this sort of high-grade material?'

'Very confident, Herr Doktor.'

'Excellent. You know, this couldn't have come along at a better time. The South German Industries Utilization Company is applying to the American State Department for increased funding. Your man's information will be an important part of that case. At this morning's meeting I shall be recommending that the exploitation of this new source be given top priority here in Vienna.'

He collected the poker off the hearth and jabbed violently at the glowing embers of the fire. It wasn't too difficult to imagine him doing the same to some human subject. Staring into the flames, he added: 'With a matter of such personal interest to me, I have a favour to ask, Herr Gunther.'

'I'm listening, Herr Doktor.'

'I must confess I had hoped to persuade you to let me run this informer myself.'

I thought for a minute. 'Naturally I should have to ask his opinion. He trusts me. It might take a little time.'

'Of course.'

'And as I told Nebe, he'll want money. Lots of it.'

'You can tell him I'll organize everything. A Swiss bank account. Whatever he wants.'

'Right now what he wants most is a Swiss watch,' I said, improvising. 'A Doxas.'

'No problem,' Müller grinned. 'You see what I mean about the Russian? He knows exactly what he wants. A nice watch. Well, leave that to me.' Müller replaced the poker on its stand and sat back contentedly. 'Then I can assume you have no objections to my proposal? Naturally you will be well-rewarded for bringing us such an important informer.'

'Since you mention it, I do have a figure in mind,' I said.

Müller raised his hands and beckoned me to name it.

'You may or may not know that I suffered a heavy loss at cards quite recently. I lost most of my money, about 4,000 schillings. I thought that you might like to make that up to 5,000.'

He pursed his lips and started nodding slowly. 'That sounds not unreasonable. In the circumstances.'

I smiled. It amused me that Müller was so concerned to protect his area of expertise within the Org that he was willing to buy me out of my involvement with Belinsky's Russian. It was easy to see that in this way the reputation of Gestapo Müller as the authority on all matters relating to the MVD would be ensured. He slapped both his knees decisively.

'Good. I'm glad that's settled. I've enjoyed our little chat. We'll talk again after this morning's meeting.'

We certainly will, I said to myself. Only it would probably be at the Stiftskaserne, or wherever the Crowcass people were likely to interrogate Müller.

'Of course we'll have to discuss the procedure for contacting your source. Arthur tells me you already have a dead-letter arrangement.'

'It's all written down,' I said to him. 'I'm sure you'll find everything is in order.' I glanced at my watch and saw that it was already past ten o'clock. I got up and straightened my tie.

'Oh, don't worry,' Müller said, clapping me on the shoulder. He seemed almost jovial now that he had got what he wanted. 'They will wait for us, I can assure you.'

But almost at the same moment the library door opened and the slightly irritated face of the Baron von Bolschwing peered into the room. He raised his wristwatch significantly and said, 'Herr Doktor, we really must get on now.'

'It's all right,' Müller boomed, 'we've finished. You can tell everyone to come in now.'

'Thank you very much.' But the Baron's voice was peevish.

'Meetings,' sneered Müller. 'One after another in this organization. There's no end to the pain of it. Like wiping your arse with a car tyre. It's as if Himmler were still alive.'

I smiled. 'That reminds me. I have to hit the spot.'

'It's just along the corridor,' he said.

I went to the door, excusing myself first to the Baron and then to Arthur Nebe as I shouldered past the men coming into the library. These were Old Comrades all right. Men with hard eyes, flabby smiles, well-fed stomachs and a certain arrogance, as if none of them had ever lost a war or done anything for which they ought to have been in any way ashamed. This was the collective face of the new Germany that Müller had droned on about.

But of König there was still no sign.

In the sour-smelling toilet I bolted the door carefully, checked my watch and stood at the window trying to see the road beyond the trees at the side of the house. With the wind stirring the leaves it was difficult to distinguish anything very clearly, but in the distance I thought that I could just about make out the fender of a big black car.

I reached for the cord of the blind and, hoping that the thing was attached to the wall rather more firmly than the blind in my own bathroom back in Berlin, I pulled it gently down for five seconds, then let it roll up again for another five seconds. When I had done this three times as arranged, I waited for Belinsky's signal and felt very relieved when I heard three blasts of a car horn from far away. Then I flushed the toilet, and opened the door.

Halfway back along the corridor leading back to the library I saw König's dog. He stood in the middle of the corridor sniffing the air and regarding me with something like recognition. Then he turned away and trotted downstairs. I didn't think there was a quicker way of finding König than by letting his crapper do it for me. So I followed.

At a door on the ground floor the dog stopped and whined a little bark. As soon as I opened it, he was off again, scampering along another corridor towards the back of the house. He stopped once more and made a show of trying to burrow under another door, to what looked like the cellar. For several seconds I hesitated to open it, but when the dog barked I decided that it was wiser to let him through rather than risk that the noise would summon König. I turned the handle, pushed, and, when the door didn't budge, pulled. It came towards me with only a gentle creak, largely concealed by what sounded at first like a cat mewing somewhere down in the cellar. Cool air and the horrible realization that this was no cat touched my face, and I felt myself shiver involuntarily. Then the dog twisted round the edge of the door and disappeared down the bare wooden stairs.

Even before I had tiptoed to the bottom of the flight, where a large rack of wine concealed me from immediate discovery, I had recognized the painful voice as belonging to Veronika. The scene required very little analysis. She was sitting in a chair, stripped to the waist, her face deathly pale. A man sat immediately in front of her; his sleeves were rolled up and he was torturing her knee with some bloodstained metal object. König stood behind her, steadying the chair and periodically stifling her screams with a length of rag.

There was no time to worry about my lack of a gun, and it was fortunate that König was momentarily distracted by the arrival of his dog. 'Lingo,' he said looking down at the brute, 'how did you get down here? I thought I locked you out.' He bent down to pick the dog up and in the same moment I stepped smartly round the wine rack and ran forwards.

The man in the chair was still in his seat as I clapped both his ears with my cupped hands as hard as I could. He screamed and fell on to the floor, clutching both sides of his head and writhing desperately as he tried to contain the pain of what were almost certainly burst eardrums. It was then that I saw what he

260

had been doing to Veronika. Sticking out of her knee joint at a right angle was a corkscrew.

König's gun was even now halfway out of his shoulder-holster. I leaped at him, punched hard at his exposed armpit and then chopped him across the upper lip with the edge of my hand. The two blows together were enough to disable him. He staggered back from Veronika's chair, blood pouring from his nose. I needn't have hit him again, but now that his hand no longer covered her mouth, her loud cries of excruciating pain persuaded me to deliver a third, more vicious blow with my forearm, aimed at the centre of his sternum. He was unconscious before he hit the ground. Immediately the dog stopped its furious barking and set about trying to revive him with its tongue.

I picked König's gun off the floor, slipped it into my trouser pocket and quickly started untying Veronika. 'It's all right,' I said, 'we're getting out of here. Belinsky will be here any minute with the police.'

I tried not to look at the mess they had made of her knee. She moaned pitiably as I pulled the last of the cords away from her bloodstained legs. Her skin was cold and she was shaking all over, clearly going into shock. But when I took off my jacket and put it about her shoulders, she held my hand firmly and said through gritted teeth, 'Get it out, for God's sake get it out of my knee.'

With one eye on the cellar stairs in case one of Nebe's men should come looking for me now that my presence upstairs was overdue, I knelt down in front of her and surveyed the wound and the instrument that had caused it. It was an ordinary-looking corkscrew, with a wooden handle now sticky with blood. The sharp business end had been screwed into the side of her knee-joint to a depth of several millimetres, and there seemed no way of removing it without causing her almost as much pain as had been caused by screwing it in. The slightest touch of the handle made her cry out.

'Please take it out,' she urged, sensing my indecision.

'All right,' I said, 'but hold on to the seat of your chair. This is going to hurt.' I drew the other chair close enough to prevent her kicking me in the groin and sat down. 'Ready?' She closed her eyes and nodded.

The first anti-clockwise twist turned her face a bright shade of scarlet. Then she screamed, with every particle of air in her lungs. But with the second twist, mercifully she passed out. I surveyed the thing in my hand for a brief second and then hurled it at the man whose ears I had boxed. Lying in a corner, breathing stertorously between groans, Veronika's torturer looked to be in a bad way. The blow had been a cruel one, and although I had never used it before, I knew from my army training that sometimes it even caused a fatal brain haemorrhage.

Veronika's knee was bleedily heavily. I searched around for something with which to bandage her wound, and decided to make do with the shirt of the man I had deafened. I went over to him and tore it off his back.

Having folded the body of the shirt, I pressed it hard against the knee and then used the sleeves to tie it tightly. When the dressing was finished it was a good looking piece of first-aid work. But her breathing had turned shallow now, and I didn't doubt that she would need a stretcher out of there.

By this time, almost fifteen minutes had elapsed since my signal to Belinsky, and yet there was no sound that anything had yet happened. How long could it take his men to move in? I hadn't heard so much as a shout to indicate that they might have encountered some resistance. With people like the Latvian around, it seemed too much to expect that Müller and Nebe could have been arrested without a fight.

König moaned and moved his leg feebly like a swatted insect. I kicked the dog aside and bent down to take a look at him. The skin underneath his moustache had turned a dark, livid colour, and from the amount of blood that had rolled down his cheeks, I judged that I had probably separated his nose cartilage from the upper section of his jaw.

'I guess it'll be a while before you enjoy another cigar,' I said grimly.

I took König's Mauser out of my pocket and checked the breech. Through the inspection hole I saw the familiar glint of a centre-fire cartridge. One in the chamber. I hauled out the magazine and saw another six neatly ranged like so many cigarettes. I slammed the magazine back up the handle with the heel of my hand and thumbed back the hammer. It was time to find out what had happened to Belinsky.

I went back up the cellar stairs, waited behind the door for a moment and listened. Briefly I thought I heard breathing and then realized that it was my own. I brought the gun up beside my head, slipped the safety off with my thumbnail, and came through the door.

For a split second I saw the Latvian's black cat, and then felt what seemed like the whole ceiling collapsing on top of me. I heard a small popping noise like a champagne cork, and almost laughed as I realized that it was all the sound of the gun firing involuntarily in my hand that my concussed brain was able to decode. Stunned like a landed salmon I lay on the floor. My body hummed like a telephone cable. Too late I remembered that for a big man the Latvian was remarkably light on his feet. He knelt down beside me, grinned into my face before wielding the cosh again.

Then the darkness came.

35

There was a message waiting for me. It was written in capital letters as if to emphasize its importance. I struggled to make my eyes focus, only the message kept moving. Blearily, I picked out the individual letters. It was laborious, but I had no choice. Finally I pieced the letters together. The message read: 'CARE USA'. It seemed important somehow, although I failed to understand why. But then I saw that this was only one part of the message, and the second half at that. I swallowed nauseously and struggled through the first part of the message, which was coded: 'GR.WT 26lbs. CU.FT. o' 10".' What could it all mean? I was still trying to understand the code when I heard footsteps and then the sound of a key turning in the lock.

My head cleared agonizingly as I was hauled up by two pairs of strong hands. One of the men kicked the empty cardboard Care package out of the way as they frogmarched me through the doorway.

My neck and shoulder were hurting so bad that my skin turned to gooseflesh the second they held me under my arms, which I now realized were handcuffed in front of me. I retched desperately and tried to get back on to the floor where I had felt comparatively comfortable. But I remained supported and struggling merely made the pain more intense; and so I allowed myself to be dragged along a short, damp passageway, past a couple of broken barrels and up some steps to a big oak vat. The two men sat me roughly in a chair.

A voice, Müller's voice, told them to give me some wine. 'I want him to be fully conscious when we question him.'

Someone put a glass to my lips, and tilted my head painfully. I drank. When the glass was empty I could taste blood in my mouth. I spat in front of me, I didn't care where. 'Cheap stuff,' I heard myself croak. 'Cooking wine.'

Müller laughed, and I turned my head towards the sound. The bare lightbulbs burned only dimly but even so they managed to hurt my eyes. I squeezed the lids hard shut, and then opened them again.

'Good,' said Müller. 'You've still got something left in you. You'll need it to answer all my questions, Herr Gunther, I can assure you.'

Müller was sitting on a chair with his legs crossed and his arms folded. He looked like a man who was about to watch an audition. Seated beside him, and looking rather less relaxed than the former Gestapo chief, was Nebe. Next to him sat König, wearing a clean shirt, and holding his nose and mouth with a handkerchief as if he had a bad attack of hayfever. On the stone floor at their feet lay Veronika. She was unconscious, and but for the bandage round her knee quite naked. Like me she was also handcuffed, although her pallor indicated that this was an entirely redundant precaution.

I turned my head to the right. A few metres away stood the Latvian and another thug whom I hadn't seen before. The Latvian was grinning excitedly, no doubt in anticipation of my further humiliation.

We were in the largest of the outhouses. Beyond the windows the night looked in on the proceedings with dark indifference. Somewhere I could hear the low throb of a generator. It hurt to move my head or my neck, and it was actually more comfortable to look back at Müller.

'Ask anything you like,' I said, 'you'll get nothing out of me.' But even as I spoke I knew that in Müller's expert hands there was no more chance of my not telling him everything than there was of me naming the next Pope.

He found my bravado sufficiently absurd as to laugh and shake his head. 'It's quite a few years since I conducted an interrogation,' he said with what sounded like nostalgia. 'However, I think you'll find that I haven't lost my touch.' Müller looked to Nebe and König as if seeking their approbation, and each man nodded grimly.

'I bet you won prizes for it, you half-sized bastard.'

At this utterance, the Latvian was prompted to strike me hard across the cheek. The sudden jerk of my head sent an agonizing pain down to my toenails and made me cry out.

'No, no, Rainis,' Müller said like a father to a child, 'we

must allow Herr Gunther to talk. He may insult us now, but eventually he will tell us what we want to hear. Please don't hit him again unless I order you to do it.'

Nebe spoke. 'It's no use, Bernie. Fräulein Zartl has now told us all about how you and this American fellow disposed of poor Heim's body. I wondered why you were so inquisitive about her. Now we know.'

'In fact we now know a great deal,' said Müller. 'While you have been having a nap, Arthur here posed as a policeman in order to gain access to your rooms.' He smiled smugly. 'It wasn't too difficult for him. Austrians are such docile, law-abiding people. Arthur, tell Herr Gunther what you discovered.'

'Your photographs, Heinrich. I imagine that the American must have given them to him. What do you say, Bernie?'

'Go to hell.'

Nebe continued, unperturbed. 'There was also a drawing of Martin Albers' headstone. You remember that unfortunate business, Herr Doktor?'

'Yes,' said Müller, 'that was very careless of Max.'

'I dare say you must have guessed that Max Abs and Martin Albers were one and the same person, Bernie. He was an old-fashioned, rather sentimental kind of man. He just couldn't pretend to be dead like the rest of us. No, he had to have a stone to commemorate his passing, to make it look respectable. Really, a typical Viennese, wouldn't you say? I should think you were probably the person who tipped off the MPs in Munich that Max was due to arrive there. Of course, you weren't to know that Max was carrying several sets of papers and travel warrants. You see, documents were Max's speciality. He was a master forger. As the former head of SD clandestine operations section in Budapest, he was one of the very best in his field.'

'I suppose he was another bogus conspirator against Hitler,' I said. 'Another fake entry on the list of all those who were executed. Just like you, Arthur. I have to hand it to you: you've been very clever.'

'That was Max's idea,' said Nebe. 'Ingenious, yes, but with König's help not very difficult to organize. You see, König commanded the execution squad at Plotzensee, and hanged conspirators by the hundreds. He supplied all the details.'

'As well as the butcher's hooks and piano wire, no doubt.'

'Herr Gunther,' said König indistinctly through the handkerchief he kept pressed to his nose, 'I hope to be able to do the same for you.'

Müller frowned. 'We're wasting time,' he said briskly. 'Nebe told your landlady that the Austrian police thought you had been kidnapped by the Russians. After that she was most helpful. Apparently your rooms are being paid for by Dr Ernst Liebl. This man is now known to us as Emil Becker's advocate at law. Nebe is of the opinion that you were retained by him to come to Vienna and attempt to clear him of the murder of Captain Linden. I myself am of this opinion. Everything fits, so to speak.'

Müller nodded at one of the uglies, who stepped forward and collected up Veronika in his pylon-sized arms. She made no movement, and but for her breathing which became louder and more difficult as her head lolled back on her neck, one might have thought that she was dead. She looked as if they had drugged her.

'Why don't you leave her out of this, Müller,' I said. 'I'll tell you whatever it is you want to know.'

Müller pretended to look puzzled. 'That surely is what remains to be seen.' He stood up, as did Nebe and König. 'Bring Herr Gunther along, Rainis.'

The Latvian hauled me to my feet. Just the effort of being made to stand made me feel suddenly faint. He dragged me a few metres to the side of a sunken circular oak vat which was of the dimensions of a good-sized fish-pond. The vat itself was joined to a rectangular steel plate which had two wooden semi-circular wings like the leaves of a large dining table, by a thick steel column which went up to the ceiling. The thug carrying Veronika stepped down in the vat and laid her on the bottom. Then he got out and drew down the two oak leaves of the plate to form a perfect, deadly circle.

'This is a wine press,' Müller said matter-of-factly.

I struggled weakly in the Latvian's big arms, but there was

nothing I could do. It felt like my shoulder or collarbone was broken. I called them several filthy words and Müller nodded approvingly.

'Your concern for this young woman is encouraging,' he said.

'It was her you were looking for this morning,' said Nebe. 'When you walked into Rainis, wasn't it?'

'Yes, all right, it was. Now let her go, for God's sake. I give you my word, Arthur, she knows absolutely nothing.'

'Yes, that's true,' Müller admitted. 'Or at least not much. So König tells me anyway, and he is a most persuasive person. But you'll be flattered to learn that she still managed to conceal the part which you played in Heim's disappearance for quite a while. Isn't that so, Helmut?'

'Yes, General.'

'But in the end she told us everything,' Müller continued. 'Even before your impossibly heroic arrival on the scene. She told us that you and she had enjoyed a sexual relationship, and that you had been kind to her. Which was why she had asked you for help when it came to getting rid of Heim's body. Which was why you came looking for her when König took her away. Incidentally, I must compliment you. You killed one of Nebe's men quite expertly. It's a great pity that a man of your formidable skills will never work for our Organization after all. But a number of things remain a puzzle, and I expect you, Herr Gunther, to enlighten us.' He glanced around and saw that the man who had laid Veronika into the vat was now standing by a small panel of electric switches on the wall.

'Do you know anything about making wine?' he asked, walking round the vat. 'The crushing, as the word suggests, is the process whereby the grape is squeezed, bursting its skin and releasing the juice. As you will no doubt be aware it was once done by treading the grapes in huge casks. But most modern presses are pneumatic or electrically operated machines. The crushing is repeated several times, and thus is an indication of the quality of the wine, with the first press being the best of all. Once every bit of juice has been squeezed out, the residue – I believe Nebe calls it "the cake" – is supplied to a distillery; or, as is the case on this small estate, it is turned into fertilizer.'

Müller looked across at Arthur Nebe. 'There, Arthur, did I get that right?'

Nebe smiled indulgently. 'Perfectly right, Herr General.'

'I hate to mislead anyone,' Müller said with good humour. 'Even a man who is going to die.' He paused and looked down into the vat. 'Of course at this precise moment it is not your life which is the most pressing issue, if I may be permitted that one tasteless little joke.'

The big Latvian guffawed in my ear, and my head was suddenly enveloped with the stink of his garlicky breath.

'So I advise you to make your answers quickly and accurately, Herr Gunther. Fräulein Zartl's life depends on it.' He nodded at the man by the control panel who pressed a button which initiated a mechanical noise, gradually increasing in pitch.

'Don't think too harshly of us,' said Müller. 'These are hard times. There are shortages of everything. If we had any sodium pentathol we should give it to you. We should even look to buy it on the black market. But I think you'll agree that this method is every bit as effective as any truth drug.'

'Ask your damned questions.'

'Ah, you're in a hurry to answer. That's good. Tell me then: who is this American policeman? The one who helped you dispose of Heim's body.'

'His name is John Belinsky. He works for Crowcass.'

'How did you meet him?'

'He knew that I was working to prove Becker's innocence. He approached me with an offer to work in tandem. Initially he said that he wanted to find out why Captain Linden had been murdered, but then after a while he told me that he really wanted to find out about you. If you had anything to do with Linden's death.'

'So the Americans aren't happy that they have the right man?'

'No. Yes. The military police are. But the Crowcass people aren't. The gun used to kill Linden was one which they traced back to a killing in Berlin. A corpse which was supposed to be you, Müller. And the gun checked back to SS records at the Berlin Documents Centre. Crowcass didn't inform the military police for fear that they might spook you out of Vienna.'

'And you were encouraged to infiltrate the Org on their behalf?'

'Yes.'

'Are they so certain that I'm here?'

'Yes.'

'But until this morning you had never seen me before. Explain how they know, please.'

'The information that I supplied on the MVD was designed to draw you out. They know you like to consider yourself an expert in these matters. The thinking was that with information of such quality, you yourself would take charge of the debrief. If I saw you at this morning's meeting I was to signal to Belinsky from the toilet window. I had to pull down the blind three times. He would be watching the window through binoculars.'

'And then what?'

'He was supposed to have brought agents to surround the house. He was meant to have arrested you. The deal was that if they were successful in arresting you, then they would let Becker go free.'

Nebe glanced over at one of his men, and jerked his head at the door. 'Get some men to check the grounds. Just in case.'

Müller shrugged. 'So you're saying that the only reason they know I'm here in Vienna is because you made some signal to them from a lavatory window. Is that it?' I nodded. 'But then why didn't this Belinsky have his men move in and arrest me, as you had planned?'

'Believe me, I've been asking myself the same question.'

'Come now, Herr Gunther. This is inconsistent, is it not? I ask you to be fair. How am I supposed to believe this?'

'Would I have gone looking for the girl if I didn't think there were going to be agents arriving?'

'What time were you supposed to make your signal?' asked Nebe.

'Twenty minutes into the meeting I was supposed to excuse myself.'

'At 10.20 then. But you were looking for Fräulein Zartl before seven o'clock this morning.'

'I decided that she might not be able to wait until the Americans showed up.'

'You're asking us to believe that you would have risked a whole operation for one – ' Müller's nose wrinkled with disgust ' – for one little chocolady?' He shook his head. 'I find that very hard to believe.' He nodded at the man controlling the wine press. This man pushed a second button and the machine's hydraulics cranked into gear. 'Come now, Herr Gunther. If what you say is true, why didn't the Americans come when you signalled to them?'

'I don't know,' I shouted.

'Then speculate,' said Nebe.

'They never meant to arrest you,' I said, putting into words my own suspicions. 'All they wanted to know was that you were alive and working for the Org. They used me, and after they found out what they wanted, they dumped me.'

I tried to wrestle free of the Latvian as the press began its slow descent. Veronika lay unconscious, her chest swelling gently as she continued breathing, oblivious to the descending plate. I shook my head. 'Look, I honestly don't know why they didn't turn up.'

'So,' said Müller, 'let's get this clear. The only evidence that they have of my continued existence, apart from this rather tenuous piece of ballistic evidence you mentioned, is your own signal.'

'Yes, I suppose so.'

'One more question. Do you – do the Amis – know why Captain Linden was killed?'

'No,' I said, and then reasoning that negative answers were not what was wanted, added: 'We figured that he was being supplied with information about war-criminals in the Org. That he came to Vienna to investigate you. At first we thought that König was supplying him with the information.' I shook my head, trying to recall some of the theories I had come up with to explain Linden's death. 'Then we thought that he might somehow have been supplying the Org with information in order to help you to recruit new members. Switch that machine off, for God's sake.'

Veronika disappeared from sight as the press closed over the edge of the vat. There were only two or three metres of life left to her.

'We didn't know why, damn you.'

Müller's voice was slow and calm, like a surgeon's. 'We must be sure, Herr Gunther. Let me repeat the question – '

'I don't know – '

'Why was it necessary for us to kill Linden?'

I shook my head desperately.

'Just tell me the truth. What do you know? You're not being fair to this young woman. Tell us what you found out.'

The shrill whine of the machine grew louder. It reminded me of the sound of the elevator in my old offices in Berlin. Where I should have stayed.

'Herr Gunther,' Müller's voice contained a gramme of urgency, 'for the sake of this poor girl, I beg you.'

'For God's sake . . .'

He glanced over at the thug by the control panel and shook his squarely-cropped head.

'I can't tell you anything,' I shouted.

The press shuddered as it encountered its living obstacle. The mechanical whine briefly rose a couple of octaves as the resistance to the hydraulic force was dealt with, and then returned to its old pitch before finally the press came to the end of its cruel journey. The noise died away at another nod from Müller.

'Can't, or won't, Herr Gunther?'

'You bastard,' I said, suddenly weak with disgust, 'you vicious, cruel bastard.'

'I don't think she'll have felt much,' he said with studied indifference. 'She was drugged. Which is more than you will be when we repeat this little exercise in say – ' he glanced at his wristwatch ' – twelve hours. You have until then to think it over.' He looked over the edge of the vat. 'I can't promise to kill you outright, of course. Not like this girl. I might want to squeeze you two or three times before we spread you on the fields. Just like the grapes.

'On the other hand, if you tell me what I wish to know, I can

272

promise you a rather less painful death. A pill would be so much less distressing for you, don't you think?'

I felt my lip curl. Müller winced fastidiously as I started to swear, and then shook his head.

'Rainis,' he said, 'you may hit Herr Gunther just once before returning him to his quarters.'

36

Back in my cell I massaged the floating rib above my liver which Nebe's Latvian had selected for one stunningly painful punch. At the same time I tried to douse the lights on the memory of what had just happened to Veronika, but without success.

I had met men who had been tortured by the Russians during the war. I remembered them describing how the most awful part of it was the uncertainty – whether you would die, whether you could withstand the pain. That part was certainly true. One of them had described a way of reducing the pain. Breathing deeply and gulping could induce a light-headedness that was partly anaesthetic. The only trouble was that it had also left my friend prone to bouts of chronic hyperventilation which eventually caused him to suffer a fatal heart-attack.

I cursed myself for my selfishness. An innocent girl, already a victim of the Nazis, had been killed because of her association with me. Somewhere inside of me a voice replied that it was she who had asked for my help, and that they might well have tortured and killed her irrespective of my own involvement. But I was in no mood to go easy on myself. Wasn't there anything else I could have told Müller about Linden's death that might have satisfied him? And what would I tell him when it came to my own turn? Selfish again. But there was no avoiding my egotism's snake's eyes. I didn't want to die. More importantly, I didn't want to die on my knees begging for mercy like an Italian war-hero.

They say impending pain offers the mind the purest aid to concentration. Doubtless Müller would have known that. Thinking about the lethal pill he had promised me if I told him whatever it was he wanted to hear helped me to remember something vital. Twisting round my handcuffs, I reached down into my trouser pocket, and tugged out the lining with my little finger, allowing the two pills I had taken from Heim's surgery to roll into my palm.

I wasn't even sure why I had taken them at all. Curiosity perhaps. Or maybe it was some subconscious prompt which had told me I might have need of a painless exit myself. For a long time I just stared at the tiny cyanide capsules with a mixture of relief and horrific fascination. After a while I hid one pill in my trouser-turnup, which left the one I had decided I would keep in my mouth – the one that would in all probability kill me. With an appreciation of irony that was much exaggerated by my situation, I reflected that I had Arthur Nebe to thank for diverting these lethal pills from the secret agents for whom they had been created to the top brass in the SS, and from them to me. Perhaps the pill in my hand had been Nebe's own. It is of such speculations, however improbable, that a man's philosophy consists during his last remaining hours.

I slipped the pill into my mouth and held it gingerly between my back molars. When the time came, would I even have the guts to chew the thing? My tongue pushed the pill over the edge of my tooth and into the corner of my cheek. I rubbed my fingers over my face and could feel it through the flesh. Would anyone see it? The only light in the cell came from a bare bulb fixed to one of the wooden rafters seemingly with nothing but cobwebs. All the same I couldn't help thinking that the outline of the pill in my mouth was very much visible.

When a key scraped in the mortice, I realized that I would soon find out.

The Latvian came through the door holding his big Colt in one hand and a small tray in the other.

'Get away from the door,' he said thickly.

'What's this?' I said, sliding backwards on my backside. 'A meal? Perhaps you could tell the management that what I'd like most is a cigarette.'

'Lucky to get anything at all,' he growled. Carefully he squatted down and laid the tray on the dusty floor. There was a jug of coffee and a large slice of strudel. 'The coffee's fresh. The strudel is homemade.'

For a brief, stupid second I considered rushing him, before

reminding myself that a man in my weakened condition could rush about as quickly as a frozen waterfall. And I would have had no more chance of overpowering the huge Latvian than I had of engaging him in Socratic dialogue. He seemed to sense some flicker of hope on my face however, even though the pill resting on my gum remained undetected. 'Go ahead,' he said, 'try something. I wish you would; I'd like to blow your kneecap off.' Laughing like a retarded grizzly bear he backed out of my cell and closed the door with a loud bang.

From the size of him, I judged Rainis to be the kind who enjoyed his food. When he wasn't killing or hurting people it was probably his only real pleasure. Perhaps he was even something of a glutton. It occurred to me that if I were to leave the strudel untouched, Rainis might be unable to resist eating it himself. That if I were to put one of my cyanide capsules inside the filling then later on, perhaps long after I myself was dead, the dumb Latvian would eat my cake and die. It might, I reflected, be a comforting thought as I left the world, that he would be swiftly following me.

I decided to drink the coffee while I thought about it. Was a lethal pill hot-water-soluble? I didn't know. So I popped the capsule out of my mouth, and thinking that it might as well be that pill which I used to put my pathetic plan into action, I pushed it into the fruit filling with my forefinger.

I could happily have eaten it myself, pill and all, I was so hungry. My watch told me that over fifteen hours had passed since my Viennese breakfast, and the coffee tasted good. I decided that it could only have been Arthur Nebe who had instructed the Latvian to bring me supper.

Another hour passed. There were eight to go before they would come to take me back upstairs. I would wait until there was no hope, no possibility of reprieve before I took my own life. I tried to sleep, but without much success. I was beginning to understand what Becker must have felt like, facing the gallows. At least I was better off than he was: I still had my lethal pill.

It was almost midnight when I heard the key in the lock again. Quickly I transferred my second pill from my trouser-turnup to my cheek in case they decided to search my clothes. But it was not Rainis who came to fetch my tray but Arthur Nebe. He held an automatic in his hand.

'Don't force me to use this, Bernie,' he said. 'You know I won't hesitate to shoot you if I have to. You'd best get back against that far wall.'

'What's this? A social call?' I dragged myself back from the door. He tossed a packet of cigarettes and some matches after me.

'You might say that.'

'I hope you're not here to talk about old times, Arthur. I'm not feeling very sentimental right now.' I looked at the cigarettes. Winston. 'Does Müller know you're smoking American nails, Arthur? Be careful. You might get into trouble: he's got some strange ideas about the Amis.' I lit one and inhaled with slow satisfaction. 'Still, bless you for this.'

Nebe drew a chair round the door and sat down. 'Müller has his own ideas of where the Org is going,' he said. 'But there's no doubting his patriotism or his determination. He's quite ruthless.'

'I can't say I'd noticed.'

'He has an unfortunate tendency to judge other people by his own insensitive standards, however. Which means that he really does believe you are capable of keeping your mouth shut and allowing that girl to die.' He smiled. 'I, of course, know you rather better than that. Gunther is a sentimental sort of man, I told him. Even a little bit of a fool. It would be just like him to risk his neck for someone he hardly knew. Even a chocolady. It was the same in Minsk, I said. He was perfectly prepared to go to the front line rather than kill innocent people. People to whom he owed nothing.'

'That doesn't make me a hero, Arthur. Just a human being.'

'It makes you someone Müller is used to dealing with: a man with a principle. Müller knows what men will take and still stay silent. He's seen lots of people sacrifice their friends and then themselves in order to keep silent. He's a fanatic. Fanaticism is the only thing he understands. And as a result he thinks you're a fanatic. He's convinced there's a possibility that you might be holding out on him. As I said, I know you rather better than that. If you had known why Linden was killed I think you would have said so.'

'Well, it's nice to know somebody believes me. It'll make being turned into this year's vintage all the more bearable. Look, Arthur, why are you telling me this? So I can tell you that you're a better judge of character than Müller?'

'I was thinking: if you were to tell Müller exactly what he wants to hear, then it might save you a lot of pain. I'd hate to see an old friend suffer. And believe me, he'll make you suffer.'

'I don't doubt it. It's not this coffee that's helped to keep me awake, I can tell you. Come on, what is this? The old friend and foe routine? Like I said, I don't know why Linden was canned.'

'No, but I could tell you.'

I winced as the cigarette smoke stung my eyes. 'Let me get this straight,' I said uncertainly. 'You're going to tell me what happened to Linden, in order that I can spill it to Müller, and thereby save myself from a fate worse than death, right?'

'That's about the size of it.'

I shrugged, painfully. 'I don't see that I've got anything to lose.' I grinned. 'Of course, you could just let me escape, Arthur. For old times' sake.'

'We weren't going to talk about old times, you said so yourself. Anyway, you know too much. You've seen Müller. You've seen me. I'm dead, remember?'

'Nothing personal, Arthur, but I wish you were.' I took another cigarette and lit myself with the butt of the first. 'All right, unpack it. Why was Linden killed?'

'Linden had a German–American background. He even read German at Cornell University. During the war he had some minor intelligence role, and afterwards worked as a denazification officer. He was a clever man, and soon had a nice racket going for himself, selling Persil certificates, clearances for Old Comrades, you know the sort of thing. Then he joined the CIC as a desk-investigator and Crowcass liaison officer at the Berlin Documents Centre. Naturally he kept up his old black-market contacts and by this time he had become known to us in the

Org as someone sympathetic to our cause. We contacted him in Berlin and offered him a sum of money to perform a small service, on an occasional basis.

'You remember I told you about how a number of us faked our deaths? Gave ourselves new identities? Well, that was Albers – the Max Abs you were interested in. His idea. But of course the fundamental weakness of any new identity, especially when it has to be done so quickly, is that one lacks a past. Think of it, Bernie: world war, every able-bodied German between the ages of twelve and sixty-five under arms, and no service record for me, Alfred Nolde. Where was I? What was I doing? We thought we were very clever in killing off our real identities, letting the records fall into the hands of the Amis, but instead it merely created new questions. We had no idea that the Documents Centre would prove to be quite so comprehensive. Its effect has been to make it possible to check every answer on a man's denazification questionnaire.

'Many of us were working for the Americans by this stage. Naturally it suits them now to turn a blind eye to the pasts of our Org members. But what about tomorrow? Politicians have a habit of changing policy. Right now we're friends in the fight against Communism. But will the same hold true in five or ten years' time?

'So Albers came up with a new scheme. He created old documentation for our more senior personnel in their new identities, himself included. We were all of us given smaller, less culpable roles in the SS and Abwehr than were possessed by our real selves. As Alfred Nolde I was a sergeant in the SS Personnel Section. My file contains all my personal details: even dental records. I led a quiet, fairly blameless kind of war. It's true I was a Nazi, but never a war-criminal. That was somebody else. The fact that I happen to resemble someone called Arthur Nebe is neither here nor there.

'Security at the Centre is tight, however. It's impossible to take files out. But it is comparatively easy to take files in. Nobody is searched when they go into the Centre, only when they leave. This was Linden's job. Once a month Becker would deliver new files, forged by Albers, to Berlin. And Linden would file them in the archive. Naturally this was before we found out about Becker's Russian friends.'

'Why were the forgeries done here and not in Berlin?' I asked. 'That way you could have cut out the need for a courier.'

'Because Albers refused to go anywhere near Berlin. He liked it here in Vienna, not least because Austria is the first step on the rat-line. It's easy to get across the border into Italy, and then the Middle East, South America. There were lots of us who came south. Like birds in winter, eh?'

'So what went wrong?'

'Linden got greedy, that's what went wrong. He knew the material he was getting was forged, but he couldn't understand what it amounted to. At first I think it was mere curiosity. He started photographing the stuff we were giving him. And then he enlisted the help of a couple of Jewish lawyers – Nazi-hunters – to try and establish the nature of the new files, who these men were.'

'The Drexlers.'

'They were working with the Joint Army Group on war crimes. Probably the Drexlers had no idea that Linden's motives for seeking their help were purely personal and for profit. And why should they have done? His credentials were unquestionable. Anyway, I think they noted something about all these new SS personnel and Party records: that we kept the same initials as our old identities; it's an old trick with building a new legend. Makes you feel more comfortable with your new name. Something as instinctive as initialling a contract becomes safe. I think Drexler must have compared these new names with the names of comrades who were missing or presumed dead and suggested that Linden might like to compare the details of a file held on Alfred Nolde with the file on Arthur Nebe, Heinrich Müller with Heinrich Moltke, Max Abs with Martin Albers etc.'

'So that's why you had the Drexlers killed.'

'Exactly. That was after Linden turned up here in Vienna, looking for more money. Money to keep his mouth shut. It was Müller who met him and who killed him. We knew that Linden had already made contact with Becker, for the very simple reason that Linden told us. So we decided to kill two flies with one swat. First we left several cases of cigarettes around the warehouse where Linden was killed in order to incriminate Becker. Then König went to see Becker and told him that Linden was missing. The idea was that Becker would start going round asking questions about Linden, looking for him at his hotel and generally getting himself noticed. At the same time König switched Müller's gun for Becker's. Then we informed the police that Becker had shot and killed Linden. It was an unlooked-for bonus that Becker already knew where Linden's body was, and that he should return to the scene of the crime with the aim of taking away the cigarettes. Of course the Amis were waiting for him and caught him red-handed. The case was watertight. All the same, if the Amis had been even half efficient they would have discovered the link between Becker and Linden in Berlin. But I don't think they even bothered to take the investigation outside of Vienna. They're happy with what they've got. Or at least we thought they were until now.'

'With what Linden knew, why didn't he take the precaution of leaving a letter with someone? Informing the police of what had happened in the event of his death.'

'Oh, but he did,' said Nebe. 'Only the particular lawyer he chose in Berlin was also a member of the Org. On Linden's death he read the letter and passed it across to the head of the Berlin section.' Nebe stared levelly at me, and nodded seriously. 'That's it, Bernie. That's what Müller wants to find out if you know or not. Well, now that you do know, you can tell him, and save yourself from being tortured. Naturally, I would prefer it if this conversation remained a secret.'

'As long as I live, Arthur, you can depend on it. And thanks.' I felt my voice crack a little. 'I appreciate it.'

Nebe nodded in acknowledgement and stared around him uncomfortably. Then his gaze fell upon the uneaten slice of strudel.

'You weren't hungry?'

'I've not got much of an appetite,' I said. 'One or two things on my mind, I guess. Give it to Rainis.' I lit a third cigarette.

Was I wrong, or had he really licked his lips? That would have been too much to hope for. But it was surely worth a try.

'Or help yourself if you're feeling hungry.'

Nebe really did lick his lips now.

'May I?' he asked politely.

I nodded negligently.

'Well, if you're sure,' he said, picking the plate up off the tray on the floor. 'My housekeeper made it. She used to work for Demel. The best strudel you ever tasted in your life. It would be a pity to waste it, eh?' He took a big bite.

'I never had much of a sweet tooth myself,' I lied.

'That's nothing short of tragic in Vienna, Bernie. You are in the greatest city in the world for cake. You should have come here before the war: Gerstner's, Lehmann's, Heiner's, Aida, Haag, Sluka's, Bredendick's – pastrycooks like you never tasted before.' He took another large mouthful. 'To come to Vienna without a sweet tooth? Why, that's like a blind man taking a trip on the Big Wheel in the Prater. You don't know what you're missing. Why don't you try a little?'

I shook my head firmly. My heart was beating so quickly that I thought he must hear it. Suppose he didn't finish it?

'I really couldn't eat anything.'

Nebe shook his head pityingly, and bit once more. The teeth could not be real, I thought, surveying their white evenness. Nebe's own teeth had been much more stained.

'Anyway,' I said, nonchalantly, 'I'm supposed to be watching my weight. I've put on several kilos since coming to Vienna.'

'Me too,' he said. 'You know, you should really – '

He never finished the sentence. He coughed and choked all in one jerk of his head. Stiffening suddenly, he made a dreadful blowing noise through his lips as if he had been trying to play a tuba, and fragments of half-chewed cake rolled out of his mouth. The plate of strudel clattered on to the floor, followed by Nebe himself. Scrabbling on top of him, I tried to wrestle the automatic from his grasp before he could fire it and bring Müller and his thugs down on my head. To my horror I saw that the gun was cocked, and in the same half second Nebe's dying finger pulled the trigger.

But the hammer clicked harmlessly. The safety was still on.

Nebe's legs jerked feebly. One eyelid flickered shut while the other stayed perversely open. His last breath was a long mucoid gurgle smelling strongly of almonds. Finally he lay still, his face already turning a blueish colour. Disgusted, I spat the lethal pill out of my own mouth. I had little sympathy for him. In a few hours he might have watched the same thing happening to me.

I prised the gun free from Nebe's dead hand, which was now grey-skinned with cyanosis, and having unsuccessfully searched his pockets for the key to my handcuffs, I stood up. My head, shoulder, rib, even my penis it seemed were hurting terribly, but I felt a lot better for the grip of the Walther P38 in my hand. The kind of gun that had killed Linden. I thumb-cocked the hammer for semi-automatic operation, as Nebe himself had done before coming into my cell, slipped off the safety, as he had forgotten to do, and stepped carefully out of the cell.

I walked to the end of the damp passageway and climbed the stairs to the pressing and fermentation room where Veronika had died. There was only one light near the front door and I went towards it, hardly daring to glance at the wine press. If I had seen him I would have ordered Müller into the machine and squeezed him out of his Bavarian skin. In another body I might have risked the guards and gone up to the house, where possibly I could have tried to arrest him: probably I would just have shot him. It had been that kind of day. Now it would be as much as I could do to escape with my life.

Switching out the light I opened the front door. Without a jacket, I shivered. The night was a cold one. I crept along to the line of trees where the Latvian had tried to execute me and hid in some bushes.

The vineyard was bright with the lights of the rapid burners. Several men were busy pushing the tall trolleys which carried the burners up and down the furrows to positions which they apparently judged important. From where I sat, their long flames looked like giant fireflies moving slowly through the air. It seemed as if I would have to choose another route to escape from Nebe's estate.

I returned to the house and moved stealthily along the wall, past the kitchen towards the front garden. None of the ground-floor lights were on, but one at an upper-floor window lay reflected on the lawn like a big square swimming-pool. I halted by the corner and sniffed the air. Someone was standing in the porch, smoking a cigarette.

After what seemed like forever, I heard the man's footsteps on the gravel, and glancing quickly round the corner I saw the unmistakable figure of Rainis lumbering down the path towards the open gates where a large grey BMW was parked facing the road.

I walked on to the front lawn staying out of the light from the house, and followed him until he got to the car. He opened the car boot and started to rummage around as if looking for something. By the time he closed it again, I had put less than five metres between us. He turned and froze as he saw the Walther levelled at his misshapen head.

'Put those car keys in the ignition,' I said softly.

The Latvian's face turned even uglier at the prospect of my escaping. 'How did you get out?' he sneered.

'There was a key hidden in the strudel,' I said, and jerked the gun at the car keys in his hand. 'The car keys,' I repeated. 'Do it. Slowly.'

He stepped back and opened the driver's door. Then he bent inside and I heard the rattle of keys as he slipped them into the ignition. Straightening again, he rested his foot almost carelessly on the running-board, and leaning on the roof of the car, smiled a grin that was the shape and colour of a rusting tap.

'Want me to wash it before you go?'

'Not this time, Frankenstein. What I would like you to do is give me the keys for these.' I showed him my still-manacled wrists.

'Keys for what?'

'Keys for handcuffs.'

He shrugged, and kept on grinning. 'I got no keys for no handcuffs. Don't believe me, you search me, you find out.'

Hearing him speak, I almost winced. Latvian and soft in the head he may have been, but Rainis had no idea of German grammar. He probably thought a conjunction was a gypsy dealing three cards on a street-corner.

'Sure you've got keys, Rainis. It was you who cuffed me, remember? I saw you put them in your vest pocket.'

He stayed silent. I was beginning to want to kill him badly.

'Look, you stupid Latvian asshole. If I say "jump" again you'd better not look down for a skipping-rope. This is a gun, not a fucking hairbrush.' I stepped forward a pace and snarled through clenched teeth. 'Now find them or I'll fit your ugly face with the kind of hole that doesn't need a key.'

Rainis made a little show of patting his pockets and then produced a small silver key from his waistcoat. He held it up like a minnow.

'Drop it on the driver's seat and step away from the car.'

Now that he was closer to me, Rainis could see by the expression on my face that I had a lot of hate in my mind. This time he didn't hesitate to obey, and tossed the little key on to the seat. But if I had thought him stupid, or suddenly obedient, I made a mistake. It was fatigue, probably.

He nodded down at one of the wheels. 'You'd better let me fix that slack tyre,' he said.

I glanced downwards and then quickly up again as the Latvian sprint-started towards me, his big hands reaching for my neck like a savage tiger. A half second later I pulled the trigger. The Walther fed and cycled another round into the firing chamber in less time than it took for me to blink. I fired again. The shots echoed across the garden and up the sky as if the twin sounds had been bearing the Latvian's soul to final judgement. I didn't doubt that it would be heading earthwards and below ground fairly quickly again. His big body crashed face first on to the gravel and lay still.

I ran to the car and jumped into the seat, ignoring the handcuff key underneath my backside. There was no time to do anything but start the car. I turned the key in the ignition and the big car, new by the smell of it, roared into life. Behind me, I heard shouts. Collecting the gun off my lap, I leaned out and fired a couple of rounds back at the house. Then I threw it on the passenger seat beside me, rammed the gear stick forward, hauled the door shut and stamped on the accelerator. The rear tyres gouged at the driveway as the BMW skidded forward. For the moment it didn't matter that my hands were still manacled: the road ahead lay straight and down a hill.

But the car veered dangerously from side to side as I released the steering for a brief second, and wrestled the gear into second. My hands back on the wheel I swerved to avoid a parked car and almost put the BMW into the side of a fence. If I could only get to Stifstkaserne and Roy Shields I would tell him all about Veronika's murder. If the Amis were quick they could at least get them for that. Explanations about Müller and the Org could come later. When the MPs had Müller in the cage, there would be no limit to the embarrassment I was going to cause Belinsky, Crowcass, CIC – the whole rotten bunch of them.

I looked in the wing mirror and saw the headlights of a car. I wasn't sure if it was chasing me or not but I pushed the already screaming engine even further and almost immediately braked, pushing the wheel up hard to the right. The car hit the kerb and bounced back on to the road. My foot touched the floor again, the engine complaining loudly against the lower gear. But I couldn't risk changing into third now that there were more bends in the road to negotiate.

At the junction of Billrothstrasse and the Gürtel I almost had to lean over in order to steer the car sharp right, past a van hosing down the street. I didn't see the roadblock until it was too late, and but for the truck parked behind the makeshift barrier that had been erected I don't suppose I would have bothered to try and swerve or stop. As it was, I turned hard left and lost the back wheels on the water on the road.

For a moment I had a camera obscura's eye view as the BMW spun out of control: the barrier, the US military policemen waving their arms or chasing after me, the road I had just driven down, the car that had been following me, a row of shops, a plate glass window. The car danced sideways on two wheels like a mechanical Charlie Chaplin and then there was a cataract of glass as I crashed into one of the shops. I rolled helplessly across the passenger seat and hit the door as something solid came through the other side. I felt something sharp underneath my

286

elbow, then my head hit the frame and I must have blacked out.

It could only have been for a few seconds. One moment there was noise, movement, pain and chaos; and the next there was just quiet, with only the sound of a wheel spinning slowly to tell me that I was still alive. Mercifully the car had stalled so my first worry, which was of the car catching fire, was allayed.

Hearing footsteps on shards of glass and American voices announcing that they were coming to get me I shouted my encouragement, but to my surprise it came out as little more than a whisper. And when I tried to raise my arm to reach for the door handle I lost consciousness again.

37

'Well, how are we feeling today?' Roy Shields leaned forward on the chair beside my bed and tapped the plaster cast on my arm. A wire and pulley kept it high in the air. 'That must be pretty handy,' he said. 'A permanent Nazi salute? Shit, you Germans can even make a broken arm look patriotic.'

I took a short look around. It appeared to be a fairly normal hospital ward but for the bars on the windows and the tattoos on the nurses' forearms.

'What kind of hospital is this?'

'You're in the military hospital at the Stiftskaserne,' he said. 'For your protection.'

'How long have I been here?'

'Almost three weeks. You had quite a bump on your square head. Fractured your skull. Busted collarbone, broken arm, broken ribs. You've been delirious since you came in.'

'Yes? Well, blame it on the föhn, I guess.'

Shields chuckled and then his face grew more sombre. 'Better hold on to that sense of humour,' he said. 'I've got some bad news for you.'

I riffled through the card index inside my head. Most of the cards had been thrown on the floor, but the ones I picked up first seemed somehow especially relevant. Something I had been working on. A name.

'Emil Becker,' I said, recalling a manic face.

'He was hanged, the day before yesterday,' Shields shrugged apologetically. 'I'm sorry. Really I am.'

'Well you certainly didn't waste any time,' I remarked. 'Is that good old American efficiency? Or has one of your people cornered the market in rope?'

'I wouldn't lose any sleep about it, Gunther. Whether he murdered Linden or not, Becker earned that collar.'

'That doesn't sound like a very good advert for American justice.'

'Come on, you know it was an Austrian court that dropped his cue-ball.'

'You handed them the stick and the chalk, didn't you?'

Shields looked away for a moment and then rubbed his face with irritation. 'Aw, what the hell. You're a cop. You know how it is. These things happen with any system. Just because your shoes pick up a bit of shit doesn't mean you have to buy a new pair.'

'Sure, but you learn to stay on the path instead of taking short-cuts across the field.'

'Wise guy. I don't even know why we're having this conversation. You've still not given me a shred of evidence why I should accept that Becker didn't kill Linden.'

'So you can order a retrial?'

'A file is never quite complete,' he said with a shrug. 'A case is never really closed, even when all the participants are dead. I still have one or two loose ends.'

'I'm all cut up about your loose ends, Shields.'

'Perhaps you should be, Herr Gunther.' His tone was stiffer now. 'Perhaps I ought to remind you that this is a military hospital, and under American jurisdiction. And if you remember, I once had occasion to warn you about meddling in this case. Now that you've done exactly that, I'd say you've still got some explaining to do. Possession of a firearm by a German or Austrian national. Well, that's contrary to the Austrian Military Government's Public Safety Manual for a start. You could get five years for that alone. Then there's the car you were driving. Quite apart from the fact that you were wearing handcuffs and that you don't appear to be in possession of a valid driving licence, there's the small matter of driving through a military checkpoint.' He paused and lit a cigarette. 'So what's it to be: information or incarceration?'

'Neatly put.'

'I'm a neat kind of fellow. All policemen are. Come on. Let's have it.'

I sank back on my pillow resignedly. 'I'm warning you,

Shields, you're likely to have as many loose ends as you started with. I doubt if I could prove half of what I could tell you.'

The American folded his brawny arms and leaned back on his chair. 'Proof is for the courtroom, my friend. I'm a detective, remember? This is for my own private casebook.'

I told him nearly everything. When I had finished his face adopted a lugubrious expression and he nodded sagely. 'Well, I can certainly suck a bit of that.'

'That's good,' I sighed, 'but my tits are getting a little sore right now, babe. If you've got questions, how about you save them till next time. I'd like to take a little nap.'

Shields stood up. 'I'll be back tomorrow. But just one question for now: this guy from Crowcass – '

'Belinsky?'

'Belinsky, yeah. How come that he quit the game before the period was up?'

'Your guess is as good as mine.'

'Better maybe.' He shrugged. 'I'll ask around. Our relations with the Intelligence boys have improved since this Berlin thing. The American Military Governor has told them and us that we need to present a united front in case the Soviets try the same thing here.'

'What Berlin thing?' I said. 'In case they try what here?'

Shields frowned. 'You don't know about that? No, of course, you wouldn't, would you?'

'Look, my wife is in Berlin; hadn't you better tell me what's happened?'

He sat down again, only on the edge of the chair, which added to his obvious discomfort. 'The Soviets have imposed a complete military blockade on Berlin,' he said. 'They're not letting anything in or out of the Zone. So we're supplying the city by plane. Happened the day your friend got his own personal airlift. 24 June.' He smiled thinly. 'It's kind of tense up there from what I hear. Lots of folk think that there's going to be one almighty great showdown between us and the Russkies. Me, I wouldn't be at all surprised. We should have kicked their asses a long time ago. But we're not about to abandon Berlin, you can depend on it. Provided everybody keeps their heads, we should get through it all right.'

Shields lit a cigarette and put it between my lips. 'I'm sorry about your wife,' he said. 'You been married long?'

'Seven years.' I said. 'What about you? Are you married?'

He shook his head. 'I guess I never met the right girl. Do you mind me asking: has it worked out all right for you both? You being a detective and all.'

I thought for a minute. 'Yes,' I said, 'it's worked out just fine.'

Mine was the only occupied bed in the hospital. That night a barge slipping down the canal woke me with its bovine-sounding horn, and then abandoned me to stare sleeplessly at the dark as the echo of it fled into eternity like the bray of the last trump. Staring into the void of the pitch-black darkness, my whispered breathing serving only to remind me of my own mortality, it seemed that, seeing nothing, I could see beyond to what was most tangible: death itself, a lean, moth-eaten figure shrouded in heavy black velvet, ever ready to press the silent, chloro-formed pad over the victim's nose and mouth, and to carry him to a waiting black sedan to some dreadful zone and DP camp where darkness never ends and whence no one ever escapes. As light returned to press against the window bars, so too did courage, although I knew that Death's Ivans held no high regard for those who met them without fear. Whether a man is ready to die or not, his requiem always sounds the same.

It was several days before Shields returned to the hospital. This time he was accompanied by two other men who from their haircuts and well-fed faces I took to be Americans. Like Shields they wore loudly cut suits. But their faces were older and wiser. Bing Crosby types with briefcases, pipes and emotions restricted to their supercilious eyebrows. Lawyers, or investigators. Or Corps. Shields handled the introductions.

'This is Major Breen,' he said, indicating the older of the two men. 'And this is Major Medlinskas.'

Investigators then. But for which organization?

'What are you,' I said, 'the medical students?'

Shields grinned uncertainly. 'They'd like to ask you a few questions. I'll help with the translating.'

'Tell them I'm feeling a lot better, and thank them for the grapes. And perhaps one of them could fetch me the pot.'

Shields ignored me. They drew up three chairs and sat down like a team of judges at a dog show, with Shields nearest to me. Briefcases were opened, and notepads produced.

'Maybe I should have my twister here.'

'Is that really necessary?' said Shields.

'You tell me. Only I look at these two and I don't think they're a couple of American tourists who want to know the best places in Vienna to nudge a pretty girl.'

Shields translated my concern to the other two, the older of whom grunted and said something about criminals.

'The Major says that this is not a criminal matter,' reported Shields. 'But if you want a lawyer, one will be fetched.'

'If this is not a criminal matter, then how come I'm in a military hospital?'

'You were wearing handcuffs when they picked you out of that car,' sighed Shields. 'There was a pistol on the floor and a machine-gun in the trunk. They weren't about to take you to the maternity hospital.'

'All the same, I don't like it. Don't think that this bandage on my head gives you the right to treat me like an idiot. Who are these people anyway? They look like spies to me. I can recognize the type. I can smell the invisible ink on their fingers. Tell them that. Tell them that people from CIC and Crowcass give me an acid stomach on account of the fact that I trusted one of their people before and got my fingers clipped. Tell them that I wouldn't be lying here now if it wasn't for an American agent called Belinsky.'

'That's what they want to talk to you about.'

'Yeah? Well maybe if they were to put away those notebooks I'd feel a little easier.'

They seemed to understand this. They shrugged simultaneously and returned the notebooks to the briefcases.

'One more thing,' I said. 'I'm an experienced interrogator

292

myself. Remember that. If I start to get the impression that I'm being rinsed and stacked for criminal charges then the interview will be over.'

The older man, Breen, shifted in his chair and clasped his hands across his knee. It didn't make him look any cuter. When he spoke, his German wasn't as bad as I had imagined it would be. 'I don't see any objections to that,' he said quietly.

And then it began. The major asked most of the questions, while the younger man nodded and occasionally interrupted in his bad German to ask me to clarify a remark. For the best part of two hours I answered or parried their questions, only refusing to reply directly on a couple of occasions when it seemed to me that they had stepped across the line of our agreement. Gradually, however, I perceived that most of their interest in me lay in the fact that neither the 970th CIC in Germany, nor the 430th CIC in Austria knew anything about a John Belinsky. Nor indeed was there a John Belinsky attached, however tenuously, to the Central Registry of War Crimes and Security Suspects of the United States Army. The military police had no one by that name; nor the army. There was however a John Belinsky in the Air Force, but he was nearly fifty; and the Navy had three John Belinskys, all of whom were at sea. Which was just how I felt.

Along the way the two Americans sermonized about the importance of keeping my mouth shut with regard to what I had learned about the Org and its relation to the CIC. Nothing could have suited me more and I counted this as a strong hint that as soon as I was well again, I would be permitted to leave. But my relief was tempered by a great deal of curiosity as to who John Belinsky had really been, and what he had hoped to achieve. Neither of my interrogators gave me the benefit of their opinions. But naturally I had my own ideas.

Several times in the following weeks Shields and the two Americans came to the hospital to continue with their inquiry. They were always scrupulously polite, almost comically so; and the questions were always about Belinsky. What had he looked like? Which part of New York had he said that he came from? Could I remember the number of his car?

I told them everything I could remember about him. They checked his room at Sacher's and found nothing: he had cleared out on the very day that he was supposed to have come to Grinzing with the cavalry. They staked out a couple of the bars he had said he favoured. I think they even asked the Russians about him. When they tried to speak to the Georgian officer in the IP, Captain Rustaveli, who had arrested Lotte Hartmann and me on Belinsky's instructions, it transpired that he had been suddenly recalled to Moscow.

Of course it was all too late. The cat had already fallen into the stream, and what was now clear was that Belinsky had been working for the Russians all along. No wonder he had played up the rivalry between the CIC and the military police, I said to my new American friends of truth. I thought myself a very clever sort of coat to have spotted that as early on as I had. By now he had presumably told his MVD boss all about America's recruitment of Heinrich Müller and Arthur Nebe.

But there were several subjects about which I remained silent. Colonel Poroshin was one: I didn't like to think what might have happened had they discovered that a senior officer in the MVD had arranged my coming to Vienna. Their curiosity about my travel documents and cigarette permit was quite uncomfortable enough. I told them that I had had to pay a great deal of money to bribe a Russian officer, and they seemed satisfied with that explanation.

Privately I wondered if my meeting with Belinsky had always been part of Poroshin's plan. And the circumstances of our deciding to work together: was it possible that Belinsky had shot those two Russian deserters as a demonstration for my benefit, as a way of impressing upon me his ruthless dislike for all things Soviet?

There was another thing about which I kept resolutely silent, and that was Arthur Nebe's explanation of how the Org had sabotaged the US Documents Centre in Berlin with the help of Captain Linden. That, I decided, was their problem. I did not think I cared to help a government that was prepared to hang Nazis on Mondays, Tuesdays, and Wednesdays, and to recruit them for its own security services on Thursdays, Fridays, and Saturdays. Heinrich Müller had at least got that part right.

As for Müller himself, Major Breen and Captain Medlinskas were adamant that I must have been mistaken about him. The former Gestapo chief was long dead, they assured me. Belinsky, they insisted, for reasons best known to himself, had almost certainly shown me someone else's picture. The military police had made a very careful search of Nebe's wine estate in Grinzing, and discovered only that the owner, one Alfred Nolde, was abroad on business. No bodies were found, nor any evidence that anyone had been killed. And while it was true that there existed an organization of former German servicemen which was working alongside the United States to prevent the further spread of international Communism, it was, they insisted, quite inconceivable that this organization could have included fugitive Nazi war-criminals.

I listened impassively to all this nonsense, too exhausted by the whole business to care much what they believed or, for that matter, what they wanted me to believe. Suppressing my first reaction in the face of their indifference to the truth, which was to tell them to go to hell, I merely nodded politely, my manners verging on the truly Viennese. Agreeing with them seemed to be the best possible way of expediting my freedom.

Shields was less complaisant however. His help with translation grew more surly and uncooperative as the days went by, and it became obvious that he was unhappy with the way in which the two officers appeared to be more concerned to conceal rather than to reveal the implications of what I had first told him, and certainly he had believed. Much to Shields's annoyance, Breen pronounced himself content that the case of Captain Linden had been brought to a satisfactory conclusion. Shields's only satisfaction might have come from the knowledge that the 796th military police, still smarting as a result of the scandal involving Russians posing as American MPs, now had something to throw back at the 430th CIC: a Russian spy, posing as a member of the CIC, with the proper identity card, staying at a hotel requisitioned by the military, driving a vehicle registered to an American officer and generally coming and going as he pleased through areas restricted to American personnel. I knew that this would only have been a small consolation for a man like Roy Shields: a policeman with a common enough fetish for neatness. It was easy for me to sympathize. I'd often encountered that same feeling myself.

For the last two interrogations, Shields was replaced by another man, an Austrian, and I never saw him again.

Neither Breen nor Medlinskas told me when at last they had concluded their inquiry. Nor did they give me any indication that they were satisfied with my answers. They just left the matter hanging. But such are the ways of people in the security services.

Over the next two or three weeks I made a full recovery from my injuries. I was both amused and shocked to learn from the prison doctor, however, that on my first being admitted to the hospital after my accident, I had been suffering from gonorrhoea.

'In the first place, you're damned lucky that they brought you here,' he said, 'where we have penicillin. If they'd taken you anywhere but an American Military Hospital they'd have used Salvarsan, and that stuff burns like Lucifer's spitball. And in the second, you're lucky it was just drip and not Russian syphilis. These local whores are full of it. Haven't any of you Jerries ever heard of French letters?'

'You mean Parisians? Sure we have. But we don't wear them. We give them to the Nazi fifth column who prick holes in them and sell them to GIs to make them sick when they screw our women.'

The doctor laughed. But I could tell that in a remote part of his soul he believed me. This was just one of many similar incidents I encountered during my recovery, as my English slowly improved, enabling me to talk with the two Americans who were the prison hospital's nurses. For as we laughed and joked it always seemed to me that there was something strange in their eyes, but which I was never able to identify.

And then, a few days before I was discharged, it came to me in a sickening realization. Because I was a German these Americans were actually chilled by me. It was as if, when they looked at me, they ran newsreel film of Belsen and Buchenwald inside their heads. And what was in their eyes was a question: how could you have allowed it to happen? How could you have let that sort of thing go on?

Perhaps, for several generations at least, when other nations look us in the eye, it will always be with this same unspoken question in their hearts.

38

It was a pleasant September morning when, wearing an ill-fitting suit lent to me by the nurses at the military hospital, I returned to my pension in Skodagasse. The owner, Frau Blum-Weiss greeted me warmly, informed me that my luggage was stored safely in her basement, handed me a note which had arrived not half an hour before, and asked me if I would care to have some breakfast. I told her I would, and having thanked her for looking after my belongings, inquired if I owed any money.

'Dr Liebl settled everything, Herr Gunther,' she said. 'But if you would like to take your old rooms again, that will be all right. They are vacant.'

Since I had no idea when I might be able to return to Berlin, I said I would.

'Did Dr Liebl leave me any message?' I asked, already knowing the answer. He had made no attempt to contact me during my stay in the military hospital.

'No,' she said, 'no message.'

Then she showed me back to my old rooms and had her son bring my luggage up to me. I thanked her again and said that I would breakfast just as soon as I had changed into my own clothes.

'Everything's there,' she said as her son heaved my bags on to the luggage stand. 'I had a receipt for the few things that the police took away: papers, that kind of thing.' Then she smiled sweetly, wished me another pleasant stay, and closed the door behind her. Typically Viennese, she showed no desire to know what had befallen me since last I had stayed in her house.

As soon as she had left the room, I opened my bags and found, almost to my astonishment and much to my relief, that I was still in possession of my $2,500 in cash and my several cartons of cigarettes. I lay on the bed and smoked a Memphis with something approaching delight.

I opened the note while I ate my breakfast. There was only one short sentence and that was written in Cyrillic: 'Meet me at the Kaisergruft at eleven o'clock this morning.' The note was unsigned but then it hardly needed to be. When Frau Blum-Weiss returned to my table to clear away the breakfast things, I asked her who had delivered it.

'It was just a schoolboy, Herr Gunther,' she said, collecting the crockery on a tray, 'an ordinary schoolboy.'

'I have to meet someone,' I explained. 'At the Kaisergruft. Where is that?'

'The Imperial Crypt?' She wiped a hand on a well-starched pinafore as if she had been about to meet the Kaiser himself, and then crossed herself. Mention of royalty always seemed to make the Viennese doubly respectful. 'Why, it's at the Church of the Capuchins on the west side of Neuer Markt. But go early, Herr Gunther. It's only open in the morning, from ten to twelve. I'm sure you'll find it very interesting.'

I smiled and nodded gratefully. There was no doubting that I was likely to find it very interesting indeed.

Neuer Markt hardly looked like a market square at all. A number of tables had been laid out like a café terrace. There were customers who weren't drinking coffee, waiters who did not seem inclined to serve them and little sign of any café from where coffee might have been obtained. It seemed quite makeshift, even by the easy standards of a reconstructed Vienna. There were also a few people just watching, almost as if a crime had occurred and everyone was waiting for the police. But I paid it little regard and, hearing the eleven o'clock chimes of the nearby clock tower, hurried on to the church.

It was as well for whichever zoologist who had named the famous monkey that the Capuchin monks' style of habit was rather more remarkable than their plainish church in Vienna. Compared with most other places of worship in that city, the Kapuzinerkirche looked as if they must have been flirting with Calvinism at the time that it was built. Either that or the Order's treasurer had run off with the money for the stonemasons; there wasn't one carving on it. The church was sufficiently ordinary for me to walk past the place without even recognizing it. I might have done so again but for a group of American soldiers who were hanging around in a doorway and from whom I overheard a reference to 'the stiffs'. My new acquaintance with English as it was spoken by the nurses at the military hospital told me that this group was intent on visiting the same place as I was.

I paid a schilling entrance to a grumpy old monk and entered a long, airy corridor that I took to be a part of the monastery. A narrow stairwell led down into the vault.

It was in fact, not one vault, but eight interconnecting vaults and much less gloomy than I had expected. The interior was simple, being in plain white with the walls faced partly in marble, and contrasted strongly with the opulence of its contents.

Here were the remains of over a hundred Habsburgs and their famous jaws, although the guidebook which I had thought to bring with me said that their hearts were pickled in urns located underneath St Stephen's Cathedral. It was as much evidence for royal mortality as you could have found anywhere north of Cairo. Nobody, it seemed, was missing except the Archduke Ferdinand, who was buried at Graz, no doubt piqued at the rest of them for having insisted that he visit Sarajevo.

The cheaper end of the family, from Tuscany, were stacked in simple lead coffins, one on top of the other like bottles in a wine-rack, at the far end of the longest vault. I half expected to see an old man prising a couple of them open to try out a new mallet and set of stakes. Naturally enough the Habsburgs with the biggest egos rated the grandest sarcophagi. These huge, morbidly ornamented copper caskets seemed to lack nothing but caterpillar tracks and gun turrets for them to have captured Stalingrad. Only the Emperor Joseph II had shown anything like restraint in his choice of box; and only a Viennese guidebook could have described the copper casket as 'excessively simple'.

I found Colonel Poroshin in the Franz Joseph vault. He smiled warmly when he saw me and clapped me on the shoulder: 'You see, I was right. You can read Cyrillic, after all.'

'Maybe you can read my mind as well.'

'For sure,' he said. 'You are wondering what we could possibly have to say to each other, given all that has happened. Least of all in this place. You are thinking that in a different place, you might try to kill me.'

'You should be on the stage, Palkovnik. You could be another Professor Schaffer.'

'You are mistaken, I think. Professor Schaffer is a hypnotist, not a mind-reader.' He slapped his gloves on his open palm with the air of one who had scored a point. 'I am not a hypnotist, Herr Gunther.'

'Don't underestimate yourself. You managed to make me believe that I was a private investigator and that I should come here to Vienna to try and clear Emil Becker of murder. A hypnotic fantasy if ever I heard one.'

'A powerful suggestion, perhaps,' said Poroshin, 'but you were acting under your own free will.' He sighed. 'A pity about poor Emil. You're wrong if you think that I didn't hope you could prove him innocent. But to borrow a chess term, it was my Vienna gambit: it has a peaceable first appearance, but the sequel is full of subtleties and aggressive possibilities. All that one requires is a strong and valiant knight.'

'That was me, I suppose.'

'*Tochno* (exactly). And now the game is won.'

'Do you mind explaining how?'

Poroshin pointed to the casket on the right of the more elevated one containing the Emperor Franz Joseph.

'The Crown Prince Rudolf,' he said. 'He committed suicide in the famous hunting lodge at Mayerling. The general story is well-known but the details and the motives remain unclear. Just about the only thing we can be certain of is that he lies in this very tomb. For me, to know this for sure is enough. But not everyone whom we believe to have committed suicide is really quite as dead as poor Rudolf. Take Heinrich Müller. To prove him still alive, now that was something worthwhile. The game was won when we knew that for sure.'

'But I lied about that,' I said insouciantly. 'I never saw Müller. The only reason I signalled to Belinsky was because I wanted him and his men to come and help me save Veronika Zartl, the chocolady from the Oriental.'

'Yes, I admit that Belinsky's arrangements with you were less than perfect in their concept. But as it happens I know that you are lying now. You see, Belinsky really was at Grinzing with a team of agents. They were not of course Americans, but my own men. Every vehicle leaving the yellow house in Grinzing was followed including, I may say, your own. When Müller and his friends discovered your escape they were so panic-stricken that they fled almost immediately. We simply tailed them, at a discreet distance, until they thought that they were safe again. Since then we have been able to positively identify Herr Müller for ourselves. So you see? You did not lie.'

'But why didn't you just arrest him? What good is he to you if he's left at liberty?'

Poroshin made his face look shrewd.

'In my business, it is not necessarily politic always to arrest a man who is my enemy. Sometimes he can be many times more valuable if he is allowed to remain at large. From as early as the beginning of the war, Müller was a double agent. Towards the end of 1944 he was naturally anxious to disappear from Berlin altogether and come to Moscow. Well, can you imagine it, Herr Gunther? The head of the fascist Gestapo living and working in the capital of democratic socialism? If the British or American intelligence agencies were to have discovered such a thing they would undoubtedly have leaked this information to the world's press at some politically opportune moment. Then they would have sat back and watched us squirm with embarrassment. So, it was decided that Müller could not come.

'The only problem was that he knew so much about us. Not to mention the whereabouts of dozens of Gestapo and Abwehr spies throughout the Soviet Union and Eastern Europe. He had first to be neutralized before we could turn him away from our door. So we tricked him into giving us the names of all these agents, and at the same time started to feed him with new information which, while of no help to the German war-effort, might prove of considerable interest to the Americans. It goes without saying that this information was also false.

'Anyway, all this time we continued to put off Müller's defection, telling him to wait just a little longer, and that he had nothing to worry about. But when we were ready we allowed him to discover that for various political reasons his defection could not be sanctioned. We hoped that this would now persuade him to offer his services to the Americans, as others had done. General Gehlen for example. Baron von Bolschwing. Even Himmler – although he was simply too well known for the British to accept his offer. And too crazy, yes?

'Perhaps we miscalculated. Perhaps Müller left it too late and was unable to escape the eye of Martin Bormann and the SS who guarded the Führerbunker. Who knows? Anyway, Müller apparently committed suicide. This he faked, but it was quite a while before we could prove this to our own satisfaction. Müller is a very clever man.

'When we learned about the Org we thought that it wouldn't be long before Müller turned up again. But he stayed persistently in the shadows. There was the occasional, unconfirmed sighting, but nothing for certain. And then when Captain Linden was shot, we noticed from the reports that the serial number of the murder weapon was one which had been originally issued to Müller. But this part you already know, I think.'

I nodded. 'Belinsky told me.'

'A most resourceful man. The family is Siberian, you know. They returned to Russia after the Revolution, when Belinsky was still a boy. But by then he was all-American, as they say. The whole family were soon working for NKVD. It was Belinsky's idea to pose as a Crowcass agent. Not only do Crowcass and CIC often work at cross purposes, but Crowcass is often staffed with CIC personnel. And it is quite common for the American military police to be left in ignorance of CIC/Crowcass operations. The Americans are even more Byzantine in their organizational structures than we are ourselves. Belinsky was plausible to you; but he was also plausible, as an idea, to Müller: enough to scare him out into the open when you told him that a Crowcass agent was on his trail; but not enough to scare him as far as South America, where he could be of no use to us. After all, there are others in CIC, less fastidious about employing war-criminals than the people in Crowcass, whose protection Müller could seek out.

'And so it has proved. Even as we speak Müller is exactly where we want him: with his American friends in Pullach. Being useful to them. Giving them the benefit of his massive knowledge of Soviet intelligence structures and secret police methods. Boasting about the network of loyal agents he still believes are in place. This was the first stage of our plan – to disinform the Americans.'

'Very clever,' I said, with genuine admiration, 'and the second?'

Poroshin's face adopted a more philosophical expression. 'When the time is right, it is we who shall leak some information to the world's press: that Gestapo Müller is a tool of American Intelligence. It is we who will sit back and watch them squirm with embarrassment. It may be in ten years' time, or even twenty. But, provided Müller stays alive, it will happen.'

'Suppose the world's press don't believe you?'

'The proof will not be so hard to obtain. The Americans are great ones for keeping files and records. Look at that Documents Centre of theirs. And we have other agents. Provided that they know where and what to look for, it will not be too difficult to find the evidence.'

'You seem to have thought of everything.'

'More than you will ever know. And now that I have answered your question, I have one for you, Herr Gunther. Will you answer it, please?'

'I can't imagine what I can tell you, Palkovnik. You're the player, not me. I'm just a knight in your Vienna gambit, remember?'

'Nevertheless, there is something.'

I shrugged. 'Fire away.'

'Yes,' he said, 'to return to the chess board for a moment. One expects to make sacrifices. Becker, for example. And you of course. But sometimes one encounters the unexpected loss of material.'

'Your queen?'

He frowned for a moment. 'If you like. Belinsky told me that it was you who killed Traudl Braunsteiner. But he was a very determined man in this whole affair. The fact that I had a personal interest in Traudl was of no special account to him. I know this to be true. He would have killed her without a second thought. But you –

'I had one of my people in Berlin check you out at the US Documents Centre. You told the truth. You were never a Party member. And the rest of it is there too. How you asked for a transfer out of the SS. That could have got you shot. So a sentimental fool, maybe. But a killer? I will tell you straight, Herr Gunther: my intellect says that you did not kill her. But I must know it here too.' He slapped his stomach. 'Perhaps here most of all.'

He fixed me with his pale blue eyes, but I did not flinch or look away.

'Did you kill her?'

'No.'

'Did you run her down?'

'Belinsky had a car, not me.'

'Say that you had no part in her murder.'

'I was going to warn her.'

Poroshin nodded. '*Da*,' he said, '*dagavareelees* (that's agreed). You are speaking the truth.'

'*Slava bogu* (Thank God).'

'You are right to thank him.' He slapped his stomach once again. 'If I had not felt it, I would have had to kill you as well.'

'As well?' I frowned. Who else was dead? 'Belinsky?'

'Yes, most unfortunate. It was smoking that infernal pipe of his. Such a dangerous habit, smoking. You should give it up.'

'How?'

'It's an old Cheka way. A small quantity of tetryl in the mouthpiece attached to a fuse which leads to a point below the bowl. When the pipe is lit, so is the fuse. Quite simple, but also quite deadly. It blew his head off.' Poroshin's tone was almost indifferent. 'You see? My mind told me that it was not you who killed her. I merely wanted to be sure that I would not have to kill you as well.'

'And now you are sure?'

'For sure,' he said. 'Not only will you walk out of here alive – '

'You would have killed me down here?'

'It is a suitable enough place, don't you think?'

'Oh yes, very poetic. What were you going to do? Bite my neck? Or had you wired one of the caskets?'

'There are many poisons, Herr Gunther.' He held out a small flick-knife in his palm. 'Tetrodotoxin on the blade. Even the smallest scratch, and bye-bye.' He pocketed the knife in his tunic and gave a sheepish little shrug. 'I was about to say that not only may you now walk out of here alive, but that if you go to the Café Mozart now, you will find someone waiting there for you.'

My look of puzzlement seemed to amuse him. 'Can you not guess?' he said delightedly.

'My wife? You got her out of Berlin?'

'*Kanyeshna* (Of course). I don't know how else she would have got out. Berlin is surrounded by our tanks.'

'Kirsten is waiting at the Mozart Café now?'

He looked at his watch and nodded. 'For fifteen minutes already,' he said. 'You'd best not keep her waiting much longer. An attractive woman like that, on her own in a city like Vienna? One must be so careful nowadays. These are difficult times.'

'You're full of surprises, Colonel,' I told him. 'Five minutes ago you were ready to kill me on nothing more tangible than your indigestion. And now you're telling me that you've brought my wife from Berlin. Why are you helping me like this? *Ya nye paneemayoo* (I don't understand).'

'Let us just say that it was part of the whole futile romance of Communism, *vot i vsyo* (that's all).' He clicked his heels like a good Prussian. 'Goodbye, Herr Gunther. Who knows? After this Berlin thing, we may meet again.'

'I hope not.'

'That is too bad. A man of your talents – ' Then he turned and strode off.

I left the Imperial Crypt with as much spring in my step as Lazarus. Outside, on Neuer Markt, there were still more people watching the strange little café-terrace that had no café. Then I saw the camera and the lights, and at the same time I spotted

Willy Reichmann, the little red-haired production manager from Sievering Film Studios. He was speaking English to another man who was holding a megaphone. This was surely the English film that Willy had told me about: the one for which Vienna's increasingly rare ruins had been a prerequisite. The film in which Lotte Hartmann, the girl who had given me a well-deserved dose of drip, had been given a part.

I stopped to watch for a few moments, wondering if I might catch sight of König's girlfriend, but there was no sign of her. I thought it unlikely that she would have left Vienna with him and passed up her first screen role.

One of the onlookers around me said, 'What on earth are they doing?' and another answered saying, 'It's supposed to be a café – the Mozart Café.' Laughter rippled through the crowd. 'What, here?' said another voice. 'Apparently they like the view better here,' replied a fourth. 'It's what they call poetic licence.'

The man with the megaphone asked for quiet, ordered the cameras to roll and then called for action. Two men, one of them carrying a book as if it was some kind of religious icon, shook hands and sat down at one of the tables.

Leaving the crowd to watch what happened next, I walked quickly south, towards the real Mozart Café and the wife who was waiting there for me.

AUTHOR'S NOTE

In 1988 Ian Sayer and Douglas Botting, who were compiling a history of the American Counter-Intelligence Corps entitled *America's Secret Army: The Untold Story of the Counter-Intelligence Corps*, were asked by a US government investigative agency to verify a file consisting of documents signed by CIC agents in Berlin towards the end of 1948 in connection with the employment of Heinrich Müller as a CIC advisor. The file indicated that Soviet agents had concluded that Müller had not been killed in 1945 and that he was possibly being used by Western Intelligence agencies. Sayer and Botting rejected the material as a forgery 'counterfeited by a skilful but rather confused person'. This view was corroborated by Colonel E. Browning, who was CIC Operations Chief in Frankfurt at the time the documents were supposed to have been produced. Browning indicated that the whole idea of something as sensitive as the employment of Müller as a CIC advisor was ludicrous. 'Regretfully,' wrote the two authors, 'we have to conclude that the fate of the chief of the Gestapo in the Third Reich remains shrouded in mystery and speculation, as it has always been, and probably always will be.'

Attempts by a leading British newspaper and an American news magazine to investigate the story in detail have so far come to nothing.

READ MORE IN PENGUIN

In every corner of the world, on every subject under the sun, Penguin represents quality and variety – the very best in publishing today.

For complete information about books available from Penguin – including Puffins, Penguin Classics and Arkana – and how to order them, write to us at the appropriate address below. Please note that for copyright reasons the selection of books varies from country to country.

In the United Kingdom: Please write to *Dept. EP, Penguin Books Ltd, Bath Road, Harmondsworth, West Drayton, Middlesex UB7 0DA*

In the United States: Please write to *Consumer Sales, Penguin USA, P.O. Box 999, Dept. 17109, Bergenfield, New Jersey 07621-0120.* VISA and MasterCard holders call 1-800-253-6476 to order Penguin titles

In Canada: Please write to *Penguin Books Canada Ltd, 10 Alcorn Avenue, Suite 300, Toronto, Ontario M4V 3B2*

In Australia: Please write to *Penguin Books Australia Ltd, P.O. Box 257, Ringwood, Victoria 3134*

In New Zealand: Please write to *Penguin Books (NZ) Ltd, Private Bag 102902, North Shore Mail Centre, Auckland 10*

In India: Please write to *Penguin Books India Pvt Ltd, 706 Eros Apartments, 56 Nehru Place, New Delhi 110 019*

In the Netherlands: Please write to *Penguin Books Netherlands bv, Postbus 3507, NL-1001 AH Amsterdam*

In Germany: Please write to *Penguin Books Deutschland GmbH, Metzlerstrasse 26, 60594 Frankfurt am Main*

In Spain: Please write to *Penguin Books S. A., Bravo Murillo 19, 1° B, 28015 Madrid*

In Italy: Please write to *Penguin Italia s.r.l., Via Felice Casati 20, I–20124 Milano*

In France: Please write to *Penguin France S. A., 17 rue Lejeune, F–31000 Toulouse*

In Japan: Please write to *Penguin Books Japan, Ishikiribashi Building, 2–5–4, Suido, Bunkyo-ku, Tokyo 112*

In Greece: Please write to *Penguin Hellas Ltd, Dimocritou 3, GR–106 71 Athens*

In South Africa: Please write to *Longman Penguin Southern Africa (Pty) Ltd, Private Bag X08, Bertsham 2013*

BY THE SAME AUTHOR

March Violets

Berlin, 1936. The city was full of March Violets, late converts to National Socialism in the early and prosperous years of the rule of Germany's Great Persuader – Adolf Hitler. For Bernie Gunther business was booming, especially in the missing-persons field. But somehow he couldn't bring himself to like it.

So when Ruhr industrialist Hermann Six hired him to find the men who had murdered his daughter and son-in-law and walked away with a priceless necklace, Gunther was glad for the variety.

'Different, distinctive and well worth your while' – *Literary Review*

The Pale Criminal

A brutal murderer on the streets isn't unusual for Berlin in 1938, but this one's killing young Aryan girls, and the Jew who has been framed proves innocent.

Embarrassing. And Obergruppenführer Heydrich doesn't want a pogrom: German insurance companies would suffer. So – a little blackmail, and private eye Bernie Gunther finds himself on the trail of the real killer, pursuing some very high-powered suspects through the crankiest sub-cultures of Nazism . . .

'Blends high-powered story-telling with a surprisingly rich piece of historical re-creation' – *Independent*